LOST IN TAROT LAND

LOST IN TAROT LAND

CHRONICLES OF TAROTLAND

KILLIAN WOLF

Grim House
Publishing

ISBN: 978-1-951140-16-8

Developmental editor: Clairie Kavanaugh - claeriekavanaugh.com
Copyeditor: Sara Lawson - sarasbooks.com
Cover design: Logan Keys - coverofdarknessdesign.com
Conlanger: Christian Thalmann - twitter.com/thalmach
Map designer: Zentra Brice
Header designer: Etheric Designs - etherictales.com/etheric-designs
Formatter: Michael Davie - grimhousepub.com/plans-pricing

To the reader who dreams about fairy tales and escaping to different dimensions. This is for you.

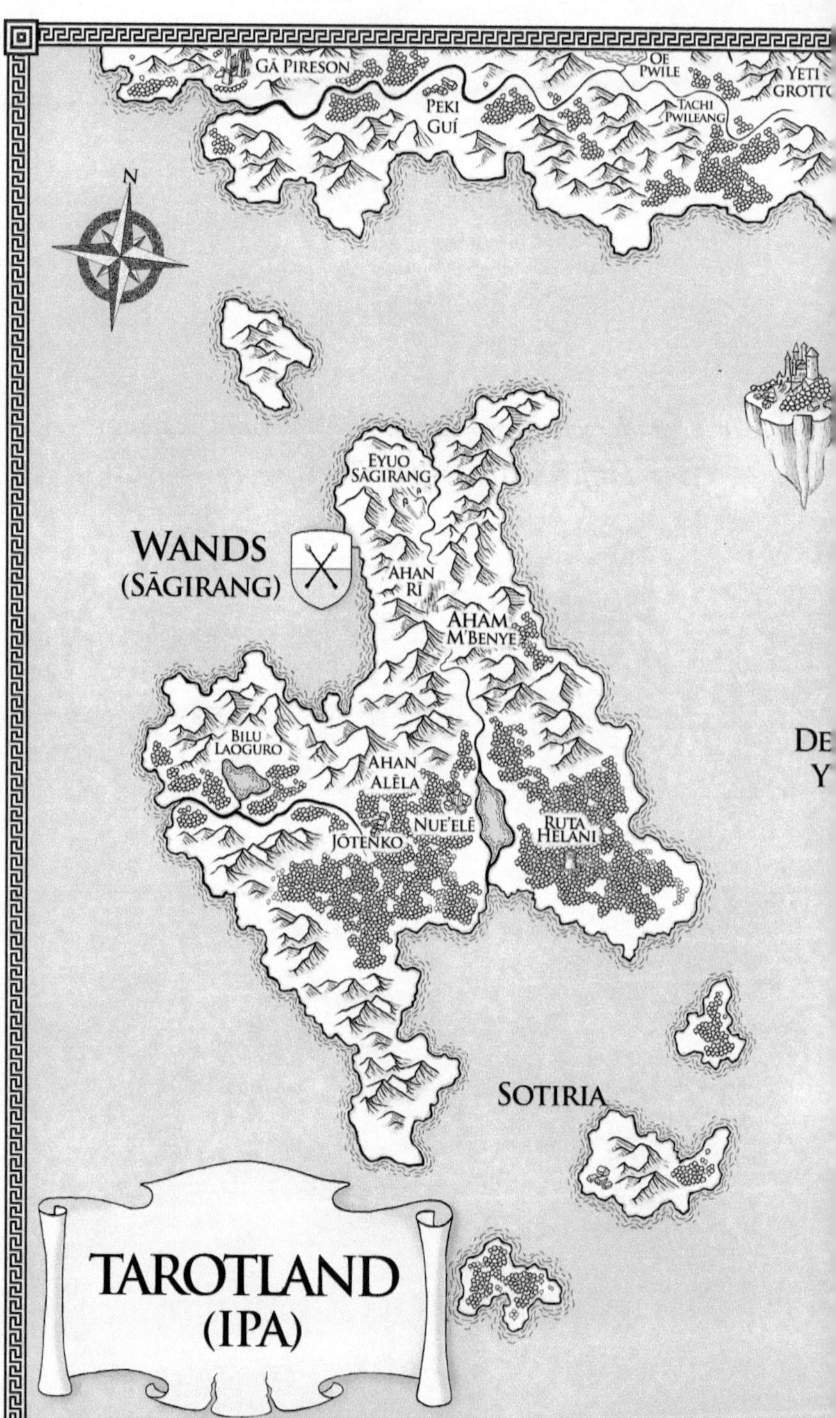

GĀ PIRESON
PEKI GUÍ
OE PWILE
YETI GROTTO
TACHI PWILEANG
N
EYUO SĀGIRANG
WANDS (SĀGIRANG)
AHAN RĪ
AHAM M'BENYE
DE Y
BILU LAOGURO
AHAN ALĒLA
NUE'ELĒ
RUTA HELANI
JŌTENKO
SOTIRIA
TAROTLAND (IPA)

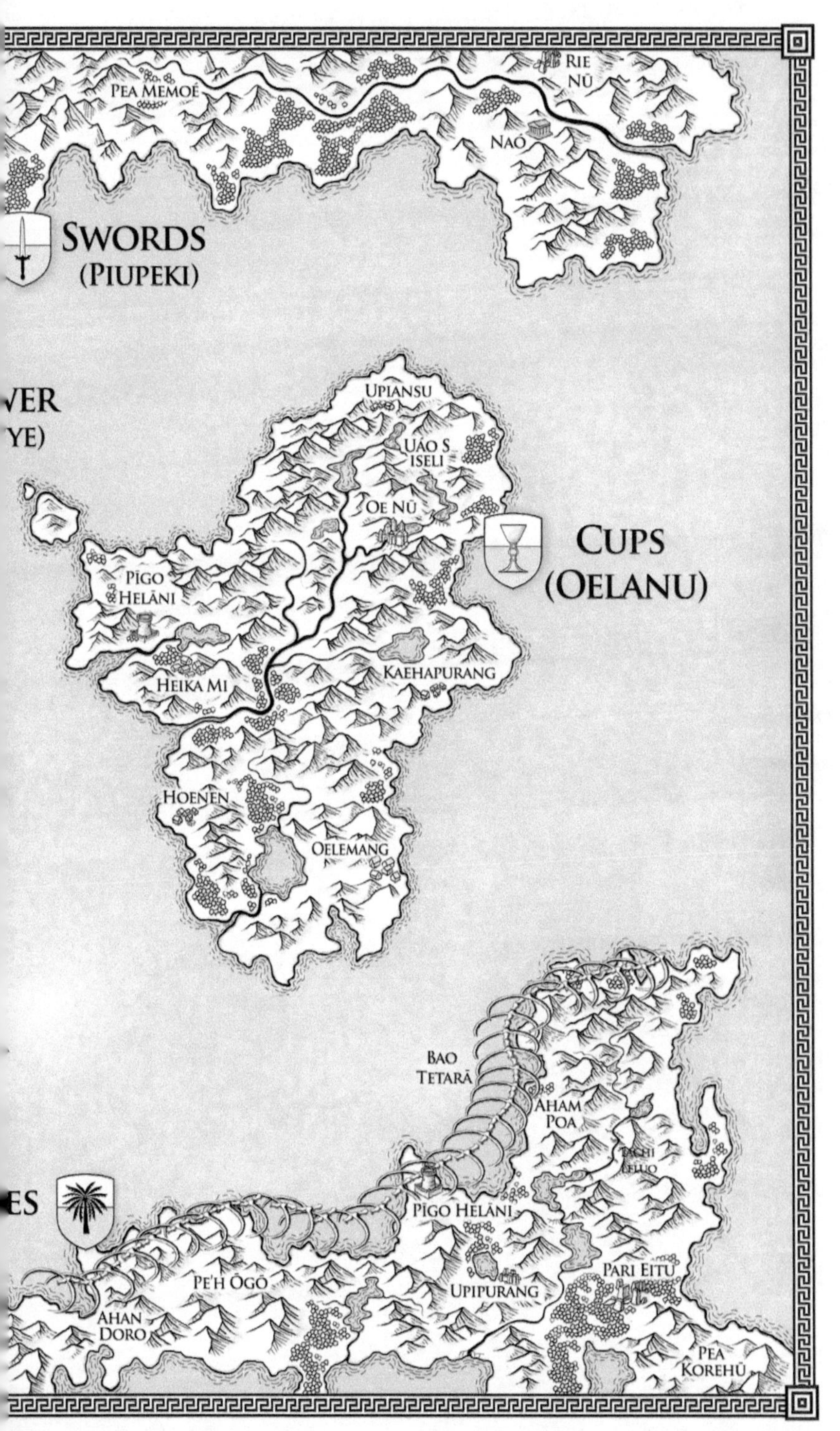

PEA MEMOÉ
RIE NŪ
NAÓ
SWORDS
(PIUPEKI)
VER
YE)
UPIANSU
UÁO S ISELI
OE NŪ
CUPS
(OELANU)
PĪGO HELĀNI
KAEHAPURANG
HEIKA MI
HOENEN
OELEMANG
BAO TETARĀ
AHAM POA
PĪGO HELĀNI
PARI EITU
UPIPURANG
ES
PE'H ŌGŌ
AHAN DORO
PEA KOREHŪ

1

My father only left me one thing when he went off to prison: a three-card monte trick. Thanks to necessity and my lucky *Alice in Wonderland* deck, it's now my ticket to survival.

Tuning out the live dark cabaret band playing in the background, I shuffle the cards on the standing table, smirking to myself as my customer, a middle-aged man who looks like he's about to teach a math class and not spend his afternoon at a creepy carnival, smacks his forehead. Poor guy came in to see a medium. Too bad he didn't walk into the psychic's tent before meeting me. Stifling a grin, I pull out my favorites, holding them up one by one. "I have three cards. The first card is a Mad Hatter," I lay it upside down on the table. "The second card is also a Mad Hatter, and the third card"—I hold it up so he can see it—"is the Cheshire Cat." I set them both upside down on the table. "All you have to do is follow Cheshire. Ready?"

"I'm ready!" His eyes are glued to where he thinks the

Cheshire Cat is, and I start moving them around, switching their placements slowly, then quicker, and slow again, intending to throw him off.

Truth is, it doesn't matter how fast or slow I move the cards. My game is rigged. It takes a sleight of hand of the three-card monte to know how to switch a card before even putting it down. But by changing the speed, he won't think I'm cheating him. Gaining his trust is my incentive. Ironic coming from me since I don't trust anyone. I mean, can you blame me though? I wouldn't even trust me.

Twice in a row, he gets it wrong. Which is perfect.

I give him a little push. "Have no fear, this one's on me. In fact, if you get it right, I'll owe *you* a dollar." I wink.

My customer pushes his glasses to the bridge of his nose as he leans over my table, rubbing his hands together.

After moving them around a good ten times, I stop, keeping them face down in a horizontal line. "Where do you think Chesh is?"

He points to the card on the right. I smile, giving him an apologetic smirk, and flip it over to show. . . "A Mad Hatter. I'm so sorry."

"Awwww. . . How'd you do that? I swear I kept my eyes on it the whole time."

I chuckle and flip the rest over, showing Cheshire in the middle where he started.

"Wow, you're good." He pulls out a twenty from his back pocket. "Keep the change."

"Thanks." I take it and stick it in my back pocket, along with my deck of cards. Sonja doesn't need to know about this little tip, especially since she's getting everything on this man's card once I swipe it with my wireless card skimmer. That is, if he has one.

"So, you're doing a séance?" I ask.

"Yeah. I'm not sure I believe in it, but a friend of mine told me Sonja is the real deal. I really want to communicate with my late wife."

"Oh, I'm so sorry." Keep him talking, Soren. "Do you have a photo of her?"

He quirks a brow.

"For the séance, I mean." I need to see his card. I should have done that first. Sonja will kill me if this was a waste of time. I have to get close enough to a customer for the skimmer to work. But it's not always that easy.

"Oh, yeah. Here." He pulls out his wallet, showing me a pocket-sized photo of a lady with curly black hair. I catch a glimpse of his watch as he turns his wrist. "Wow, nice watch!"

Are those diamond dials? Guess I was so focused on my card trick I hadn't noticed.

"Aw, this? Thanks, it was my grandfather's, then my dad's."

"Oh, nice! Only thing I've had passed down to me is this old charm." I hold up my wrist to show a little silver teacup.

"Well, hey, it's the memories that make an object valuable at the end of the day."

"That couldn't be more true."

I still didn't catch a glimpse of his credit card. Time to improvise.

"Can I get you anything to drink while you're with the medium?" I point to the bar several feet away, next to the center stage. "They have the best blackberry mead here."

Sweat beads adorn his forehead. "Yeah, that sounds great,

actually. Thanks." He opens his wallet pouch, twisting his features. "Uh, looks like I'm all out of cash. I'll have to use my card. . ."

"We take cards!" I smile.

Over his shoulder, Sonja waves her last customer out of the seance tent behind him; I give her a slight nod and hold up a finger. Wait.

"It looks like she's ready for me. I'll just get something to drink after."

"It's no bother, I can ring you up at the bar and get the card back to you while you're in there," I say, crossing my fingers behind me.

He darts his eyes back at Sonja's tent.

"It'll be fast, I promise. It's getting late in the day and the mead does run out. It's really good," I sing, showing him my award-winning smile.

"Alright, you twisted my arm. You seem like a nice girl."

My heart skips a beat as he pulls out his card, covered in foil. Dang, they're getting smart. Who taught him to do that? Foil blocks all skimming transactions. No wonder he seemed hesitant to take it out. Good thing I checked.

His glasses slide down his nose

"I'll guard it with my life." I take it and hold it up to my heart. "And she'll charge you as soon as I'm back with it, don't worry."

He smiles over his shoulder at me as he walks into her tent.

Notes of cotton candy and caramelized popcorn tickle my nostrils as I check to make sure no one is behind me. My table is set up right between the fortune teller's tent and my foster mother's séance tent.

I hum to myself and swipe the customer's credit card in the skimmer.

My first rule of the game is don't get caught. That's been my philosophy since the day that asshat social worker dumped my sister and me in our shitty foster home together. Except now the reward will be much higher than measly table scraps. Not that I hadn't had run-ins with the law before, but this time, I've joined a traveling show where I can put my talent for magic to good use.

I don't have "psychic abilities" or whatever, not that any of it is real anyway, but I can't exactly join the freak show. And I don't consider myself a thief. I do what I have to.

Six months ago, I used my favorite three-card monte trick on a couple at a park. I had no idea I was trying to con a couple of con artists, but it granted me enough lucky stars to be fostered by them. Albert and Sonja Nelson, the proud owners of this freakish carnival.

Is what I'm doing messed up? Yep. Do I care? Not one bit. It's what I'm good at, and after almost nine years of fending for myself, I finally found a family who teaches the important things in life. Like how to survive in a messed-up world.

Something rattles behind me and I glance over my shoulder as Tarotland's finest contortionist stretches her leg high over her dusty top hat adorned with a string of skulls.

A matching necklace drapes from her neck to the chair she balances on. She smiles at me behind twisted red lips that reach almost to her ears. I wave and turn back to the skimmer, my foot tapping impatiently on the outdoor carpet. Really? She has to set up here, now?

Tarotland Circus is creepy. We don't exactly attract family

folk, but more of the demented-adult types that are aching for a scare in mid-June. The ones who can't wait for Halloween. Whatever tickles their fancy. Some kids would kill to live the Addams Family life. Me? I've had my fill of creepy to last a lifetime.

All I know is that this scanner had better hurry up before this guy starts wondering where his card went.

The skimmer screeches and my eyes widen. Please don't tell me it's stuck. . . Oh no. . . Second rule of the game is to be quick about it. Crap!

I cancel the transaction, tap on the side of the device a few times, and swipe again. My pulse races as I steal a glance at the séance tent in front of me. Between the music and chattering carnival goers, I can't hear anything inside.

Come on, work. . . Okay, if worst comes to worst, this doesn't work, and we'll just have to get the next customer.

Rustling comes from inside the tent and I step back. Shit, are they finished already?

Tripping over the edge of the fortune teller's tent behind me, I hop back to catch my balance only to trip over the tent's stake and land on my ass. Ow! Damn being clumsy!

"You okay, sugar?" I turn my head to face the contortionist's sad, jester-like grin, and a groan escapes my lips. I quickly tuck the skimmer in my back pocket, away from prying eyes. Having landed with a perfect view of the inside of the psychic's tent, something shiny catches my eye. Probably a crystal ball or something. As I sit up, the shiny thing moves too quick to be an inanimate object. I squint to try to see what it is, half expecting there to be someone standing there. Except there isn't, and whatever the shiny thing was is too small.

"Yep, just dandy," I say. She offers me a sorry look and I shrug it off. Picking myself up off the ground, I wipe some grass off my two-toned leather pants. My right side is white and my left side black. With a tight black tube top, I fit right in, but unfortunately, the clothes are easy to stain.

The shiny object moves again inside the tent. This time, I catch it coming from a glass tank. Curiosity urges me forward, and before I know it, I'm inside the fortune teller's tent and peeking into the tank. A small spider with a black, translucent exoskeleton crawls toward me. If I didn't see it just moving around, I'd think it was part of a brooch. Its body isn't only shiny and the size of a dime, it looks like stained glass with ruby red shards splattered in a mosaic-like pattern.

"I hope you're not afraid of spiders."

I gasp and spin around. A lady a few inches taller than me wearing a friendly smile and intense blue eyes stares at me.

"Nope, not at all." Spiders have never bothered me. "My sister, on the other hand, she'd be screaming. I should bring her in here later," I snicker.

"You have a sister?" Her eyes fix on me, and I stop myself from pulling a face.

"Mm-hmm. What type of spider is that?"

"Phidippus speculum. They're a hybrid between the jumping spider and the mirror spider. I must say that red hair of yours could stop traffic."

I smirk and turn back to the spider, placing my fingers on the glass and mimicking the way it moves. Despite having four pairs of eyes, her two large ones give her an adorable appearance. Her body tilts to the side as she stares at me inquisitively, almost puppy-like. "Not one like I've ever seen."

"Sorry, I shouldn't stare." She turns to face the spider. "They're rare. Would you like to hold her?"

"Uhh. . .I should really get back. . ." The fortune teller is already taking the lid off the tank before I finish.

"My name's Madame Asteria. You must be Soren, Sonja's foster child."

I chuckle. "Yep. And you're the new fortune teller. I'm surprised you didn't go for Madame Arachnea." She smiles behind her long brown curls as she lowers her hand into the tank.

Peeking over my shoulder, Sonja's tent is still closed. They've been in there forever; I wonder what they're talking about. The spider attaches to her fingers as she lifts it up.

"Open your hand."

I do and she lowers the spider to the tips of my fingers. It crawls to the center of my hand, its eight legs tickling my skin. I stiffen. Again, not afraid of spiders, but I've never had one crawl on me before and it feels weird. A nervous giggle escapes my breath. The spider jumps onto my shoulder, and I hold my breath.

"Oh, please, don't be frightened."

I tuck my chin into my neck, afraid if I move, I might lose it. Without warning the spider jumps off me and glides across the tent. I gasp and try to follow its movements with my eyes. It lands on a glass display case at the far end of the tent.

Sharing a glance with Madame Asteria, she nods at me. I take it as a cue to follow.

I make my way through her dusty red carpet, passing a round table draped with a burgundy tablecloth. At the far corner is a black and white pin-striped single couch with a burgundy velvet pillow. Incense smothers my nostrils as I inch up to where the spider sits, legs sprawled out on the door of the glass. "Hey there," I whisper. It twitches a leg. Inside the case, a gold glare grabs my attention. The back of the case is a mirror, and my reflection stares back at me. My bright red lips match my wavy red hair. And right in front of me, being held by a frame stand, is a single Tarot card with a thick gold trim. In the center is a world that's not Earth. . . I squint, tracing the five black pearl islands over gold waves. A purple shimmer ripples across it and I do a double take.

The waves start to move. Like a magnetic pull, I can't take my eyes off the card. How is it doing this? A pirate ship emerges through the waves, and a sea serpent whips its tail, like a moving picture. Then the ship grows bigger—that or the image is zooming toward the ship—and lands on a guy a little older than me. Beautiful, tall, and with subtly pointy ears. His fierce dark eyes stare somewhere into the distance. Orange veins ripple inside his irises and he lets out a violent scream. I gasp and the image vanishes; the card returns back to its original form.

The spider's mosaic glass pattern reflects off the glass, and I snap my attention back to it. My heart pounds in my chest. I'm out of breath from just standing here. I snap my gaze back to the card. Did that just happen?

"See anything you like?"

I glance at Madame Asteria and smile nervously. No, that wasn't real. I mean, obviously not. I've gotten too much sun, duh. I squint back at the gold trim edges of the card. "Is that real gold?"

"That's right," she smiles, making her way over.

"Woah. . . I've never seen a Tarot card like it. You really have a rare collection of things."

She puckers her lips and scoops the spider from the glass.

"Not that I'm calling your pet a thing. . ." Nice going, Soren.

"It's fine. Her name's Philo."

"That's a pretty name." I say, shaking off the strange vision I just had. Is that what fortune tellers see when they read cards? "So, how come there's only one card? Don't Tarot cards come in. . .sets?"

"Oh, it's incomplete. And"—she holds her hands out, letting Philo walk freely over them—"that one's a collector's item."

"Why don't you sell it?" Shit, a pawnbroker would know what to do. Probably melt it for the gold.

"Too valuable to sell. Besides, no one would want only one Tarot card. This particular one is number twenty-one and is the Tarot's World Card—different from other World Cards you may have seen."

"I never paid much attention to other Tarot card decks, but I remember the original having a woman on it. I glance back at it, and another purple glare washes over the surface. My breath hitches.

"No one really knows the true origins of Tarot. But yes, the one you're thinking of is also very old." She smiles curtly at me.

"I didn't know that."

"Hey, Sore-ren! Mom's freaking out over there!"

My face pales. Crap! "Uh, sorry! I have to go!"

Madame Asteria is already making her way back to Philo's tank, with her back to me. I glance at the card, and without giving it a second thought, I push the glass in, and it pops open. I glimpse back at Asteria, her back is still to me. The sounds of the busy carnival have muffled the glass door opening. Quickly, I swipe the card, and replace it with a different one laid out on the shelf. She would have to check the actual card before she notices it missing. I stick the stolen black and gold card in my pocket. Sonja doesn't have to know about this either. I can pawn it to stash more cash for my own place, or if this skimmer doesn't work, I'll have this as a bargaining chip.

I rush past Asteria and meet my foster brother, Bradley, at the entrance of the tent. Sonja and Albert's real son. Fourteen and immature as hell. I never hated my name so much until I met him.

Madame Asteria follows me out. "Maybe you can come back for a reading sometime."

I scoff internally, forcing a smile as I leave the tent. She's nice and all, but I don't believe in that stuff. I'll drink some water and shake it off. Visions aren't real.

Besides, with a valuable like that one, I'm sure Sonja will kick the fortune teller out as soon as I tell her what I did and how much I got for it. I'll probably never see Asteria again.

"Hurry up, sore loser! She's pissed. Have you been hiding in there this whole time?"

"Shut up and stop calling me that. Is the customer pissed off?"

"Nah, he forgot all about his credit card. Mom had him in a deep trance with her hypnotic séance crap. She told him you just didn't want to disturb him."

"Oh, good, good." A sigh leaves my lips and I make a dash to the tavern to get his mead.

I meet Bradley back at the entrance to Sonja's dark tent, but before I can walk inside, she barges out of the closed curtains and grabs my arm, almost spilling the beverage.

"Where the hell have you been?" Sonja's large hoop earrings reflect the sunlight.

"I. . .uh. . .the skimmer got stuck and then—"

"Got stuck? Did you get the information? Why didn't you come get me?"

"You said never to disturb—"

"You could have found Albert or Bradley."

"Sorry."

"Ha ha. Soren's sorry," Bradley muses.

I scowl at him. "You're an idiot."

"Well, no time to lose." Sonja holds her hand out. "Let me have it."

I hand her the credit card and receipt. She turns back to the tent and looks over her shoulder.

"This better have worked, or it's a double shift for you tomorrow."

Awesome. Rolling my eyes, I turn to Bradley. "Have you seen Talia?"

He shrugs. "I saw her around the food stands, but that was like three hours ago."

Great. "I better go find her to get ready to go." I try to keep her far away from thievery and crap as much as possible. If I can at least protect my little sister from turning out like me, I'll have done something right in my life.

"Why do you overprotect her anyway? She's not even your real sister."

"And you're not my real brother. So what?"

"And we hate each other."

"That's because you're a dick," I snap. He snickers. "You don't know what it was like in the group home. We've both been through a lot. I care for her as if she were my real sister. You know, like some friends do?"

"No friends that I know of."

"Well, I feel sorry for you."

He narrows his eyes and turns his gaze to the floor. I almost feel bad for him. Almost.

"She'll disappoint you, eventually. People always do."

I scoff and turn toward the pink and orange sun setting behind the food stands. A crowd of people stand around the live band next to the tavern, while a few vendors start packing up.

I don't trust easily. But with Talia, it's different. Maybe because she's younger than me and depended on me for protection at the group home. He can eat shit though, I trust her more than I trust him or his parents. Social workers have told me I really need to start letting my guard down if I ever want a forever family. Pah. Yeah, right. Nothing lasts and trusting only makes it worse.

The band plays their final song and people start clapping and cheering. I gotta hand it to Albert and Sonja; they manage to attract guests to their creepy carnival everywhere we go. Six months with them and they've scammed hundreds of people from California to Louisiana. Thankfully, they agreed to foster Talia too, so long as I help them with their little heists.

They're not the best lot, but, hey, one more year and I'll be an adult. Well, one year and three days technically. But who's counting?

"No, no. It's missing. I had it on my wrist."

I snap a look back at Sonja's tent. Mark is standing outside it, panic in his voice. What's going on?

"Your watch, was it, dear? And you're absolutely certain it couldn't have fallen off?"

"Rolexes don't just fall off, lady."

"Alright, let's all just calm down. It must be here somewhere. I'll help you look."

I step toward them. The man pants frantically as he searches the grass outside the tent.

"It's not here. It isn't anywhere. It has to be back in your tent."

"We already looked, but we can look again." Sonja opens the curtain wider, motioning a hand to let him in.

Sweat drips off his forehead as he darts back inside.

My eyebrows rise to my forehead. Eesh. This is not what we need. A missing expensive watch could blow our whole operation. Two hands cover my eyes from behind.

"Guess who?"

"Ha ha. Not now, Talia, this customer is about to lose his shit."

"What's going on?"

"The customer we were working lost his Rolex and probably thinks one of us stole it."

Talia puckers her lips as she toys with the *Alice in Wonderland* charm on her bracelet. It's similar to mine, but hers is the white rabbit, while mine is a teacup. It's sort of our thing. My mom giving me this charm is one of the last memories I have of her.

The man bellows from inside the tent. "I'm calling the

cops! They'll do a thorough search." He storms over to a tree to place the call.

"Is that really necessary? I said I'd help you look." Sonja shoots me a stare and I walk over.

"You didn't steal anything from him, did you?" she whispers.

"What? How? I only took his credit card and stepped away. I'm not that stupid."

Her eyes snap to Talia. "How about you?"

"She wasn't even here," I hiss, planting a hand on Talia's shoulder. Her mouth hangs open. She isn't used to being accused of stealing. A few minutes later Albert shows up. Sonja must have texted him.

"Well, the best I can do is undo the tent, so that we can see clearly," Albert says as he opens the flap of the door wider.

"It could have been any one of these freaks," the customer shouts. I grimace. He's actually not wrong, but still, calling us freaks is low. Seriously though, how would his watch have just disappeared? I sure as hell didn't take it. But. . .crap, he's going to think it's me because I gave him a compliment. Who wears a Rolex to a circus anyway?

About twenty minutes later, two cop cars pull into the entrance and park right outside the tents.

"Come on, let's give them some space." I nudge Talia over to the side of Madame Asteria's tent. The contortionist isn't there anymore, so I sit her down on the now-empty seat.

Two cops get out of their cars. My face deadpans as I recognize the one with tight braids pulled back on her head. "Shit."

"What's wrong?"

"I know the woman cop. That's Officer Brown. I've had a few. . .run-ins with her."

"That's Officer Brown? Good thing you're not in trouble."

"Mm-hmm." Good thing, but I'd still rather not be in her line of sight.

Albert walks over to speak to the officers, his hands on his hips. The customer starts walking over to the tent. The other cop follows him. A few of the carnies circle around to see what the commotion is all about. I attempt to ignore their footsteps shuffling through the grass as I try to listen in.

"Ma'am, do you mind if we check your tent, please?" Officer Brown asks.

"Go ahead. He already checked, but that's fine." She throws her hands up in the air and follows them inside. Moving a bit closer, I catch wind of a few words. "He could have dropped it anywhere in the park."

"What do you think is gonna happen?" Talia whispers.

"Shush. Let me hear."

"Well, I'm out." Wolfman, one of the carnies who got close enough to watch, waves at me and I wave back. Good. Leave. This ain't no show.

"There it is! In there!"

My mouth hangs open. Holy shit, he found it? I cock my head to the side and glance down at Talia. "See? He did drop it, I'm sure—"

"Who is Talia Landry?"

Confusion flickers on my face as the male cop walks out of the tent holding my backpack and my sister's wallet. My eyes widen as I stare down at my sister. "You didn't steal it, did you?"

"W-what? No!"

Right, of course not. I take a step back so that she can get up, but she stays put. I clear my throat and tilt my head toward the cop. "He's calling you. . . You have to say something."

"Talia Landry?"

Sonja and Albert rush out of the tent, followed by Officer Brown.

Her brows scrunch, and she slides off her seat. "Um. . .I'm Talia. . ."

"Oh, there's more, yeah? Why are there two wallets in here? You, who is Soren Vyris?"

His Cajun accent resonates in my ears. "That's me. And because we share a bag."

The cop looks up from my picture ID in his hand as my open backpack dangles from his arm. "Can you tell me why you had this watch in your bag then, Ms. Vyris?"

No freaking way. My eyes slowly land back on Talia. No. . . She couldn't have. . . Could she? Talia's face pales as she stares at me. Shaking her head, she shrugs, her eyes wide.

"I didn't take it, I swear. I wasn't even in there!" Talia's voice breaks. Officer Brown steps forward past her partner.

"I've got this, Boudreaux. I know this one."

Ah, crap, here it comes.

"Ms. Vyris! Why am I not surprised to see you here? Are we graduating from convenience store jewelry and onto expensive watches?"

My cheeks flush, aware that people are watching. Even though I know the circus has pretty much cleared out, her voice is loud. I shake my head. "No. I don't know how that got there." She looks straight at Talia.

I speak instead. "I have no idea how it got there, but we sure as hell didn't steal shit, and you can leave my sister out of this. She didn't do anything." Crap! Officer Brown raises her eyebrows and chin as she drops her eyes at me. Dammit, Soren, for once, why can't you keep quiet?

"You best check that attitude, young lady. This would be the third time this month we've had a problem with you."

Behind Brown, Officer Boudreaux rummages through our bag and takes out something that looks like it could be another credit card or ID. After he returns the watch to the man, he holds the card up, takes another look at the man, and shakes his head. "Looks like they stole more than just a watch."

My mouth falls open. We're definitely being set up. I dart my eyes around the premises. Where did Bradley go? That creep. . . It had to have been him. He's the only one who had been lurking around here while I had the skimmer.

"This watch is a family heirloom," the customer says. "I almost drove away without it, and my identity could have been stolen. You better believe I'm pressing charges! Some séance! It was probably all bullshit." He points his finger at Sonja's chest. "You really had me fooled!"

Albert cuts in and blocks him. "Take it easy, she's the real deal. None of this is her fault."

"Talia, it's okay. Just go sit down," I tell her.

"Well, I'm afraid, Mrs. Jackowitz, if he wants to press charges, he can. And unfortunately, thanks to the shared bag, Miss Vyris is an accomplice. I'm gonna have to take them both in."

"What!" My voice squeals.

Oh, this cannot be happening. And not to Talia. "Please,

don't take my sister in. I swear we did not steal. We're being set up." My throat dries up as Sonja and Albert shoot me a hard steel look. I gulp.

"And who exactly is setting you up?" Officer Brown asks.

My heart hammers in my throat. Rule number three? Yeah, this is the worst one. If rule number one fails, I have to take the blame, so my foster parents don't get arrested. It makes sense because I'm a minor and will be given less time. If my foster parents get caught. . .we're all screwed. Not only will we lose the circus, but we'll all go right back into the system. I can't rat out Bradley. I have no proof it was him and his parents will deny it. That bastard. He wanted to get rid of us from the start.

"Ms. Vyris? Are you done fabricating the lie you're fixin' to tell us?"

I choke on a sigh. Shit. "It was me. Just please, let Talia go."

"I hate to say this, but no can do. He's pressing charges, so I have to take you both in." She lowers her voice. "Listen, I know you've been working through your problems, but we've had numerous cases with you." She turns to Sonja. "I have to put aside my feelings and do what the law tells me."

"N-no!" Talia cries. "But I didn't do it! *Soren!*"

"Soren Vyris and Talia Landry, you have the right to remain silent. . ."

Rolling my eyes as they read us our rights, I bow my head as they stick us both in different police cars. I cannot freaking believe this is happening right now. As we pull out of the park, I take one last look at the large Tarotland Circus sign. There, standing next to the giant, creepy, jester-like grin of the demented clown entrance, Bradley waves goodbye with a menacing sneer.

2

PROCESSING TOOK HOURS. THE INFAMOUS MUGSHOT after waiting in line to take them, fingerprinting, more waiting, and now being stuck in this disgusting holding cell with a cluster of obnoxious girls. To make it worse, the floor is sticky, it smells of urine, and I'm pretty sure I saw a rat. Not to mention, I've been stuck in tight leather pants for hours. But nothing, none of that, comes close to how much I hate my sister being stuck in here with me.

"So, what happens now?" Talia's eyes are bloodshot from crying, and she's sitting with her legs, prickled with goose bumps, against mine.

"I don't know, Talia. We just have to wait till Sonja and Albert bail us out."

"How long will that take? That girl over there said she's been here for six hours!"

"I don't know."

"Great, thanks."

I look at her sympathetically. She doesn't deserve this. "Hey, why don't we talk about something else?"

She purses her lips and keeps her eyes locked straight ahead at the gray wall. I sigh and lean back in my seat.

"At least your birthday is in three days," she says. Here we go.

Pinching the bridge of my nose, I sigh.

"Then one more year and you can leave."

"I won't leave you behind," I say.

"Sure."

"Hey. Stop that. Would I have left you at the center if I didn't care about you?" I ball my fist and look off to the side. How could she think I would leave her after all this? I mean, really! I've done everything I can to make sure we do not get separated, which is hard, as we're not even related. Normally siblings get separated anyway so I really had to "talk the talk" to get her adopted with me. "I can't believe you'd still think I'd abandon you," I huff.

"No, but this time will be different. You'd be leaving me with a family."

I see her point, but there's no way I'd leave her with them. . . What can I do though? I can't adopt her. "Listen to me, even if I do move out, I'd get a job and stay nearby. Heck, maybe I'd still be at the circus. I'd still see you every day. And then in four years. . . you'll be eighteen."

"Four years though!"

"Four years go by quick. It won't be so bad; I'll figure something out. Besides, my eighteenth birthday is an entire year away anyway. What else do you want to talk about?"

"Maybe my mom will be able to get me after all this." Her voice cracks as she slumps on the bench.

"Yeah. . ." I place a hand on her shoulder. "Hopefully. But till then, you have me."

"But you always say you can hardly trust yourself!"

"True. . . I do say that, but that's because I don't trust anyone besides you. And sometimes I have to do what I don't want to. But you should know that with you, it's different."

"You know, if you learned to trust people, things might be easier for you. You know, when you're out on your own."

I give her an indulgent smile. "Yeah, maybe. . ." Bullshit. With everything she's been through in her life I still don't understand how my sister can be so trusting.

Talia went into foster care three years ago when the police went into her home after her mom's ex-boyfriend called the cops for negligence. Talia was an only child, eleven years old, and playing a video game while her mom wasn't home. I think they found illegal substances around the house; Talia doesn't talk about it. But if her mom gets cleaned up and gets her act together, at least there's some hope.

Me on the other hand. . . There's no one coming for me. Mom has been in St. Germain's Hospital all the way down in Florida for dementia since I was eight. For about a year, it was just me and my dad against the world. Until he didn't come home one night. He told me he was out working, but I knew all those sleight-of-hand card tricks weren't just for show. I waited and waited, until finally, a social worker came to pick me up.

I trace my little teacup charm with my fingers as a memory

of me at seven years old flashes through my mind. Suddenly, I'm sitting in the living room watching cartoons.

My mom's in the kitchen. I can see her through the open doorway having a serious conversation with somebody at the table, no phone nearby. Her tone is strict, worried, like when she's mad at me for running in the house and tripping over my toys. Except, I know my father is outside in the yard.

I hop off the couch and walk over to see who she's speaking to like that and startle when a black spider with a red hourglass on its back stares right back at her.

"Oh, honey, come!" Her eyes beam at me and she waves me over. "There's nothing to be afraid of."

Curiosity pushes me forward; besides the fact I trust my mom with every fiber of my being, I know she would never put me in harm's way.

My eyes widen as a spider crawls on her hands. "Cup your hands. Like this."

I cup my hands and hold them up to her as she meets my hands with hers, edging the spider to climb onto mine.

"So pretty," she says. "Don't worry, it won't hurt you."

I giggle as its legs tickle the back of my hands and it runs up my arm. My mom's face goes blank, and I hold my breath.

"Aletha, don't you do it!"

"Mommy?"

"I will kill you if you do, don't you dare! Aletha, I'm warning you!"

My knees quiver and I step back as her features drastically change from being kind, to frightened, and now menacing. The spider crawls around my neck, and my shoulder jerks up. My mom grabs a frying pan off the stove and swings it high over her head.

"Let her go!" she yells.

"Mommy, no!" I scream, bringing my arms up to block her from hitting me and forgetting all about the spider.

My father bursts into the kitchen and runs up to her, grabbing the pan from her hands.

"Diana, what on God's earth are you doing? Were you going to hit Soren?"

My mother gasps, "No, I—"

Tears stroll down my face. I gape at her as her hands shake and confusion spreads across her face. She shakes her head rapidly and starts to mumble inconsistencies. About a black widow spider wanting to kill me. But she had befriended it before.

I think that was when my father realized she was unwell.

The spider drops from my back and my father—pale in the face—squashes it with his shoe. My mother shrieks and starts hitting my dad on his back.

She said he murdered her *friend*. The same one she just tried to kill. It made no sense. Back then I hadn't known about the venomous black widow spider. My dad was so angry she had brought it into the house, but he seemed more overwhelmed about my mother's sudden changes. After that, she was diagnosed with early dementia, and was soon considered a danger to others and herself.

But I don't talk about that with Talia. I do wish I could see her, though, not that she remembers me. The last time I had visited her was with my dad. Back then, I didn't know what was wrong with her; now, I'm old enough to know they had her so drugged up, she didn't recognize me. It's not like I can go on my own with no money. And the Nelsons would never take me. I clear the lump in my throat. Maybe someday I can see her.

We sit in silence for the next couple of hours. Correctional officers come in, call a few names, come back, drop off newbies, and repeat.

"How long have we been here?" She breaks our silence.

"Feels like a lot longer than six hours," I say with a sigh. We got arrested around six p.m.; it took like two hours to process us. "I don't know, it could be anywhere between four and six in the morning."

"Oh my god, I'm so tired."

"I know. Me too. We'll be out soon."

"How do you know?"

Her forehead crinkles. I can tell she's really scared about being here. To be honest, I'm a bit frightened, too, but I'm trying to hide it for her sake. "Hey, you know how Alice gets caught by the Queen of Hearts, and the entire time she pretends to be someone else until she learns how to defeat her?"

"Yeah."

"They say that one interpretation of the Queen of Hearts is that she is a reflection of Alice's troubles that she learns to overcome."

"So? What's that got to do with being stuck in jail?"

"Nothing. I'm just trying to distract you. But also, maybe try pretending we're not really here."

"I'd give anything to be able to escape to Wonderland right now."

"Me, too, kid. But also, there's a lesson in this somewhere. When Alice returns home from Wonderland, she's stronger and braver than she was before, after learning so much and conquering her issues."

Talia stares blankly at me.

"Just be strong, Talia, we'll get through this."

The C.O. drops another girl in. I try to avoid eye contact with anyone who comes in here, so I just keep looking straight ahead. Not tryin' to fall asleep in here either.

"What'd you two clowns do?"

A stubby girl around sixteen with pink spiky hair snaps me back to the present.

"What?" So much for avoiding eye contact.

"You two are dressed like you just walked out of a circus."

"That's because we did."

"Ohh, attitude!" The girl holds her hands up and moves her body in a circular motion. "So, what are you in for? Must've been something bad to get locked up these days."

"Nope. They just hate me." And it was my third strike.

"How 'bout her?"

Talia sucks in a breath but stays quiet.

I shrug. "Nothing. She shouldn't be here."

"Ha. Guilty by association, huh?"

Talia turns her cheek.

"What? Don't wanna talk to me?"

"She's shy."

The girl walks over, and I lean in.

"Can't be too shy round here, kid. You'll get eaten alive."

"Hey, just leave her alone, alright?"

"Know what? I don't feel like leaving her alone cause I'm bored as shit. How you like that?"

Alright, now I stand to face her. "Oh, you're bored? How 'bout I give you some entertainment then?" I push two fingers against her chest hard enough to make her take a step back. "I said, leave her the hell alone."

"Soren, it's not worth it," Talia calls after me.

The girl pushes forward with her chest, but I don't budge. We face off for a few seconds. She stares at me, and I don't flinch.

"Soren, come on. Do you want more time?"

"Fine, I'll leave your little girlfriend alone." She spits.

"She's my sister, bitch."

"Whatever, *bitch*."

"Ooooooooo!" someone yells. "There's gonna be a fight up in here!" Shouts come from the other girls as they jump up in excitement, slapping Pinky on the shoulder to edge her on. I ready myself just in case.

The door opens and everyone shuts up. "Oh, I better not be hearing there's 'bout to be a fight." The correctional officer slams the door behind her and looks everyone in the eye, one at a time. I swallow.

"Ladies." She eyes her clipboard. "Everyone stand."

Another correctional officer walks inside, moves past her, and starts cuffing girls, starting at the entrance of the holding cell. I share a look with Talia who's nervously biting her bottom lip. *"It'll be okay,"* I mouth.

"Ey, where we goin?" Pinky asks as she's being cuffed.

"To the open bay," the C.O. responds.

My heart hammers in my chest. If they're moving us to

sleeping units, that means either the Nelsons haven't bailed us out yet, or they aren't going to at all.

Once Talia and I are cuffed, we follow the C.O. out of the holding cell. Single file, and with the other officer behind us, we're led up narrow gray stairs to a noisy open bay area where the general population of inmates are spending the weekend.

There are four bunks in each cubicle, and thankfully, Talia and I are placed in the same unit. Less thankfully, Pinky is assigned to one of the remaining bunks. A weeping girl is in the other.

A correctional officer stands at the entrance of the unit giving us instructions on what to do with our clothes.

With my back to them, I quickly change to the orange jumpsuit left on my bed. I take the bottom bunk so that Talia could take the top. It's easier for me to keep an eye on her that way. Once changed, I take my belongings and place them in the gray tray on the bed, as instructed. They already collected my phone when I got here, but now they want my clothes too.

"How do I know y'all are gonna keep my stuff with what I came in with?" Pinky demands.

"Because I'm putting a sticker with your inmate number on the trays."

"Lemme see it."

While Pinky keeps her distracted, my fingers move inside my pants pocket and I slip out my deck of playing cards and the Tarot card I stole earlier. I discreetly stick it in the pocket of my jumpsuit, take my tray, and hand it over to the C.O.

At least I'll have something to look at while I'm here.

That one's a collector's item. . . Too valuable to sell.

And I don't trust correctional officers.

"Inmates. Get ready for count in a few minutes." The C.O. turns around, carrying four trays, and leaves us to our own devices.

I lie back on the bed, and Talia sits on the edge of it.

"Soren," Talia whispers. "Are the Nelsons going to get us out of here?"

"Don't worry, I'm sure they will."

"A-are you sure?"

"I'm sure they're just being slow. We'll be out of here before you know it. Okay?"

She nods.

"Y'all talk a lot of shit," Pinky says.

"Shut up," I snap.

Pinky lays her head down on her mattress and covers her eyes. "Whatever," she muffles. "Too tired for this shit."

I grab Talia's hand. "Be strong, okay? Like Alice."

An hour passes and the C.O. walks back around. "Ladies, get up for count."

We all stand up at the corners of our beds.

The C.O. looks down at her clipboard, takes a finger, and goes down a list. "Virus?"

Pinky snorts. I arch an eyebrow.

"Virus, Sorn? Who is Virus, Sorn?"

"You mean Vyris, Soren?" Why the hell can't anyone ever get my name right? Laughter erupts through the room and I roll my eyes. Idiots. "Veerees," I say. More laughter bellows throughout. "It's Greek."

"Think you're being funny?"

"I'm just telling you how my name is pronounced."

"Do you want to get out of here, or do you want to spend

the weekend down in solitary? Let's try it without attitude, you ready?"

"Yes, ma'am."

"Good. "Veerees," she scribbles something next to my name.

"Landry, Talia."

Talia's voice shakes. "Here."

She calls out the other two names and then leaves.

After "lights out" is called, I lie on my back, facing the top bunk. Open bay sounds like the Trans-Siberian Orchestra of snores, and it's impossible to fall sleep.

Luckily, Talia was able to, but that girl can sleep through a hurricane. I take out the Tarot card and spin it around in my hand, letting my mind wander. Whoever created this card sure had an imagination. How cool would it be if this map were real?

Maybe it would be a place where Talia and I wouldn't be running from creepy foster parents and in constant trouble with the law.

A purple light swipes the face of the card, outlining the gold trim and black engravings of the land over the gold sea. Goose bumps make the hairs on my arms stand on end. Fierce eyes resurface in my memory, and I shake the image away. It was a trick of the light. That's all.

Something tickles my neck and a shriek escapes my throat as Philo pops out of nowhere and crawls down my arm! "Woah, where did you come from?" I whisper loudly, looking around me to make sure I didn't just wake anyone up. She must have hid in my clothes back at the carnival. It's strange I didn't feel her or see her at all this whole time.

Pinky stirs in her sleep, but then her snoring continues.

Philo jumps on the card, and a strange magnetic pull forces it out of my hand. The card drops on the floor.

I reach down to pick the card up when an odd smell of saltwater assaults my nostrils. It takes me a few minutes to realize the smell is coming from the card and not around me. A bright white light emanates from the card, and I inch back on the bunk. The room starts to spin, wait—no, it's not the jail room that's spinning, a whirlpool is opening from the hole on the floor!

Philo jumps into the whirlpool, and I gape. Strong winds whip around me and a magnetic force starts pulling me down. Forget the spider! Save myself!

Panic constricts my lungs as I spin around, jerking my body sideways, trying to grab onto something, anything. The bed, the leg of the bunk! I dig my nails into the mattress but the force from the hole dragging me down is too strong. I'm pulled in and the last thing I grab is the edge of the floor until I'm ripped away and sucked down.

And I fall fast. And hard. Down into an unknown abyss.

Next thing I know, I land with a deafening, sharp splash.

3

M

Y LUNGS BURST OPEN IN FURIOUS WATER-regurgitating coughs. Disoriented, I open my eyes and choke on a gasp. Staring down at me from my right is a man with no eyes. His long black hair is dripping wet, and a gaping hole in his cheek reveals his skull underneath. Strands of flesh hang loosely over the hole.

My eyes roll to the back of my skull as my head hits the floor.

Unfamiliar whispering voices hover over me.

What language is that?

A low snarl jerks me awake. My vision comes into focus and I'm met with a dark shape prowling over me. A pair of burning scarlet eyes and shaggy black fur comes into view.

That. . .that can't be a. . .wolf? I open my mouth to speak, but saltwater and humidity scratch at my throat; my chest feels like it's been stabbed with twenty icicles. I clutch my chest and gasp, too slow and weak to get away from the beast.

Two guys and a girl in a brass-geared wheelchair block me in. One of the men to my left—tall, bald, and burly, with chocolate skin—puts his hand on the wolf's chest, pulling her away from me. "*E onī, Iéle. Pitano to kivenete a eki iesī.*" he says.

The woman speaks next, *"N'twa'r a n'eakeang?"* Water drips from her hair, down her face, flashing her skull beneath her skin. Lightning strikes and I scramble back.

A faded memory of the skeleton resurfaces in my mind. "Where am I?" I mumble as I wipe my eyes.

The lady dries her face with a cloth and her skin comes back to reveal the face of a girl around her early twenties with wet hair and rosy cheeks.

They exchange glances and the girl in the wheelchair reaches into a bandolier full of glass bottles. She selects one filled with a clear liquid and offers it to me.

"W-what is it?" My throat scratches again. I'm hesitant to take anything from someone who was a skeleton a minute ago, but I'm dying of thirst. "Is it water?" The lady offers me a smile, uncorks the top, and nudges the bottle to me again. I reach over and take it. With one motion, I pour it into my throat and swallow.

My mouth twists, and I push down the bile rising in my throat. The bottle falls from my hands, and I grab my throat. A high-pitched laugh erupts from the long-haired guy at my right.

"Licorice? I thought it was water!" I gag.

The wolf growls at my sudden outburst, but the lady in the chair holds her back.

The medium-height guy with long black hair and red

lipstick grins as he picks the bottle back up with matching painted nails and hands it to the lady.

"Good. Now we can understand each other," she says. "Who are you and where did you come from?"

"Oh, so you do speak English," I say.

Confusion flickers on their faces. The woman twists the bottle in her hands. "You drank a translation potion."

I quirk a brow and stare at the nasty drink. Yeah, right.

"Well? It's not every day someone falls from the sky and almost drowns." Her tone sounds accusatory, as if I had meant to almost drown.

My face blanks. "Falls from. . .the sky?" I peer up at tumultuous clouds formed overhead as a few icy raindrops start to patter down on my face. A purple hue seeps down from the moon and a shimmery violet light swirls through the sky. I'm instantly reminded of the Tarot card. . . But how. . .? Okay, I chuckle. I see what's going on here. I'm dreaming. Duh. I must have fallen and hit my head. Come to think of it, I rub the back of my head. It hurts.

The burly man leans in and with a thick accent I've never heard before, he says, "We are late now. I raise anchors, yes?" My eyes flick up to him and stop at his ears that form subtle tips. He's large, a tower of a man, strong. He looks like he could grab the skinny long-haired guy with one arm and throw him far. He wears a long coat down to his knees. Dark stripes decorate his neck and hands. A drop of water drips down his brow from his bald head, leaving an impossible trace of his skull visible. He wipes it away, and his skin reappears where the water was. I gape at him.

Without waiting for a response, he squints at me before turning on his heel and disappearing behind us.

Anchor? The ground moves beneath me, lifting me upward and then down. I mean, I know I fell into the ocean, hence the almost drowning bit, but. . . I guess it just registered that I'm on a boat. Because I was just in jail.

"Here, have some water this time." The guy with the long hair to my right offers me a canteen. Narrowing my eyes, I stare at it. Raindrops patter on his arm, and it's almost as if the rain melts away his skin to reveal his skeletal hand. This must be a nightmare.

"It's alright. It's real water. I promise." He grins as he dries his face with his other hand. Strange dream.

I slowly take it and wet my lips before swallowing. Yep, water. I chug a few long gulps, my chest still heaving from the fall.

"How'd you end up at sea?" he asks.

My eyes widen. "I-I don't know. One minute I was with my sister in a jail cell, and the next I was. . .falling."

"That's curious," the woman says. I squint hard at her wheelchair. It's different than any I've ever seen before with gears and bottles and brass and copper tubing. I crane my neck up and notice a light gleaming down on us through the mist. A gas lamp? "Who are you people?"

A deep growl snaps my attention back to the black wolf.

"I'm Ajax, but you can call me AJ, and that's Tessa," he says. Tessa nods at me. "And the one who was just here is Kaehante. And you are?"

"Soren."

"Well, Soren, you're lucky we found you in time, you'd either have ended up dead or eaten. . .basically just dead."

I frown. The cold wind tousles my hair. I bring my knees to my chest, wrapping my arms around me.

AJ, now crouched on his feet, glances at Tessa. "So, what now?"

"Nothing. Wait for Nkella to decide."

"She needs to get out of those wet clothes."

"Who's Nkella?" I ask.

"He's the captain of the ship. Welcome aboard the *Devil's Gambit*," he says with an apologetic wince.

The *Devil's Gambit*. My mind takes me to the pirate ship that had come to life on the Tarot card. This can't be happening.

Heavy footsteps approach from behind. AJ stands and I swallow.

A deep, husky voice cuts through the air. "Have her stand under the light."

AJ extends his hand out to me, and I take it, still wet and freezing, I climb onto my feet and pull on my jail uniform pants to separate them from my skin. Not uncomfortable at all.

Tessa reverses, giving us room as AJ steadies me to stand beneath the hanging gas lamp.

"Be easy on her, eh, Captain? She's incredibly disoriented from her fall."

"Hnn. She would be. The question is from where did she fall, daí?"

I take him in as he approaches. A pirate captain's hat sits snugly on top of black curly hair hiding a double looped earring on one. . .subtly pointy ear. I squint. He has on a long coat that guards his neck, and he wears boots on his feet. His accent is the same as the other guy who was here earlier, what was his name? Kae— something? But although he's shorter and slimmer, he's more of a leaner build. What *are they?*

"She says she doesn't know."

Nkella holds his hand up; AJ stops talking. His eyes fix on mine, intense and unforgiving. "Answer," he hisses.

Those eyes. . . I gasp, recalling how the card changed and showed me a pair of dark, angry eyes. *His* eyes. "I—I've seen you before. . ."

A muscle under his eye twitches and his gaze narrows. He gets closer and grabs my right arm. I gasp and backpedal, but he tightens his grip. His full lips curl up as I struggle to move my arm back. He raises my sleeve by force with his other hand.

"Hey!" I manage to say and then stop as I stare down at what he's looking at. A tanned marking resembling a spiraled spiderweb shows on the inner side of my forearm. My lips part. How the hell—?

"She is one of them." His voice is low and deep, but also velvety. It takes me a moment to collect myself.

"One of who?" I twist my wrist back from his grasp.

His dark irises flash an amber glow, like magma in molten rock. I gasp. His frown deepens, and he leans in.

"*Utwa,*" he hisses. "Take her to the brig."

"Wait. What?" What the hell did he just call me? "What does that mean?"

"Wait, Captain." AJ steps forward. "I don't think she came from the Tower. That's a long fall. No one could survive that."

"*Bancha!*" He whips back to face him. "She has the mark. Disoriented or not, she is one of them."

"But. . ."

"AJ. . ." Tessa warns behind him.

"To the brig." He whips around to face me again. "Or back to sea. You choose."

AJ deflates and walks up to me.

"Wait—" I stammer. "I'm not a. . .whatever that is. I can explain."

Nkella raises a brow and crosses his arms. "'*Splain.*"

"I. . ." I put my hand in my back pocket. Could it still be there? Feeling for a wet card, I pull out the thick, gold and black World Card. "I was sitting in a jail cell, when this suddenly opened up a portal. . ." Yeah, Soren, that didn't sound crazy at all.

AJ and Tessa gasp behind Nkella but his eyes are unflinching, his expression the same. Until he scowls deeper—just when I thought it wouldn't be possible.

He snaps the card from my hand and holds it up. "Any questions?"

AJ shakes his head. "But—she speaks a different language."

"Daí? And who knows or cares what they speak on the Tower? Enough arguing with me. To the brig."

AJ moves forward and takes me by the arms.

"Wait! What's the Tower? And I need that card! It's my way home!". . .I think. AJ grabs my elbow and gently urges me forward. I stumble a bit but he steadies me. I could try to fight. . .but I know I won't win. The captain is bigger and stronger, and let's face it, I'm on a freaking ship! There's nowhere to go but back into the water.

"Don't fuss or it'll be worse. You don't want him to call

Kaehante to take you down, or worse. . .have him do it himself."

He steers me down three flights below deck on a wide-enough ramp until we reach a dark and narrow staircase to the side of a dusty corner stacked with sandbags. I swallow as I step one foot down first with him behind me, his hand on my shoulder.

"You don't need to touch me. I have nowhere to go."

He removes his hand, and I step further into the darkness. At the bottom of the stairs, gas lamps illuminate a small, narrow hallway.

"What's the Tower?" I ask.

AJ shakes his head as he takes out the key. "That's some amnesia you have there. Might have a concussion."

"No, I'm fine. What's the Tower?" I repeat.

"Tower Island?" He quirks a brow and I raise mine.

"Still not ringing a bell."

He purses his red lips and opens the iron bars of my new prison cell. "Where do you say you're from, then?"

"Louisiana."

His brows draw together. "Where is that?"

I snort. "A state. . .in America. . .? *Hello.*"

His face blanks and he shrugs. Oh, right. I forgot I'm dreaming. I catch a view of his bare wrist and notice a similar marking, except it is different than the one I have. I squint, and right in front of me, it goes from a strange symbol to what looks like a roman numeral. . . Tattoos that can change form, what else am I going to dream about?

"In you go," he waves toward the inside of the cell which is actually a cage. A literal cage with a bucket in the corner. Gross.

"Great, thanks." I strut inside and turn to face him as he closes the gate and tucks the key into his pocket. Damn, I was hoping for a "hanging the key on a wall with a dog guarding it" scenario. Except, not that wolf out there. Hell, no.

He notices me still staring at his wrist. "What?"

"It. . .changed."

"Oh, that would be the potion working. Written translations take a little longer than speech, usually."

Why did I even ask? Just more nonsense I don't understand. "So what now?" I ask.

He gives me an apologetic look. "Just hang tight, I'll see about bringing you some food later, 'kay?"

"Wait. Before you go, can I ask you a question?"

His forehead wrinkles and he nods.

"What did your captain call me?"

"Utwa."

I ball my fist. "I don't know what that means, but all I can say is he's wrong and I don't appreciate being judged and then thrown in jail for it." I cross my arms.

AJ rubs his chin and squints at me. "It means spy."

"I'm not a spy."

He stays quiet.

"But anyway, how come I heard that word then and not spy? Wasn't that potion meant to translate?" Look at me, catching my own dream in a lie.

His long hair moves down his arm, and he pushes it over his shoulder. "You really don't know any of this, do you?"

I shake my head.

"The language potion doesn't work perfectly on the Ipani

since they're oumala. Even bound ones. Or anything coming from something oumala, or magical, for that matter."

Oumala? Bound ones? I narrow my eyes at him. He might as well be speaking his language.

"Especially with how illegal these potions are, we can't always get our hands on a very good one, so they're not so reliable."

"What's an oumala?"

"Well, Nkella is, obviously." He chuckles at the last word.

My face blanks and he continues. "Oumala are magical beings, non-humans, and ouma means magic. The native Ipani people and animals who came before us are all oumala. Most have had their magic bound to prevent them from using it."

"Non-humans? Your captain isn't. . .human?"

He laughs and shakes his head. I gape at him.

"Look, basically you'll only understand us when we speak Imboe, even if Nkella speaks it. But you won't be able to understand the oumala languages, like Ipani. The potion won't work on them."

"Why do I feel like the more answers I get, the more confused I am?"

"I don't know, but I better get back to the main deck before they send for me."

He turns and heads out, shutting the door with a clank, and snuffing out the only lights coming in from the hall. Leaving me alone, wet, and in a dark prison cell on a pirate ship. Now all I have to do is wake up.

4

I HAVE TO BE DREAMING. RIGHT? GOOSE BUMPS prickle my skin from my arms down to my toes. I wish I could take these wet clothes off and change into something dry.

My nose twitches and I sneeze. That felt real. This all feels real. But if it is real. . .then. . .I shudder. I'm going crazy. None of this can possibly be real! I mean, come on!

Pirates? A language translator drink? And then there's. . .I touch the inside of my arm. Only in a dream would a mysterious tattoo appear on my skin. I squint through the dark cell to study it, but I can't see my fingers if I lay them out in front of me.

I have so many questions—or I would if I weren't dreaming! The least they could do is leave me a torch. I guess I shouldn't expect much from pirates. AJ seems nice enough. But he has to follow orders, I get it. That captain is a grade A asshole. Kind of hot. . .but definitely a jerk. Okay, Soren, stop talking to yourself and try and think of your next move.

I sneeze again. "Ow." That one hurt. My nose is too cold. I don't have many options. Except maybe, try to wake up?

A tiny light pops on my shoulder and scurries down to my arm. I startle. A reflective spider scuttles down to the back of my hand. "Philo? Where did you come from?" She moves her body to look up at me with those big eyes of hers, then she disappears in another pop of light. I gasp.

Okay, yeah, this is definitely a dream. I shake my hands, then my head, jump up and down, and try wiggling my toes and fingers, although that's kind of tough because—have I mentioned how cold I am? If anything, this is helping to keep me warm. When that fails, I start slapping myself with both hands on my cheeks.

"Do you normally hit yourself?"

I choke on a breath. "Who said that?"

"I did." A low soothing voice comes from behind and I spin around.

"Who?"

"Me!"

I whirl toward the bars. Now it's coming from where I had been facing.

What the heck? "Where are you?"

A moment later, he doesn't answer. I back up and hit the wall behind me. A silvery-blue swirl appears beside the bars to my left, and my jaw drops as it spins itself to reveal a face covered in long, messy strands of blue and purple hair. Two horns curl back, a long snout, and two wing-like fins from either side of its floating head faces me. . . *Floating head?* My back slides down against the wall, shocked from my own hallucination. Because, what else could it be? A serpent-like body swooshes behind him, appearing only momentarily as it swims in thin air, before disappearing again, along with its head.

"That drink did more than just translate words. . ."

"What drink?" His head reappears and I yelp.

"You might want to keep quiet. I hear there's a Devil on this ship." He has a deep, almost gurgling voice, with a hint of amusement.

"W-who are you?" I ask.

He floats closer, and I can see his little legs and paws underneath his floating body. He resembles a dragon. . .but also, a sea serpent? That flies? "What are you?"

"I think the real question is"—he spins around on his head so that he gleams at me from upside down while his body disappears—"who are *you*? You are not from this world." He inches closer and sniffs under my chin. I squeeze my eyes shut and turn my cheek. "I can smell it."

"I'm Soren. And I'm not from here. . ."

"No, you're not. You smell different. From another world. But which one?"

"Which one?"

"Yes, which one?"

"Which. . .world?"

"Well, you're not from this one. So, you must be from another."

"Uhh. . .Earth. . ."

"Well, why didn't you just say so?" he sings.

"Because. . ." Okay, not answering that. I'm dreaming, remember? If not, I'm talking to a hallucination. I slap my forehead. "Why can't I wake up?"

"I believe, for one to wake up, they need to first be asleep." He grins.

I cover my face and sigh into my knees.

"What's the matter?"

Glumly, I move my face to the side. "I just want to wake up."

"Why do you want to be asleep so badly?" he gurgles.

My chest tightens. "Because. . .if I'm not dreaming. . .then that means I really did fall through a portal, and I won't be there for my sister who really needs me right now. And she'll get sent back into the system." Tears well up in the corners of my eyes. "She'll think I abandoned her."

"I don't know what a system is," he gurgles, "but it seems to me that not believing what you see is hindering your ability to watch for yourself, all because you're worried about someone else, who should be depending on themselves?"

I look up. "She's just a kid."

"And you're a prisoner on a pirate ship." His grin widens and he licks his sharp teeth. I'm suddenly aware that he's not just here for a friendly chat.

I back up against the wall of the cage. Okay, Soren, time to wake up. I'm not about to be eaten by some made-up dragon thing in my own nightmare. I squeeze my eyes shut. *Go away. It's my dream. Go away.*

When I open my eyes, his body slithers in the air, and his nose presses up against mine. I wince. My heart starts to thump loudly in my ears.

"Oh, don't worry. I'm not hungry." He disappears with a pop only to reappear a few paces away from me. "I like to save all my food in my cave for when I am."

My shoulders relax a bit with a sigh of relief. Unless he means to save me for later. "You're not going to try to eat me?"

"I haven't decided."

"And why's that?" I'm not sure how I'd be able to defend myself in here.

"I wouldn't want to eat something of value." He rolls on his back so that he's facing me upside down. "Why are you in a cage?"

I'm afraid to answer that. What if this strange mark tells him I'll taste better or something? Or he'll take me as prisoner for his own gain? I can't trust anything or anyone in this place. "How'd you even get in here, anyway?"

"Do you want me to leave?"

"That depends. Can you help me out of here? Or are you going to plot to eat me?"

"Help you? I only came because I saw a pretty little spider and thought, yum! But found you instead."

I wince at the mention of him finding me. "Philo?"

"Oh, do you know it?"

"As much as someone can know a spider, I suppose."

"Hmmmm. . . . . ." He spins himself upside down again.

"Will you stop doing that? You're making me dizzy."

"Oumala spiders, or any other oumala animals don't usually appear to just anyone. It must like you for some reason."

"Oumala spiders? Are you an oumala?"

"Me? Nooo. I'm a drakon."

"A dragon?" I was right then.

"Dra-kon."

"Okaay. . . And the drink I took wouldn't work on you if

you were an oumala? I'm just trying to make sense of all this."

His laugh comes out as a wheeze this time. "Oumala animals can't talk. My species came here long ago. But we are fully assimilated into this world which makes me part-oumala I suppose. I can talk, you see? But, I can also go into the *Aō* dimension—the spirit world that the oumala animals can travel through." He disappears and reappears to show me. Huh. That's neat.

My mind wanders to Madame Asteria's tent when Philo was out of her tank, then disappeared, and then reappeared to me in jail. So, Philo is an oumala spider.

I gaze up at his floating body. "What's your name? Do you have a name?"

"Of course I have a name, don't you? It's Katergaris."

"Kater-what?"

"Katergaris," he repeats.

"Kater. . .garis," I repeat slowly. "I'll just call you Gari."

He rolls over on his back and hums. "Accepted."

Great. Now I'm on a first name basis with my hallucination, and I've given it a nickname. At least, now, I no longer think he wants to eat me. Unless he always has in-depth conversations with his food.

"I've been to Earth. I don't like it much, it smells bad."

I chuckle. "I guess it depends where you go."

"I don't know the name of the place, but it was dark and wet, and it smelled of feces. So, I left." He spins his head around again.

"Gross. It sounds like you ended up in a sewer. There are much nicer places."

"Hmmm. . ." His body shimmers through the darkness as

he floats above my cell. "How did you end up a prisoner on the *Devil's Gambit*?"

"You know this ship's name? Why is it called that anyway?"

"Everyone knows this ship. And it's called that because a Devil captains it."

I gasp. "Nkella?"

"Who else?"

I swallow. "Why do you say he's a Devil?"

Gari swims through the air, his head nears my face, and he grins. "In this world, you'll find—"

"Oh, please, don't tell me nothing is like it seems, or some other crap."

"I was going to say, in this world, everything is exactly how it should be. Why. Are. You. Locked. Up?" His voice lowers to a deep gurgle as he backs me into a corner.

I hesitate, but then show him my arm to reveal the marking. "When I dropped—from, I guess, Earth—they rescued me from drowning. But then. . ." I move my arm up.

"Now, that is curious." His tail shimmers as he wraps it around my arm. "You're one of them," he whispers.

"Why does everyone keep saying that? How can I be "one of them" if I'm from Earth?"

"So are they."

I raise a brow. "What?"

"Anyway, as I was saying"—he unravels my arm—"this world is called Ipa to the Ipani but Fateland to the humans, and everyone in it gets marked. Like yours, except yours is special. To get marked as a Devil, you have to do something really bad."

I choke on a gasp. "Really bad? What kind of marks?" I

peer down at my arm, at the slight image of the web shining from Gari's glow.

"I believe in your world. . .they call it the Tarot?"

My head snaps up. "What? Tarot? Are you kidding?"

A snickering hiss escapes him. I think that's a laugh. "Most of the time, but not now."

"So, I left Tarotland Circus to get locked up at a Tarot. . .land! Guess that makes sense as well since I got sucked into a portal made from a Tarot card!"

"What is a circu—?"

Heavy boots sound from outside the door. I quickly climb to my feet and walk to the bars. Gari makes a shushing sound and disappears into my peripherals.

The door slowly opens, allowing the soft lights of the hall to come through and a silhouette emerges from the shadows, a wolf following behind. Nkella. The Devil.

I stare at the leather-clad captain, and our eyes lock. His face tightens as we take the measure of one another.

I swallow, trying to slow my breathing and the elevated beating of my heart as he stops in front of the metal bars. His gaze doesn't leave my face.

"Who are you talking to?" A hint of the hickory and vanilla rum escapes his breath.

"No one."

His lips curl into a frown. "More lies."

I sniffle.

He takes out the World Card and flips it around in his hand. "You say you used this to come here." His voice is dark and smooth; it makes the hair at the back of my neck stand on end.

I nod. In the light, I can see his features more clearly. Subtle pointed ears, sharp incisors, not particularly long ones but definitely more pronounced than a human's, and flawless, young, tanned skin with dark stripes on his neck and hands. Intense dark eyes search my face. He looks human but isn't. I really didn't imagine it. "You're so young. How'd you get to be captain of a ship?" I mean, he only looks a few years older than me, but I would expect someone older to captain a ship.

"I stole it."

"Right. Pirate," I mumble. I can't stop staring at him. I avert my gaze, not wanting to be rude.

He continues to spin the card in his fingers as he stares at me skeptically. "AJ thinks you came from somewhere else. I'm having a hard time believing this."

"I swear I did. I fell through a portal. I'm telling you the truth." I cannot believe the phrase "I came through a portal" just came out of my mouth.

"Go on then." He unlocks the gate and hands me the card. "Go back home." The wolf blocks the exit as if I would dare try to push him or the wolf out of the way to run out. A purple shine sweeps the card as I flip it around to inspect the back. "I-I don't know how."

"Convenient."

"I don't know how it works. It was by accident."

"You are lying." He raises his chin, showing his scrutinizing stare below his captain's hat, dim light outlining razor-sharp cheekbones.

"I'm not lying." I sneeze again and stare at the card. How did it happen before? I had been inspecting it when Philo popped out of nowhere. Then there was a strange magnetic force as it dropped on the floor. Next thing I knew, I was falling in.

Here goes nothing. I drop it on the floor. A muscle in his cheek flexes as he stares at me, expectantly. Nothing happens.

"Liar," he hisses.

"You know, if I knew how it worked, I'd be out of here by now."

He grimaces and steps forward with determined intensity. My head sinks into my chest. Inching back, I slowly bend down to pick the card up. As I do, I stifle a gasp. An image of a black stick, with dark green vines twirling tightly around it appears. A purple crystal point sits on the top. I hold the image side of the card toward me, the back of my hand facing the captain. He stares at me. The image disappears again.

"Utwa."

"I'm not a spy."

His frown deepens, and he snaps the card from my hand, locks the iron bar, and turns away. Not very conversational, huh?

"Wait," I say. He pauses and glances down at his shoulder. I don't know what I'm going to say, except, "please let me go."

I watch as the captain disappears back through the door. My throat clogs. I'm gonna be stuck here in this prison cell forever. Probably die of hypothermia.

"Come, Iéle." The wolf gives me one last growl before following him out, and once again, I'm left in the pitch-black brig, his dark gaze leaving an impression in my mind. I guess I'm a criminal no matter what dimension I'm in.

Wait—what am I saying? I fell into a different world. . .with pirates! And now the card that brought me here can change its image? What the hell is that supposed to mean? My heart hammers in my eardrums as I grab onto the black steel bars. How am I going to get out of here? I lift my sleeve to inspect my spiderweb marking. One thing is for sure, the World Card definitely showed me an Ace of Wands—I'm not proficient in Tarot, but I remember what some of them are from working at the circus.

But why did it change to that? Could the card be trying to tell me something? I need to get home to Talia, and the only way to do that is by getting that card back, but something tells me that isn't going to be as easy as just dropping it on the floor. I don't know why but I think my mark and that card are connected somehow.

Minutes pass and I find myself sliding back down against the wall as overwhelming exhaustion befalls me. That, and I think I'm getting sick from being cold and wet.

A bang jerks me awake. For a split second, I forgot where I was. Also, I fell asleep? If that's not confirmation that I was never dreaming, I don't know what is. Dread twists my stomach into knots. Talia. . .

Thunder roars outside and I sit up.

Another bang hits the ship, jerking it sideways. What the hell is going on? Loud shouting comes from above deck. What hit the ship? I gasp and get to my feet. Is it a storm, or are we under attack?

The ship sways again, and I fall against the bars.

Water seeps in from the top of the cell, splashing me in the face. I have to get out of here. Frantically, I search my hair for my hairpin and thrum the lock with the tip of my thumb. I stick the pin in and move it up and down. The ship jerks again, and I drop my pin. My breath hitches. Dropping to the bottom of the cage, I start feeling through the metal bars in the dark. It could have fallen anywhere in the cracks! A blue light glows above me.

"Still think this is a dream?"

"Gari?" I gaze up at him, his pupils narrowing into slits as he stares at me, his body shimmering behind him. I gulp. Not a dream. Not a hallucination. . . But if this. . .thing. . .was going to hurt me, it would have done so already, right?

More yelling comes from outside.

His gurgling voice sings down from the top of the cage. "If you don't get out now, you'll surely drown."

"Yeah, I got that, thanks!"

"What are you doing on the ground then?"

"Gari, if you're not going to help me get out of here, stop distracting me! I lost my lockpick!"

"If you need help getting out, all you need to do is ask, you know."

I flick him a glance. The ship gets hit with another bang, flinging me across the cage. I scramble up, ignoring the sharp shooting pain in my elbow. "You can get me out of here?"

"I suppose you can hop on my back. Then I can pop us out of here!" he giggles.

My heart skips a beat, and I involuntarily move away from him. Ride on his back? *Pop* out of here? As much as I desperately want to get out of here, what if he takes me to that cave of his so he "can save me for later"?

He widens his grin, showing long sharp fangs and disappears.

Great. Very helpful. Maybe he senses I don't trust him.

A moment later, he reappears.

"Take a bite out of this." His tail reaches over as I lean on the thick metal cage; the tip of his tail holds onto something like it's a finger.

"What is it?"

"It'll get you out. Just one small bite, not too big, and you'll be able to go through those bars."

My lips part as I take the item. Some of it crumbles to the floor. "It's just a cookie."

"You might want to hurry. Or you can come with me."

Ignoring his last offer, I raise the cookie to my nose. It smells kind of like peppermint. Last time I took something without understanding what it was, I almost choked. "What will it do to me?"

"It'll make you fickle"—with a pop, he disappears and then reappears—"like me."

"So. . .invisible?"

"Something like that." He floats on his back. "Think of it like a specter."

"Hmmm. . . A ghost?"

"In a way." He gurgles a laugh.

"I don't know about this." I bring the cookie down.

"Just long enough to get you out of the cage and above deck, unseen. One *perfect* bite, and you'll be invisible till port, allowing you enough time to get away. *If* you make it to port, that is."

Unease settles in my gut as I scan the cookie, smelling it again as if its true nature will appear. "Why are you helping me?"

His eyes narrow as his body disappears first, then his head, leaving his eyes and his grin before they're both gone.

"Gari? How much is a perfect bite?" I spin around. "Gari? Did you really leave this time? Katergaris!" Do I trust he's telling the truth?

More water pours in from above the ceiling boards and splashes my feet. I press my back against the gate. Leave it to me to get myself stuck in an impossible situation. The ship's going down, and I'm about to die. I bring the cookie to my lips. Do I trust a disappearing oumala-drakon thing that just gave me a cookie?

No, I do not. Do I have a choice? Well, when the alternative is to drown anyway, I guess eating a magical, potentially-harmful cookie for a chance at escape is the only choice I've got.

I could have gone with him, but I didn't trust that either.

A blast roars from above, and I almost drop the cookie. I think that was a cannon. I better move.

Here goes nothing. I stick my tongue out to taste it. Sweet peppermint tickles my taste buds as I take a bite, chew, and swallow. That wasn't so bad. I kind of want another piece. I nibble on another bite when a tingling sensation starts from the top of my head and swooshes down my spine. The tingling increases and it starts to feel like dozens of fire ants are swarming my body, down to my toes. The darkness of the brig lightens to a dull gray and I can see my hands in front of me. What the? Still tingling, I'm starting to lose feeling in my fingers. The cookie falls to the puddle on the ground. Waste of a perfectly good cookie! Wait—what's happening? Did it work? I take a step back, forgetting that I was leaning against the cage and a second later, I'm facing the square metal that was holding me in. I look at my hands and arms and my mouth slackens. I'm completely see-through!

I'm. . .I'm. . .a specter! It worked! I got out!

The ship rocks back and forth, and although I can barely feel it, I can still see it happening. Time to go before this cookie wears off and I really do drown.

The floorboards creak beneath my feet. I might be invisible, but I'm not weightless. I'll still need to be careful. I walk up the narrow stairs and stop at the dimly lit ramp with what appears to be an artillery room to the left. Even in the blackness of night, everything is a monotone gray, and I can see all the details happening. Is this how oumalas and drakons see? Funny, considering Gari's hair is so colorful.

A large figure eclipses the light from my path out of here, and I hold my breath. A black hooded robe draping down to the floor hides the figure from being seen. A white expressionless mask covers his face. But what makes my hair stand on end are his eyes—or lack thereof—staring at me. Or right through me. I can't tell if he can see me, but I cannot make out any pupils. It's like. . .dark, depthless smoke is the only thing inside of that mask.

His robe is being clasped to his shoulder by a small reflective emblem in the shape of a shield with what looks like a tower at its center.

A sword swings from behind, the blade slicing through the hooded figure's neck.

A squeal escapes my throat and I jump to the side, hitting my shoulder against the wall. The figure spins on his heel—completely unhurt!

Kaehante towers behind him, wielding his sword, fashionably spinning it around, readying himself as if he didn't notice it didn't do anything the first time. I stumble back, the noise around us masking my movements.

The figure steps into the blade, impaling himself as he grabs Kaehante by the throat. His fist turns into smoke—yet still holds the shape of his hand as he reaches inside Kaehante's orifices. Smoke seeps out from his ears, then his nose and mouth. A choked cough escapes his lips; I realize the smoke must be poison or something. I feel the wooden wall behind me with my fingertips and start to slowly slide against it. If this masked guy is killing him, I don't want him to find me next.

The ship soars to the left, a large wave of water pouring over Kaehante. And with it, a skull flashes in place of his face; I do a double take. His smile beams into the hooded figure's dark shadowy eyes. A bang sounds from behind them, and green gas envelops the figure. Kaehante stumbles to the ground as the masked stranger dissolves into a whirl of smoke, letting the sword drop to the floor with a clang.

Kaehante wipes his wet face as it returns to normal.

Tessa sits in her chair with a small cannon attached to the side of it, greenish-gray smoke swirls out of the barrel. Kaehante exchanges a nod with her as she turns and drives down the ramp.

I don't allow myself time to process what I just saw.

Pushing back Kaehante's skull-face from my mind, I bolt up the ramp, past the two other levels, and onto the main deck.

Someone jumps over my head and lands on their feet. Nkella's coat billows against the strong winds. He runs to the front of the ship, swings his arm, and tosses something out. He turns and throws himself to the ground, covering his face. A giant boom of green fire blazes from where he threw the object, which now I'm assuming was some kind of green fire grenade. Suddenly, I feel like I was safer in that cage.

AJ appears from the sideline pulling on a thick rope and fighting against gusts of strong winds. He fights the hair covering his face as he takes out a round blue bottle, which I assume is another bomb, but then opens a small door on the side of the ship, sticks the bottle in, and twists.

What the hell was that?

"That should be enough to keep the sails steady!" AJ yells over the winds.

A low motor rumbles from behind me and I jump back as Tessa drives up in her steam-geared wheelchair. My eyes widen as I can now see the clear bottles filled with a lime green liquid in her hands. She tosses one at the captain, and he catches it.

A black hooded figure with a white mask lands behind him. He spins around but Tessa had already shot her mini cannon at him, letting out some sort of poison gas.

The figure goes out in a whirl of smoke like the last one.

Nkella's fierce eyes greet her as she zooms past. "They are here for the girl," he spits. I stifle a gasp. Does he mean me?

"Give her to them!" Kaehante shouts from below. Blood drains from my face.

They look around as if waiting for more to come. But a moment later, the sea calms down.

"They are not getting her this way." Nkella declares.

Whew. Wait—this way? What does he mean by that?

"Or"—AJ shouts back while climbing on a rope ladder to my right—"they're here feeling out our whereabouts since it's getting close to curse day!" The whole ship lifts us from the side. I fall and slide to the right, hitting the boards blocking me from falling off as AJ flies off the ship but holds on with one arm.

The ship slams down, hitting the sea with a hard splash. Water completely covers the deck. I hear Kaehante scream something as he dashes upstairs to take the wheel. No idea what he said, but either way, it wasn't for me. The captain bolts over to the far corner of the ship where Tessa has fallen out of her chair and is struggling to flip it over. AJ swings back onto the ship, lands on the main deck, and hauls the ropes down, bringing up a sail. Dripping wet, he passes me and runs toward the ramp.

I catch a glimpse of his skull and shut my eyes, pressing my hands to my mouth, not wanting to see any more skeletons. I'm going to get myself killed out here, but if I go back and we capsize, I'll drown.

Something hits the ship again and I fall on my back. Something large—like a giant tentacle—grabs onto the edge of the ship right above my head. I choke on a scream and scramble farther along the wall. What the hell was that! The ship lifts again, and this time, more of the creature's body surfaces above the water, showing that it wasn't a tentacle at all.

My heart plummets to the floorboards as the body of a

giant serpent lifts the other side where Tessa and the captain are. Nkella grabs one of the glass bottles from Tessa's chair and throws it at the sea beast; it erupts in a green burst of fire and gas.

I shield my face as a bright green light sweeps the deck, and then I press myself against the wall of the ship.

A high-pitched squeal bursts out of the serpent, shattering my eardrums, but it doesn't dwindle. I think that only pissed it off. The sea calms as it sinks back down into the ocean, and I steady myself onto my feet. I can no longer see AJ, but I catch a view of Kaehante at the wheel turning it as the captain yells something at him, most likely giving him a command.

Tessa, now back on her chair and ready, is mixing something inside another bottle. I guess the sea serpent—or whatever the hell that was—isn't gone yet? Or are they preparing just in case? The ship makes a sharp turn as Kaehante steers the ship.

The sea serpent whips its tail from below and rips a hole into one of the sails at the front end of the ship.

Nkella runs toward the sail right when the sea serpent lifts its head over the vessel, opens its mouth, and snaps toward Tessa. It could probably consume half the ship in one bite.

Nkella spins around and lunges after Tessa. Just as he reaches her, he takes out a sword and the serpent opens its mouth wide and gulps. They both disappear inside the serpent's mouth; panic shoots through me as I press myself harder against the rail behind me. Kaehante jumps over the railing from the quarterdeck, sword in hand, but just as he lands, the serpent screeches as its body convulses. Its mouth opens wide as Nkella holds a sword plunged into the roof of the serpent's mouth, the rest of his body shielding Tessa.

My knees weaken, and I grab onto the rail. Drool pours off Nkella and Tessa like a sticky substance. I think I'm gonna be sick.

Another strong gust of wind pushes the sails, and the ship makes a turn. My eyes widen as realization strikes—Kaehante had to let go of the wheel.

The serpent whips its head up, shaking furiously from side to side. It plunges below, the tip of its tail whacking one of the front masts as it buries its head under water.

Tessa takes another bottle from her satchel as she drives her wheelchair back toward the ramps. Holy cow, she's a badass! I catch a glimpse of her pouring in another mixture as she makes —from what I can guess—another liquid bomb.

AJ comes out from the ramps with two cannonballs gripped between his arms. He sticks them into a cannon. Nkella holds him back, telling him to wait.

"Reef the foretop!" Nkella yells, running up to the wheel and switching places with Kaehante who is now readying himself with the cannon while Tessa prepares more grenades.

AJ nods and runs toward the ripped sail just as something hits the ship, causing him to slide across the deck. The serpent has returned, eyes slit and pulling back, ready to strike.

Kaehante and Nkella start shouting back and forth while AJ stares at the sail, then looks toward Tessa and Kaehante. He throws his hand down in a furious grunt, whips out a sword, and runs toward the serpent. Three against one giant beast? The ship jerks and I topple. Did Nkella just slam the ship into it?

Harrowing sounds of a storm gather overhead as water droplets start to fall.

Panic hammers at my throat. The storm is getting worse. If the sail doesn't get fixed, they're battling two monsters at the same time. Maybe I can figure out what to do about the tear, while they deal with the beast.

I reach the rope ladder and attempt to climb but my hand goes through it.

Uh-oh. I went through the bars. . .how am I meant to climb the rope? Now that I think about it, I've been able to feel cold winds, but not the droplets of water.

Wait, how am I standing on deck then?

My foot falls through the floorboard and I scream. No! Stay on deck!

My foot comes back up.

Ohh. . .I stare back at the rope ladder and then down at my hands. I squeeze my eyes shut. *Climb.*

The wet, scratchy texture of the rope fills my palm. Yes!

Placing one hand over the other, I start to climb. One hand, one foot, and then the other two. Winds shake the rope and I hold on for dear life, pressing my face against it. I climb a few more paces before looking down. Tessa is no longer on deck. Where did she go?

Kaehante fires a cannon and the whole ship vibrates with a bang. I yelp and squeeze my eyes shut. I open one eye, hoping to see the serpent gone, with a pool of blood tainting the water but nope. It's whipping to the other side of the ship now.

Seriously, why is it after the ship?

Okay. Keep climbing. I have to fix the mast, even though I have absolutely no idea what I'm doing. . .or I could climb back down, jump on a side boat, and escape this whole thing. But, honestly, I don't want to get in the ocean with that thing in the water—and who knows what else is in it. That and something tells me they don't have life jackets. What would I do anyway? Paddle until I hit land in a random general direction during a storm?

As I climb higher, the winds pick up. Goose bumps run from the top of my head down to my feet but I'm trying hard not to pay attention to the cold. Gripping the rope tightly with both hands, I reach the top. With my heart lunging in my throat, I glance down to see how high I am. This was definitely a bad idea.

The wind smacks the sail hard and a part of it hits me in the face, momentarily blinding me. I've never even sailed before! How am I supposed to fix this?

Shouting coming from below distracts me, but I force myself to keep my wits. Pay attention, Soren! I'm not dying out here!

With great effort, I grab onto the torn sail and pull it hard with my right arm, gripping the ladder with the other. The sail doesn't even budge. I'm not strong enough to do this.

The ship jerks sideways and I grab onto the wood, choking on a scream.

I'm such an idiot. Why did I think I could do this?

As the ship steadies, I get my bearings. Because they're busy fighting a freaking sea serpent and I don't want to drown. Wind pushes the mast to my right, and I push it back, grabbing onto the tear, accidentally making it worse.

Crap.

The wind gets blocked out momentarily, as I study the sail.

Thinner rope going across the wooden pole ties the rest of the sail, keeping it strapped in. Okay, I think I know what I need to do. I need to unravel it first and pull the sail down and wrap it so that the wind no longer passes through the tear.

I reach for the end to start unraveling it, but it's too far away and tied in a knot. Plus wet. Have you ever tried to untie wet rope?

Yep. I'm an idiot.

A claw pops out in front of me, and I almost fall back. Gari's eyes and jester-like grin appear over the rope as he cuts it in one fluid motion. I gasp as I reach to grab it and let out a sigh of relief.

I look up to thank him, but he's already gone.

Hoping it works, I use all my body weight to tug it down and wrap it around, pulling it under and over. But now, how do I tie it?

An explosion bursts my ears as a bright pink light sweeps the sea. Spots circumvent my sight. After a few seconds, my vision refocuses.

The ship hits something hard, as it rumbles underneath and almost sends me flying off. Time to get down.

I wrap the sail under and over, tucking it in, hoping the knot will be tight enough to at least get us through the storm.

As I finish my messy handiwork, the sea settles, and I stare down. The serpent seems to have disappeared. Tessa is back on deck with shattered glass bottles on the floor. Kaehante searches overboard for what I assume is the serpent.

I make my way, carefully, down the rope ladder—which I never want to climb again. And turn to face AJ, who is ready to climb up to fix the sail, confusion contorting his features.

5

I SUCK IN A BREATH AND HOLD IT. AJ SQUINTS AT THE giant masts as he whips his long hair behind him. He still can't see me. It's not like he'd suspect it was me; he thinks I'm still in the brig. Who else would he think fixed the sail though? How common are these specter cookies?

On that note, I slide past AJ as he stares, stunned, at the sail. I guess my options now are either to go back to the brig and wait for this cookie to pass—and hope to God no one comes down to find I'm not there before I'm visible again—or find a hiding spot and, the moment we dock, book it to find someone I can ask for help. Neither of those choices sound secure, but I mean, I really thought I was in more danger being trapped in a cage with water pouring in and not knowing if the ship was going to go down!

The floorboard creaks as I take a step toward the ramp and pause. AJ is now climbing up the sail, Nkella is somewhere at the back of the ship, but Kaehante and Tessa are still nearby. They don't seem to notice.

I tiptoe across the deck. A few more paces and I can hide within the ramps. Then, I guess, it's back to the cage to pretend I never left. I hope this invisibility doesn't last much longer.

I take another step, and a sea breeze tousles my hair. My nose itches. Oh no. I hold my breath. Don't sneeze. Don't sneeze. . .

Achoo.

I cup my hands over my nose and mouth, eyes wide. Holding my breath, I make a dash for the ramp, the floorboards moving and creaking as I sprint. Tessa and Kaehante exchange a glance and stare at the position I stopped. With my back facing the ramp, I can either run down, or keep very still.

Kaehante takes a few quick steps forward and waves his hand out, touching the air as I inch back.

"Hnn. . ." He cranes his neck to look at Tessa and shrugs.

"It wasn't Nkella. He doesn't get sick," she says.

"The girl?" he asks.

Tessa straps a bottle to a leather belt and ties it to the side of her chair. "Who, Soren? We wouldn't hear her sneeze from up here. Someone should go check on her."

Oh no. They'll see I escaped.

AJ, having finished undoing my handiwork and properly fixing the sail, jumps down and heads toward us.

Kaehante takes out a handkerchief from his coat pocket and wipes his bald head. "Send AJ. I'm still checking the *Gambit.*"

AJ walks up from behind Kaehante. "Send me where? Hey, the strangest thing happened to that sail. . ."

Okay, good, keep them distracted, AJ. As I turn, the floor creaks again. I cuss under my breath. Damn squeaky ship.

Tessa holds out a finger to shut AJ up as she and Kaehante stare in my direction. I back into a barrel and accidentally budge it. Kaehante's forehead wrinkles, then his eyes widen.

My skin tingles, and suddenly, aches and pains starting at my feet, elbows, and knees swarm my body.

"Oh, Lordy," AJ smacks his face, shutting his eyes. Tessa and Kaehante gasp. A cool breeze passes over my body; goose bumps run up my legs and. . .my butt? I look down. Oh my god! I drop to the floor behind the barrel and cover myself.

"What is going on?" Nkella's voice booms from the steering overhead. His heavy boots start to make their way down the steps. "Why aren't you checking the ship? We are late," he says with an emphasis on the *t*.

Kaehante quickly unbuckles his coat and hands it to me, his eyes glued to the floor as he does. Blushing hard, I take it gratefully and drape it around me.

Stupid cookie. I should have known it wouldn't have made my clothes invisible too!

Nkella walks around to where we are and stops at the looks on their faces, then he turns his gaze toward me. His eyes narrow and his frown deepens as he stares me up and down.

"You." His deep raspy voice makes my bones shake.

I grip Kaehante's heavy coat, wrapping it tighter around me, and slide into the crevice between the barrel and the wall. At least Kaehante is big and his coat reaches to my feet.

His gaze turns dark and dangerous. "What are you doing out of the brig?"

My throat dries as I search for the right words.

Placing a hand at the back of his head, AJ takes a step forward. "Don't be so hard on her, Captain. She probably felt the ship getting wrecked and got out somehow. . ."

"Yes, how?" He spins back to AJ, pointing his finger against his chest.

"Hey, I didn't get her out!"

"She was invisible," Kaehante chimes.

Nkella snaps his attention to Kaehante, then back to me. "More ouma? What else do you have?" he hisses.

"Me? Nothing! I—"

"More lies!"

"Cap—" AJ starts.

"Enough of you!" He swings his arm to shut AJ up, but the man only cocks his head back and shakes it with a roll of his eyes.

"I'm just saying, you're jumping to conclusions. Honestly, I think she's telling the truth."

"How would she get out if she didn't have help? Unless she has magic. Which, she claims she does not, daí? Someone tell me then"—he spins around—"how would she make herself transparent and escape a thick metal cage?"

AJ sighs deeply and Nkella sighs louder between his teeth, making it sound more like an angry hiss as he whips back around to face him. They keep arguing about me as Tessa drives past me, glancing in my direction but disappearing down the ramp.

Was I supposed to follow her? Afraid to make a move and have Nkella possibly lose it and throw me overboard, I stay put. I mean, as much as I'd love to be off this ship, if he's going to toss me off, I'd at least like my clothes first.

A few minutes later, Tessa comes back holding a few garments in her hand. My eyes skim her wheelchair. A black pedal is under her left foot, a white one for the other. "Here, you should put these on, they'll be warmer."

I graciously take them and hold them to my chest, wrapping them and Kaehante's coat tight. "Thank you. . ."

"She has the web!" Nkella grits his teeth as AJ throws his hands in the air.

Tessa cranes her neck to AJ and shouts, "Go check the rest of the ship and stop arguing with your captain."

Nkella closes in on AJ's face, grimacing. Kaehante, who had been quietly standing by, grabs a rope, making himself useful. This is one small crew. Is this really all of them?

Nkella snaps his gaze between me, Tessa, and the clothes I'm holding. AJ's eyes widen at the clothes, and he turns away.

"Tessa. What are you doing?" Nkella's voice came a tad softer than when he was speaking to AJ.

"The girl needs warm clothes. The ones she came with are soaked, and she's clearly catching a cold."

"Why do I care if she catches cold, daí?" He strides over to me and I inch back.

"Nkella." Tessa's voice is rigid and commanding and I gasp. "She didn't even like those pants. What's it to you if Soren wears them?"

She?

Nkella scowls. He gives me a long lingering look that makes my insides quake. I swallow and grip Kaehante's coat around me even tighter.

"Let her borrow them so we can get on with the night. We're running late as it is."

"She's utwa," he says with a growl. "They likely came here looking for her." His upper lip shows his sharp incisor as he grimaces.

"Wait a minute," AJ comes back around. "You really think the attack was because they were looking for her?" He points a finger toward me.

"Give her to them," Kaehante says, "if the Empress wants her back."

A lump forms in my throat. The Empress?

Nkella's gaze doesn't leave me as he frowns. "Not like this."

"In which case, you'll need her alive, won't you?" Tessa remarks. "Do you really want to waste time having us care for her if she gets ill?"

He needs me alive to give me to *them?* My eyes switch from her to Nkella. I'm good with being alive, but not to be given to anyone—let alone some mask-wearing, hooded figures with smoke for eyes and arms.

AJ clears his throat dramatically. "Just because she fell from the sky doesn't mean the Minor Arcana Army was here looking for her. You know, because um, it's about to be *curse day* and they'd be here looking for *us* anyway! Have you all lost your minds?"

Arcana. . .army? About a dozen questions swim through my mind. The card, how it changed to an Ace of Wands, Gari's words about the Tarot. . .the Empress!

Nkella lets out a grunt and an almost inaudible "fine" under his breath. His eyes narrow, a tiny flare of amber illuminates his irises as he stares at me. "Dry your clothes, then give those back." Turning on his heel, he heads back toward the wheel. He turns his head slightly to his shoulder. "Take her back until I figure out what to do with her."

I don't know what Tessa's relationship is with the captain, but he listens to her. I'm glad she's here.

At least AJ is still on my side. "Okay, then. Guess I'll just go back to my room. . .you know, the cold, damp, uncomfortable cage."

Nkella pauses, looking over his shoulder, but doesn't say anything. Then he keeps walking.

For some reason, he thinks the attackers were here looking for me. He could have handed me over but fought them instead. Unless, he didn't think about this until now and regrets not handing me over.

Not like this.

Or he's planning something.

"Right," Tessa says. "I trust you won't fight us to get back to the brig?"

I shake my head.

"Go on and get dressed. AJ will be there shortly to bring you a meal." She turns to the others, driving off behind me. "Right, then, let's check the rest of the ship for damages and we should be on our way."

"Did anyone notice which island the Arcana soldier was from?" AJ asks as he turns away.

"The Tower," Kaehante mutters as he leaves in the other direction, leaving me completely alone.

"In that case, they know something's up. Maybe they did sense Soren on the ship, since you know, they're all psychic at the Tower," AJ calls over his shoulder.

That sends chills down my spine. Psychic soldiers? What kind of a place is this?

Are they really going to let me walk myself back to my cell? Like I'm some dog who's been told to go to her cage after peeing on the carpet? When no one follows me down the ramp, I decide that confirms it. Let's face it. They know I have nowhere to go, and the captain seems to trust his crew will watch over me since he doesn't care whether I rot in the brig or go overboard—as long as I'm not loose on his ship.

Speaking of dogs, where's that wolf?

As I make my way, slowly—and I mean I'm in no hurry to get back to sitting in a damp cage which I'm sure is practically under water right now—I take a peek around the corners of the ramps. On the floor beneath the deck is a small kitchen area to the right with a kitchen island, bags stacked on bags of what I assume could be flour and who knows what other cooking ingredients. On the other side, is a hall to my left.

I look behind me to make sure no one is following me and give in to my curiosity.

A hall with four rooms on each side covered by wool curtains is lit by a gas lamp at the far end; the lamp hangs above an open wooden door with a tub and sink. The first room to my right is closed by a heavy wool curtain. I peek inside and see a small bed, a table with a gas lamp on it, stacks of leather-bound books and quills, and a small closet full of gadgets and neatly folded clothes. This must be Tessa's room. My eyes land on some of the pages with scriptures on them. Wait, I recognize some of those. . .

Quirking a brow, I inch forward to take a peek. Without touching anything, I gloss over the open pages. Call me crazy, but these words are in Greek! Maybe ancient Greek. . . I mean, I never studied it before even though I know I'm from Greek descent, but I know what it looks like.

But how would Tessa know Greek if this is another world? My eyes narrow as I back out of her room. Very strange. They were speaking a different language when I woke up on deck, but it didn't really sound like Greek. . . Although, now that I think of it, maybe it did a little? But the words Nkella and Kaehante have spoken. . .that's not a language I have heard before. More importantly though, what does any of this have to do with the Tarot? Not to mention there's an Minor Arcana. . .

The room across from Tessa's is tidy with an extra set of large boots by the bed. Kaehante's room, maybe? I noticed the captain's quarters are at the far end of the ship, with its own entrance, so it can't be Nkella's, and AJ's feet have to be smaller. . .

The next room is empty with a neatly-made bed and a single closed chest. It doesn't look like anyone's been in here for some time, although it's not completely empty. The adjacent room is wide open and empty. I pass that one and reach two other rooms that I can only assume belong to AJ and another empty room. I turn back to the half-empty room, and my eyes land on a necklace with a symbol of what looks like a palm tree on it. I wonder who stayed here before.

Growling comes from behind me, and my eyes widen. I spin around to find the wolf's glowing red eyes leering back at me, teeth bared, head low to the ground.

"Easy there, girl. . . I'm just leaving." I press against the closed wool curtains and inch back to the ramp as she follows me with her gaze. A second later, I'm out of the hallway and she dissolves into black fog. Oumala wolf. Interesting. That explains why she wasn't there during the sea serpent attack. A shiver runs down my spine. That's creepy. Means she's always watching.

I peek at the level down below to find rows of hammocks. Despite the tiny crew, there is definitely room for a lot more crewmates. The level below, just before reaching the narrow set of stairs leading to my dreaded destination, is filled with a dusty mess of weapons, cannons, coal, and more stacked sandbags. I better tuck myself into my cage before the wolf comes back and eats me this time. That'll take care of me for the captain. I now realize why he doesn't care that I walk alone. I was never alone.

Knowing that there are warm rooms with beds in them makes me dread the brig even more. I'll even take one of the hammocks. Anything would be better than the cage.

As I step into the cold wet cage, the bottoms of my feet ache when they touch the uneven metal. I wince as I take off Kaehante's coat and hang it on the door of the open cage. I don't even know why I care about hanging up my captor's clothing but I sure as hell am not going to close the cage on myself like a good little prisoner. And there's nowhere else to put it besides the wet floor.

But that would be mean considering he did lend it to me. He could have just let me stay naked. Why didn't he? Honestly, most of them aren't exactly mean. . .for pirates. . . Makes me feel like there's something more going on here. I unravel the clothes Tessa gave me. The look on Nkella's face when he saw her hand them to me. . .

What did she mean by "she didn't even like these"? Who

was she talking about? Could it have been a girl who stayed in the half-empty room I saw?

I quickly put them on over my dirty—yet mostly dry—body. A loose-fitted red blouse hangs past my butt over black pants torn at the hems. I can't complain, they're comfortable, and I'm no longer cold and wet. Not to mention, they're not the ugly orange jail clothes I came here wearing. The sleeves hang at my elbows, showing my newly emerged spiderweb marking. I run my fingers over it. I wonder if the Greek I saw on those pages has anything to do with this mark. . . It's not like I can bring up seeing those pages though, they'll know I was snooping.

I pick up the jail clothes sitting in a puddle, check the pockets, and frown at my *Alice in Wonderland* themed playing cards. Luckily, only the outer cards are wet. The rest seem fine. I stick them in the baggy side pocket of these new pants and hang the jail clothes on the cage door next to Kaehante's coat.

Reaching the back of the cage, I find a dry spot and settle down when I hear someone climb down the steps. I hold my breath, expecting it to be Nkella ready to interrogate me again but relax my shoulders when I see AJ's friendly face. He holds a metal tray in both hands with what looks like a bowl of soup, a spoon, and cup. He sets it down inside the cage and I scurry over.

"Alright, spill it," he says. "Did you eat something to make you invisible?" His makeup is washed away, and he has his black hair up in a bun.

"Yes. . .I had a cookie. . ."

He lowers Kaehante's coat from the cage along with my

garments and locks the cage. "That explains it. You ate an *ouma ipononchi*."

"Huh?"

"A magic cookie. I'm starting to doubt you were telling the truth about coming from another world. I really wanted to believe you."

"What? Why? I *am* from anoh—"

"How did you get the cookie then? Not to mention, these things take skills. Say you are telling me the truth. You could have died."

My face pales. "What?"

He searches my face. "If you eat too much of one at once, you risk never coming back. Your body won't be able to digest food while you're invisible, so eventually you'll starve or die of dehydration."

My eyes widen. That stinking, good-for-nothing, son of a —Did he do this to kill me? I knew I never should have trusted Gari. That one's on me, I was desperate for a way out of here.

"So, where'd you get it from then? I'm trying to help you here, but I can't if you don't talk to me."

"An oumala visited me and gave it to me so that I wouldn't drown in case the ship sank." I blurt out.

AJ's eyes widen. "An oumala animal would have to be comfortable with you, Soren. . ."

"It said it was a drakon."

"Oh. . . Oh!" He wipes his face. "Nkella better not find out about that then."

I relax my shoulders. "It came in here, curious about me. And then popped back in to save me in case I drowned. What was I supposed to do? Not take his help? The ship was being struck. I really thought it would sink."

AJ cocks his head and shakes it. "Ship wasn't going to sink. It'll take a lot more than that to bring us down. The sea serpent delayed us, but we would have gotten out of there."

"Didn't look like it."

"You helped." He smiles. "Also, Tess is a great engineer. Any damage and she'll be able to handle it. Anyway, eat your supper. You'll want your energy for tomorrow and you don't want to get sick. Oh, and next time, if you do eat another cookie, never do it on an empty stomach. It's more dangerous that way. It reaches your bloodstream quicker, yeah?"

"I didn't think I had a choice."

"Fair enough."

"Hey, everyone keeps mentioning how late you all are. Late for what?"

His face blanks. "Uhh. . . We need to make it to land before. . ." he lowers his voice "curse day."

"W-what's curse day?"

"Never mind that. Problem is, between stopping to rescue you and dealing with the serpent, we're at sea for another day and will arrive in port the next morning. We'll make it before curse day, though. We left with room to spare. Nkella is just overly cautious."

Another day stuck in a cage at sea? I think I'm gonna be sick. . . "When is curse day?"

"The day after tomorrow."

The day after tomorrow? What day was it today? Oh. . . "The day after tomorrow is my birthday. And I'm a prisoner in another dimension. What else could go wrong?"

"Your birthday, huh? And how old will you be turning?"

"Seventeen. You guys have birthdays in this world too?"

He chuckles. "Of course we do. I better get back before Nkella thinks we're conspiring," he says with a smile. I snort.

"Tell Kaehante thank you for me? I think I was too embarrassed to say it earlier."

He slants a smile and shuts the door behind him.

After devouring my soup, which was more like broth and onions, I huddle in a corner to try to get some sleep. But my mind keeps whirling about all sorts of stuff.

Finally, I fall asleep to the back and forth rocking of the sea and the waves crashing against the ship.

I dream I'm back at Tarotland Circus. Talia is beside me holding a cone of cotton candy as we both watch the Amazing Sword Swallower drop a long sword down his throat and take it out like it was nothing. Something catches my eye near the popcorn stand beside the stage. Philo is hanging from the roof of the stand, beckoning with her glistening glass body for me to follow, so I do. Before I reach her, the scene changes to a ship. Thunderclaps sound as rain starts pouring down; I start to panic. No, no, no! Why am I back here? I need to get back to Talia.

A large shadow appears in front of me. I can't make out who it is, but two glowing red eyes glare back at me, as two horns form at the top of his head. I swallow, getting the sinking feeling I know who this is. Captain Nkella. I step back. The Devil doesn't move, but even though I can't make out the features of his face, I can feel his grimace between the shadows leering back at me.

Gari's face appears above his; he offers me a cookie.

I gasp, remembering the peppermint cookie from earlier. "Katergaris?"

"What happened to calling me Gari?"

Gesturing at the cookie, I cross my arms. "No, I don't want it."

"But without it, you'll never get back to Talia."

"I could have died eating the last one you gave me! And for what? Nothing, because I'm back in the brig!" I gasp, realizing this is a dream.

"I did tell you to eat very little." His blue and purple fluff glistens as his body swims through the air like an eel. The images of the ship and the storm fade around me as it becomes the prison cage, the image of the captain gone with it.

"No. You said the perfect piece, whatever that meant!"

"Nonetheless, you're back in the brig because you got yourself caught."

I cross my arms. "And you didn't tell me my clothes would fall off!"

He giggles. "They didn't have to fall off, you know, you need to be more determined with your thoughts!"

"What? What kind of dream is this anyway?"

His jester-like smile sends chills running down my spine.

He vanishes and I startle awake. Rain patters on the rocking waves outside. I lean my head against the wall, letting myself drift back to sleep—this time without drakon oumala creatures lurking in my mind.

6

I MUST HAVE WOKEN UP AROUND TEN TIMES throughout the night, confused about being on a ship, in another world, and behind bars. Okay, so that last one isn't that surprising.

The door creaks open and I stiffen. Hopefully, it's AJ at the door with breakfast. I roll over on my elbow to push myself off the hard metal and quickly withdraw.

Nkella stands at the foot of the cage, long coat down to his shins, one popped collar taller than the other, giving him an edgy look. He narrows his eyes at me. "Let's go, utwa." His husky voice ties my stomach to a knot.

I sit up. "Where are we going?"

"You can join the crew for a meal. Then you will work." He opens the cage to let me out.

"Work?"

"Or you can stay here and starve all day. You choose."

His expression is rigid and unwavering as he glues his eyes

to the floor, his leg keeping the cage door open. No idea who changed his mind, and I'm not dumb enough to ask. I hurry out, catching a whiff of his warm hickory and leather fragrance as he leads me back up the ramps and onto the main deck. Notes of baked bread tickle my nostrils, and my mouth begins to salivate.

I think about asking him what kind of work he wants me to do, but since he refuses to make eye contact, I decide to keep my mouth shut. I'm sure someone will tell me.

On the main deck, Kaehante, Tessa, and AJ sit around two barrels pushed together. Plates of food cover the tops of the barrels as they ramble away. Nkella nods me over in silent command before walking off in the other direction. A deep growl greets me from the foot of the table as the wolf slightly lifts her head at the sight of me. Oh, great. It's you again.

AJ stands and pulls up a tall stool. "Morning, Soren. Sit. I baked fresh bread."

Stomach rumbling, I quickly sit. "Is the captain not joining us?"

"He already ate." AJ cuts a piece from the loaf and places it on the plate in front of me.

Tessa nods, taking a bite of a piece of bread. "Yes, he always eats fast and then gets up before anyone finishes."

"Go on, try the bread," AJ encourages.

"Thanks. . .so. . .does this mean I'm no longer a prisoner?"

Kaehante flicks his eyes up at me and looks over his shoulder. My guess is he's looking to see if Captain Devil is around.

Tessa smiles. "Baby steps. Eat."

I lift the piece and inspect it. "Umm. . . This isn't gonna. . .do anything weird to me, is it?"

AJ chuckles. "Nope. It's safe. Promise." He pulls his hair back in a ponytail.

I take a bite and break off a piece of hard bread. Ow. I slowly chew through the tough dough, careful not to break a tooth. Hiding my disappointment, I smile at AJ who looks over at me, eagerly.

"Well? Do you like it?"

My eyes water as I swallow and take another bite. "Delicious." I don't understand it. . .it smells so good, yet it tastes like. . .well, like nothing. I guess he tried. I'm honestly too hungry to care. The cool morning breeze blows through my hair as I devour the rest of my piece. When I'm finished, I'm still famished. I guess there isn't much to eat onboard.

"Sorry. . ." AJ finally says as Kaehante snickers. "I know it isn't great. My taste buds haven't been the same since—"

Tessa interrupts him. "Don't worry. I'm putting together a list of supplies and food ingredients we need when we reach port. Salt being one of them."

"Right, and I will get you that list when I go back to the kitchen." AJ sips his cup. "Hm. You should come help me."

"Work in the kitchen?" I ask.

He nods.

That doesn't sound too bad. "Yeah, okay." Not having Nkella leering at me from behind sounds good, and AJ seems cool to be around. A scoff comes from my left; I glance at Kaehante.

"You think Nkella will allow her to touch his food?" Slow deep laughs come from the back of his throat. Unease settles in my stomach.

"I can still try. I need help down there anyway." AJ takes

another bite. "Or you can try talking to him, Tessa. He listens to you."

"I already got her out of the brig. I'm not going to push it."

"He'll probably set her to sweeping the ship." Sunlight glistens on the beads of sweat at the top of his bald head and the tips of his pointy ears. He leans over and grabs a piece of AJ's uneaten bread, but AJ smacks his hand away. Kaehante grunts.

"Fine. Go ahead, you big oaf." AJ pushes his plate toward Kaehante who takes it unapologetically. "It's not like any of us actually need to eat."

Kaehante shrugs a shoulder and smirks as he sticks the whole piece in his mouth.

It's not like any of us actually need to eat. Last night's attack and their transformation into skeletons whenever the seawater hit them resurfaces in my memory.

"Well, I hope he won't put her with me, that's for sure." Tessa says.

I shake the memory away and bite my cheek. "Why not? Am I that repulsive?"

She laughs and shakes her head. I purse my lips.

AJ leans in and whispers, "She mixes dangerous explosives. You don't want to uhh. . .accidentally get caught up."

I gasp. "Oh. . . ." The liquid bombs.

"Yes," Tessa says. "I'm running out of certain solutions, which is why the bombs were so weak against the sea serpent. I don't have much to work with, but I think I can use some of what is left to make do in case it comes back. . .or something worse."

"Something worse than a giant sea serpent?" Then I remember the masked men.

"Busy day," Tessa says.

"Don't you need more people to steer the ship while you're fighting?"

AJ and Tessa exchange a look.

"I've just been wondering why your crew is so small."

"Well, we're meeting my girlfriend tomorrow at Dempu Yuni. We had to split up to avoid capture." His features twist as he struggles to find the right words. "Anyway, she went to go find us some magic plants we need."

"For. . .curse day?"

Tessa snaps a look at AJ, raising her eyebrows, then settles on me. "Yes and no. We need supplies, but we need to be on land for curse day. Too dangerous to be on sea."

"Not to mention," AJ says, "we have potions that take care of a lot of the sailing."

I break another piece of stale bread and stick it in my mouth. "What do you mean potions for sailing?"

AJ points to where the wheel is above our heads. "There's one for the actual steering, one for the masts—although, that one has been running low which is why you saw me and Kaehante struggling with the ropes. But with the right amounts, it's usually smooth sailing."

I look over to the wooden panels as a memory of him sticking a glass bottle and turning it inside a small door resurfaces. So that's what that was.

"It's her birthday tomorrow, this one!" AJ abruptly announces.

Tessa breaks a piece of bread and stuffs it in her mouth. "Really? How old are you turning?"

"Seventeen."

"Ah, not much younger than those three," she says. "Well, hopefully you will no longer be a prisoner and we can do something far away from the captain on curse day, yeah?"

I'm not sure how to take about half of that in.

"Five minutes!" Nkella yells from his quarters.

"How old is Nkella?" I ask.

"He's nineteen," Tessa says.

"Wow. He seems older."

"Yes, he carries himself like he's a lot older, but he had to grow up fast. He holds a lot of responsibility on his shoulders."

"He's been through a lot," AJ adds.

"We all have." Kaehante swigs back the last of his drink before pushing himself to his feet. His heavy boots sound on the wood as he leaves to climb the steps leading up to the quarterdeck.

"I know the feeling." My eyes drop to the mark on Tessa's wrist and then the one on AJ's. What does it all mean? I tug on my sleeves, not wanting to stir up a conversation about my own mark.

"So, what language do you speak?" I ask, changing the subject.

"*Keo sa'l Imboe,*" AJ says, "but we just call it Imboe."

I remember the word from when he first explained the language potion to me. When I don't say anything, he continues.

"It's a mixture between ancient Greek and *keo sa'l Ipani.*"

I knew it! I almost bounce on the balls of my feet as I lean in. "You're Greeks? But wait, how's that possible? I thought this was a different world."

"The ancients came from another world hundreds of years

ago, but much of that knowledge is lost. Except a few things that have been carried down over the ages."

Interesting. "And the captain?"

"He speaks Imboe, too, but his native tongue is Ipani. He's from Danū, also called Pentacles."

"Pentacles?"

Tessa, who has been closely watching the exchange, narrows her eyes at me. Probably unsure if whether I'm telling the truth or not about not knowing any of this. I feel like AJ is the only one onboard I can trust, but for how long? Trust never came easy for me, but hell, I need an ally. I really hope I can work with him in the kitchen.

Humidity mixed with salt tinges my senses. I pull my hair back, wrapping it in a tight ponytail and letting the cool breeze sweep the back of my neck. Something catches my eye between the clouds far in the distance and I squint. At first, I think it's just part of the cloud formation, but as the clouds part, I realize it looks more like. . .a land mass. . . "What's that?"

AJ cranes his neck. "What's what?"

"That enormous thing way up there!" I shoot up from my seat and scurry to the edge of the deck.

AJ and Tessa don't move. "Still not sure what you're looking at."

"Are you kidding me? That large chunk of land floating in the sky!"

"Oh *that?*" AJ nudges his seat back. "That's Tower Island."

My jaw drops. "*That's* Tower Island? The tower place you all think I came from? *A literal floating island?* I mean, an island that. . .f-floats? In the sky?" My voice squeaks and suddenly a pressure weighs down on my head. I stumble back a little. AJ catches my arms and steers me back to my seat.

He looks at Tessa with an "I told you so" stare.

Her face softens. "Are you going to be okay?"

I try to bring my pounding heart back to a normal pace. Okay, there are disappearing drakons that talk. I can believe in a floating island. "Do all your islands float?"

Tessa giggles. "No. Only that one."

"But *why* does it float?"

"It's floated for longer than we've been alive. Rumors say the Empress raised it herself long ago," she says.

"The Empress." I repeat. The one I've been accused of knowing. The one who's supposedly looking for me. "Wait—how long ago could she have done that if it was before you were all born? How old is she?"

"Rumors say she's immortal," AJ says.

I bark out a laugh, but the looks on their faces tell me they're serious. My smile fades. "And that army?"

"Belongs to her." Tessa says.

I gulp.

"Well, we best get a move on." Tessa reverses from the table and turns toward the ramps. AJ stands and motions with his head for me to follow. I do so quickly.

As we edge the top of the ramp, Nkella steps down from the quarterdeck. "No. Not you."

"What? I thought—"

"You will work with Kaehante today, helping him in the armory."

My eyes widen as I look to AJ for help. "Ima have to do what now?"

"Come on, Cap. Let her be in the kitchen with me," he says, shifting his weight to one leg. "You know I need the help."

"So you two can conspire?" He cocks an eyebrow at AJ who tilts his head to the sky, and lets out a heavy sigh.

"Not even to sweep the deck?" AJ says.

"That is your job." Nkella winks at AJ, which catches me off guard.

AJ passes me an apologetic glance and I wince as I watch him walk down the ramp without me. . . So close.

Nkella turns back to me, hardening his face, as if I hadn't just seen a hint of humor on it. I raise my chin, as if challenging him to say something to me. I don't want to go back to the brig, but it's not like me to stand down or cower. Since I've been here, I feel like that's all I've done, but that's because I've been out of my depths. But now, being out of that disgusting cage makes me want to prove myself. If anything, I can't get back to Talia if I'm stuck being a prisoner. A muscle in his cheek flexes.

Kaehante climbs down the steps from the quarterdeck and stops when he reaches us. "Captain?"

"She will help you today." His eyes remain on me as he speaks.

Kaehante's face deadpans. "What? Why?"

"I do not trust her to be anywhere else."

The feeling's mutual. His dark gaze lingers, and I study his eyes, trying to catch those fiery specks that sometimes appear, but they're not there.

"I trust my gunman to keep an utwa in line."

I glower at him, then stare at the burly gunman. Kaehante has barely spoken a word to me since I got here, aside from lending me his coat. He did suggest turning me over to those creepy masks—and then there's his skull face. I shudder. But I think all of them are like that.

They exchange a few words in Ipani—the one the potion I drank doesn't translate.

Nkella gives me one last scrutinizing stare before he spins on his heel and moves upstairs back to the wheel. I gape at Kaehante, who looks conflicted and bewildered.

"So, uhh," I ask, "what are we doing today?"

"Oi." He runs a hand down his face and turns to leave. "Come on." I run after him.

Below deck, he leads me to an artillery room with cannons sticking out of holes and cannonballs rolling in all directions. That can't possibly be safe.

"During the attack, we got hit by the Minor Arcana Army. They went for our weapons. This mess is dangerous for the ship. Collect all the cannonballs and stack them in a tidy corner over there." He points to the far corner of a long room.

I swallow.

He walks to pick up four cannonballs, two in each hand, and stacks them neatly on the other side. I follow his lead, pick one up, and nearly drop it. "Oof."

"Heavy?" He smirks.

"Nope, I can do it." It'll just take me longer. I stretch my back and take a gander at the floor. "How many cannonballs are there?"

"I don't know. Two hundred, maybe."

"Why do you need so many?"

"Most came with the ship. But it is better to be safe than sorry."

"Didn't look like it did anything to the sea serpent last night," I mutter under my breath. He cranes his head at me and shakes it.

"That is because there are only a few of us. Loading these takes hard work and time."

"Got it." A few drops of water hit me on the head, and I glance up. We're at sea-level here, so that must be from rain buildup.

"After this, we have to scrub the floor in case there is any gunpowder."

"I thought the captain didn't want me cleaning."

He chuckles. "No, he doesn't want you snooping around the berth or the stern."

"Huh?"

"Our living quarters," he answers flatly.

"Oh."

"Well, get to work." He turns to leave.

"Wait, where are you going?"

"To check the sails, cables, anchors. Around here we are a small crew. We each do more than our own specialties."

"That makes sense." He turns to leave again. That's the most I've heard him talk since I got here. "Hey, Kaehante?"

He looks at me from the corner of his eyes, frowning.

"I just wanted to say thank you. . .you know, for lending me your coat last night."

He fully faces me and slowly approaches. "Who are you really? The captain doesn't trust you."

I swallow as he approaches. "And you? Do you trust me?"

"Not sure. I heard you speaking a language that's not from anywhere around here."

"English."

"En-glish," he repeats. "Hn. We shall see if we can trust you. For now"—he points to the floor—"cannonballs."

"Right. On it."

Despite Kaehante's large and terrifying stature, and the fact he suggested turning me over to the Minor Arcana, there's something about him that displays loyalty and honor. Maybe it was the way he lent me his coat to protect my modesty, or the way he is with his crewmates. I feel like he's the type of person where once they consider you family, they'll protect you till the end. That won't be me though. His honor is to his captain, who hates me. But I can still respect it.

I stare at the giant pit of cannonballs as he leaves me to it. Sweat beads along my brow and I haven't even started yet.

Bending down, I pick up a cannonball and stack it neatly with the others. The next one I roll over and then pick it up to make it tidy. I start rolling a few at a time to make it easier on myself. This isn't so bad. At least I'm getting exercise, and it's better than being stuck in a cage. I keep the pace for about twenty minutes, my mind going to Talia, how I got here, the strange mark on my arm, Gari, Philo, and then it spirals to Madame Asteria and how pissed she probably was to find her collector's card missing. Ha. Some collector's piece, eh? I wonder if she has any idea about this place, or if she really bought the card from some collector.

Either way, I can't remain stuck on a ship moving cannon-balls forever. I need to find a way back. But the only way I know is the same way I came here. Even though I couldn't get it to work when Nkella was taunting me. . .I was probably just nervous. Who wouldn't be? He's. . .intense. AJ stands up to him though. I wonder what's up with those two.

I stack another cannonball on the top of a pile, but then one from the bottom escapes and rolls off to the side. I run after it and almost bump my head on a barrel. So, there's gunpowder in here, huh? I've never seen gunpowder before. Curiosity urges me forward and I lift the heavy wooden lid off the barrel. It's half full of black powder. Only half? This is an uneven cannon to gunpowder ratio. A drip of water hits my head again. A few more drips run off the side and land in the inside of the barrel. Oops. I wipe my hair and cover the powder with the lid. It'll be fine.

I continue stacking cannonballs until I hear heavy footsteps and voices coming down the ramp. I keep working.

"A twakom palo?" Nkella's voice rings through the wood.

"Ko nalo utwa, kum. Dira'y e sao raí. "

"Nong gichachi?"

"Hāyan tileni muni? Helāni poé a sesirang onje n'unne ipa, mollisi. "

"Kh. *Hehive.*"

They pause and I look behind me to see them both standing, staring at me. What were they just saying?

Nkella's frown deepens. *"Ko kwela mū."* At that remark, Kaehante lifts his brows and glances at the floor. He turns and heads back up the ramp.

Ko kwela mū.

I don't know why, but the way he said it, and the way Kaehante reacted to it makes my stomach twist in a knot.

I wish that potion worked on the Ipani language too. And

they both speak Imboe. Bastards. They purposely didn't want me to understand.

"Come on, lunchtime," Kaehante says over his shoulder, taking off without me.

I place a cannonball on the pile and follow him. Back up the ramp, I hear my name and I stall, pressing my ear against the wood.

"Do you think Soren can stay in one of the rooms tonight? It doesn't feel right, her being in the brig."

Kaehante's voice answers back. "AJ," he pauses for a second, "do not get attached."

AJ falls silent.

I gulp. They mean to get rid of me. Turn me over to that army or kill me. I have to get out of here ASAP. I need to get that card back so I can figure out what it was trying to tell me and get the portal to open. I'm running out of time.

Tessa's voice comes next. "So, you must be excited to see your girlfriend tomorrow? Finally, huh?"

"Yeah, can't wait. I feel bad about having to split up."

"I understand." Tessa says. "It was necessary, or they would have caught her. She's helping a lot by finding the ingredients for us though, eh?"

"I know, but I'll just die if anything happens to her."

I suck in a breath and step around the ramp. AJ looks up, his eyes soft as he looks at me, but I can tell he's forcing his voice to sound excitable.

"Hey, Soren! How's it going?"

"Fine." My eyes fall to Nkella who is silently crouched down with his head pressed against his wolf's. I take a seat next to AJ, careful not to disturb whatever is going on between those two.

On the table is a plate of dry meat, bread, and a canteen. A moment later, Nkella looks up. "It's good news. Iéle reports we should expect clear waters, no attacks."

Turning back to the wolf, he places a hand behind her ears and scratches. He whispers something else and a second later, a loud popping sound rings in my ear just as she vanishes.

"Bye, Moon," AJ sings.

"She will continue to scout a bit further and will be gone for a while." He stretches his legs and sits diagonally across from me, avoiding my gaze. His coat hangs from one of his legs, and his shirt is unbuttoned at the top, showing a few of his Ipani stripes and the semblance of a tattoo. His eyes move to mine and his brows furrow.

I quickly look away. "So," I say, "Iéle means moon." And they can communicate, interesting.

His gaze remains on me. "Hn."

"Yeah, good job." AJ slants a smile.

"How do you say wolf in Ipani?"

AJ glances at Kaehante who is busy chewing his food. After a few awkward seconds of me feeling stupid for attempting small talk, Nkella replies with a grunt.

"*Ruh.*"

"Sorry?"

"Ruh. It means wolf." He uncorks his flask and takes a sip, the warm scents of hickory and vanilla blending with the leathery smell of his coat.

"Ruh. Cool."

I take a bite of the bread and hold it in my mouth. It's stale. And tasteless. I chew slowly then swallow.

We eat in silence for a few minutes before Nkella gets up from his seat and walks away. My shoulders relax a bit. It's not like they eat in silence with him; it is definitely my being here that is making things awkward. Maybe having a bit more of that cookie wouldn't be such a bad idea. If only it hadn't fallen into a puddle under the cage.

Nkella wasn't lying about clear waters today, though I guess it was Iéle who "said" it. Nothing but blue skies all around, a stark contrast to last night's tumultuous storm. With the rocking of the ship and the cool breeze occasionally breaking the warmth of the sun, I can almost pretend I am lounging on a catamaran, living a perfectly normal dream and not mindlessly having to move cannonballs with a floating island defying the laws of physics overhead.

A bead of sweat drips off Kaehante's brow and he lifts his sleeves up to his elbows, showing his marking of what looks like a horse's head and a tiny pentacle on its brow. I stare at it for a second and cover my mark as if they don't already know what mine looks like. He catches me looking at him and I smile.

"So, what does your mark mean?" I ask.

His brows rise as he sticks a piece of jerky in his mouth. "Knight."

"Oh. . .wow." My mind goes to the Tarot cards. With his broad stature and sword, I guess that makes sense.

"Knight of Pentacles," he clarifies.

"Why Pentacles?"

"Because that is where I am from."

"Before the Moirai invasion, it was called Danū," AJ says. "Some of the Ipani still call the islands by their original names. We do too. I mean, we, on this ship."

Dare I ask. . . "Why is that?"

Kaehante squints at me and takes another bite. He looks at Tessa and she shakes her head.

"I don't think she is lying about not knowing," she whispers.

"Because I'm not."

"There are four major islands," Tessa declares, "Wands, Cups, Swords, and Pentacles."

"All ruled by this. . .Empress?" I ask.

AJ nods, taking a sip of his water and swallowing. "As you can see, we don't plan on obeying the Empress any longer. Haven't for a long time now."

"So where are you two from?"

"I'm from a small island off the southern coast of Wands called Sotiria and Tessa is from Cups. Nkella and Kaehante, as you already know, are both from Pentacles."

"Well, one thing's for sure. You're not the pirate stereotypes. . ."

They exchange glances and laugh. "We do what we have to, but not much pillaging goes on with this crew," Tessa says.

Guess I should consider myself lucky. I finish off my meal and my stomach grumbles. That was definitely not enough food. I run my hand down my pants and feel my deck of cards. I forgot I had these; that should get my mind off eating. "How about some entertainment?"

"What do you have in mind?" AJ asks. I reach into the pocket of my borrowed pants and pull out my deck of cards.

He gasps. "That's not. . . Is that the Tarot?" he whispers. Tessa leans in. Kaehante has his head tilted back as he observes.

I laugh. "No, this is a regular set of playing cards. Well, except for the fact that they're themed in Alice and Wonder-land—uhh. . .a story from my world."

"Oh. What do you do with them?"

"They're meant for playing games, but I use them for stage tricks," I say, cautiously aware of avoiding the word magic with these guys.

I shuffle the cards in my hand, remove the two jokers, and count twenty-six, leaving two stacks of twenty-six cards. "AJ, split one of these decks in the middle."

He picks up one of the sides and splits the deck right down the middle, "Like this?"

"Yep, just like that!" I take one of those sides and set it apart. Then, take the un-split deck, shuffle it again as they all sit quietly watching as I do, and spread the cards in my hands, facing him. "Now, pick a card, don't let me see it."

He does so.

"Great, now memorize that card and stick it back in the deck." Watching closely where he places it, I stick my finger in between, and with a sleight of hand, shuffle the cards, sticking his chosen one at the back. "Now, I'm going to lose your card. Ready?"

He smiles and nods. When I've done that, I drop the cards on one of the cut piles.

"You know what?"

They all lean in.

"I'm not convinced the card is lost enough," I start shuf-fling them a different way, and their eyes widen. I start dropping cards on the table, secretly keeping the same order, and once I'm done, I gather them all up again. "Now AJ, count how many cards are on that pile you cut over there."

He picks up the lonely pile and counts, stopping at thirteen.

"Okay, then, everybody ready?" Starting from the top, I count the cards slowly, stopping on the thirteenth card. I flip the card over and show the eight of diamonds, with a drawing of the White Rabbit on the inside. "Is this your card?"

His eyes beam as he sits back and claps. "How did you do that?"

Kaehante squints. "Magic?"

"Trickery." A husky voice comes from behind me and the hairs on the back of my neck prickle my skin. I didn't even hear him approach. Nkella steps to my side and picks up a card. I hold my breath, letting it out slowly.

"Well, yeah, that's the point." I say.

"She counted them. More proof she is a liar." He snaps.

"Oh, come on, Nkella, it's just for fun."

Nkella grimaces and cocks his head to the side, eyes narrowing at AJ. "Captain."

"What?"

"You will call me Captain, enough calling me Nkella, daí?"

Kaehante's eyes fall to the ground and Tessa looks from Nkella to AJ whose jaw has dropped to the table.

"Oh my god, are you seriously pulling rank right now?"

"You need to learn respect," Nkella hisses.

"Fine! Cap-*tain*, you need to lighten up!"

Nkella grimaces.

"Alright, you two. Break it up." Tessa holds her hands out. "That's enough testosterone for one day."

Nkella turns his eyes to me. "Do another."

I gulp. "Another?"

"Yes."

"Oh. . .okay. . .Like a different trick or the same one—"

"Another."

"Fine, alright." I gather the cards and separate my two Mad Hatter jokers and my black ace of spades Cheshire Cat card, setting the rest of the card deck on the table.

He picks one up, disrupting my game. "What are these images?"

"They're from a story my mom used to read to me when I was little." My fingers automatically go to reach my little teacup bracelet around my wrist.

"Hn." He sets them back down, his eyes growing softer as he sits, intrigued by the images, the fact that it's from a story, or the actual card game.

"I've been feeling more and more like Alice since I got here," I mutter under my breath.

I tuck the deck away and hold the three cards in my hand. "This one doesn't involve counting cards." I swallow hard. I'm taking a bit of a risk with this one because if he does think it's magic, I'll be back to square one. "For this trick, follow the black card."

He stares, unmoving. I show him the card, then set each of them face down on the table. Pointing again to the card I told him to follow, I slowly move them around. When I stop, I ask him, "Which is your card?"

"Kh." He taps his finger on a card. "I am not bancha. It is

this one." He turns it over to find one of the Mad Hatter jokers. Confusion plasters his face as the others gasp.

AJ laughs loudly. Nkella snaps his eyes to mine, and I suck in a breath.

"Trickery."

I shuffle the cards back and smirk.

"You are a liar and a cheat," he hisses.

"It's only a game." AJ says. "How did you do it?"

I slant a smile. "A good Magician never reveals their secret." Uh-oh. Poor choice of words.

"Magician, daí? Hn." He picks up a card and inspects it. "And you want us to trust you?"

Kaehante groans and lets out a chuckle in the end. "You are not helping your case. Come on, back to work."

I tuck the cards in my back pocket.

To my surprise, Nkella's twirling the World Card in his hands. He keeps it on him? He looks up at me and narrows his eyes, the soft light accentuating the Ipani stripes on his neck and the subtle point of his ears sticking out from his hair.

"I can show you how I do the card trick if you want?" I ask.

"Koj."

I'm guessing that means no. "Okay then." I turn to follow Kaehante down the ramp and steal a glance at Nkella still sitting, inspecting the Tarot card. Concentration hardens his face. A second later, I see him stick it back inside his coat. A smirk curls on my face, and I put a pep in my step as I head back to work.

The rest of the day goes by quickly. Kaehante only comes in a few times to wipe the cannons, check up on me, and give me a bucket of water and a sponge to scrub the floor. For the most part, I'm left alone while he helps the crew with the rest of the ship and Nkella steers.

Come dinnertime, we have broth and more bread; I cannot wait for a decent meal, if I'll ever have one again.

I lean over the ship's railing and stare out at the sea. The ebb and flow of the waves crashing against the ship soothes me as I try to deal with how surreal this all still is to me. I hope Talia is okay. At this point, she'll never forgive me for abandoning her. But maybe it's better that she's mad at me and not worried something happened to me. A soft motor approaches by my side.

"Are you alright, dear?"

I smile down at Tessa, "I'm fine. Just worried about my sister."

"Well, that's curious."

"What's curious?"

"I think you and the captain have a lot more in common than you know."

I stifle a laugh. "Oh, yeah, we have loads in common." I stare back out to sea.

"The girl whose clothes you're wearing belonged to Nkella's sister."

I gasp and point to my blouse. No wonder he didn't want me wearing it. "Belonged?"

She nods, sadly. Oh. . .that's who they were talking about before. Now I feel terrible wearing it. I wouldn't want some stranger I think is a spy wearing my dead sister's clothes either.

"I should. . .go change my clothes. . ."

"No, he'll get over it. She didn't like that outfit anyway.

Said it washed away her complexion." She chuckles. "Of course, she looked fine in it, but it's a little torn."

I smile. What's her angle?

"Well, it's bedtime. We have to be up early for port."

"Right, I guess I'll go lock myself up then."

"Actually."

"Hm?" I had already started walking away.

"I managed to convince him it wouldn't make a difference if you stayed in a room or not, seeing as how you escaped once already. He only grunted in response, but. . ." she tilts her head for me to follow as she backs up her chair. "Come."

"Really?" I follow her down to the crew's quarters, my heart skipping a beat. She leads me to the narrow hall I had snuck into before and points me to a room beside the one I suspect is AJ's. The wool curtain is rough to my touch as I move it to the side and lay my eyes on the one thing apart from my sister I've been yearning for the entire time I've been stuck on this ship. A bed! I turn back around to thank Tessa but she's already gone back to her room. I drop my deck of cards on the side table and lay my dirty body on the tan mattress.

I knew I'd win at least one of them over. A sly smile crawls on my lips. This just makes it so much easier to steal back that card and get the hell out of here.

"Uh, come in." I sit up on my elbows as AJ pushes himself through the curtain, my jeans and tank top hanging from his elbow and a jug and bowl in his hands.

"I brought your dry clothes, a bowl of warm water, and a hand cloth." AJ smiles, setting the jug, bowl, and cloth on the table next to my deck of cards.

I take the clothes from his hands and set them down, eying the warm bowl. Am I meant to use that small bit of water to wash myself?

"Oh, and there's a bath at the far end of this hall."

Oh, good. "Thank you."

"My pleasure. I guess if you're going to want something, get Tessa to convince the captain. I tried to get you a room earlier, but Nkella never listens to me."

"What's the deal with you two anyway?"

He shrugs and falls on the bed, his long hair spilling on the sheets. "Neither of us are good at taking orders. But we all voted for him to captain the ship, including me, so I can't complain."

"Are you regretting that decision now?"

"No, not really."

Huh. Not the answer I was expecting.

"He just puts his goals before ours sometimes, and I call him out on it. But he is a good captain and"—he sits up on his elbows—"unfortunately you'll probably never get to see this side of him due to. . .unfortunate circumstances"—he nods to my mark with his nose—"but he does care about all of us. He's devoted his life to the fight against the Empress, so fighting with him will just make our voyage harder."

"Got it." Okay, so maybe he doesn't hate Nkella like I thought. I can't ask him to help me with my plan then, he might try to stop me, or worse—tell Nkella.

"How did you two meet?" I ask.

"That's a long story." AJ smiles. "About a year ago, Nkella, his sister Ntaoru, and his cousin Kae—you know Kaehante— tried to escape Danū."

I didn't realize Kaehante and Nkella were cousins. When I don't speak, he carries on.

"Because it's under siege." He glances at me. "Things in Danū are bad."

"Oh."

"They got caught. Escaping Danū is impossible, I was surprised he succeeded. The entire island is blocked off. From what Kae and Nkella told us, they tried leaving one at a time. Kaehante got hit in the back with an arrow and when Nkella went back for him, he got caught as well, taken and tortured." I stifle a gasp, imagining Nkella being tortured.

"How did he get out? I mean, he obviously did eventually."

"He won't talk about it, but he made it to Oleanu on a raft. He was so badly injured, he was close to death. I was with Tessa when we found them, and she took him in and looked after his wounds."

"How did you meet Tessa?"

"I met Tessa when I was tarovelling through Oleanu with my ex-boyfriend." He stares up at the ceiling. "My current girl-friend, Lāri, and I were just friends back then, and she was staying with Tessa. We were there trying to break up oumala animal fights." He pauses, taking a breath. "Nkella helped us when he got his strength back. Then, in return, we helped him to go back for Kae and his sister. . ." His voice trails off. I wonder what happened to her but decide not to ask.

"That's quite a big payment for helping you to break up animal fights," I say.

He glances at me. "He brought us into his plan to over-throw the Empress, and it was a pirate's life ever since. We even helped him steal a ship." He pats the bed.

It makes more sense now that I've learned they're not just pirates looking to loot. A bunch of questions swarm through my mind but I suppress the urge to ask them. I need him to go to sleep so I can carry on with my mission, not to mention, none of this is any of my business. What happened to Nkella's sister? Why is Danū under siege? I have to remind myself that none of it is my problem.

"Well," he gets up. "I'm glad you're not a prisoner

anymore. And for the record, I always believed you were telling the truth."

"How could you know for sure?" I for one wouldn't let myself place blind trust in people.

"I can tell when people are lying. You weren't."

I chuckle. "Thanks, AJ."

"I'm right next door if you need anything." He walks out and closes the curtain. I'm gonna miss that guy. Under different circumstances I would have wanted to keep him as a friend. Crossing my fingers, I'm successful at getting the card to work. I'll spend all night trying to get that portal to open. If worst comes to worst, I'll just have to drop it back in his coat when he's not looking. But it worked once before, so it has to again, right?

After I wash up in lukewarm water with a cloth and change out of Nkella's sister's clothes, I stare at the ugly jail clothes I wore when I came here. Sighing, I put them on and stick my card deck in my pocket, I sit with my back against the wall, listening to the conversations between the other crew through the curtains. Not trying to get sleepy, it's better to wait until they're all asleep first before I make my move.

"Pesky *bohhibe*. Chewed through my socks. That was my last pair."

Tessa laughs through the curtain. "I'll add socks to the list, AJ."

"And bohhibe killer. Soren, do you have bohhibe in your world?"

"I don't know what those are. So, no."

"They're these tiny flying monsters with small eyes, and

toothed beaks. They eat cloth and they're hard to kill because they're oumala and just pop up whenever!"

I stifle a laugh. "Yikes. I'm glad we don't have those on Earth."

Kaehante clears his throat, followed by heavy boots on the wooden floor. "You talk too much, daí? I am going to relieve the captain and take an early shift. I will wake you up in a few hours, AJ."

Shit. Of course they're taking shifts! Someone has to steer the ship. What am I going to do?

"Right. Sorry, Kae. It won't be so bad when we get more of the steering potion."

Kaehante grunts.

"And it doesn't help that Iéle is off patrolling the area instead of on ship."

Oh, right. . .that makes things easier for me though. I can sneak past Kaehante. . .I hope.

After about twenty minutes, the light in the hall outside my curtain is snuffed out. Snoring fills the area and I edge myself to the foot of the bed. After a few beats, I'm convinced they're all asleep. Sucking in a breath and holding it, I tiptoe outside, barefoot so as not to not make any noise or catch Kaehante's attention at the wheel.

Cold wind smacks my face as I reach the top of the ramp. The water glistens in the moonlight as the rhythmic splashing of the waves against the ship sends a current of calmness through my bones. I feel kind of bad sneaking into Nkella's room after what AJ told me. Behind all that badassery, there must be kindness inside him.

But no. I can't stay here. I need to go back for Talia, but

also for my life. I don't belong here. And even though AJ and Tessa seem nice, one mishap could make them change their minds about me. And Kaehante tolerates me but he's the same as the captain. Yep. It's time to go. And this is my only chance.

I traipse around the main deck and fight the wind up the steps to the quarterdeck. To my right, something has Kaehante distracted at the wheel; his head is tucked under it while he tinkers with something. The loud winds must have muffled my footprints.

Taking a deep breath, I sprint to the next set of stairs that lead to the captain's quarters. It's only three steps, so I take them all at once and quickly tuck myself into an alcove, pressing myself tightly against the wall. Strong winds wrap my hair around my face as I glance back at Kaehante who is now looking straight toward the bow. My heart hammers in my throat as what I am about to do settles into my reality.

I pull my hair behind my ear. Okay, hold it together. I can do this. I'm a stealthy carnival con artist queen. I've got this.

I glance over my shoulder, past the rear of the ship, and out to the open ocean. He's going to make me walk the plank if he catches me, I know it. My stomach ties itself into a knot. Focus, Soren. I've made it this far. Do it for Talia. I fix my eyes back on the door.

God, I hope his wolf is far, far away in the ouma dimension. And not watching me.

No, if she were here, she would have caught me by now.

I inch to the captain's bedroom door. Turning the knob, I suck in a breath and hold it. This is so incredibly stupid. If I get caught. . .I shouldn't think about that. I need to steal the card back so I can figure out a way home. I slowly push the door open to a room with sheer beige curtains covering glass windowpanes across each wall. A slight breeze passes through my hair and I notice one of his windows is open, letting in the dim lighting from the gas lantern on his balcony.

My eyes skim the captain's bedroom. A brown rug lies underneath a bed in the center of the room. Wooden arrows and a bow lean against a desk all the way to the right. Straight ahead and next to the desk is a small round table with a carving knife and an unlit candle on top; next to the table is a chair with his coat draped over it. Bingo. The bad news is, Nkella is lying on his stomach on the right side of the bed, his head facing in the other direction but still too close to his coat for comfort.

I swallow and take my first step, squeezing my eyes shut. I expect the floorboard to creak but it doesn't. My shoulders drop and I carry on, walking on the soft carpet masks my steps even more. Keeping an eye on him, I can't help but notice the dips and curves of his lean back muscles as they rise up and down with each deep breath. Thick Ipani stripes almost criss-cross his back but instead form blade-like points at his spine. They're like tiger stripes, only thicker and straighter—just a shade darker than his skin.

His matted hair is tousled in different directions. He looks so peaceful, almost innocent. Like he could never be. . .a Devil. I still wonder what he did.

My foot lands on a loose floorboard. It squeaks and I hold my breath.

A low groan escapes his lips, and he starts to move.

My body tenses. Quickly, I bend my knees, preparing to

hide in front of his bed. He flips himself on his back and covers his eyes with his arm. He's still asleep. Whew—that was close.

Strange symbols are tattooed across his pecs, inked right over the Ipani stripes coming down from his shoulder blades and nearly touching at the middle of his chest. I have to fight myself to not stare at them. My eyes wander down his muscular torso and stop at his wrists. On his left, he has a marking, brown like mine but of the number *XV*. On the other, is a *0*. Curious.

Something tickles my arm and I almost shriek in alarm. I bite my tongue as Philo pops out of the Aō dimension with her mosaic black and red body shimmering in the dim light. She jumps into his coat, and I reach to grab her, now taking long strides to his bedside.

As I pull up a flap of his jacket, I catch her glare over a pocket until she disappears inside. That's where the card must be. Makes sense as Philo seems to be attracted to its where-abouts. I cautiously stick my hand into the inside of the pocket, careful not to make any ruffling sounds with the fabric and slowly lift the card up, revealing its black and gold glare. Booyah!

A hand grabs my leg and I suck in a sharp breath. I drop the card and flick my gaze to Nkella's hard stare. My stomach dips.

His grip intensifies as he swiftly switches positions, lunging up and grabbing my arms instead. I try to back up.

"I'm sorry—"

"What do you think you are doing?" He pushes himself up fast as hell and backs me into the corner between his desk and the wall.

"I—"

Shadows dance across his face and the intensity in his sharp eyes twists my stomach into knots. A chain hangs from his neck with a round, black, tarnished pendant, decorated with a black winding tree on its face. Like the one I had seen in the empty room.

My eyes flick up as I'm suddenly aware of him being aware at my staring at his chest. My cheeks flame.

His jaw clenches. "Stealing from me?" Hatred flashes in his eyes and those fiery specks illuminate his irises for a second. Suddenly I'm out of breath despite not having moved.

Stealing? I mean, usually but. . . "How can it be stealing? It's my card."

"So, you finally admit you are one of them." His deep husky voice lingers in my ears. I shiver.

"W-what? How? No, I mean—I came with it."

"I should have known to keep you in the brig. You are going back."

"No please. . .I'm sorry. I just want to go home."

"Don't we all, utwa."

"I'm not a spy." I say again for the gazillionth time. "What will it take for you to believe me?"

His face darkens. "What is stopping me from killing you right now?"

My face pales. "Why don't you then?"

He ignores my last words and puts his hand at the back of my neck and squeezes it, pushing me forward. "Let's go."

"Because you need me alive, don't you?" I try to squirm from his grip but his hold tightens in immeasurable strength. "Why?"

"Move."

Sighing, I let him lead me out of the room.

"I can go back to my room. I promise I'll stay there this time."

"People make many promises. The only ones they keep are the ones that serve themselves."

"That—Okay, that is not always true."

"Kh."

"I promised my sister I would always be there for her. And I left." Tears well up in my eyes.

"You prove my point."

"No! I left by accident. Because that stupid card opened a portal and dropped me here!"

"Quiet. You wake up the crew."

"The only reason I had was because—"

"I don't care."

My breath shutters as a tear rolls down my face. There's no point with him. He's a heartless pirate who will never in a million years believe anything I say. Because I'm one of them. Whoever they are.

My stomach sinks as he steers me back to the brig.

"Please, you can trust me. I only want to go home. I don't mean any harm. It's an accident, me being here."

He takes a right turn instead of a left to the brig and guides me into a tiny room. "Where are we going?"

He doesn't answer and I start to squirm even harder, pulling at his hand. "Let go of me. Where are you taking me?"

He pushes me down to a chair at the back of the room. I try to stand but he's already taking my arm and strapping it down with a rope. I yank my arm, and with brute force, he jerks me down hard as he ties me quickly. A giant lump forms at my throat and my lungs constrict. The rope wraps around my torso, binding my hands on my lap.

"Why are you doing this? You can trust me. I fixed your sail! Or. . .tried to anyway."

"I trust no one."

"What are you going to do to me?"

He steps back and folds his arms. An image emerges from behind him, a low prowling stance, and scarlet eyes. Iéle. The wolf is back.

"Who are you?" he hisses.

My eyes move back to his cold stare. "I'm Soren. . .I told you that already."

"Hn." He tilts his head. "Iéle?"

The wolf's head prowls low as she fixes her snarling stare on me. I stiffen. My skin prickles as the temperature plummets and I can see my breath. "Wait—what's happening?"

"Each lie you tell, Iéle will use her ouma."

I squeeze my lips together and push my head back. A strong magnetic force concentrates my focus to Iéle, forcing me still. Her eyes peer into mine, her magnetism drawing me in deeply. And for a second, I only see her.

The air around me grows icy. The moisture on the skin of my face leaves me all at once and my throat dries up. Then my tongue absorbs the remaining saliva I have left. And now I desperately need water.

"I will ask again. Who are you?" Despite his raspy voice interrupting his magnetism, my eyes remain on the wolf.

I lick my peeling lips. "I—I'm Soren, just a girl. I'm not related to the Empress in any way." My throat scratches as I speak. "I didn't come from the Tower. Please—" I clear my throat. "I need water."

"Iéle."

The wolf's magnetism grows stronger. My heart rate intensifies, and my insides start to ache. I cough. I'm so dehydrated. "Water. . ." Spots start to emerge from my peripherals as dizziness overwhelms me. "Please. . ."

"Who are you?" He repeats.

"I'm. . .not. . .lying."

"Fine. Did you come from the Tower?"

"No." My voice croaks. "Water."

A slow hiss escapes his lips. "Iéle, now."

My vision darkens and the wolf's glowing stare snuffs out of the cold cell. A popping sound blankets the room in deafening silence, and I can no longer see or hear anything around me.

I don't understand. Where did the wolf go? Where's Nkella?

A heavy pressure drops from my head, pulling me down, as if I'm suddenly falling leagues below water. But I'm not underwater; I can still breathe the cold air. What is happening?

Something tickles my hand and before I realize I can't actually move my limbs, I try to pull it back. The pressure has gone down to my feet, cocooning me in some sort of heavy force field. I try wiggling my fingers and toes but even that is no use.

Despite the darkness that has fallen over the room, I can still move my eyes down to my hand to see what's there.

A single spotlight illuminates an isolated spot in my hand and I open my mouth to scream. But no sound comes out.

A large, blue parasite-like creature sits on the back of my

hand. It turns its round-shaped head to my face and reveals no eyes, just rows upon rows of sharp teeth lined in circles. Screaming inaudibly, I try jerking my hand back again but no matter how hard I try, I am paralyzed in this chair. My heart hammers at my throat. The parasite creature inches to the tip of my index finger, leaving a slimy residue on my skin. My eyes widen as it touches the tip of my finger with its teeth and bites off an inch.

My mouth opens wide to shriek in agonizing pain. But no sound comes out.

Blood surges out of my finger and it takes all the energy I have inside me to try to move. To scream. To kick. But nothing I do works. The slug continues to gnaw on my hand, inch by inch, eating all the way down until my index finger is gone.

The pain makes my brain go fuzzy. The world around me spins as I watch the creature move onto my middle finger until blood is streaming down to the black abyss. I'm being eaten alive!

"*Somebody help!*" I try to say.

Nkella's voice echoes inside my ears as his tall stature breaks through the darkness. "Are you ready to answer my questions now?"

I scream again; this time my voice echoes loudly.

"Did you fall from the Tower?" he asks calmly.

"No!" I yell. My throat burns as I'm finally able to speak.

The parasite takes another bite out of my hand and I yell, tears pouring down my face, still unable to move.

"What do you know of the Minor Arcana?"

"Only that it's an army, and only because your crew told me."

"Lies. Are they really dead?"

Oh my god, my hand—my whole arm is throbbing. "What?"

"Can they be brought back?"

"I—What!"

He grunts. "Iéle."

"No. Stop, please—"

The wolf leaps from the darkness and lands on my chest. My breath pants. "I'm not lying!" I try to fight the force field to lift my chin away from the wolf's snarling teeth. Her heavy paws squeeze down on my shirt; her sharp claws pierce my skin. She inches back, opens her mouth to show her large fangs, and sinks them into my stomach.

Struggling to move, I scream until my voice gets snuffed out again and I'm yelling uncontrollably although no sound emerges.

I watch as the wolf rips through my flesh, blood oozing from me as she takes my innards out and swallows them whole. Every fiber of my being shrieks in pain as my surroundings start to fade away. And I realize I'm either dying or already dead.

And then she stops. With my heart at my throat, I gaze clearly into her prying red eyes, and she jumps off. I—I'm not dead?

Tears stream down my face as the rest of the room comes into view. I gape down, expecting to see blood everywhere and my body in shreds, but instead. . .everything is still intact. I wiggle my fingers, the pain no longer there.

My lips part. "But. . .I don't understand! It was all fake?"

"Have you had enough yet? Are you ready to speak the truth?"

My eyes flick up to meet his serious gaze. "I was not lying."

He lifts his chin. "Kh."

Iéle sits by his feet, her eyes no longer glowing but still fixed on me.

"Did you come from the Tower?"

"For the last time, no."

"Next time, it won't be an illusion."

I swallow. "Just kill me then, if you're not going to believe me." My voice cracks.

A low hiss leaves his throat, and he flicks the card in his hand. "What do you know about this card?"

"Just that it brought me here."

"What else?"

I swallow.

Iéle's eyes give a glow.

"It changed." I blurt.

"Daf? What changed?" He moves toward me. "The card?"

"Yes."

"How?"

"W-when you gave it back to me to see if I could get it to take me home and I dropped it on the ground. . . When I went to pick it up, it changed."

He squints his eyes at the card. "What did it show?"

"Umm. . .a wand with a purple crystal at the top, covered in a vine."

"The Ace of Wands?"

"Yes."

"Why?"

"I have no idea, and that is all I know! Please, just. . .leave me alone."

"Ntaoru."

"What?"

"Have you seen her?"

Fuzziness clogs my memory and then I recognize the name. "Your sister?"

"So you do know her."

"Only because AJ told me about her."

He lifts his chin, his eyes narrowing down at me.

"I told you I'm not from that Tower. . .Island. . .place. I don't know the Empress. And for the last time, I am *not* from here."

"Hn. Either you're very good, you're telling the truth, or your memory was wiped. But I still do not trust you. Let's go."

"Makes two of us," I hiss.

"How did you get ouma then, daí?"

"Magic?"

He grunts as he unties the rope.

"Katergaris. A drakon visited me." Sorry Gari, but I'd very much like to keep my limbs.

"Hn."

The magnetic hold Iéle had over me releases. I can finally move again. My knees quiver as I stand, and he grabs me by the neck like he did earlier and guides me out of the room.

I don't even ask him where he's going this time or try to talk. In fact, I'd rather never speak to him again. He leads me back to the brig. The disgusting metal cage I started in. Why did I have to sneak out of the perfectly cozy room AJ and Tessa got me? I could have enjoyed a full night's sleep in an actual bed. But instead, I went ahead and got myself caught. And imprisoned. Again.

Nkella slams the cage shut and locks it. His dark eyes stare at me, emotionless.

"Could I at least have some water?" I ask, mad at myself for betraying my wish to never want to speak to him again.

He scoffs, turns on his heel, and once again leaves me in the dark wet prison that is my life. Without a drink of water.

"You're still here?" A blue electric light pops in front of me and Katergaris's fluffy head spins upside down, its body following his lead.

"Go away, Gari. I'm not in the mood."

Gari looms over my head but doesn't speak.

"He really is the Devil."

"Well, he couldn't be anything else," his voice gurgles.

"I'm never getting out of here, am I?"

"I gave you the chance of getting out of this cage. You keep getting yourself back in."

"No, I mean I'm never getting out of this world. I need to go home."

"Want? Or need?"

I lift my head up from my knees. "What?"

"You say you need to go back for your sister. But, if so much time has passed, won't your sister be figuring things out?"

"She's a kid. And I don't want her to think I abandoned her."

"You can make it up to her later, can't you?"

"Your point?"

"You never mentioned *wanting* to go back. . ."

Ha. That's because I'll be going back to the Nelsons and waiting until I'm eighteen to leave. "It doesn't matter what I want."

"Doesn't it? Some of the people here want their freedom. So, they fight for it."

"And how am I supposed to fight for my freedom if I don't know my feet from my ears in this place?"

He giggles.

"I have nothing to fight with here. I was just tortured by a wolf and her hallucinogen power. Even the pain was a hallucination." I shiver. "I'm nothing. Powerless."

"Oh, I'm not so sure."

I quirk a brow. "What do you mean?"

"You have the mark."

I roll my eyes and sigh. "Yeah, much good that's done."

"Didn't you mention something about the Quartermaster Card changing for you?"

"Quartermaster?"

"The World Card. It won't change for anyone else."

I swallow a breath. "It won't?"

"If it changed for you"—he spins on his back—"then that's where you need to go. Perhaps, it shows you what you want. And if going home is truly what you want, then you must find what it was showing you. . ."

"The Ace of Wands. . ."

"Ah! Then that's what you need to find in order to get back to your sibling. See? I'm always of use."

"Uh-huh." I cross my arms. "How do I know I can trust

you? The last time I did, I ate a danger-cookie that could have killed me."

"It got you out of this cage, didn't it?" His tail whips around from his disappearing body and touches his cheek. "And I told you not to eat the whole thing."

"Hmm. . . Fine, but why would the Quartermaster Card show me the Ace of Wands instead of my actual home?"

"I don't know much about the cards, but I do know this. . ." His head turns clockwise so his eyes leer into mine. "Each card does something, and the aces carry enough power to do *anything*."

"Anything?"

"Anything," he sings. "Well, maybe not anything." His body is sinuous above my head. "The Ace of Wands, being the card of new beginnings as is said, cannot be used by the ones in chains."

I blink. "Meaning a prisoner? It can't be used by me?"

"Oh, it's nothing *you* have to worry about, more for the one in internal chains. Like a poor soul bearing the curse of the Devil Card." His head turns upside down as his body stays the same. "You see?"

"A Devil like Nkella? That's probably a good thing." A spark of hope ignites under my skin. Maybe I don't need the World Card. Maybe my only hope is to get away from these undead pirates and find the Ace of Wands. If what Gari is telling me is true, and the World Card is a Quartermaster that shows me how to get what I want, then that's what I have to do.

"Gari, thank you. I know what I have to do now."

"Do you know where you're going?" he gurgles. "The Ace of Wands is protected from the Empress in the Isle of Wands."

"No. But first, I need to get far away from here. Wait—why is it protected *from* the Empress?"

"That, I haven't a clue. All I know is, she can't cross the barrier that protects it. If she gets her hands on it, Ipa is doomed." He sings the double "oo" in doomed.

Not my problem. "Can you take me there?" I gaze up at him and he backs away.

"Drakons are being hunted in the Isle of Wands right this moment. I cannot take you. We would be shot down or hunted inside the Aō."

Shot down or hunted. "No matter. I'll find my way to that card. Tomorrow, we dock, and that's when I'll make my move."

8

I didn't sleep a wink. When it wasn't phantom memories of parasitic worms eating at my hands, it was Iéle's menacing stares coming back to haunt me. But worst of all, it was fear that kept me awake. Fear about being stuck in close proximity with some oumala captain who could use his wolf to harm me in ways I never thought imaginable. I mean, why make me hallucinate? It's bad enough the wolf can literally eat me, but the fact that he can change my perception of reality at will. . .feel pain and make me nearly die of thirst or go crazy with dementia. Ah, there it is. *Crazy with dementia.* Like my mother.

My blood curdles. I don't care if running away means I'm alone in this strange world before I can find that Ace of Wands card. I'm getting off this ship.

The door to the room clicks open and a familiar growl greets me. I bring my legs up to my chest. Nkella rushes inside with his pirate captain's hat on his head and unlocks the gate.

I hesitate to get up. "Why?" I ask him.

"Why, what?"

"Why let me out at all?"

"You got out once. I'm not letting you out of my sight, *rikwa*."

"What did you call me?"

"Thief."

"Right." Guess he realized I'm not an utwa after all. "Takes one to know one," I tell him.

I try moving past him but he blocks my path, his permanent scowl on his face. I gasp as he grabs my wrists and slaps cuffs on them.

I pull on the chains. "Really?"

"Walk."

Biting back a response, I speed walk up the ramps and meet the rest of the crew on the main deck by the ship's exit. Tessa is speaking to Kaehante and AJ; I inch over, readying for when they let down that wooden ramp to my freedom. AJ's facial muscles are solid and angular as his gaze drops from my eyes down to my wrists, and then to Nkella. He shakes his head, and I relax my shoulders. I wasn't sure if Nkella spoke to them about me before letting me out, but by the evil glares AJ's giving Nkella, *he* doesn't think I'm some thief.

I stand next to him as Tessa continues talking.

"Happy birthday," AJ whispers.

I glance at him and part my lips. "Thanks." I had forgotten my birthday was today. Some birthday this has started out to be. Wait, that means it's been two days since I've left Talia by herself. My stomach sinks down to the kelp.

Tessa raises her voice an octave. "AJ and Nkella will go to

the tavern to meet Lāri and book us the room for the evening while Kaehante and myself will head to town to collect supplies."

Nkella bows his head down to the wolf. "You go with them, Iéle. Make sure they stay safe." Iéle whines loudly. That's the first time I've heard her make any sound other than a growl.

AJ laughs. "Won't let you into the tavern, eh? Poor girl."

The wolf growls.

Nkella gives her a glare. "Iéle." He says, his voice stern.

She lets out a snarling bark and I ball my fists. Yeah Iéle. Stay with them. The wolf turns to face me and bows her head. A shiver runs down my spine; I nudge closer to AJ. Stupid wolf.

Tessa continues. "A quick rundown on what we're getting while in town. Oh, and we'll bring everything back to the ship before calling it a night. No reason to bring it into the inn with us. Right, so thread for the sail, barrels of water. . ." She steals a glance at Kaehante holding two barrels in each arm. *Yeesh*, he's strong. "Food—I have your shopping list AJ—and if we can find them, potion ingredients to keep the ship running."

She continues with the list when Kaehante murmurs. "We're going to have to make two trips."

"And of course the *hū raku* that your girlfriend has collected for my chair cannons, AJ." Those must be the poison bomb things.

"Don't forget we also need some more *Indakepoa* for Soren," AJ adds.

My brow quirks. "Hm?"

"To keep your language translation."

Oh, the nasty licorice drink. Yeah, no thanks. I won't be here for that. I give him a fake smile and nod.

"I have some in my room, but it doesn't hurt to get more," Tessa says.

"Great, let's go!" AJ jumps in place. "Lāri has been waiting long enough!"

I inch closer to AJ, but Nkella plants his heavy hand on my left shoulder. "You come with me."

"Yeah." I roll my shoulder from his grip. "I know." He wants to keep his eye on me. Whatever. As long as his wolf goes in the opposite direction.

Kaehante lowers the ramp onto the rocky ground and Tessa drives down first. I watch as the three of them, wolf included, head off to the left of a forked path up ahead.

With Nkella walking behind me, I follow AJ who leads excitedly toward the right, passing a row of boats and ships docked near what looks like a market. The acrid smell of seafood assaults my nostrils. Laughter from a tavern not too far in the distance emerges through the trees. We climb up four moss-covered stone steps leading toward its entrance. A large sign hangs over the door that reads **Κέρβερος ταβέρνα**. I watch as the potion works its magic and the words morph into Cerberus Tavern.

A guitar band plays inside the tavern mixed with sounds of chatter and laughter. I scan the grounds for any kind of pathway. He'll have to leave me out of his sight at some point, to go to the bathroom or something while we're in there. My eyes fall to a tree with a poster nailed to its trunk. Words, in what I assume belong to the Imboe language, changes to English after a few seconds and in big letters it reads: *"Say no to Magic. If you see something, say something."* Red graffiti in a big *X* inside a circle is drawn over it. Huh. interesting.

AJ picks up speed and bursts through the doors, ready to see his girlfriend. The music grows louder with the door opening. I choke on a laugh. Poor guy, he's been desperate to see her for days.

A busty woman with pointy ears and bright pink lips pushes herself close to Nkella, blocking the entrance. Nkella ignores her, turning his cheek, and for a split second, he has his eyes off me. I crane my neck out into thick shrubbery and trees. A nearby horse whinnies. I'm not about to steal a horse, but I doubt I can outrun Nkella.

And yet. . . He lets out a hoarse "kh" and opens the door, pushing the woman aside, and blocking the entrance.

This might be the dumbest idea I've had in a long time but. . .I book it.

Sprinting out into the shrubbery with my hands still chained together, I jump over a few rocks and plants and make a dash for it.

I don't look back.

No idea where I'm going, but I don't care. I can't stay a pirate prisoner.

Run.

I'll worry about my chains later; I've gotten myself out of worse.

Just run.

Find somewhere to hide, then ask someone for directions to Wands. My heart pounds in my chest as I lift each knee, jumping over roots and shrubbery as I go.

I vault over another bush, almost twisting my ankle as I trip and fall. Catching myself with my tied arms, I quickly steady my footing. Blood on my hand catches me by surprise and my eyes flick around me.

A trail of blood leads to a man's torso pinned to the bark of a tree from his neck and chest. Maggots eat at his innards.

I choke on a scream and backpedal. Mud smears his face and arms. Slightly pointy ears and stripes the same color as the mud on his skin. An Ipani. His eyes are rolled back, and a horrible gurgling sound escapes his throat. How the hell is he still alive?

The rapid beats of heavy footfalls speed behind me. I dare not to look. A look behind me is time wasted. Get up and run.

My heart pounds in my chest as the footsteps grow louder. I only make it a few steps when something shoves me from behind and I hit the ground inches from the live torso. Slamming my hands against the ground, I let out a shriek.

My chest heaves as I gaze up at Nkella's scornful stare.

"And where did you think you'd go without the World Card, daí? Your way home. More proof you were lying." He scoffs. He doesn't seem bothered by the bleeding torso.

"Your crew said I wasn't the only one who'd passed through," I rasp, trying to scurry away from the dead man. "World of magic? I figured I'd either find another way or another card."

His eyes narrow down at me, and with one motion, he grabs onto my shirt and pulls me to my feet. I quickly let go of the arm I had instinctively grabbed. Holy shit, he's strong. He shoves me back a little and steps forward, trapping me between him and a different tree behind me. His scornful gaze, intense and threatening.

His breath brushes my cheeks as he presses his face too close to mine. "Each time you make me angry, you will pay."

I swallow.

He grabs onto my chains and pushes me forward. "Walk."

Tears sting my eyes as I take shallow breaths. What the hell was on that tree? How could that thing still be alive? In a few seconds, I went from trying to escape to having my wits scared out of me. He pushes me inside the tavern and immediately steers me to the right.

Clanking of glass, music, and laughter rings through my ears.

"Hey, watch it. Stop pushing me."

"Climb up there." He points to a long wooden pallet crafted to be some sort of stage with three wooden poles sticking up from it.

The one to the far right is empty, the one in the middle has a drunk, beat-up blond guy tied to it with his head bowed. Nkella shoves me closer to the one on the left, also empty. I give him a confused stare as he pushes me to stand in front of it, takes my wrists and again cuffs me so that my arms are behind the pole. Jerk.

"What is this?" I ask.

"Payment for my anger."

Each time you make me angry, you will pay. My face pales. "What do you mean?"

He snickers a low laugh, one that's full of menace. "I wonder how much you'll go for."

My breath leaves my lungs. H-he's going to sell me? He takes one long look at me before he turns on his heel to head for the bar.

A dry lump forms in my throat. I tug on my chains from behind the pole and yank hard. If escaping was top priority when I got off the ship, now it's life or death. The image of the bloody living-dead torso keeps forcing itself into my mind; I block it out for the twentieth time. I've got to get out of here.

Nkella reaches the bar. The barkeep takes out a notepad and checks for what I'm assuming are available rooms.

AJ pushes his way through the crowd and steps up to the bar with a look of urgency on his face.

"AJ!" I yell, hoping he'll see me and come to my rescue. If anyone would let me go, it'd be him, right?

He whispers something to Nkella who then looks around. Without a glance in my direction, they pull away from the bar and disappear into the noisy tavern. No! Where are they going?

A tall human man with graying clipper cut hair under a small roundish black and gold pointy hat glances at me from behind a couple. He has a vulpine smile and a long nose. His hat sort of resembles that of a pope but in a lower magnitude. He wears black on black robes with a set of keys hanging from his belt. My awareness of being vulnerable up on this stage is heightened and I avert my eyes, trying to see where AJ took Nkella. AJ wouldn't leave me here like this. He'd at least put up a fight against Nkella. Wouldn't he?

AJ dashes out from the crowd and stampedes out the door. Nkella isn't behind him. After a few minutes, it dawns on me that they really left me alone.

No, this can't be right. Nkella needs me for something. Unless he changed his mind. Maybe after I tried stealing the card back, he decided I'm more trouble than I'm worth. Ugh I'm so stupid. I should have slept in that cozy room last night and conserved my energy to escape today. I should have waited for my chance instead of trying to get a card to work without even knowing how.

I yank on my cuffs again. I don't know why I keep doing that; it's not like I'm going to loosen them. The guy on the floor next to me gurgles something unintelligible. I glance down as he bobs his head forward. Oh man, I hope he doesn't yak right here.

I glance up to see the tall man hasn't taken his eyes off me. "Take a picture, it'll last you longer." Do they even have cameras here? "Draw a picture then." The man gets up and I gulp. Great way to bring attention to myself. Just great.

He pushes himself past tables and steps up to the stage. My chest heaves as he looks me up and down. He climbs onto the wooden level and takes a look toward my back. My cheeks flush. I try to lunge forward even though I know I can't go anywhere.

That's when I lock eyes with Nkella. Intensity deepens in his eyes as he switches from me to the man inspecting me. A hollow ache twists in my chest. I try my best to keep a straight face as I raise my chin and stare back at him.

A finger touches the inside of my arm where my mark is, making me jolt. I snap my gaze to my arm.

"Now that's curious. Who are you?" the man asks.

"Wouldn't you like to know?" is all I manage in my attempts for gumption.

"Ah!" he yelps and I jump, gaping at him as a tiny bit of blood oozes from his finger. "Why, hello!" he says.

Philo sprints down my arm and pops back into her dimension. I swallow a gasp. That was weird. I hadn't seen Philo since

I snuck into Nkella's room. I thought she had gotten scared and left for good.

"I wondered why a human was being sold. Unless you used magic, which is strictly forbidden." He walks back around to face me, and I notice a metal clasp holding his collar together in the shape of the spiderweb on my arm. "Which is why *he* is here," he looks down at the dude. I press my lips. Not about to start telling this creep how I ended up in this world. Who knows where that'll take me this time. My eyes linger on his metal spiderweb clasp.

It looks just like the mark on my arm.

"But that mark you have"—he chafes his chin—"and that naughty little spider. . ." He glances down at his thumb. A prickle of blood tinges his skin and he lifts it up to his mouth and licks it off. "Maybe you should come with me."

With his same hand he strokes my cheek, giving me a smile. "My name's Demitri." A shiver runs down my spine as I turn my cheek.

The guy next to me lets out a loud and disgusting belch. I do a double take. Gross.

Demitri takes his hand back and frowns in the direction of the drunk mess on the floor next to me. He flicks his eyes back to me and says, "Don't go anywhere" with a smirk. "I won't be long."

I let out a long shaky breath. What does he know about my mark?

"You're welcome," the blond dude sings.

"For what? Stinking up the place? It's bad enough I'm tied up next to a beat-up slurring drunk."

The guy laughs. "I wish I were drunk. Sadly, just beat up."

My breath hitches and I turn my neck. "Wait. Your accent!"

"*Your* accent," he slurs.

"No seriously, say something again!"

"*Smonthing. . .a-gain.*"

"Oh wow, someone really hit you hard on the coconut huh?"

He giggles. "Coconuts."

"I mean your head, you fool."

He sighs deeply, his head hanging to the side. "Why couldn't I have been the Fool? Why did I have to get branded as a Magician in a world where magic is outlawed?"

"Dude, I'm serious, where is your accent from?"

He squints at me and starts to get up, struggling with the chains holding him back. "No, now so am I," he says, sounding a bit more coherent. "I'm from Boston."

I screw up my face. "You don't sound like you're from Boston. . ."

"Hey, just because I'm from Boston doesn't mean I have a Boston accent! And really? That's your response?"

"No, you're right. Sorry. Just nervous. Oh my god. . . So, you're from Earth too. . ."

His features twist. "What are you doing here? I thought I was the only one."

"Long story." Nervous about that man coming back, I steal a glance toward the bar and catch him asking the barkeep something. The lady turns to look at me then searches the tavern. She's probably looking for Nkella.

"Well, as I've found out," he says, snapping my attention back to him, "I'm not the only one who's passed through this world from Earth. And apparently doing so makes me a Magician and a bad guy."

His teeth chatter and I squint at him. His lips have a blue tinge to them, and he has white flakes at the corners of his eyes. They must have dosed him good with something; it's hotter than Hades out here. How can he be cold? "Yeah, they think I'm some evil witch from Tower Island or something."

"And do you practice magic?" he asks.

My eyes rise. "What? No! Duh. . .I mean, do you?"

"Yeah, actually, that's kind of how I ended up here."

"You? Magic. From Earth?"

"There's a lot of magic on Earth, you just have to know where to look."

"I mean. . . I guess there is hoodoo and stuff in Louisiana, but. . ."

"You never thought it was real."

I shrug.

"My name's Harold, by the way."

"Soren."

"Nice to meet you. So, what brings you to the prisoner's stage in this fine tavern of a distant magical land?" His blue eyes beam as he smiles back at me, showing his teeth. The frostiness that was just there has gone away.

"You seem awfully cheery for being a prisoner."

"Eh, I'm optimistic."

"Optimistic? There's a man cut in half and pinned to a tree outside. . . and somehow, he's still alive! How are you optimistic?"

"Oh, that? Yeah, I've gotten used to it. People don't die here. Unless the Empress in the Tower wants them to."

My face deadpans. "What do you mean they don't die? If I didn't just see it for myself, I would have no idea what you're talking about."

"I don't know that much about it except—it was punishment for something they did—treason or something or other. Eternal suffering is worse than death and all that."

I blink rapidly. The more I learn about this place, the faster I want to get home. I sigh. "When I fell. . . I fell into the ocean and got rescued by pirates. The captain thinks I'm an utwa, which means spy, I guess."

"Ah, yep, that'll do it."

"You?"

"Long story about how I got here. . .but, I was not rescued by pirates, I was taken by some evil bastards who want to sell me to some pirates"—he nudges to a different set of crewmen —"so that I can make some nasty potions for them."

I furrow my brows. "What kind of nasty potions?"

"You seriously do not want to know."

"So, if you got yourself here, how do you plan on going back?"

"Why? Are you trying to go back?"

"Umm. . .heck, yes? That's all I want to do. . ."

"Maybe I can help."

"You?" I chuckle. "Dude, no offense, but it kinda looks like you're in the same spot as me."

"Hear me out. I can get you back the same way I got myself here. I'm a Magician after all, right?"

I squint at him, then peer back into the tavern to see if I find AJ or Nkella anywhere.

"Okay. . .so what can I do?"

"Convince your captain to buy me and get me on board your ship. He can get me to Wands, which is where I wanted to go anyway, and I can get you home."

My pulse quickens at the mention of Wands. "I need to go there too," I say.

"Why? What do you know about Wands?"

Should I tell him about the cards? Maybe not yet. "I heard there's something there that can get me back."

"Hmm. . .possibly. So, will you do it?"

"Ha! Me? Convince the captain to listen? All he does is look at me and call me a spy. He put me up here. He plans to sell me to the highest bidder."

"Just try to talk to him when he comes back. What's there to lose?" His pleading eyes stare back at me as we both struggle with our arms tied behind us.

"*If* he comes back, you can try talking to him. So far, it looks like they've left me here to rot."

"Umm. . .yeah, about that, I've been here for a while and my language potion ran out."

My face pales. Crap. I might actually need that too now.

"From what I've learned I could possibly make it permanent. But I haven't been able to find more, and the plant I need to make it grows in Wands."

"I don't know if I can help. . ."

"Just try, please. I'm begging you. Don't let me go with those creeps. You don't know what I've seen. . ."

"He's never going to listen to me."

"Just tell him what I told you. Trust me."

I jerk my head back. "Yeah. . .I'm not very good at that."

"What? Trust? Fine, then don't trust me. But the way I see

it, we're both from Earth and that means we're all we've got. What'd you have to lose?"

"Rikwa." The Captain appears in front of me and I gasp. Where did he come from? I was just looking for him.

"What are you two talking about?" He darts a look to Harold. "Anyway, time to go."

"Go?"

"Kh. Do you want to stay?"

"I thought—" I glance at Demitri who is now approaching. Oh. Oh no. He's only uncuffing me because. . .because I've been sold.

"Daí?" He turns to face Demitri.

"I've been waiting for you. How much for the girl?"

Nkella flicks his eyes to me and the corner of his lips curl upward, as an evil gleam fills his eyes.

I am so screwed.

9

"SHE IS NOT FOR SALE."

My heart leaps back up to my chest. I'm not? Then what the hell was the point of all this?

Demitri takes a step toward Nkella. "What do you mean she's not for sale?" He raises his voice over the music. "She's on the platform. She has to be."

"Not for sale." He repeats as he reaches behind me and grabs hold of my cuffs.

"I'll give you three hundred gichang," Demitri offers.

"Kh."

"Five hundred gichang then."

He uncuffs me and I roll my wrists. What the hell is going on?

Nkella's lips curl as he whips around and presses his face close to Demitri. "Why do you want her, daí? Do you know her? Have you seen her before?" He steps forward, forcing Demitri to step back.

"One thousand gichang."

Nkella raises his brows. "Is she that valuable to you?" He crosses his arms. "Tell me"—his eyes scan the man's clothes—"since you wear the robes of the Empress's advisor, why doesn't the Empress come and collect the girl herself?"

Demitri's eyes search Nkella's face. "I'm not aware of anyone, other than the Divine Empress herself with a mark like that one"—he motions to my arm—"and I am certain if Her Divinity knew, the girl wouldn't be here." He narrows his eyes. "How did she fall into the likes of you, *pirate*?"

Nkella lifts his chin and glances at me from the corner of his eye. I look back at Harold who's been watching us with a nervous look on his face. I forgot he can't understand anything.

For a moment they stare at each other, none of them moving until Nkella straightens his back. "Hn. She is not for sale."

Wow, he's not giving in. I have to admit, I am surprised as hell.

"If the girl with that mark has committed a crime, then she should come with me so that the Empress can decide her fate."

Nkella lets out a deep grunt from the back of his throat but doesn't look like he's about to back down. "Call the Minor Arcana then. I will wait."

I choke on a gasp. What is he doing?

Three men walk through the tavern door. Two of them are human, but one is Ipani with long, thick braids under a red head scarf; his slightly pointed ears and the stripes on his neck give it away. They're all wearing boots, long coats, and have a look in their eye like they're ready for a fight. Must be pirates.

Demitri glances over his shoulder at them and then back at

us. "Fine. Keep her, vermin. But I will find out why she has that mark." He gives me one last long look before he spins on his heel and heads out the door. Nkella turns back to untie me.

"I thought you were going to sell me," I say.

"I don't agree with keeping slaves."

My jaw drops. "Did you *have* to tie me up and make me think you were?"

He flashes an impish smile. "No."

I ball my fists.

"Hate to interrupt, but mind helping a fella out then?" Harold says with urgency in his voice.

Nkella squints at him, then snaps back to me. "Time to go." He grabs my arm but I pull back.

"Wait."

"We have lost enough time. Because of you."

"Because of me? How? Wait. Can you"—I mutter a sigh—"*buy* him?" I nod toward Harold.

"Daí?" Confusion flickers his features. "Why would I do that?"

"You need potions, right? He's a Magician and can make potions."

"Tessa makes potions."

I give Harold an apologetic look. "Do you have anything else you can offer? He already has someone on the ship who can do that."

It's weird having to repeat myself in English to both, and the translation potion translating me to Nkella, while Harold and Nkella can't understand each other. It's also useful how the potion makes me translatable to people here as well, despite it tasting disgusting. This whole place is one strange mind freak.

"Tell him I have plants from Piupeki, I can mix anything," he says, hints of desperation in his voice.

I repeat it to Nkella, and he lets out a grunt.

"Why are you grunting? Because he's a Magician? You're looking for magic, aren't you?"

He stares at me and then at Harold. "He is human."

"Yeah, and? So is your crew."

He grunts again. "What is in it for you?"

"He says he can get me home, and I'll be out of your hair. So, win-win for you, eh?"

"Hn." He turns to Harold and glances at his wrist. "Does he know how to use *Solerig* and *Taevenye*?"

"He wants to know if you know how to use Solrig and Taveny? Sorry, I have no idea how to pronounce—"

"Yeah, all of them," Harold says. "Well, not all but I can make plenty of potions."

I nod at Nkella. "He says yes."

"Does he have any with him?" he asks.

I translate to Harold, but he shakes his head.

"He needs passage to Wands," I tell him.

"Hn." Nkella purses his lips. "We are going to Wands."

"We are?" My heart skips a beat. All this and all I had to do was wait?

A muscle under his eye jumps. "We are now. There has been an incident and we have to move."

Oh. "I thought you had to stay on land. We're going back on the ship?"

Nkella is already reaching behind Harold. He breaks his cuffs in one strong yank. I suck in a breath.

"Ei!" a man calls from across the tavern. I snap a look toward him and realize it's one of the pirates who came in.

Harold jumps down. "Yeah, now would be a good time to leave." The three men approach, and Nkella stands in their way. They exchange a few words in Ipani.

"Soren. . ." Harold warns. "Those are the guys."

I quirk a brow in his direction.

"The ones I'm being sold to," he whispers.

Oh crap.

Nkella looks at Harold, then back at the men. He shakes his head. "Koj."

The Ipani with the red headscarf twists his face and smiles at his friends. Then glances back to Nkella with an amused expression on his face. "Koj?"

Nkella shoves Harold and me toward the door and we start walking. One of the humans has a heavy beard, double loop earrings in both his ears, and huge muscles. The other man is skinny, with a bald head. The bearded man grunts, swings his arm, and punches Nkella in the face.

I gasp and stumble into Harold. The music stops playing and silence hits the tavern as Nkella doesn't take his eyes off the floor. A fiery glow flashes momentarily behind his eyes. Nkella squares his jaw. As the glow dims out, my stomach twists. Whenever his eyes have glowed, he's been either annoyed or angry. But so far, no one's hit him in the face in front of me. I back up.

A woman screams, and chairs and tables scrape against the floor as people get up to leave the tavern.

I flick my eyes to Harold to see if he saw that, but he has his face glued to his pockets as he searches for something.

The man with the beard swings at Nkella for a second try. Nkella blocks his blow with his right arm and twists the man's arm quickly, making him stumble to the ground. The skinny, bald one goes for him, and with his left arm, Nkella blocks his blow and double punches him in the face with the same arm. That leaves the Ipani with the braids cracking his knuckles.

Eying the door, I inch away from the fight, my eyes still glued to Nkella who is now in full on hand-to-hand combat with the three pirates. Some people have cleared out of the bar, while others who weren't so lucky to make it to the exit have taken refuge on the other side of the tavern.

The Ipani grabs Harold's shoulder. Nkella glances over to us and in a beautiful set of swift blocks and attacks, he brings the two men to the ground, lunging to help Harold.

Harold balls his fist and swings his arm upward, clocking the man in the nose before Nkella reaches him and kicks the guy behind the knees. Braid guy hits the floor.

Meanwhile, I've been standing around like a goon. This is the perfect chance, while Nkella is busy, for me to make my escape. I turn to leave and come face to face with a fourth Ipani man. My face almost slams into his chest and he grins. He has a pointy beak of a nose and chalk-white spiky hair. He wears a half-empty suspender belt with bottled bombs on it. Holy hell. When did he come in? I step back but he grabs me with full strength, spins me around and brings me close to his chest by the nape of my neck.

The others, now getting up from the floor, circle around us. I glance at Harold who has straightened his posture, ready to get his hands dirty, although Nkella doesn't look like he'd let anyone in his fight. His eyes, hungry for more, pause when he sees me struggling to break free.

The Ipani grips me tighter, pulling me into his glass bottles. "We walk out with the Magician, or the girl dies."

I scream as the man covers my mouth with his other hand. I squirm as hard as I can; Nkella isn't going to care if I die or not.

"Let's go," my captor says to Harold. Nkella holds out his hand, blocking Harold from moving. Or at least I thought he was. He forcefully grabs onto the back of Harold's neck and pulls him in.

"Let her go or I kill the Magician."

My eyes widen. What did he say?

"A trade then."

"That is not going to work either," Nkella hisses. "Let her go, or the Magician dies."

I squint at him. The tension increases as they both stare at each other. They are at a standstill. The man chuckles and loosens his grip slightly.

I reach for his pinky covering my mouth and yank down hard. The man yells. I backfist him in the nose and kick back to his balls. The man topples down. I swing around and kick him in the head for good measure. I turn to look at Nkella. Why would he do that? A quizzical look is sprawled on his face as he glares at me. He lets Harold go.

"Let's go!" Harold backs me toward the door and the two men inch closer. Nkella is about to swing first when—

Harold throws something on the floor, and in an instant, a

bright blue light blinds the entire tavern, followed by a lot of blue smoke. A bitter tang of the gas coats my tongue as dizzying nausea boils down my stomach. The floor drops below me as if I've suddenly been dropped inside a carnival tilt house.

I can't see a thing, but Harold grabs my shoulder and guides me out the door. My knees quiver as I struggle for balance.

I wince as the bright yellow daylight blinds me even more as we step foot onto the gravel. I topple over a nearby tree root and use it as a crutch to lean on. Harold guides Nkella out behind me, carrying the injured Ipani man over his shoulder, dangling the half-empty bottles by his belt.

Why is he bringing him with us?

"Hey, I hope you had a plan in there!" Harold shouts at Nkella. Nkella hardens his face at Harold's raised pitch. I'm about to translate but then Nkella smirks and lets out three cold laughs. Something tells me I don't need to translate for the captain to understand what Harold's upset about.

He did just threaten to kill him if that pirate didn't let me go. Which is perplexing as hell to me right now, but one thing at a time.

"What the hell was that?" I ask. "The blue bomb thing."

"Something I picked up when I got here. It only gives us enough time to escape so we need to move."

"Was it a bomb?"

"No one in there was harmed, but they will be unconscious for about ten minutes."

"Ten minutes?" I gasp. "How come it didn't affect us?" I mean it took me for a spin, but I'm not unconscious.

"That's part of the magic. I concentrate on who I want it to work on. Sorry for the aftereffects."

"Wait a minute. You had a bomb with you the whole time you got captured?"

Harold shakes his head. "It's a long story, but without my belt, I was saving that one for when I really needed it."

"More than being sold to pirates?"

Harold raises his brows and nods.

Okay then. . . "What about him?" I ask, pointing to the white haired man over Nkella's shoulder.

Nkella drops the man on the ground. The man grunts as he curls up, struggling to get to his feet. Harold leans in and unbuckles the man's belt.

"I'll take my belt back, thank you very much." Round bottles with different color liquids clang together from the belt loop as he takes it and ties it around his waist.

Nkella furrows his brows at him, then at me.

I shrug. "Apparently, it's his."

Nkella grimaces and peers down at the Ipani man. "What is so important about him?" Nkella points to Harold who doesn't seem bothered by the question until I remember he still can't understand anything.

"Magician."

"Hn. What do you want with him?"

The man starts to chuckle. Nkella grabs him with one arm and displaying inexplicable strength and speed pins him to the tree behind me. I yelp as I move out of the way.

"Answer or die."

I swallow, glad for once that his short commands aren't geared toward me.

He increases his grip around the man's neck until he croaks out an answer.

"Daí?" Nkella loosens his grip only enough to let the man breathe.

"Potions. He can make them."

Nkella hisses behind his teeth. "Tell me something I don't know a Magician can do. Why do you need potions?" He pins him harder against the tree.

"*Rikorō garisi.*" The man croaks out.

Nkella's face darkens. His hand shakes as he grips the man's neck so tight, he starts to turn blue and his eyes bulge. I clasp my hands to keep them from shaking. He loosens his grip and the man wheezes. "You are. . .a disgrace. . .to our kind."

"Koj. . ." the beak nose mutters, tears wetting the corner of his eyes. "*Ja e'r a la cā n'jamae poé.*"

"Not like this." Nkella reaches back with his fist, about to knock the guy out.

"Wait!" he hacks. "I. . .can help."

Nkella doesn't lower his fist but doesn't strike either.

"I can take you. . .where. . .they're taking her. I saw you and your friend looking for someone."

I flick a glance at Harold who has his eyebrows raised, clueless about what's going on, but with fear plastered over his face. Taking who? I hope he doesn't mean AJ's girlfriend. . . I gasp. Is that why we're going back to the ship?

"I already have a tracker." Nkella swings back.

"No, please. Don't kill me. I know who's behind all the trafficking."

"Daí?" Who?"

"Kind of running out of time here, guys." Harold casts a glance at the tavern. "We really have to go."

Nkella ignores him, not that he can understand, but I'm sure as hell not going to interrupt.

"Speak." He loosens his grip and lets the man fall to the floor.

He rubs his throat. "I don't know his name. But I've seen him. Your tracker won't know who to look for."

Nkella glowers at him. "The moment you prove useless, I kill you." He reaches to his back, which is covered by his coat, and pulls out a small rope. He stuffs it into the Ipani man's mouth and ties it around the back of his head. Then he takes out his cuffs and locks the man's hands together. I stuff my hands in my pockets. So glad that's not me right now. Nkella picks him up by his chest and shoves him forward.

"Walk." The man stumbles forward. "We have to go. The tavern will call the Minor Arcana Army for use of magic."

I try letting him pass me as he shoves his new prisoner in front of him.

"Kh. You two walk in front of me," Nkella tells us.

"It's not like I'm going to take off running again." I mutter, shoving past him. "There's nowhere to escape to." Who knows what he'll do to me if he catches me, and those creepy soldiers are going to be swarming this area any minute. Why did he save me in there?

Harold falls into step beside me as we make it down the mossy stones and back out to the market area platform.

AJ calls out to us from the main deck of the ship. Nkella picks up his pace and we follow suit.

"Wait." Harold pauses. "Uh. . .Soren? You didn't tell me you were on the *Devil's Gambit.*"

I flick my eyes to where he's looking. The black pirate ship I came in. I hadn't even given a thought to looking behind me while I was plotting my escape and hadn't yet seen the outside of the ship. Three large masts watch over the pitch-black wood of the vessel. The figurehead is a decorative shiny black skull—possibly obsidian or something like it—with large glistening rubies for eyes and teeth and two shiny red horns on its head.

"Have you heard of it?" I ask.

"Have I heard of it? Everyone has. . .This only means that badass captain who threatened to kill me is. . .is. . ."

"The Devil?"

"So you do know."

"I know he's a jerk," I mutter under my breath.

"Right. Um. . ." He backpedals. "Thanks for all your help in getting me out of there, but uh—"

"You will walk." Nkella bumps him from behind.

He groans under his breath and mutters, "What have I gotten myself into now?"

"I tried to warn you."

"No, you didn't. You told me you wouldn't be able to convince him. To be honest, it wasn't hard seeing as how he needs my skills."

"And he threatened to kill you."

"I thought he had a plan!"

I stay quiet, that question still lingering at the front of my mind. Did he have a plan? Why would he want to save me instead when he needs the Magician's skills?

"Nkella Mikiroro." Demitri steps from the shadows, blocking the ramp. "I know who you are now."

"*Captain.*" Nkella hisses. "And what are you doing next to my ship?"

"Last I checked, I can stand anywhere I want."

"Move."

"Slow down, Devil. Shouldn't you be staying on land tonight?"

"It appears I have more pressing issues," Nkella says between gritted teeth. Demitri shifts his gaze over to the new Ipani prisoner and then to me, then glances past us to the tavern.

"Goodness me, what a mess you've all made. That's not the only tavern on the island you know. I can get you a good rate at the Columns."

"Stop wasting my time."

"You owe me for him." Demitri points to Harold with his chin.

Nkella looks over his shoulder at Harold. "Daí? *You* were selling him?"

"That's right."

"Then you should have collected your *gichang* from the other men."

"And yet, I did not, so he hasn't been sold. As of now, you're stealing him."

AJ and Kaehante approach the top of the ramp. "What's the holdup?" AJ calls.

Nkella motions them down with two fingers. Kaehante swings his legs over the rail and jumps down, landing heavy on the wooden ramp. He grabs hold of the prisoner.

"To the brig," Nkella tells him. Kaehante gives one nod and drags the man up with him. I hold my breath. What does that mean for me? And also. . . "You didn't tell me he was the one who was selling you," I whisper to Harold.

"I did tell you not to trust him."

Nkella reaches into his belt and pulls out a leather pouch. He reaches inside and takes out a handful of his currency and drops them into Demitri's hand. My mouth drops. He actually. . .paid it.

AJ whistles.

"I do not have time for this. You have your gichang. Now, go."

Demitri holds one up to the light. My eyes widen. They're not just gems, they're pressed rubies in the form of imperfect circles and have some sort of insignia on them.

"Minted in Danū, these are worth quite a lot. Much obliged." He pours his payment into his own pouch. "May Her Divinity take pity on your soul." Demitri bows his head to Nkella before turning to leave. His eyes narrow at me and Harold. "See you soon," he mutters under his breath. And he leaves.

"What the hell does he mean by that?" I ask no one in particular.

Without answering, Nkella runs up the ramp. He doesn't even look down to see if we're following him. None of the crew are looking either. Something bad definitely happened. I pause at the foot of the ramp.

If I stay, I'm left here with this creep, fending for myself, and possibly looking for passage with some other creepy pirates. If I go, I might end up right back in the brig. . .

And with a roommate. But at least I'll be heading to Wands. Harold passes me and boards the ship. Guess he keeps his promises, even if it is to the Devil. Taking a deep breath, I step on the ramp.

A hauntingly deep whistling sound erupts from the sky. I pause and look up.

Overhead, falling like bombs to the island, are black smoke-like trails, almost solid in color. They land with thuds, one after the other, and the same masked soldiers I saw on the first night on the ship stand as the smoke clears.

I jump on board. Kaehante slams the ramp shut and quickly unties the ropes.

Harold starts to help him. Leaning forward to watch the Minor Arcana Army, I catch a glimpse of Demitri talking with one of them. "That is a strange man indeed."

"He works for the Empress, but is just an opportunist," Harold says.

"Who's this?" Tessa drives herself closer to me and Harold.

"A Magician." Nkella responds.

Tessa's eyes widen.

"For what?" AJ asks.

"To make potions," Nkella says.

"Lāri will make the potions with Tessa."

"Lāri isn't here," Nkella says.

"We don't even have the ingredients yet." AJ raises his voice. I look around the ship.

"What happened to Lāri? Weren't we meeting her here?" I ask.

AJ snaps his gaze at me, and his chest starts to heave as he balls his fists. He snaps his attention back to Nkella.

I think this confirms it. . . AJ's girlfriend was the girl the prisoner was talking about.

"We are going to Wands to get the ingredients," Nkella says.

"We need to rescue my girlfriend!"

My mouth parts. Oh, no. . .

Nkella sighs deeply, takes a step toward AJ and places his hand on his shoulder.

"I would never leave her behind. You know that."

AJ lets out a few shaky breaths and nods rapidly.

Kaehante approaches. "Do we have a heading, Captain?"

Nkella moves toward the gas lamp. "Iéle."

The wolf appears from behind Tessa and sits at his feet. Nkella bends his knees and presses his head against the wolf's. For a few moments, they sit in silence. Harold stands by me as he observes the exchange.

"Great. . .and he has a wolf as a familiar."

"Mhmm."

Tessa tilts her head for us to follow her. She leads us over to the side of the ship while AJ and Kaehante are now untying the ropes. She takes out two glass bottles with clear liquid inside them and hands them to Harold and me. He takes it and thanks her. She smiles and nods in understanding. In one swig, he chugs the bottle.

I, on the other hand, hesitate.

"You're gonna want to drink that if you want to be able to communicate here," Harold says. "Don't forget, it doesn't last forever."

"Yeah, yeah." I take the bottle from Tessa. "But I really hate licorice." I drink it slowly, nearly gagging.

"Just shoot it, like it's medicine."

Tessa laughs. "Now I can understand you," she tells Harold.

"Hi, I'm Harold."

"My name is Tessa." She tells him who Kaehante and AJ are.

I scan the main deck. The afternoon sun burns the top of my head. No sign of the prisoner so I'm guessing Kaehante was successful in locking him up. "Tessa?"

"Yes, Soren?"

"Please don't let Nkella put me in the brig with the new prisoner."

"I do not think he would do that."

And I don't think she knows what he's capable of. A phantom memory of Iéle's glowing red eyes makes me shudder.

"AJ," Tessa calls over her shoulder. A doleful look makes his face appear somber as he stares at his inner arm. His eyes flick to us but he remains silent. "Are you alright, dear?"

He shakes his head. He shows us his wrist, and a small *0* has appeared on it.

"What does that mean?" I ask.

Nkella breaks his concentration with Iéle and gets closer. "The Fool."

I shoot him an irritated look. "Really? He's pissed off. Can't you see he's upset?"

"No, he's right." AJ says. I quirk a brow.

Harold leans in. "The Fool doesn't mean what you think it does."

"What's it mean then?"

"My journey has begun." A somber look appears on AJ's

face. Nkella puts his hand on his shoulder and squeezes it. "It also means this isn't going to be easy."

Nkella curls his lips at me, his eyes narrow and scrutinizing. Maybe talking back to him isn't a great idea given my current position on his ship. He turns back to Iéle and bends a knee.

"W-what happened?" I ask AJ.

He squeezes his eyes for a moment and swallows. "We searched everywhere. Until I found this at the back of the tavern." His voice cracks and he takes out a brown scarf from of his pocket. It has a black feather embroidered on one of the ends. "She's an unbound Ipani girl. We took too long to get here. They must have caught her a few hours before we docked."

I stare at the scarf and guilt constricts my stomach. "That's hers?"

He nods.

I don't know what to say; there's nothing I can say.

"They keep them in cages," AJ's voice croaks. "I don't even want to think what they're doing to her—" His voice cuts off.

Tessa approaches with the soft hum of her chair. "Don't go there," she says. "We will reach them. If they left a few hours ago, Nkella will steer this ship fast. Especially with Iéle's help. We may be a small team, but we're efficient. You know that."

"Wait," Harold interrupts. "Is this the whole crew then?"

"Yep." AJ lets his arms fall to his sides.

"AJ, why don't you go get some rest," Tessa says. "I'll get lunch ready and they can help me put stuff away. Get yourself cleaned up."

"No. I need to stay busy. I'll rest when we have her."

Harold steps forward. "How can I help?"

"Well, you can help take the water barrels down to the kitchen," Tessa tells him. "We weren't able to get any gunpowder so we'll have to be strategic with the little bit we have. I'll make more *hū raku* bombs."

"I can help with those as well," Harold adds, tightening a strap on his belt.

"Yes, having a Magician on board will be useful. I only studied steam engineering but have learned bits about potions here and there. What we needed was floating and transparency potions for the ship's engine box." She reverses her wheelchair, getting ready to turn.

"This ship has an engine?" I ask.

"It's an added adjustment I made for our plan to reach the island."

"You weren't able to find any, I'm guessing?" Harold asks.

"No, we were on our way from Oleanu. Lāri had split up to go to Sotiria to grab some of her own stash, trying to avoid going to Wands. It was meant to save us the trip."

"How was she getting there?" Harold asks. "Seems like it would have been easier not to split up."

"No kidding," AJ says. "Lāri's power enables her to shape-shift into an eagle."

"Woah." I exchange a glance with Harold. I hadn't considered the kinds of different magical oumala out here.

"She never wanted to be bound, but now look what happened."

No one responds to that. What is there to say?

Nkella finally glances up and Iéle turns, runs toward the edge of the ship, and leaps. Before reaching the water, she disappears into the Aō dimension. I'll never get used to that.

"Iéle has their scent." He leaps over the steps up to the wheel, and Kaehante joins him.

"To Sāgirang, right, Captain?" Kaehante bellows.

"Iéle heard mention of the Karst Temples there. If that is where they are taking the trafficked Ipani and Lāri, I want to know the exact route they take. Iéle is tracking them." He moves his captain's hat down, "we'll catch up. And then they'll pay." I watch as Nkella pulls out a bottle with an orange solution from a compartment near his station and sticks it to the wall nearest the wheel, twisting it clockwise. The masts are all raised at once; the wind pushes my hair back.

This is some ship.

I glimpse at Harold and AJ lifting a barrel down the ramps, and I run after them to help.

Tessa, who's carrying a few bottles in a bag on her lap, drives down in front of us and says, "When you finish there, I'll show you to your room, and then I'll show you what we have as ingredients and potions we can use. We'll need something for when we catch up to those pirates. This won't be an easy fight."

10

"So, how come you're in a wheelchair?" Harold asks Tessa as we stand by on the main deck, waiting to push some more barrels down.

"Why are you so blond?" she retorts.

I snort and shove him. I cannot believe he just asked her that.

Harold screws up his face. "What? Was that too blunt? Sorry. . ."

Tessa chuckles. "I like you," she says. "I like bluntness and honesty. I was born not being able to walk. But, in Oleanu, where I'm from, these chairs aren't common. Actually, you don't see them at all. I always felt out of place there, except when I'm in the water."

Harold's face reddens. "Sorry. . ."

"Don't be." Tessa smiles. "It's all I've ever known. I don't have a problem with it."

"Don't let that fool you," AJ says as he pushes a barrel past us. "She's a badass."

"Yeah, she is," I mutter, as I pick up two bags full of food Tessa and Kaehante managed to buy. We follow AJ down the ramp toward the kitchen.

"I never felt like I belonged with my people." Tessa continues. "Or anywhere. . . but then one day, I met a Hermit. He had been all over the world and was a Magician—yes, but so much more than that. He taught me about steam engineering and about being independent. I owe him everything."

"Where is he now?" I ask.

She shrugs. "Off being a Hermit. He took me as a student, but I always knew it would be temporary."

AJ and Harold push the last barrel into a corner of the kitchen, and I set down the two bags of food on the table next to a cast-iron stove.

"But still," she continues, "I hope I'll see him again."

"I hope you do too." I give her a smile.

Heavy footsteps reach the entrance of the kitchen and a familiar feeling of dread lands in my stomach.

Nkella's husky voice makes the hair on my arms stand on end. "Tessa, we will be gaining speed as soon as we are farther from port."

"That's fine. I'll be down here preparing a meal while AJ is up there." She looks at us. "I don't like full speed on the main deck."

Trying to avoid eye contact, I start into the kitchen, putting away the food they brought. They didn't manage very much though. A few vegetables, fruit—

Nkella steps behind me, and I hold my breath. He hasn't spoken a word to me since the tavern and I'm so afraid he's going to take me back to the brig. The last thing I want is to be roommates with that new creepy prisoner. He takes a broom out of a closet and just when I think he's going to hand it to me, he hands it to Harold.

"Our crew is small, but we split the tasks other than our own personal ones."

"No problem," Harold says, taking the broom. "Makes sense."

"Good." He turns his focus to me. His eyes narrow. I grit my teeth.

"Oh, so you trust him with the cleaning but not me," I blurt.

"Your job is with Kaehante. You will sleep in the bunk tonight, but make no mistake, rikwa. You are still my gembella."

"Your what?"

"My prisoner. Maybe *gembella chacheang*, comfortable prisoner. For now. That will depend on how you behave. But prisoner, nonetheless." He turns on his heel and heads out the kitchen.

Why didn't he just let that guy at the tavern kill me?

Harold whistles. "What did you do to piss him off?"

AJ snaps his eyes up at me. "Yeah, you weren't in your room this morning. What happened?"

I lower my gaze to the floor. "I. . .uh. . . I messed up. I tried sneaking into Nkella's room to steal my card back."

"Oh, lordy." AJ smacks his face.

"You certainly did mess up." Tessa chimes. "You'll have to work extra hard to gain his trust now."

"I don't think it'll matter anyway," AJ says under his breath. "But I mean. . .she just wants to get home, guys."

"And I don't blame you for that," Tessa tells me, "but you did make things harder for yourself."

"I know. He tried to sell me earlier."

Her eyes widen. "He what?"

"He would never do that," AJ says. "As unorthodox as that was, he wanted to see if anyone recognized you."

My brows furrow. "Huh?"

"He could have done that without tying you up with a fake price tag, which is why I was confused, but I didn't question it because. . .well, I was looking for. . ." He trails off, and I nod. "But now I see why he did that. You really pissed him off." He laughs.

"Yeah, it was hilarious." I dig the tip of my shoe into the floorboard.

"Lucky, he didn't think Demitri recognized you then," Harold said. "I was out of translation potion so I couldn't understand what was going on, but he looked *very* interested. And take it from me, when that creep takes interest in you, you're in trouble."

Tessa tilts her head. "Who took interest in Soren?"

"The guy who wanted to buy me," I answer. "He said his name was Demitri."

"Oh, that's the Hierophant. The Empress's advisor," AJ says. "He maintains the worship of the Empress among the humans, and tries to do the same with the Ipani, but everyone scoffs at that."

"Yeah," Harold says. "I don't believe he's honest about his title, but that's just me."

AJ shakes his head. "You're not the only one who thinks that."

"Well, he didn't recognize me," I say. "I've never met him in my life, but he gave me the creeps." My brows knit together. "Nkella told him to call the Minor Arcana if he really thought I belonged with the Empress. Why would he do that? If Demitri is the Empress's advisor, wasn't Nkella risking him actually. . .you know, bringing down the Arcana soldiers? Aren't you guys running *from* them?" At least that's what I gathered from the fight they had with them the other day.

"He must have been calling his bluff," Tessa says.

AJ flicks his long hair back and crosses his arms. "Which means Nkella thinks Demitri is up to something."

Harold takes his broom and starts sweeping around where we're standing.

That gives me an uneasy feeling. If Demitri believed I belonged with the Empress and thought they were searching for me, then he should have called the army himself, it being his job. Unless he wanted me for himself. . .

"Harold," Tessa starts, "I overheard whiffs of Nkella's conversation with Demitri outside the ship. He was selling you to pirates?"

Harold nods. "That was a ruse. He wasn't selling me. He had me up there for collection, to make it look legit. I'm telling you; that guy is not to be trusted."

"Do you know what those pirates wanted with you?" she asks him. "Obviously they wanted you for your skills, but for what?"

"All I know is, they have an operation in Wands involving some really dangerous potions, and Demitri is in on it. The fact that Demitri accepted payment for me, instead of making more of a fuss over me, only meant that he didn't want to blow his cover. It would have looked weird if he had just let Nkella get away with stealing me, but even weirder if he hadn't accepted the payment. It would have made it look like he needed a Magician for something. Which is illegal here."

I gasp. "The last thing he said was, 'I'll see you soon.' He has no intention of letting us stay with this crew." I stare at him.

"Don't worry," Tessa chimes, "you're safe with us. And I need to report what you're telling me to Nkella."

Harold nods.

Tessa puts her chair in reverse. "That's enough chatting for now. Let's get on with it, shall we? Lots to do."

AJ claps his hands together. "Let's get you two sorted, shall we?"

Harold stays behind to pick up what he had started sweeping with a dustpan while AJ and I reach the hallway with the rooms.

AJ turns to me. "It's going to be a long night and you haven't slept, have you? I'll talk to Kaehante for you, so that you can rest, eh?"

"Are you sure? Because I don't want to end up in the brig with that creep."

"It'll be fine. Kaehante doesn't want you falling over his cannons. Nkella will listen to Kae, don't worry."

"If you're sure. . ."

A tired look washes over AJ's face as he motions for me to enter my room. "I'm sure, go on then."

I look into his dark brown eyes. Poor guy. "AJ. . . Are you going to be okay?"

He gives me a modest shrug. "I'm really scared." His voice cracks.

I step toward him and hold my arms out. His brows furrow as I pull him into a hug. "You look like you could use a hug," I say. He wraps his arms around me and sighs into my shoulder.

"AJ. . . I'm so sorry."

He pauses for a beat and clears his throat. "We have to stay positive. *I* have to stay positive."

"No, I mean, I can't help but feel this is my fault." I pull away from his embrace. "If you guys hadn't stopped for me. . ."

"No, no. This isn't your fault. We couldn't just let someone drown. That's not who we are. Don't even give it another thought."

I force a smile.

Harold steps up behind me. "Sorry to interrupt."

"Harold!" AJ spins on his heel, "Your room will be"—he takes a step back and points to his left—"right in here."

"Thanks, I'd drop my bags in there but. . .I don't have any," he chuckles. He takes a step and walks inside. "I have to say, this is a nice ship."

AJ looks Harold up and down and then glances at me, rubbing his chin. "Hmm. . . If all goes well, maybe we can find you both some clothes when we get to Wands. They have nice markets there."

Not that I'm planning on going shopping, especially since I don't have any money or. . .gichang, but I can't help being curious about the markets in this world.

"I'm sorry your birthday hasn't been great," AJ says,

turning to me. "But I think I have something that'll make things easier for you while you're here.

I quirk a brow as he shuffles to his room and digs something out of a bag.

"It's your birthday?" Harold peeks his head out of his room.

"Yeah, it's okay. I'll make it up when I get back." If there's even a home to get back to at this point. What will the Nelsons say after I've disappeared for so long? Will the police be looking for me? Or will I return as a fugitive since I disappeared from jail? After forty-eight hours, what is there left for them to do? I'll be spending my time looking for Talia in the system, and then apologizing to her for the rest of my life.

AJ comes back out of his room holding a satchel. "Come into your room and hold out your arm."

I quirk a brow as I walk into my room and the others follow.

"Let's cover that mark, shall we?" AJ plops down on my bed as Harold takes a corner chair.

"Cover it?" My eyes widen as he pulls out a small glass vial of what looks like concealer and a few thin branches with different colored tips. I take off my jacket and pull up my sleeve.

Hovering over my arm for a closer look, Harold squints at my mark. "What is your mark? I hear everyone is going crazy about it. Oh!" He sits upright and curses under his breath.

"Great. So you know what this means?"

He laughs out loud. "No wonder everyone here thinks you're a spy or something."

"Care to share it with the class?"

"That mark is the same mark seen on any Empress-related insignia. No one has seen her bare arms, but she must have the same mark. No one else has it."

"Ah. Great. And none of you thought to tell me that?" I stare at AJ, and he glances up at me.

"To be fair, none of us knew if you were telling the truth or not. Except me, of course, but a lot was going on. Now hold still." AJ grips my arm as he works.

"Demitri was wearing it around his neck," I say.

"Yep, because he acts as her advisor." Harold leans toward AJ. "You'll want to draw a replacement. She can't just go around these parts without a mark."

"What do you think those are for?" AJ nods toward the colored pencils.

"Nice. What are you going to draw on her?"

"Figured the Fool will be less conspicuous."

Harold purses his lips and nods.

I look between them both. "Great. Fitting."

"Oh, come now, the Fool isn't a bad mark," AJ says. "And I said, hold still. I want to make sure it's fully covered and won't run off easily. Plus, the numerals have to be precise." I take notice of his chipped red nail polish and smile to myself, remembering the first time I saw him with his lavish red lipstick and flowing black hair.

"I like how feminine you are," I blurt, and he smiles.

"And I'm the blunt one?" Harold says.

AJ laughs. "It's okay. I like to think of myself as fluid as the ocean. Except when I get wet, because then I'm as stiff as a literal skeleton."

I grimace. I remember the skeletons. . . Quick, change the

subject. Anything besides skeletons. "So what kind of magic do you do back home?" I ask Harold.

AJ stares at Harold. "Are you from the same place as her?"

"Different area, but yeah." He turns to me. "I'm a runecaster."

"A what?"

"You know, Norse mythology?"

"Oh, I've seen those scriptures before. So, you. . .carry runes stones and stuff?"

"Just runes. Wood, not stone." He chuckles. "And I did, but. . .they got confiscated when I got here." He lifts his wrist to show me his mark. A Roman numeral *I* decorates his wrist. "And, I also have the Fool's mark," he shows me his other wrist. "That one didn't appear until I"—he clears his throat— "changed directions in my journey."

So, a person can have two marks. My mind wanders to when I was in Nkella's room and saw the Tarot numerals on both his wrists. The *O* for the Fool, and I'm assuming the *XV* is for the Devil. There's so much about this world that I wonder about. Some marks are curses, others make you illegal like the Magician's mark, and others display you're on a journey. Why is the mark of the Devil a curse? What did Nkella do to get it? And what journey is he on?

AJ's gentle brush strokes tickle my skin and I force myself to stay still.

"You got branded with the Magician's mark because you practice magic in your land," AJ declares.

"Yep." White flecks that resemble frost appear under his eyes. He wipes them away and I squint. His fingernails are white with frost as well. I noticed that at the tavern too when his teeth started to chatter. Weird, considering it's warm in here. I bet it has something to do with his runes.

"So how did you learn how to use the magic here?" I asked, intrigue poking at me now.

"When I first got here, I met a girl. . .an Ipani girl. She showed me a lot."

"Ohhhh," I coo.

"Where did you land when you got here?" AJ asks.

"Piupeki."

AJ whistles. "Quite a difference from Wands in temperature."

Harold snickers. "I was meant to go to Jötunheim. . .er, a different world. But it's also very cold, like Piupeki. So, at first, I thought I was there until I saw all the ancient Greek in the temple I landed in. Plus, the Ipani girl who almost killed me." He chuckles.

"I'm guessing she's the one you turned out to be friends with," I say.

His eyes grow somber and look downcast. He nods. "I still need to get to Jötunheim. If you haven't noticed the frost that occasionally appears around my lips and eyes, I'm cursed. And the only way to break it is for me to face the Frost Giants who cursed my ancestors hundreds of years ago."

My eyes widen. Well, that answers why he always looks freezing. "You're going to go fight Frost Giants in some Viking world? I thought *my* life was weird."

"I know it's a lot to take in. But it's my journey, and mine alone."

"Well, in the meantime, welcome aboard the *Devil's*

Gambit." AJ smacks him on the shoulder, the liquid vial in his other hand. "We're all cursed one way or another."

"Thanks. . . And, for what it's worth, I will help the best I can with saving your girlfriend. I owe you and the captain for letting me on board."

"Hey, I helped!" I say.

"You too, Soren. You could have ignored me."

I shrug. "It wasn't completely selfless. You did say you'd help me get home."

"Even still."

"Can you do that?" AJ asks. "Can you help Soren get home?" AJ glances up and picks out a soft skin tone color that matches the color of the mark.

He nods. "And myself. I just need my runes back."

"And where are they exactly?" I ask.

"With the Empress."

I quirk a brow. "Which means?"

"They're in Rutavenye?" AJ glances up. He finishes drawing the Fool's mark in ancient Greek, which quickly changes to look like an *O* for my eyes.

Harold wipes his face and nods his head.

"Wait a minute. . ." I say, now standing up and pacing back and forth.

AJ bottles his makeup vial.

"You mean, you can't get us out of here until you get your runes back that are up in the floating Tower Island?"

"Yeah. . ."

"So how exactly are you planning on helping me?"

"I am! Just, not right away. Like I said, I need to get my runes first."

My face deadpans. "Dude, you totally used me."

Kaehante shouts from the main deck. "AJ, ropes!"

AJ jumps up. "Gotta go." He storms out of the room. My eyes fall back to Harold.

"I'm sorry." He lets his arms drop. "I needed to get out of that situation."

I sigh and sit back down. "Fair enough. How are you planning on getting your runes back?"

"Well," he sits on my bed. "My plan so far was to make the translation potion. But I have that now. Next, I guess I'll try to find a way to Rutavenye."

"Well, if that fails"—I lean in—"I haven't mentioned this to anyone but"—he leans in too—"the way I got here. . .was with the World Card."

He widens his eyes. "You mean like the *World Card*? From *this world's Tarot deck*?"

"Yeah, what do you know about it?"

"What do *you* know about it?" He pushes himself to the edge of the bed.

"Not this again."

"I'm serious. I didn't even know this place existed, so how did you find that? It was on Earth, wasn't it?"

I tell him everything, from Madame Asteria at Tarotland Circus, to going into jail, up to the point where the card opened a portal.

"Wow."

"Yup. And a drakon came to visit me while in the brig." I catch him up to speed about my plan to find the Ace of Wands card. "The drakon said it can do anything, so I'm betting it can take me back."

"Hmm. . . Maybe."

"We can both use it," I finish.

"That'd be great, but I'm not leaving here without my runes. They're—a part of me. And in order for me to finish my quest to become a runemaster, I need them."

There's so much I don't know. "And all I want is to get home."

He leans back. "I mean. . .this place is great. There's so much stuff here. Ruins, archeology. . .like ancient Greek archaeology!"

I smile thinly, my eyes growing heavy.

"You don't care about that stuff, do you?"

"I mean, I know about the ancient Greek stuff, it's all around here, but. . .I just care about getting home."

"I get that but. . . given the mark on your arm, you don't want to find out more?"

"About some random mark in a Tarotworld? Not really. It just randomly appeared out of nowhere when I got here. What's it got to do with me?"

"It's not as random as you may think. You really have no idea why that mark would come to you, do you?"

"What's the big deal?"

"What's the big deal?" he quirks a brow. "Soren, you really know nothing about Tarot cards, do you?"

"I mean, I know what they are. . ."

"Have you ever seen a mark like the one you have on the Tarot?"

"No. . .?"

"No, because it doesn't exist. So, get this. . . From what I've learned, this place wasn't only invaded by Greeks in ancient times. It would have taken a lot of power to find this place."

I blink a few times.

"What could have enough power to open a portal into another dimension?"

I shake my head. "Why don't you just tell me?"

"All I know is, my aunt used to tell me stories of the Norse gods, and one of them had the power to go through portals."

My eyes widen. "So, like, the Greek gods or something came here? I thought gods and stuff were just a myth though."

"Yeah, like magic is a myth?"

"Good point. Okay so who is she? The Empress, I mean."

"That's what I've been trying to figure out. But the only Greek beings associated with spiders that I can think of are the Moirai. But that means there would be three of them, and I've only heard of one Empress."

"The who?"

"You know, past, present, and future? One who weaves the web, one who measures it, and one who cuts it?"

I shake my head.

He sighs. "The Moirai were known as the Fates in Greek mythology."

"Oh, I think I remember that now."

"Really?"

"No."

"Alright, it doesn't matter. What matters is, if I'm right, this land was created by the Moirai, or at least one of them. And you have their mark. The question is, why."

I shrug. "No idea."

"Aren't you curious? I am, and I'm not even the one with

the mark. I mean, Soren, you have the only mark that has something to do with the ancient Greek Fates!"

I lie back against the wall. "I just don't think it's that important compared to my sister."

Harold's lips twist into a scowl. "If the Empress finds out you have that mark, or worse—know where the lost World Card is. . ." he shakes his head.

"What would happen?"

"I don't know but nothing good. Don't forget she controls people's fates with the Tarot. She turns people into faceless army soldiers against their will. Who knows what she could do with the entire collection."

I let that sink in. "Good thing she doesn't know I exist then, eh?"

AJ bursts through the wool curtain. "Hey, eat your lunch quickly. He drops a plate full of bread, vegetables, and fruits. "We're reaching full speed ahead soon."

"Thanks. How long will it take to get there?"

"Hopefully, a few hours if we can speed up enough to make up for lost time. Iéle has already found them."

Wonderful. That means the wolf is back.

"So, what are we talking about?" AJ takes a seat on the chair in front of us.

"Oh-uh." I shake my head at Harold. "Nothing. Just talking about Earth stuff."

A pained look spreads on AJ's face. "Well, I need to get back anyway. See you on the main deck." My stomach twists. I didn't mean to hurt him. I like AJ. And he just helped me by covering up the web marking on my arm.

"What was that for?" Harold asks.

I lower my voice. "When I first woke up here. . .I saw them. . .change. Like. . . they're undead or something."

"Yeah, this is the *Devil's Gambit* and the undead crew."

I screw up my face. "Undead crew?"

"I don't know all the details. I only know hearsay from people talking on the docks. They all got cursed real bad by the Empress. They're all undead, except the captain. The captain apparently has it the worst. He got cursed with the Devil Card."

"Oh. . .that's why he's the Devil. I wonder what he did."

Harold pops a few grapes in his mouth. "No idea, but I haven't heard of any other Devils around here so whatever he did, try not to piss him off too bad."

A shiver runs down my spine.

"The crew seems alright though."

"Yeah," I say. "But I don't trust AJ won't tell his captain what I say, especially if he thinks it'll help them on their mission. Nkella has been all hell-bent on my mark since I got here so. . ."

"Got it."

"By the way"—I lean in—"back at the tavern, you said people don't die here. . . You were talking about the Empress, weren't you? What does that mean exactly? Why won't the Empress allow death to occur naturally?"

He shrugs one shoulder. "My friend told me she used to, but too many people, Ipani and humans alike, started killing each other. I suppose she thought eternal pain was worse, so now every death has to go through her.

"Sounds like hell."

"Exactly what I said when I found that out."

"How though? I shudder to think anyone can have that kind of power."

"She holds the Death Card."

"The wha—"

The ship surges and I fall back against the wall. Harold topples to the floor, trying to keep his balance.

"They weren't joking about full speed!" I yell.

"I wonder what potion they're using."

I scramble to get up. "This is magic?"

"Has to be. Tessa must have already had it because they didn't mention anything about having to make it. I better get to work on what she told me."

"Yeah, just don't get seasick." I hold my stomach.

"Ha. We'll see." He leaves my room and topples over to his. I lay my head down and make use of the time AJ bought me to fall asleep. I start to doze off and the last words that ring through my head are about the Fates and my mark. What does it have to do with me? Who exactly is this Empress?

I wake to the thunderous sound of cannon fire. My heart lunges into my throat as I catapult out of the bed and through the curtain. Another bang roars around me as the walls shake. Good thing I fell asleep with my shoes on. The ship rocks and I almost fall into Tessa's room. Shouts from the main deck reverberate through the floors and I make a dash to the ramp, swallowing my drowsiness. Kaehante balances two cannonballs in one arm and three powder horns on the other. I run up to him and grab the two cannons.

"Sorry. Overslept. What's going on?"

"We sighted a ship. They are attacking us."

Another cannon blasts through the air. I nearly fall backward as the ship shakes.

I scream.

Kaehante runs toward the main deck amid the fight.

Clutching hard onto the cannonballs, I scurry against the wall of the ship. Why am I helping again? Because I want to help AJ? Because I feel like I owe him? Another blast shoots at us and I drop to the ground, a cannonball slipping from my hand. Or maybe because, if the ship goes down, I too go down with the ship. I scramble to pick the cannonballs up and climb to my feet. I can't die here; I can't let Talia think I abandoned her. Gaining my balance, I focus on Harold running down the ramp.

"Take those to Kae. I'll grab more!" He dashes past me to the artillery room.

My heart hammers and I nod. "Right." Okay, I can do this. I step onto the main deck and spot Kaehante lighting one of the cannons. Nkella screams something from above my head as I make a dash for cover under the foremast. Tessa says something back to him, but over the commotion, I can't make it out.

In the near distance, a ship with six large masts threatens us. And here I am, in a literal battle with pirates. And with no training whatsoever. Did I ever say I was a badass? Yeah, I lied.

Another fire blast surges toward us; I lunge for the cannon

Kaehante is stationed at, hitting my back against the wall. I catch a glimpse of AJ climbing onto a rope.

"Are we going to fire a cannon?" I ask Kaehante.

"Not yet. We wait until they are closer."

"But. . . They're hitting us."

"We wait."

A loud groan comes from the wheel. Kaehante's face pales. He clenches his jaw and darts his eyes to the quarterdeck. I flick my gaze to where he's looking. A black flag has risen that has a skull with devil horns and an angry smile, just like the one on the bow strip.

Below it, Tessa fights Nkella for the wheel. He grabs onto his head and topples back. She takes hold, letting him fall backward.

Why would Tessa take control of the ship?

I spin back to Kaehante. "What's going on?"

He points at the sky. "Curse day has begun."

Beyond the assailant vessel, the sun sinks into the horizon. The moon casts its light over our ship as AJ swings back on the rope, as if readying to launch himself forward.

Cannon fire blasts from the assailant ship, causing a wave to hit and splash over AJ's body. His flesh disappears and he becomes a skeleton wearing clothing. I choke on a gasp and press my back harder against the wall. As I do, I catch a glimpse of Kaehante's coat, as he turns, his hollow eye sockets momentarily stop at my gaze. I yelp. I knew I had seen them change before, but this seems more. . .permanent.

Nkella jumps to the main deck, and I startle. "Now!" he yells. Kaehante takes a cannonball, fires it up, and points for me to go to the other. I grip the cannonball in my hands and sprint to the other one, loading it just as I watched him do. He lights the ends of both cannons and I grab onto my ears, waiting for the blast.

Nothing happens.

The other ship is nearing closer, and any minute now, we're about to be blown up.

Nkella moans loudly behind me. I spin to see him gasping for air. His hat falls off his head, revealing two horn stumps protruding from within his tousled hair.

Iéle flies over my head and lands hard on all fours. She runs down the ramps, distracting Nkella. She must have come through the Aō dimension.

Kaehante relights the wick. I ready myself for a blast again as the other ship gets nearer. Why they haven't blasted us yet, I have no idea, but I don't want to find out.

The cannons don't fire. Kaehante lets out a loud grunt and he slams his fist on his cannon. He pours out one of the horns and tips it over. A clump of powder hits the floorboard. "The gunpowder is wet. How is it wet?" He scrunches his face and then looks right at me. "You."

"Me?"

"Did you open the barrel?"

"I—no. . ." Oh crap—when I was stacking cannons the other day. . . "I got curious. . ."

"How did it get wet?"

"Some water dripped but. . .very little. I didn't think it would matter."

"You doomed us," he snaps.

I shrink back. No. . . "The cannons won't fire?"

"Gun powder is useless when wet. That was our only barrel."

My pulse quickens. Crap, crap, crap. "I can fix this. . ."

Kaehante reaches to his back and takes out two guns, then turns to aim at the enemy ship.

Nkella stumbles over to one of the ropes, his balance out of sorts. I hope to God he didn't hear our exchange. He grabs on and pulls. With his other hand, he takes out a pistol and starts to fire. I take a few steps back over to the side.

Harold appears on the main deck at full sprint. "We have a problem!"

"No kidding!" I yell back and point to Kaehante and AJ who are now fully skeletal "But we also have a bigger problem—"

Harold interrupts me. "They've been sailing under the radar! That's why they needed *solerig*. I need a potion that makes things invisible, or the Empress will have her army on us in seconds."

I gulp.

Gunfire shoots back at us, and Harold and I duck.

"What's the other problem?" he asks.

"The gunpowder is wet."

His jaw drops.

"It is too late," Nkella says from over his shoulder.

"I can fix this." I repeat, unsure if he was talking to us or not.

I pass Harold to make it down the ramp. There's gotta be something we can fire the cannons with. Or maybe I can call Gari for help. He would have something magical, wouldn't he?

Harold puts his hand on my shoulder and stops me. "I'll make a potion."

I look at him, forcing my eyes to stay dry. "Tessa has bombs too. . . Take them from her, she's steering the ship."

He turns to leave to the quarterdeck.

Nkella screams. "AJ, no!"

I snap my gaze over and catch AJ, swinging all the way back on the rope, aiming for the ship, now uncomfortably close to ours. I can only tell it's AJ because he still has his long black hair underneath a bandana on his skull. A pirate holds an oumala female with her arms tied behind her, a sick grin pasted on his toothless face.

Sword in hand, AJ swings from the rope and lands his feet on their deck.

"AJ!" Nkella's voice is hoarse and deep. "It's a trap!" He and Kaehante start shooting at the ship. Nkella is about to swing after AJ when the pirate on board the other ship grabs him and pulls him off the rope. He holds him by his bony neck and in a swirl of smoke, the pirate shifts into an Arcana soldier. My mouth drops. The oumala hostage also shifts, along with the soldier who held her.

It *is* a trap.

Cannon fire roars through the night. I don't even see it coming. Nkella flies through the air but not toward the ship— toward me! He lunges and lands on top of me with a hard thud, knocking me off my feet. A cannonball hits the other side of the ship. My head arches back to stare at it. I try to get up as Nkella climbs off me. My mouth parts but no words come out. He stares at me, his eyes darker than usual as a scarlet glow forces its way behind his pupils. He saved me. . .

He jerks back, and grabs onto his head, letting out a painful wail. He clutches his stomach as he picks himself up. A swirl of scarlet magic whooshes down from his head to his feet, he lets out another groan and punches a hole through the floorboards. I stumble back.

Arcana soldiers are crossing over to the *Gambit*. Nkella spins around, whips out his pistol and starts to shoot, hitting each one on the head. They disappear in a whirl of smoke only to reappear after a few seconds.

Panic surges through my veins—we are losing this fight.

To the side, a big and bony Kaehante is fighting one off. I dart my eyes, looking for Tessa and Harold, but don't see them at the wheel. I can only hope they will be successful in making something powerful enough to get out of this.

A scarlet blast emanates from Nkella, allowing him to pull free of the masked soldiers. I choke on a gasp as the soldiers disappear.

He takes a moment to orient himself and dashes to a rope. His head shakes furiously, and I can tell he's battling with himself to stay focused. Like there's an inner conflict inside of him, a Devil trying to take over.

I feel completely useless. Kaehante was right. I doomed them with the powder. Had the cannons fired before, the Minor Arcana wouldn't be on board this ship. And AJ would be safe.

One of Kaehante's daggers shows from his belt as he shoots. I run up and grab it from his sheath. He glimpses me but doesn't object. Instead, he blasts an Arcana soldier, grabs onto a rope, and swings to the other ship. Probably to go after AJ.

Nkella does the same; only this time, an Arcana soldier appears on the edge of the rail and cuts the rope with a swing of his sword.

I scream and lean over the rail right as Nkella plummets. He hits his head on the side of the ship on the way down, and lands with an inaudible splash.

I freeze and stare down at the crashing waves.

I snap my attention to the Arcana soldier looming over me from the top of the rail.

Wind smacks my face as I stare straight into the Arcana soldier's dark voided eyes. I clutch onto Kaehante's dagger, my hand shaking as I point it at him.

For a second, I take my eyes off the soldier and look to the enemy ship for Kaehante or AJ. I can't hear Harold or Tessa over the sounds of gunfire and the roaring ocean.

The soldier jumps down, its gaze fixed on me.

It's now or never.

Letting the dagger fall to the floor, I clutch onto the rail with both hands, and without a second thought, I pull my weight over the rail and dive in after the captain.

My skin hits the icy water like bricks on cement. Pain seers through my veins as my body bursts out of the water, my lungs hungry for air. I don't know why I jumped to save my captor, but I'll justify it later. My legs kick underneath as I search for Nkella.

He must have hit his head hard. No time to think.

Just search.

Waves fight my line of sight and I dunk my head into the dark depths of the sea.

Phantom memories fly at me.

Torture.

The tavern.

Iéle's teeth sinking into my stomach.

The brig.

Where is he? Keep searching.

His menacing stares.

It doesn't matter. Search.

Something hits my leg. I spin around and grab on to whatever it is.

I pull it up; it's Nkella. He gasps for air. Clawing at the water, he grabs me and pulls me under. Kicking harder, I fight to stay afloat. I grip his shoulder with my left hand, ball my right fist, and punch him with all the strength I have left.

Right in his head.

Hopefully, a big Ipani guy can withstand more than one concussion, but it's for both our sakes. And I sure as hell am not about to let him drown me.

I lean him over my shoulder, treading water with my loose arm. Kicking furiously, I look up. How the heck am I going to get us back on the ship?

Nkella gurgles water out of his mouth. Good. he's alive. Keep kicking.

A whoosh of black smoke circles around us. Nkella starts to kick furiously, his weight dragging me down under the waves. Water fully submerges me, and I can't pull myself up from his weight. I start punching up at the water, the surface becoming more and more distant. My chest aches. I can't hold my breath any longer.

And I see black.

What feels like a second later, we're back on the ship.

Except, the inside walls are yellow with a black trim. We're not on the *Devil's Gambit*.

Water shoots out of my mouth as I start to violently cough and my chest heaves from being out of breath. I dart my gaze over to Nkella as I blink away the wetness in my eyes. I reach for him. His eyes narrow at me, a hint of scarlet glow from behind them. He parts his lips, and his brows soften.

"You. . ." He coughs. "Saved me."

"Yeah. . ."

"Bancha." he spits water from his mouth as his chest heaves. "Why? You should have let me drown."

My face hardens. I don't know what bancha means but I'm pretty sure it's an insult. "No—"

His face pales as something grabs me from behind. He reaches for my wrist but it happens too fast. He grabs at me again and this time I feel something snap away from my wrist. A second later I'm being pulled away in a cocoon of smoke. The last thing I see is Nkella's confused face. And a bright green explosion.

MY KNEES BUCKLE AS MY FEET HIT BLACK AND WHITE checkered marble. The swirling smoke that brought me here dissipates as the Arcana soldier lets me go. I block my fall with my hands as the floor moves around me and my eyes fixate on my bare wrist. My charm bracelet. The only reminder I had left of my mother. That's what snapped off. My chest tightens.

It takes me a second to realize the floor isn't actually moving. Between having been on a rocking ship, going for a swim, and freaking teleporting—uugh I think I'm gonna be sick.

"Why is she dripping on my floor?"

An orotund voice snaps my attention to a woman wearing a gold, expressionless mask, sitting on a bronze throne. The back of the throne is long, and curves to the shape of a spiderweb. To add to her grandeur, dainty golden laurel leaves adorn the crown of her head. She wears a black corset that reaches up to her shoulders, with military-fashion shoulder blades. A fan-like spiderweb collar covers her neck down to her cleavage.

"Woah. . ."

Above her, a large spiderweb spiral just like my mark glistens in gold on the wall. I stare at it in disbelief.

Whispers come from all over. *"She had fallen to sea."*

"Who said that?" I spin around, looking for where the voices are coming from. Guards stand along the walls of the room, their masked faces staring forward and unmoving. Silver emblems with a shield and tower in the center clasp their robes at the shoulder.

The room is huge. Like some sort of court or. . .duh, I guess throne room. Metallic spiders with gas lamp torches on the top end of their bodies decorate the walls between high cathedral style windows.

"Oh. In that case, it is a good thing Apeiron didn't eat her," the woman snaps.

I bring my gaze back to her. Wait—eat me? Is she talking about the serpent? "Apeiron? That sea beast has a name?"

Gasps echo through the walls. *"Do not speak to Empress Aletha directly, miss!"* I hold my hand to my lips. Oh my god—I'm. . . Am I on the floating island? Finally shaking off my disorientation. . . This woman is the Empress?

"No matter. I can handle it when someone does not know manners. To answer your question, yes, and he is very old. Pirates keep bothering him; he's quite territorial." She lifts her chin. "For My Divinity's sake, change her clothes. Do it quickly. And clean up this mess."

Large spiders with glistening blue and purple mosaic patterned bodies fall from the ceiling and enclose me. Before I can move away, a whirl of smoke whooshes from the top of my head down to my toes. They move so fast, I can't keep track, all I know is the smoke is so thick, no one standing outside of it looking in would be able to get a glimpse as spiders unravel my jail clothes and construct something new. I can't wrap my head around it, and I'm not sure how I feel about being dressed by spiders. Not that I was given a choice.

My skin prickles as they wrap me tightly in silk, pulling and cutting. My legs jerk as they make their ways down the back of my thighs, hitting my most ticklish spots.

I cup the part of my arm where the makeup is, scared it'll rub off. As soon as they finish, they ascend back over my head and the smoke vanishes, leaving me clutching my sides. Bewildered, I gape down at my legs. A skin-tight black top covering my shoulders hugs my torso as it opens at my waist like a cape. It's black with intricate web designs from top to bottom. Leggings hug my hips, and I have no guess as to how they managed to build around me. I must admit, I'm glad to finally be free of that gross orange jail suit. Luckily, they left my shoes. Not so lucky, my feet are still wet.

"There now, much better," the Empress says. "What of the captain of the ship?"

"Um."

"No, not you." She tilts her head as a spider comes down and sets itself on her neckline. It has a large oval body with a mosaic black pattern and translucent black legs. It appears similar to Philo, only larger, about the size of an orange, with black mirrors instead of red. I still as the Empress and the spider sit in silence, communicating. A memory of Nkella and Iéle flashes in my mind. I wonder if the whispering spiders are like Gari. A hybrid between Oumala and mythos. Maybe that's why they talk.

Gari's head pops out from the ether right above the Empress's head. He stares at me with his wide jester-like grin. I gasp and open my lips to speak but he shakes his head and disappears.

"He got away?" she shrieks, jolting my attention back to her. The spider jumps up and disappears up its web to the ceiling. "That's too bad. I was hoping for a show on curse day."

Curse day? She must mean Nkella and the crew! A smile curls on my face and I quickly suppress it.

She tilts her head to the right, but this time no spider is present. After a few awkward moments, my eyes start to wander around the room, casing it for an exit. Not that I'd be able to jump off a floating island.

"No deaths I'm waiting on are present. Let them suffer."

I snap my face back to her. No deaths she's waiting on? I clear my throat. "Umm. . .why am I here?"

The spiders gasp and the Empress snaps her head to look directly at me.

"Uhh. . .Your Highn—Majesty?" I take a small step back.

"You have quite the mouth on you, child. Step forward."

I inch forward.

"Closer."

I take three steps and face the Empress head-on. Emerald green eyes peer back at me from behind her gold mask. A strange sense of calmness washes over my head, followed by despair. Her gaze intensifies; now I'm met with the overwhelming power of something. . .not human, not even oumala. . .but divine. Could Harold have been right?

"One of my psychic scouts brought you. I suppose he thought you'd be of interest to me. Do you know why that is?"

"Psychic scout?"

"The soldier who brought you here. My, you aren't very sharp, are you?"

A memory of AJ saying the soldiers from the Tower are psychic surfaces in my mind. Then it drifts to the Arcana soldier who was staring at me from the rail, right before I jumped into the water. My breath hitches. She doesn't appear to know why he brought me here. Do they not speak to her? Maybe they can't speak at all.

"Speak up, girl. I haven't all day. Are you with the Devil's crew?"

Oh. I swallow. She was clearly trying to sabotage their ship. She cursed them all. If she thinks I'm one of his new recruits, that can't end well for me. "No," I say, and I'm not lying. That's the truth, I'm not part of his crew. "I was being held prisoner."

She taps her finger on the chin of her mask. She's probably trying to tell if I'm lying. "I cannot read you. I can read everyone. This is peculiar indeed." She stands and comes near me, her mask faceless, emotionless, just like her voice. "I suppose you should be thanking me if you were truly a prisoner of the ship. I saved you."

I swallow.

"What can you tell me about them? Where were they headed before my army blew them to bits?"

"I—I don't know?"

"Well, you must know something. Otherwise, if you are causing a ruckus, I have no use for you."

"Quick, she'll turn you into one of them."

"One of who?" I glance around me to see if I can spot the spiders talking.

"The Minor Arcana, miss."

My breath hitches as I scramble for words. What do I tell her? I'm not going to mess things up for the crew when they need to focus on saving AJ's girlfriend, and I don't know this world well enough to steer her in a different direction, let alone know the extent of her powers. I may resent Nkella for keeping me prisoner, but I'm no snitch.

"Well?" The Empress sits back down. "I don't have all day."

"I'm not sure what you want me to do—" I gasp. Oh, I know! "Would you like to see a card trick?" It's not exactly the information she was after but it's all I got.

She sits forward, peering at my hands from behind her mask. "How did you get cards?" Her voice rings like venom at the last word.

"Oh, these are just playing cards. They're not like yours." Maybe this was a bad idea.

"Let me see them." She holds out her hand.

I reach for my pockets when—"um. . . they were in my clothes."

"Bring her belongings!" she yells.

A spider reaches down and drops the deck of cards into my palms. I open the box and hand them to her. Thankfully, they're not wet. Spider magic?

She inspects each one, picking one at a time, bringing them up to her face. She flicks one with her other finger and when nothing happens, she moves on to the next. "What are these pictures depicting? Who are these people and the creatures drawn on them?"

I bite the inside of my cheek. I can't tell her it's from a story I grew up with; she'll know I'm not from here. "My mother had a vivid imagination. She painted them," I quickly fabricate.

"She painted all of these designs?"

I nod, hoping she doesn't detect a lie.

"Impressive. I quite like art. Where is your mother now?"

"Oh. . .she's very ill."

"Is she? Oh dear, I am sorry. I had a sister who would be able to tell your mother's future, but I cannot, I'm afraid."

"Oh, it's okay." A sister who could tell the future? Harold's theory is making sense to me now. I hope she doesn't ask who my mother is. "It's her mind. . . I haven't seen her in ages."

"Tsk-tsk-tsk. You poor dear. And what of your father?"

"I also have not seen him in years. H-he"—my voice breaks —"gave me away a long time ago."

The Empress lifts her chin to see me better. "And you feel betrayed by that, don't you?"

"I—well, yes." I'd be lying if I didn't.

"My father caused a war that got my mother killed when my sisters and I were young."

Yeesh. . .

"Then both my sisters betrayed me."

That hit me like a knife to my gut, snapping me back to reality. Talia probably thinks I betrayed her. I can't let her think that, I need to get out of here and go after that Ace Card.

"Do you have any sisters?"

"Yes. A younger one."

"My advice to you is to keep an arm's distance between

you. They'll either always want what you have or try to best you in everything you do."

Not me and Talia.

The Empress clasps her gloved hands together. "Go on then, girl. Show me your trick."

"Oh, right." I take out my two Hatters and my one Cheshire Cat, tucking the rest of the deck inside my thigh pocket. I gotta hand it to these spiders, I'm really liking this outfit. I take the cards and show her each one. Slowly, I approach the seat beside her to set them down. When the Empress doesn't budge at my offense of nearing so closely, I continue. "Keep your eyes on the cat," I show her the card. I place each one, and with my sleight of hand, switch the cards. I move them slowly. "Do you know where the cat is?"

"Of course I do. I'm not daft. You were moving too slowly." She picks up the card she thinks has the Cheshire Cat and gasps. I swallow a chuckle, unsure if she's pleased or not.

She inspects the card over and over.

"Would you like to go again?"

"Show me your numbered mark, girl."

I gulp.

"You are not a Magician, are you?"

I shake my head, stumbling back. "No, it's only a trick I swear." Yep, definitely a bad idea.

"Your mark!"

I lift my forearm, hoping to God the makeup AJ drew didn't get washed away. As the light hits it, I release a breath. Still intact. Whew.

"A Fool? You're telling the truth." The Empress stares at my arm and hands my card back.

"Yep. See? As I said, it's just a card trick," I hide my arm behind me. "I can show you how it's done, if you like?"

She nods, her interest piqued. I smile and pull the cards out again. "This is all it is." I hold out each card and carefully explain my sleight of hand. The Empress has her hands clutched together, drawn in toward her stomach. I would normally never share the secrets of my tricks, and if Talia were here, she'd be shooting me evil glares.

She's been begging me to show her how to do this for months. But desperate times call for desperate measures. Wouldn't want her to change her mind about me not being a Magician.

She carefully examines each card as I explain the sleight of hand, handing them to her to try. She holds the three cards face down on her palm like I showed her, but when she does the flip, the cards come apart and reveal the trick, instead of hiding the one on top. She tries once more and messes it up a second time.

"That's alright. Try again," I say, keeping my voice steady and sweet, just how I convinced Albert and Sonja to adopt me.

"No."

I startle.

"I never had a Fool entertain me in my court. You are sneaky yet truthful. Cunning. I can respect that." She pauses for a beat. "I've decided to keep you."

I cough. "Keep me?" An image of me dressed as a court jester doing tricks for this creepy lady in the mask surfaces in my brain and I shake it off.

"People like you and I do not trust easily. I think you'll find you'd fit right in."

I take an involuntary step back. Fit in where? Tower Island? I can't stay here.

"Hmm. . . and you're entertaining. I don't get much of that around here either. Why are you backing up?" Her voice rises.

"I—I'm not."

"Yes, you are. You just backed away from me."

"Oh, um. . .not intentionally. . .sorry."

"Sit."

She slightly tilts her head to the cushioned seat beside her. None of the Arcana soldiers guarding the walls move; eyes follow as I step over and have a seat. I sit with my legs pressed together, and my back upright. Why she wants me sitting next to her, I have no idea.

"What is your name, girl? You still haven't told me."

Because she didn't ask for it. "Soren."

"When were you born, Soren?"

"Oh, um. . ."

"I know a person's present, but not their past—but yet, I get the sense you were born today."

"Yes, today is my birthday."

"I knew it. Long ago, we only celebrated the birthdays of the gods, then that changed to a celebration only for males. Did you know?"

I shake my head.

"I didn't like that, so I made it so that everyone would have a birthday celebration."

Oh, she did, huh? Wow, she's full of herself.

"Tell me, Soren. Do you like games?"

"Games?"

"Why, yes, of course you do. That's a silly question. Come!" The Empress jumps to her feet, her lacy spiderweb gown flowing behind her. "Guards! Prepare the arena! It is Soren's birthday!"

"Umm. . .you don't have to—"

"Hush, you. And then later, you can show me another trick." Even though I can't see her expression behind the mask, I get the feeling she just smiled.

Rows of Arcana soldiers line up along the tall black marble columns of the exit. With my heart in my throat, I follow the Empress out of the grand room, the Arcana guards walking with us in between the two rows. Looking to either side of me, I try to gaze at the faces behind their masks with the mother-of-pearl sheen, but their eye sockets are like an endless void of black smoke. Their robes are adorned by silver metal clasps with the shield and tower decorations.

The masked soldier on the ship also had a mother-of-pearl sheen. As did the one who tried to kill Kaehante. So all these soldiers are psychic?

Their heads are also fully covered by black hoods. From what the crew said, Nkella's sister was made into one of them. He had asked me if they were dead. Now it makes sense. But were they turned into smoke? What's inside their hoods? How can they be walking around and following orders if they're smoke dummies?

Strong winds hit my face as the open-air halls of the Tower come into view. It's a long walk up the spiral arches until we reach the very top. The Minor Arcana doesn't skip a beat, marching in perfect union. Their expressionless masks always face forward.

The top of the Tower is freezing. I cross my arms together, rubbing my goose bumps. We step out of the arched hall to an even grander opening, with large columns along the wide circumference of the space.

"Come along."

I trudge forward as we're led to a row of seats. The Empress takes her seat facing the arena. She tilts her head in silent command for me to sit beside her. Taking my seat, I glance back at the Minor Arcana that hasn't budged. She waves her right hand, and all at once, they stomp their right leg one time. I can't take my eyes off them as they disperse to positions along the arena.

"Wait until you see my new champion." Excitement pitches her voice. "The moment I found out about her power, I thought, why use her as a faceless soldier when I can have her entertain me?"

I'm sorry, creepy lady said what? I clear my throat.

"Is there something the matter with your throat, dear?" She claps her hands. "Get Soren water!"

"No, no, I'm fine! Thank you really, I just—"

"Spit it out."

"I have a question, Your Majesty."

"Your Divinity is just fine."

"Right. . . Okay. Your Divinity."

When she doesn't respond I take it as a cue to continue. "What *are they* exactly?" Being careful not to sound too out of this world—literally.

"What are what? You're stuttering."

"Your army, I mean. . . It's just. . .I've always wondered what they are."

"Ipani prisoners, of course. Have you been living under a rock?"

"Yes, of course, but I mean. . .after—"

"My prisoners become my army—they have no agency."

"Are they. . .alive in there?"

She guffaws. "Why, of course they're alive. I am Fate incarnate."

I choke on a gasp. So she *is* a Fate.

"They won't die unless I tell them to. But then I wouldn't have a use for a dead army, would I?"

Oh, so not zombies. . . That's good. But no agency? They can't make any decisions of their own? They obviously can't use their magic, but as AJ told me, the bound ones can't either. That must be awful.

New masked soldiers with metal drums around their waists line the edges of the arena. In uniform, they start playing a slow rhythmic beat.

A figure in long purple and gold robes steps onto the center of the stadium. Their mask is a plain silver, but as far as I can see this one doesn't have any pupils or white around the eyes, just dark swirls of darkness like the others. They bring a trumpet up to a tiny hole at the lips of their mask. A moment later, high-pitched metallic tones amplify the arena.

For a split second, I forget about my current situation. And for a split moment, I lean over the edge of my seat expectantly. A pulse of excitement flickers at my wrist, and I smile back at the Empress. She gives me an elegant nod, her piercing green eyes unflinching beneath her gold mask. Right, she's calling all the shots in this charade. They have no agency. I need to remember that.

I guess they're not all added to her army, but still. . . "What about the ones who play music?"

"What about them?"

"Do they have agency?"

"No. They do only what I allow."

"Do they know?"

"Do they know they have no control, you mean? You seem very interested in the lives of prisoners. Do not be mistaken, child. Each and every one of them committed a crime."

"A crime of using their magic?"

"Magic is outlawed," she says sternly. "It is for their own good. It can kill."

"But—if you hold the Death Card—"

"Quiet now. Are you not enjoying yourself?" Her voice reaches a high pitch at the last word. "This is in honor of your birthday, Soren."

"Right, no, I mean—yes! Yes, I am. Thank you." I face forward.

The masked trumpeter lowers his instrument and faces us.

"Some have committed treason as well." She finally raises her hand and gives a wave. The drummers pick up the tempo as the masked trumpeter disappears in a whirl of smoke. The increasingly fast pace of the beating drums goes on for a few more seconds until they all stop at once. The sand of the arena settles, and we're met with a beat of silence.

An announcer who I cannot see echoes his voice through the stadium. "To the right, we have a very special oumala with powers so fast you won't believe your eyes." In a whirl of sand, a snow leopard appears on the right of the arena. It growls and its eyes glow red. Like Iéle. I lean over in my seat.

"And now, introducing our champion, our one and only Ipani fighter, Ntaoru Mikiroro!"

Wait. . . Ntaoru? Nkella's sister? She's here? My mouth drops as an Arcana soldier wearing a silver mask appears in a swirl of sand. The sand settles on the ground and she faces the leopard.

"She has magic?" I mutter.

"Controlled," the Empress says. "I allow her only to have what's needed. An Ipani with her power could do great damage. She is very tame, mind you."

Tame. Like an animal.

A masked Arcana soldier approaches holding a tray with a glass of clear liquid with a tint of green. I squint at it and then at the mask.

"That took an age," the Empress hisses without taking her eyes off the arena.

"Oh. . .I said I was fine."

The Arcana soldier pushes the tray forward. There's no way I'm drinking that. I know it's not water, but why is it a clear green? Gazing up at the mask, I do a double take. The plain silver mask changes before my eyes. Its face morphs into the features of a Drakon and winks at me.

"Gari?" I whisper.

"What did you say?" the Empress asks. Gari's face disappears from the mask, and nothing is left but the blank stare.

"N-nothing. Sorry." I take the glass and bring it down to my lap. "Thank you." Eying the liquid suspiciously, I clutch it against my stomach. If Gari is giving me this drink, it better be to get me the heck out of here.

And yet. . .the last time I ate something he gave me, it could have killed me. But it did get me out of that cell. What will this do to me?

An Arcana soldier runs into the arena holding a hot metal rod. He sticks it to the leopard's side and the leopard snaps at him. He hits the leopard again and then disappears into a cloud of smoke. I flinch and clench my teeth. This is so messed up, the poor leopard.

The leopard roars, backs up, and leaps through the air at a remarkably impossible speed, disappearing into the Aō only to reappear in front of Ntaoru. I know leopards are fast but this. . .this is unreal.

It reaches Ntaoru in a flash of yellow light and smacks her against her mask. She gets blown off the ground on impact and lands with a hard thud. My breath leaves my chest. God, that was fast. I move to the edge of my seat. Is she okay?

The Empress laughs and claps her hands.

The oumala leopard walks around the arena, its eyes glowing and staring at the Arcana soldiers. It stops to look at me and then turns its attention to the Empress.

Ntaoru picks herself up. I'm half surprised her mask hadn't fallen off, but I'm assuming it's stuck on with magic. She holds out her hand and the ground starts to shake. Some of the tinted water in the glass starts to spill over and I top it with my other hand, holding onto my seat with my feet. The Empress doesn't seem bothered.

A crooked drift rips through the arena, boiling lava seeping from deep within. But how? We're on top of a tower. "How is she doing that?"

"Her power is magnificent!" the Empress proclaims.

"But how is she making lava on top of the building?" I yell over the ripping of the arena.

"She can manipulate the land and create lava. Aren't you paying attention?"

Right, I need to stay quiet, or I'll give away that I'm not from here. My mouth gapes as the leopard jumps over the rift and Ntaoru creates a volcanic mound to block it. Then another and another as the leopard dashes through them at a dizzying speed.

Ntaoru grows another mound, but this time the leopard jumps at the wrong time and gets blundered.

Ntaoru creates a second rift, and the leopard nearly falls, its paws holding onto the edge for dear life. My throat dries and I look away. I can't watch. She's about to kill that leopard. But she literally doesn't have a choice, does she? She probably doesn't want to do this at all or is doing it to stay alive while most of her power is bound. How much of her is still in there?

I need to get out of here. I look down at the glass. Do I take the chance? But also, do I have a choice? If I don't, the Empress intends to keep me here. . .possibly forever.

The Empress leans on her seat. I wish I could see her expression. "Is she going to kill it?" I ask.

"Only if I allow it."

I gulp.

The leopard finds its position on a ledge and springs out of the rift. A second later, it has Ntaoru pinned to a mound, its teeth clenching her throat. I squeal and cover my mouth. This isn't fair. It isn't right. All this time Nkella is out there, desperately trying to save his sister, relying on a sliver of hope she's not really dead, and she's been here, being puppeteered by the

Empress. Her agency, stripped from her. And now, she's going to die from being mauled by a leopard, all for the Empress's entertainment. Okay, I'll drink this as soon as I know his sister is okay.

"Please," I beg.

The Empress doesn't say anything. She doesn't even look at me. She's too consumed by her show.

"Please don't let the leopard kill her."

This snaps her attention to me. "What?" Her voice is dark. "You don't care about the Ipani, do you?"

"I—"

"She committed treason."

"N-no! Of course not. It's just. . . She has such great power. None like I've ever seen! Wouldn't it be best to save her for something. . .greater?"

"Hmm." She curls her fingers under her chin. "Like against that traitorous rebellion."

Who? I don't know if I made it better or worse.

The Empress waves her hand, and the leopard separates from Ntaoru in a whirl of smoke. I catch a glimpse of the mark on her wrist. A spiraling spiderweb. Just like mine.

The announcer's voice makes me jump. "And the winner of this round is the oumala leopard!"

"I've never seen a mark like that before," I lie. She stares at me. I don't even know why I brought it up. I knew she had it. It's just. . .why do I have it?

"Are you mad? Or just ignorant? You should have seen them everywhere on the Tower by now."

"I mean, I've never seen it on a person." I bite my tongue.

She pauses for a beat as she stares at me. I can feel my

cheeks burning. I've messed this up, any minute now she's going to figure out I'm not from here and throw me in a dungeon or turn me into one of her mindless soldiers. "My mark is very old," she finally says. I let out a slow and steady breath. "No one else has it. Everyone who did died long ago. Of course, this was before I took the Death Card."

Everyone who did died long ago. I bring the drink to my lips, letting her words sink in. I take a gulp and swoosh notes of peppermint and cinnamon around my mouth before swallowing. Tempting to take another sip, I remember AJ's warning about what could happen if I have too much and set the glass down. I just hope it'll be enough.

"No one other than myself is worthy of this mark," she says, her voice sounding a bit distant now. As if she's remembering something. "Anyone who has it should be dead."

Should be dead. That's an odd way of saying that. . .

The arena clears and the sand settles. I sit up at the realization I have lost sight of Ntaoru.

"This next one will be even better. Have you ever seen a flying Ipani fight an oumala ostrich?"

"Can't say that I have. . ."

Her green eyes behind her mask enlarge as she twists in her seat. "Soren? Where did you go?"

I gasp and look down at my hands becoming more transparent by the second. This happened faster than last time. Is drinking it more potent than eating it? My surroundings change to a gray color as I fade into the Aō dimension.

The Empress leans on her seat and raises her hands furiously over her head. "Guards! Guards!"

Uh-oh! I start to get up but when I do, I lift off my seat. Completely weightless.

What's happening?

"Think of your clothes, Soren! Don't forget about your clothes!"

"My clothes? Gari?" Afraid to take my eyes off the Empress and the soldiers, I don't look for him. But I recognize his gurgling voice.

"Yes, remember what happened last time!"

"Oh right! So what do I do?"

"Think of what you were wearing and hold it in your mind. Let yourself float over the island, then listen to my instructions. Carefully."

"I'm all ears." I float out of the seating area as the Empress stands and guards surround her. She cries something about the use of magic and how I just vanished.

"She's not going to let that go," Gari sings. "You will have to be careful from here on out."

"Why did you give me the drink then?"

"How else were you going to get out of here? You did want to leave, didn't you?"

:Yes!"

"Well, good, because I wanted you to stay."

"What? Why?"

"But then I thought. . .nothing will get done this way," he gurgles. "It's better you go."

"Gari, what are you talking about?"

The island grounds grow smaller as I float over an overgrown mess of thorny branches intertwined to form a labyrinth surrounding the Tower. "Gari, what did the Ipani call this island again?"

"Rutavenye. It means Cloudwall. You can turn around now."

I spin myself around and see his large serpentine eyes and furry blue snout. His sparkly hair swooshes over his horns in the wind.

"Okay. How do I get down?"

"Get down?" He giggles. "Why would you want to do that? You'll dive into the water."

12

"WHAT DO YOU MEAN I'LL DIVE INTO THE WATER, Gari! Did you expect me to float around forever?"

"It's so easy to rile you up. Are you still thinking about your clothes?"

I gasp. "Yes!" Not really. . .but now I am! "Just tell me what to do next."

The biting wind of the night goes right through me as I float down from Rutavenye.

"Where is it you want to go?" He glides through the air beside me. His entire body is visible now and the silvery-blue trail of his tail follows where he goes. His twisted horns on his head glisten against the starlit sky as does the rest of his shimmery blue and purple hair. He reminds me of one of those flying Chinese dragons, except he's part drakon and part oumala.

"Well, I guess I need to go to Wands. But didn't you say they'd hunt us?"

"It'll be dangerous, but maybe that's half the fun! I hope you drank all the drink I gave you. Wands is a ways away, but it'll be a fun flight with me."

"You have an odd definition of fun. Wait. I only took a sip."

"Oh, well then, you haven't much time, have you?" He spins on his back and glides in front of me. "I was going to take you on my back, but only through the Aō. If you appear out of thin air, the Wands' Prefect will shoot you on sight. And if they find me. . ." He glides over to my other side. "They'll skin me for my fur. And I quite like my fur. . ."

"Gari! How much time do I have?"

"I haven't the slightest idea," he sings.

I shudder. "What happens when the magic runs its course?"

"You'll exit out of the Aō and you'll fall."

"I know that," I snap, feeling panic coursing through my veins. "But I came here through a portal and landed in the water. I didn't die even though I'm sure it was a far fall!" Actually, I don't remember the fall. . . I suppose the portal could have opened closer to the surface.

"Yes, but you had the World Card, didn't you? Magic was carrying you in. Oh," he gurgles, "you clearly don't have that with you now, do you?"

"No. But I'm in the Aō now, aren't I? Won't it be different? Isn't there. . .magic here?"

"The consequences are the same, I'm afraid."

And that's my luck. "Gari, what do I do?"

"Hmmmm. . ." He spins around my body as I float in the wind. "I'll be back."

"What? No, don't leave me!" He speeds ahead of me and disappears into the darkness below.

My skin prickles as the wind rushes past and I start to descend. Oh, no. . . As fast as the drink started working, it's already ending! I should have drunk more!

The gushing air races through my body. Clouds pass me by at a rapid pace, and my vision blurs. My chest tightens, and my lungs feel like they're about to collapse.

It's hard to breathe.

Nausea overwhelms me as the mountains come into view and the dark blue water gets closer and closer by the second, no longer the monotone gray. My body spins itself on its back and I know the magic has completely worn off. My eyes close as I try to shield my head.

Something big and fluffy catches me and we bounce in the air.

"Hang on, Soren."

I gasp for air, catching my breath. "Gari?"

"The one and only."

"Oh my god, Gari. . .I thought. . .I thought. . ."

"That you were plummeting to your death?"

"Yes!"

"I told you I'd be right back."

A loud sigh escapes my lips as I orient myself and grab onto his neck. How did he get so big? I guess if he can disappear and make himself small, he can stretch big enough to carry me too.

I press my face against his fur, right behind his fins. Looking over the horizon, I have a better view of this world. It's mostly sea, but there are mountain ranges up ahead. "Where are we going?"

"I found the *Devil's Gambit*."

"Oh." A mixture of feelings overwhelms me. Disappointment for starters, for not being able to escape and go to Wands. Fear of Iéle, fear of the Devil Nkella was turning into before I left, fear of what he will think or do now after he saw me vanish. But also, a buzz of excitement at seeing the crew and being in a familiar place in this world doesn't sound so bad right now.

"Don't sound too enthused. It was that or the serpent's belly."

"I'm fine!" I shout through the wind. "Thank you."

"We have company."

We do? I crane my neck and gasp. Long trails of black smoke zoom out of the sky from Rutavenye. Right, we're completely visible now. "Oh no! What are we going to do?"

"Hold on!"

Gari swoops down and I grip his body with my knees.

"Hold your breath!"

Hold my breath? My stomach lunges to my throat as he takes a deep dive straight down to the water. No no no no! The Minor Arcana nears us and materialize to our sides. One of them extends a smoky arm, but Gari dodges it. Another comes overhead from our left. I shut my eyes as Gari zigzags and spins into a cyclone motion, causing strong winds to push out all around us.

A second later, I'm taking a last-minute breath as we dive headfirst into the frigid ocean.

Once again, my bones ache at the impact of hitting water at high velocity. My body separates from Gari a little as he cuts through the water like an electric eel. I grip him tighter, bringing my legs closer and wrapping them around his core. At least I think it's his center? It's hard to tell on such a long body.

He stalls for a moment, and I try to squint through the water. But I feel like we've hit a wall or something. What's he staring at? I wish I could ask him but that would involve opening my mouth. Something moves slowly in front of us and my blood runs cold. That's not a wall.

Gari starts to back up. And that's when the thing in front of us snaps its body sideways, showing its face. Two giant yellow serpentine eyes glare at us as it opens its giant mouth, showing its long pointy fangs. The sea serpent.

13

I RESIST EVERY URGE TO SCREAM. TO SCREAM WOULD mean to drown.

Gari makes a sharp dive in front of the serpent. Deeper we go as we zip through a spot of darkness I can only imagine is a cave. His silver trail is the only thing lighting our path. I so want to look behind me to see how far away the serpent is and if he's following us, but I'm afraid if I do, I'll accidentally let go.

I'm not sure how much longer I can hold my breath but it's either drowning or being snake food. I'm not liking those options. I tap on Gari's sides as a muffled groan escapes me.

My breath is running out.

Next thing I know, we're swimming upward and my head rushes. He zooms faster, breaking us out of the water. I gasp for air. No time to think, I clutch onto his hair for dear life. The sea serpent springs from the water, and without warning, Gari zigzags to the side and away from the serpent's reach.

Water sprays my backside as a splash crashes behind us. I brave a glance behind me and no longer see the beast. It must have gone back into the water. "Yeah!" I yell. "You're not having us for dinner!"

"We're not out of danger yet."

"Right, the Minor Arcana." I squint through the night for any smoke soldiers flying around. "Maybe it's too dark for them to catch up?"

"Doubtful, but I think we may have lost them in our detour." His voice gurgles as he sing-songs, "They wouldn't check below waters."

We swim through the sky for about an hour as he moves his body into a calmer and steadier pace as we pass over Dempu Yuni, the trading post island. My hair is stuck to my skin but the rest of me is drying out. I wish those spiders had made me a jacket.

Down below, houses with their gas lamps lit look like fire ants from this high.

"Can they see us?" I ask.

"Maybe, maybe not. It's dark, but we're visible." He speeds up and I grip the knots of his fur. Seawater tickles my nostrils as he hovers closer to the surface.

"We're closing in on the ship."

"What ship?" I peer into the thick night but can't see a thing.

"You won't be able to see them. The *Gambit* is cloaked."

A hint of hope sparks in my bones. The Empress had asked the oumala spider about the captain, and she had said they got away. Harold must have been successful in making the cloaking potion.

"As we cut their cloaking blockade, you'll be able to see them and get in," he says. I wonder if I would be able to do that without Gari, because otherwise, anyone near could still see the ship. . .

"Hang on tight."

My body lifts as he speeds up and swoops down, swaying his tail from side to side. I grab onto him with my thighs and squeeze as tight as I can just as we hit the cloaking blockade. It's almost as if we're trying to go inside a balloon without popping it. I press my chest close to his back, and tuck my neck in, afraid to bounce off.

The giant masts of the ship come into view, only they're a little too close! I shut my eyes as Gari crash-lands on the bow of the ship, sending me flying off him and tumbling hard on the floorboard.

My legs drop to the floor and I sit up and rub my back. And my head. "Ow."

"Soren?" Harold's voice comes from above me and I crane my neck to see a blond-haired blue-eyed guy in front of the wheel.

"Harold? You're steering the ship?"

"Somebody has to. Where the hell did you go?" he whispers. "And what are you wearing?"

I look down and let out a sigh of relief. "At least I managed to keep my clothes on this time." I glance back at Gari. He winks at me, shrinks in size, and waves his tail right before disappearing back into the Aō dimension.

"Was that the drakon?"

"Yeah. . ." I scurry to my feet and run up to the quarter-deck. The wind picks up, and I pull my hair back. The view is a lot better from up here. My eyes fall to the wheel and a round bottle with a sage green solution strapped and connected to the center of it. Copper tubing sticks from behind the wheel and disappears into the floorboards. Huh. Interesting.

"We were wondering where you went. Nkella is angry as heck."

My heart sinks to my stomach. "Angry? With me?" The last look he gave me was confusion. What does he think happened?

"Where did you go?"

"They took me to Rutavenye."

He gapes at me and turns from the wheel. "You were up in the Tower? Did you meet the Empress?"

I nod and explain the last few hours from meeting the Empress, Nkella's sister, and the Ipani versus oumala animal fights, up until now. His face blanks as I tell him the whole story. "How did you end up captaining the ship?" I ask.

He scoffs. "I'm hardly a captain. But luckily, I had enough potions left in my belt to get things under control." He points to the bottle on the wheel and I notice he's barely done any actual steering since I got here.

"Don't you need to like. . .hold the wheel to steer it?"

"Oh, so this ship is pretty cool." He points down to a smaller bottle with a chunky orange goo inside it strapped to a different mechanism by his foot. "See that? That's like auto-drive for this ship."

"Oh, sounds pretty easy to captain this ship then."

"Well, someone still has to be here in case something happens. All the auto potion will do is keep it going straight, and if it runs out, we're on manual."

"Oh." Makes me wonder what else this ship can do.

"I ended up having to tranquilize the real captain and tie him up."

My jaw drops. "Nkella is tied up?"

"In his bed, yeah."

"You *tranqued* him?" I ask, unsure of whether to be relieved or freaked out.

"Mhmm. Don't worry, I'll untie him at sunrise."

"How did you manage that?"

"It wasn't easy but I had help. Curse day is not fun. When he got back on the ship, after you. . .disappeared, he totally raged out. His eyes went full on red-glowing like in *Dominion*. My bomb managed to blow the other ship up and get everyone back here safely, but the Minor Arcana popped back in. . .Nkella. . .or rather, the Devil inside of him, took them all at once."

"What happened to them?"

"The Minor Arcana?" He lets out a long breath. "He killed them."

My eyes narrow. "But how? The Empress holds the Death Card. You told me that."

He flicks his eyes to me.

"Oh. You mean he sent them to eternal torture."

"Which is why his curse is so scary. And what's weird is. . .they were completely lifeless. We rounded up their bodies to throw them overboard, but they finally disappeared after about half an hour."

"So, they might still be alive?"

"It didn't look like it. Usually, they vanish and return, even if impaled."

"So, Nkella's curse lets him kill the Empress's army."

Harold shrugs his right shoulder. "I'm still trying to figure it out. But"—he lowers his voice and leans in—"he doesn't remember a thing."

"How do you know?"

"He kept looking for them, saying they'll be back. Repeating the same thing over and over. We don't think he remembers anything."

"Oh, that reminds me. The Empress told me she is Fate incarnate, and she also mentioned something about her knowing people's present."

His brows furrow. "I knew I was right. That confirms she's the Fate of people's present then."

"So, what does that mean?" I ask.

He leans his head back. "Nothing good. Probably that there are two more Fates around. My guess is, being that she's the Fate of the present, she knows what everyone is doing."

My mouth gapes. "Everyone?"

"Well, she can't go into the Aō dimension. That much we've learned, right? Which makes sense of why the crew wants the ship sailing under the radar." He taps on the orange-liquid bottle.

"Why is the Empress after him, anyway?"

He shrugs. "If he can kill Arcana soldiers, what if the Devil Card is strong enough to defeat her?"

I screw up my face. "I can't even begin to wonder why that would make sense." I stare out at the sea. "Where's the rest of the crew?"

"I told them I'd keep watch tonight. Kind of felt creepy having skeletons walking around. . ."

I wipe my face. "This place is so weird. On a regular day, it appears their skeletons show up if the seawater hits them. But on curse day, they remain that way, and Nkella loses his mind.”

“Yeah.” He chuckles. “But at least they’re not Frost Giants.”

I do a double take and grunt.

He stifles a chuckle. “Why don’t you get some rest?”

“Don’t you need help?”

“No, I’ll get AJ when I get tired. We’re taking turns.”

I yawn and stretch my arms. “Okay, good night then.”

“Oh, Soren?”

I glance at him over my shoulder.

“You’re 100 percent sure it was Nkella’s sister you saw fighting?”

“It really was, yes.”

“Don’t tell Nkella.”

I gulp. “Don’t tell Nkella his sister is alive? But. . .”

“Each time Nkella gets angry, it’s a step closer to the Devil inside him coming out. I would let him find out once we’re long gone.”

I take a deep breath and hold it. When I tried to run from him back at Dempu Yuni, he said, *Each time you make me angry, you will pay.* He was trying to keep his cool. That’s why he was so calm after, up until the fight at the tavern. “Right. . .okay, I see your point.”

“Don’t worry. We’ll get out of here soon enough. That’s their problem, not ours.”

“Yeah. . . For sure.” I turn to leave and head to bed.

My eyes blink open, and I catch a glimpse of a long black coat. I take a few breaths before I remember where I am and jump out of my skin. "Nkella?"

Nkella's voice is like steel. "You were with the Empress." His eyes are sharp with intensity, his expression cold.

I swallow and clear my throat, scurrying up on the bed and covering my chest with my blanket. I'm wearing the clothes from last night, but still. "They took me to the floating island," I croak.

AJ sticks his head through the curtain. "Soren? You're back? And you met the Empress?"

"She went back to her. Utwa," he accuses.

My jaw drops, and I fling the covers off me and stand. "Seriously? I dove into the ocean to save you! And you still call me a spy?"

His eyes flash as they linger on me.

My cheeks go hot. Up until now I've gone from wearing an ugly orange prison uniform or his sister's baggy clothes. This is the first time I'm wearing something that shows my curves.

He quickly collects himself, dragging his gaze back to my face, and grimaces. "They fetched you for your reports because you are an utwa."

So much for thinking things would be different now. We're back to square one.

An amber glow flickers behind his dark irises, shadowed by his captain's hat. The horns protruding from his skull flashes in my memory. I need to not piss him off. Is the curse still active even though it's the next day?

"You're wrong," I tell him.

"Captain—" AJ starts. I stare at AJ; his face is back to being smooth with a little goatee and long black wavy hair loose around his shoulders.

"Daí? You still defend her, even now? After Lāri was taken because we were late, because of rescuing her?" He waves his hand at me.

My throat dries. I knew they were thinking it.

"First off, need I remind you, you're the one who stopped to rescue Soren," AJ states.

My lips part. Devil captain did what now?

"Kaehante spotted her."

"But you stopped. So stop pretending like you don't care."

"Until I learned she is a spy."

"But she isn't." AJ crosses his arms.

I lift my arm and show him the *O* mark AJ painted on me to show I wouldn't even want the Empress to see my mark, but it's completely washed away, revealing that damn web.

Nkella scoffs.

"AJ had covered it with makeup so that no one would recognize me," I tell him. "The Empress thinks I have the Fool's mark. If I were really her spy, I wouldn't have cared to cover it."

He snaps his gaze to AJ. "You helped her to blend in?"

"So that she wouldn't be a target."

"But you know what?" I interrupt. "While I was up there, I did become a spy."

AJ smacks his forehead. "Soren, what are you doing?"

I face Nkella head-on, our noses almost touching in this little room.

Nkella raises his chin.

"For you," I say.

"Kh."

"They're alive."

He narrows his eyes at me, unbudging.

"The Minor Arcana. I found out they're alive."

"How do you know this?"

"I was able to get some information out of the Empress," I say carefully, heeding Harold's warning.

Gaze still fixed on me, he quirks a brow and tilts his head to AJ. "Steer the ship."

AJ sighs, then nods, giving me one last glance before leaving us alone.

"Bancha." Nkella lowers his voice to a hoarse whisper. "Why would you save me?"

I cross my arms. "I still don't know what bancha means."

"It means stupid."

Great. I knew it was an insult. "First off, I saved you because AJ, Tessa, and Kaehante need their captain, and I like them. Two, I wasn't about to let anyone drown and be happy about it, and three. . ."

He flicks his eyes to the floor as if trying to decide if what I'm saying is true.

"You saved me first." I pause and clear my throat. "I almost got hit by that cannon."

"Kh." He touches his forehead, then lets out three raspy laughs. "You fool. What good are you to me dead?"

"What do you mean?"

He snickers. "Why do you think I keep you alive?"

The memory of AJ and Kaehante talking at the barrels resurfaces. *Don't get attached*, Kaehante had said. Nkella's been meaning to hand me in, this much I've gathered. "Why didn't you just give me up when the Minor Arcana was here then?"

"What good will it do if they overpower me, daí? Turning you over will be done on my terms."

I need to convince him not to turn me in. I can't get back to Talia if I'm dead. If I tell him I saw his sister fighting in that arena, he might escalate his plans on using me as a bargaining chip. Besides, Harold warned me not to say anything that would send him over the edge. His fierce dark eyes bore into me as I struggle to find the right words.

I calmly explain everything that happened and the questions I asked the Empress, but I leave out who was fighting in the arena and tell him it was a flying Ipani versus an oumala ostrich instead.

His eyes squint as I finish talking.

"You still don't believe me?"

"Maybe you tell the truth. Maybe you don't. Ko kwela mū. But. . ." He smiles. "The Empress will still want to know the truth."

"What's that supposed to mean?"

"Hn," he smirks.

"You still want to trade me for your sister." In return for some truth about who he thinks I am because of this stupid mark. That's what that means. "Even after I saved your life. Even after I spied on the Empress for you?"

His face darkens and a spot below his eye jumps. "Ko kwela mū."

My brows furrow. Those words sound familiar. . . "You've said that about me before, right? To Kaehante. . ."

"'It does not make a difference.' *That's* what it means."

I swallow the dry lump in my throat. Maybe I should have left him to drown. I thought perhaps, beneath the Devil inside, he was good. I tighten my arms around myself. "No, I guess it doesn't make a difference. So, what now then? Am I still your prisoner?"

His lip curls upward, giving me a glance at his sharp canines. "Comfortable prisoner."

"What if I try to leave?"

"Daf? Be my guest." His chin raises.

"When we get to Wands, I'll go." I have my own mission anyway.

He smirks and I get an uneasy feeling in the pit of my stomach.

"You don't think I will, do you?"

He chuckles twice.

"Why not?"

"Either you get caught again by the Arcana Army and you don't go home or you stay alive a little longer. You choose. Good luck surviving Sāgirang."

He's not convinced I am a spy after all. Also, he's bluffing; he's not going to let me walk away when we get to Wands. "What makes you so sure the Empress will kill me?"

"Why did you hide your mark?" He crosses his arms.

"Because everyone keeps telling me to. What if I tell the Empress the truth?"

"Then maybe she'll let you go home, and I'll get my sister back. We both win."

I press my lips together. At least he's not mad about me punching him in the face. Silver linings? "Part of you thinks I'm telling the truth, that I'm not some double agent."

He stretches his neck, his Ipani stripe peeking out from his coat collar. "Thank you for the information on my sister. Now go be a comfortable prisoner, or you'll be in the same cage as the current occupant."

I swallow and back away but then stop myself.

"No."

His face hardens.

I'm not letting this end like this. I'm sick of being a prisoner and I need that World Card. "Look, you can hate me all you want. And believe me, the feeling's mutual."

"Kh."

I bite down a sigh. "For some reason, I have this mark, and I don't know why."

He stares at me coldly.

"Despite what you think, I really don't. But what we do know is, the card can change for me, right?"

He rubs his chin. "Keep talking."

"You need to save a member of your crew, and the World Card is a portal, isn't it? Maybe it can even take you to your sister. But for that, you'll need me to use it. Maybe it can even show where they are."

His brows knit together. "I have Iéle."

"Fine, your wolf can find people. The World Card can get you there quicker, but you'll still have the problem of your sister being stuck as one of the Empress's agentless soldiers." When he doesn't respond, I keep talking. "The drakon told me the Ace of Wands Card can do anything. Maybe it can help get us all what we want. Maybe it can release your sister."

His frown deepens. "The Ace of Wands is protected by the Empress's magic at the Karst Temples."

"Right. And didn't you say that's where Iéle heard they're taking Lāri and the other kidnapped Ipani?" I ask.

He passes his hands over his lips, and his eyes narrow, as if considering what I'm saying. . .or unsure what to reveal. "Yes," he finally says. "It seems the card is what they are after, aside from ouma."

I scrunch my features. If the crew thinks I'm the only one who can use the World Card—a card from the Empress's Tarot deck, then— "What do the traffickers want with the Ace of Wands? Can they even use it?"

"That I do not know, and it is not my business. I care only about saving my sister, and Lāri."

"And defeating the Empress."

"Kh. That is the crew's dream. She cannot be defeated."

"But they think you're in it to try and fight her."

"I want Danū back. That is all."

"And you intend to do all that with what? Your fists? Or that Devil you keep fighting inside you?"

A small glow flashes behind his irises, but I hold my ground.

"Harold says the Hierophant—Demitri—must want me for something. Otherwise, he would have called the Arcana soldiers to take me to the Empress. But instead, he wanted to buy me for himself. Why?"

"That is what I have been trying to figure out."

I glance at my mark. "It has something to do with this. That we know. The question is what."

He chuckles to himself. "You and I both know you know the truth, gembella."

I purse my lips together. "I don't. But. . . Could it have something to do with the Ace of Wands? Demitri must be trying to use it somehow, maybe I'm just his easy ticket to do so."

His eyes widen.

"That's possible, isn't it? That's what he wants me for." I cross my arms.

He looks to the side, his brows furrowed, deep in thought. Like he's piecing something together.

"I can't imagine that would be good. He could use it for *anything.*"

"This drakon. You trust him?" His eyes flick back to me.

I clench my fist, struggling with the concept of trusting a mythical creature that accidentally almost got me killed. But then he saved me. "I think he also wants to save this land."

"The drakons came with the Empress. Just like the sea serpent."

"So did half your crew. She outlawed magic, which means he's also in danger every day he's here."

He quirks a brow, his gaze lingering on my face. Despite the hatred he displayed earlier, he seems more contemplative now. Hopefully, he's considering my words.

I need to get home no matter what happens to these people. And who knows if I can use the World Card to get out the same way I came in. That Ace of Wands seems to be my last resource if I can't figure out the former, *if* Nkella lets me practice with it. Either way, it's to his benefit that I do.

"Let us help each other," I push. "You can save your family, and I can go home. Then you'll never see me again."

His eyes narrow. Does he believe me? Would he believe any words that come out of an utwa? Or hearsay from a drakon?

Probably not. My heart starts to race and I swallow. What *would* the Empress do to me if he trades me in for his sister?

No one else has it. Anyone who does should be dead.

Yeah, she'll probably kill me. "Do we have a deal?" I stare into his dark eyes as they search mine. Trying to figure out if I'm telling the truth.

He inches closer, forcing me to back up against the wall. His scent of leather and hickory engulfs my senses as he lowers his face close to my ears. I hold my breath. "Comfortable prisoner. We have a deal, until you disappoint me."

"I won't," I whisper.

"Hn."

14

Kaehante's voice carries through the morning wind as I climb up the stern of the ship.

"And you're sure this is strong enough?" Harold tugs on a tight rope, his feet sliding against the floor.

"Yes. Very strong." Kaehante says. "It is the most useful type of knot on a ship."

Harold stops tugging on it and unravels the rope. "But it gets loose so easily."

AJ chuckles. "That's what makes it so useful. No matter how tight the knot gets, it can easily be undone. Makes it advantageous in emergencies." He cranes his neck and nods at me, his face more solemn than usual.

"Okay, try the knot again, just as I showed you." Kaehante instructs. I make my way closer to them as Harold holds out the rope, crosses the loose side over, loops it around, and then unravels it again. "Ah, sorry. I messed up."

"Try again," Kaehante says. "Soren, you try with this rope," he grabs another from behind him and lifts it toward me.

I point to my chest. "Me?"

"Yeah, that's not a bad idea," AJ says. "Seeing as how we have five to six weeks till we reach Sāgirang, you should learn the ropes in case we need you."

Sāgirang is Wands, I remind myself. "Five to six weeks? At sea?" I think I'm gonna be sick.

Creases wrinkle across AJ's forehead and guilt twists me into knots again.

"This is called a bowline, daí?" Kaehante tells me, using his inflexion as a way to ask me if I understand. It makes me think about the ways Nkella uses it. I wonder if it's an Ipani thing or a Danū thing. "First, you will loop this side of the line. Then, with the slack part, you will go underneath—"

"Comfortable gembella"—Nkella's dark voice spins me around, and Kaehante quickly turns his attention back to Harold—"take off those clothes."

My cheeks burn as I touch my intricate spiderweb garment and then my eyes fall on the clothes he's holding out to me. Oh. "I have a name, you know."

"Hn."

Reaching for the red blouse and black torn pants that belong to his sister, I hesitate. "I thought you didn't want me wearing your sister's clothes."

"I want the Empress's guises on my ship even less," he snaps. "And it is important you blend in when we get to Sāgirang."

Right. "I'll go change then." I turn to face the others. "Sorry, guys, I'll practice later."

"I'll make breakfast in a few minutes," AJ says. My stomach growls. I haven't had a decent meal in days, and no offense to AJ, I don't think I can take any more stale bread.

"Mind if I try my hand in the kitchen?"

AJ gives me a slanted smile. "That bad, huh?"

"No, it's not that, just thought I could help, is all. Seeing as how I messed up with the powder. . ." My blood drains from my face. We're going to be at sea for more than a month without gunpowder. And it's all my fault.

"What's this about the powder?" Nkella asks.

Kaehante cuts me off before I can get a word in. "It got wet. It was my fault, Captain." I part my lips and stare at Kaehante.

He squints his eyes at Kaehante then moves them to me. "Fine. Do not poison us." The corners of his lips curl into a smirk as he turns to leave.

AJ lets out a giggle and Kaehante laughs. I roll my eyes.

I watch Nkella walk back to the quarterdeck and resist the urge to smile. It's obvious to me he didn't believe Kaehante but is keeping his anger banked. Choosing his battles. Works for me.

I turn back to Kaehante. "Thank you. You didn't have to do that. I'll find a way to make it up to you. . ."

He chuckles. "None of us want to keep watching you suffer. Besides, we did not have much powder left. Had we used it, we would be out now anyway."

Unease settles in my stomach. No one's ever had my back like that before. And he barely knows me. . .why would he lie to his own captain for me? I stare at him, conflicted and confused as he continues teaching Harold how to tie a knot. No one can be that sincere, right? Especially not a pirate. I swallow. That might not be fair to AJ. . .

These aren't the stereotypical pirates, and I get that, but even still, I can't allow myself to get too comfortable around them.

Stomach grumbling, I quickly dash to my room and change clothes—God, that feels better. Although stylish, the outfit those spiders wove me was not comfortable. I finish tying up my boots and head to the kitchen.

The musky smell of wood and humidity greets me as I step onto the small cooking area.

Okay, so what do we have? Skimming the kitchen, my eyes land on a clean countertop with a single bag of flour and a smaller one of sugar. Great, at least those are two dry ingredients they keep. But I don't see a refrigerator or cooler of any kind. . . This might be a challenge. Rummaging through the cabinets, I find. . .nothing.

Just a bowl of bread rising on the countertop behind me. I'm starting to think it isn't AJ's fault he hasn't cooked a decent meal. Over to the right, near a small circular window is a burlap bag. I peek inside. Booyah! Potatoes! At least they have potatoes in this world. Okay, I think I know what I'm going to do.

Footsteps near the entrance of the kitchen. "Need any help?"

I flick my eyes over to AJ standing with a sullen look on his face. "I thought you'd want to be on the main deck, helping with the sails," I say.

"It's a straight path for now. Nkella's got it."

"I see. In that case, grab a knife and help me peel some potatoes?"

AJ grabs two knives out from a drawer and hands me one. He pulls out a bucket and takes a seat. I sit down across from him next to the sack of potatoes. "You didn't have anything else planned for these, did you?"

He shakes his head. "Kaehante grabbed that sack before rushing to get back since we weren't able to complete our shopping list. I haven't had a chance to think of what to make for Nkella."

Grabbing a potato, I begin to peel. "Do you always consider what Nkella wants to eat?"

He furrows his brows. "Hm? Oh. . . No. The rest of us get hungry but we can't taste anything so. . ." his voice trails off.

Oh. "Is that because of. . ."

"The curse. Yeah." He starts peeling quicker.

I hadn't even considered they can't taste food. And yet, they still feel hunger. That must be horrible. To be able to feel emotion, pain, hunger, but not be able to satisfy any of it. For someone stuck in impending doom, AJ really is a beacon of hope. "I'm sure you'll break the curse, AJ. . . I'm sorry this is happening to you, to all of you."

"As long as we stay dry, you won't see my bones. Except on—"

"Curse day."

He smiles. "That's right."

"So, what happens if you go for a swim?"

"We don't float, that's for sure."

I blink. "So, you'll all just sink to the bottom of the ocean? Indefinitely?"

"All except the captain." The corner of his lip curls up. "Of the four of us, Nkella is the only one who is not undead. His curse is different, as you saw." He glints up at me, a tiny smile creasing his lips, but then goes back to peeling. He finishes one and I grab it and start slicing it up in tiny slivers.

"That sounds horrible." I look back down at my potato.

He glances up. "What are you doing?"

I chuckle. "I'm making something called hash browns. I noticed you don't have any milk or butter, so these won't be as great as I could make back home, but I'm hoping it'll be something different for you guys. . ." Although now that I know they can't taste anything, I guess Nkella and Harold are the ones who will be judging it.

"Well, I'm excited then," he says, without much excitement in his voice.

"How are you holding up?"

He sighs deeply. "I'm not. I just want to find her. I'm worried sick." His voice breaks. "I'm trying not to think about it but. . . What if they've—"

I put the potato down and lean over. "Hey. No, stop it. She's a badass eagle-shifting Ipani. I'm sure wherever they have her, she's giving them hell."

"She can't go into the Aō though, Soren. Ipani can't. Otherwise, she'd be able to escape."

"Even still. I don't know her, but she sounds tough. Can't Iéle find her?"

"Nkella has her doing that already, but they must have unbound Ipani with them, as well as oumala familiars. They can throw off Iéle's scent. Especially if they're using magic."

Hmm. . . "I wonder if the drakon can find her."

His eyes flick up at me. "Do you think so?"

I shrug. "He shows up every now and then. I'll ask him if he turns up."

"Thanks, Soren. That would be helpful. Drakons aren't as instinctive and primal as wolves are." He hands me another potato and I start to slice it. A few moments pass as we continue to peel and slice before I glance at him.

"AJ?"

He looks up from his potato.

"W-why is—um. . . What did Nkella do? To be cursed as. . .the Devil, I mean."

AJ swallows and grows quiet. He glances at the kitchen entrance and lowers his voice. "He tried to kill her."

"Who?"

"The Empress. And he almost succeeded."

I gasp. That's what she meant by treason. "Were you all together?" That's probably how she got his sister too. . . "How did he almost succeed?"

"He stole the Death Card. We snuck into the Tower, found the Tarot deck while she slept, and with the Death Card in his hands, he almost slit her throat."

I snap my mouth shut; I didn't realize I had it open. "What stopped him?

"It didn't work. It isn't so easy as stealing a card, but we didn't know this back then. She woke up and caught him, knife in hand."

"How did you escape?"

"With Iéle's help and bites of ouma ipononchi."

"The magic cookies."

He nods.

"Our curses were already taking effect when we reached the

ship. The rest of us were guilty by association but. . .she took Nkella's betrayal the most personal for some reason. Ntaoru didn't get a chance to escape. The Empress had her soldiers grab her and cursed Nkella with the worst fate."

"It's bad being the Devil. . .huh?"

His eyebrows rise to the top of his head. "The longer he stays that way, the more he loses himself. But worse than that, she bound his oumala power."

"He was unbound before?" That makes sense, since his sister's was unbound.

He nods. "Do you know what happens when the Empress binds an Ipani?"

I shake my head.

"She can transfer that magic to herself or to her army. She's basically harvested his power and has the Minor Arcana killing and abusing his own people in Danū."

My jaw slackens.

"And he had to stand by and watch as his people were being killed by his own ouma. There was nothing he could do about it."

The creaking of the ship breaks our silence as it rocks back and forth. We work as I let his words sink in. I'm not sure what any of that even means—the Devil inside him. Is it literally another being sharing his body? Or is it just pent-up rage dying to come out? And what happens if—or when it does?

"Soren? I didn't scare you, did I?"

"Mmm. . . nope! Sorry, almost done. Can you turn on the stovetop?"

He gets up and lights a fire under the burner. "How are you holding up? About your sister I mean. . ."

I grab a bowl from the counter and start gathering the potato slices into it.

I swallow. "I guess like you, I'm trying not to think about what's happening over there, but it's difficult not to. If I don't stay focused on getting out of here, I'll drive myself crazy. And. . . I'm already feeling kind of crazy, so. . ." I finish slicing up the last potato and carry the overflowing bowl to the stove. Six potatoes should do it. And if it doesn't, it's still better than what they've been eating.

AJ watches as I fry the potato slices over the stovetop. It's pretty primitive in nature, just a metal slab over fire, but it's still curious to me how some things are still similar to my world.

Harold pokes his head in through the entryway. "Are you cooking hash browns?"

"Yep!"

"No way! That smells amazing!"

I chuckle. "Don't hold your breath. There's no butter, no milk, and no ketchup."

He shrugs. "Can't be too picky around here. No offense, AJ."

AJ grabs a small ceramic jug and tips it over the cooking plate. A tiny bit of oil drizzles out. "Despite my lack of taste buds, with the proper ingredients, I'm a good cook. I'll show you two someday."

"I'll be looking forward to it." I smile. Except there won't be any time for that to happen; I'm just being polite.

"I'd better start prepping the cured meat and bread for later." AJ moves past me and heads over to the bowl with the rising dough. I pass Harold a look and he comes over as I flip the hash browns.

"I think Nkella and I are finally at an understanding," I whisper, flicking a glance over his shoulder to make sure the captain himself isn't standing at the entrance.

He leans in closer and quirks a brow. "Why do you say that?"

"I think we have a plan that can help all of us."

AJ cranes his head over his shoulder, listening to us. "All of us?"

"Care to elaborate?" Harold asks.

I might as well share this with AJ, too, especially if it can help get his girlfriend back. And possibly break the crew's curse. "I told him about the Ace of Wands."

"The Ace of Wands?" AJ asks. "What do you know about that?"

"Only that the drakon told me it can do anything, maybe even get me out of here, and break your curse."

He turns around. "I thought those were just stories though."

My heart plummets. "But then why would the World Card show it to me?"

"Show it to you?" AJ takes a handful of flour from a bag and starts spreading it on a wooden cutting board. "How do you mean?"

"When Nkella came to me in the brig and tried to get me to use it to go back home, it changed its picture."

Harold's eyes widen. "The card changed?"

I give him a quick nod and cut the hash browns up to serve

them on wooden plates. "The drakon—I call him Gari by the way—said it's a Quartermaster Card."

He squints his eyes to the room. "It's worth a try, I guess. Nkella believes that?"

"He seems to think it's a possibility. . ."

AJ gives me a side-eye as he turns back to the dough. "Hmm. . ." He scratches his head.

"Well," Harold starts. "Let's hope we can get to the island before being seen. We're running low on solerig potion, so the invisibility will run out soon."

AJ stares at him. "How low?"

"It's hard to say. This isn't my magic; I'm still learning as I go."

"Looks like you're a fast learner then," AJ says as he grabs wooden forks from one of the drawers.

"I can weave my way around it." He grabs a plate of hash browns from the counter. "Besides, I like learning new things."

The three of us take the plates up to the main deck and set them on the two large barrels. Soon Tessa drives up, followed by Kaehante wiping his hands of cannon grease. I sit close to AJ and Harold, with the plate of hash browns on my lap to leave room for the rest of them. A barrel doesn't exactly make a large table. Nkella's heavy footing reaches us and I glance up.

"Dai? What is this?"

"They're called hash browns," I say. "Try some."

"They're delicious, Soren," Harold says with a mouth full of potato. "Thank you!"

I playfully elbow his arm. "No problem."

AJ sticks a forkful in his mouth. "If I had all my taste buds, I'm sure I'd be saying the same thing."

Kaehante chuckles deeply, his large shoulders moving up and down as he does.

Tessa, who has been quietly listening, pulls out a stool with her right hand for Nkella to take a seat. He stops it with his foot and curls his lips.

"You said it was okay if I cook, right?" I ask.

"Hn." He takes his seat and stabs the hash browns with his fork, bringing it up to his nose. He sniffs it, then sticks it in his mouth. I wait expectantly for him to say something but when he doesn't, I bring my eyes back to my plate.

Harold clears his throat and takes a swig from his canteen, breaking the ice. "So, we have no gunpowder. And are running low on solerig. Now what?"

"We stay unseen," Nkella says.

"Where we are going"—Kaehante scrapes his plate—"is very dangerous. We need all the weapons we can get."

"If Wands is so dangerous, can I have a weapon?" I ask. I know I should be saying Sāgirang around them, but Wands is so much easier to pronounce.

Nkella snickers between bites. "Koj."

"That means no, right?" At least, I've assumed so.

"Yes, it means no."

"So how am I going to defend myself?"

He glances up at me. "You will be safe with me."

"Well, that's comforting."

"So, what's the plan for getting the Ace of Wands?" Harold interrupts. "Soren, you said the World Card opened a portal for you, right?"

"That's right." I stick another forkful in my mouth and glance at Nkella.

"And then it changed to show you the Ace of Wands?" Harold continues.

"Mm-hmm." I cut a bit of the corner of my hash browns.

He pauses, thinking for a second.

"Sounds too unpredictable."

I flick my eyes at him.

"What do you mean?" Nkella asks, finishing off his plate. The corner of my lip curls. Looks like he liked it. Or maybe he's just hungry, seeing as how an undead person who can't taste anything has been doing the cooking with minimal ingredients.

"Shouldn't she at least practice trying to get the card to work?" Harold asks.

"Hnn..."

My heart skips a beat. If Harold convinces him to give me the card...maybe I can manage to open a portal back home...

Nkella brings his hands up to his lips and narrows his eyes at me.

I swallow my last bite and my eyes dart from him to Nkella. AJ snorts. A few seconds pass by and I start collecting their plates. AJ stops me and picks them up.

Nkella still hasn't taken his eyes off me, but I do my best not to look at him.

Tessa leans in and faces me. "Do you want to help me out today?"

"Oh?" A memory of Tessa mixing solutions together at a moment's notice to create an explosive potion to throw at the sea serpent resurfaces in my mind.

"Yes," she repeats, "we don't have a lot of material, but we'll need to make potion bombs for when we get to Sāgirang."

"You want me to help you make bombs? Me? I thought you said you didn't want me to help."

"I think you'll be fine. Harold will also be with us, but I presume he'll also be helping with the sails."

"Might be good for you to learn, Soren," Harold chimes in as he licks his fingers. I cringe.

I flick my eyes over to Kaehante. "Is it okay if I go with Tessa today?" I have no idea why I felt the need to ask him for permission.

"Hn. I am not the one you should ask, and the armory is a mess. But we have about a week at sea."

"No."

I dart my eyes to Nkella who finally spoke after minutes of staring at me. "No? No to what?"

"No to you being alone with the World Card. But with me, yes."

"Oh. . . Okay then." He seems completely unbothered by Tessa's request. I flick my gaze to Kaehante who shrugs back.

"So will you be ready to help?" Tessa asks, seemingly ignoring Nkella's hard stares.

I split my gaze away from Nkella and raise my brows to her. "Am I ready to learn how to make magic bombs?" Can I say, hell yes! Or should I pretend that I don't want to? I mean. . . They're freaking magic bombs! "I just hope I don't blow myself up."

She laughs. "So do I. An accident can mean we all go down."

I gulp.

"After she feeds the prisoner," Nkella announces.

I gape at him and exchange glances with Harold and AJ. "You want me to do what now?"

"Captain, let me do it," AJ says.

Kaehante glances up from his plate. "Does he need to eat at all?"

AJ shoots him a scornful look.

Nkella raises a brow and curls his lips. "No. You have all been right all along. The comfortable prisoner needs to earn her keep. And learn the ropes if she wants to survive on this ship. She should know what happens to traitors in the brig."

Earn my keep? I just made breakfast! "Fine. I'll feed the prisoner. What's the big deal?"

"Nothing, you'll be fine." AJ pats my hand.

I clutch the small plate with day-old bread as I slowly step on the creaky wooden steps that lead to where I used to lay my head, the brig. Apparently, they're protective over their chewy dried meat and there aren't any hash browns left, not that we'd share it with a prisoner. So, stale bread is what he's going to get. I still wish AJ or someone would have come down with me.

The drip drip drip of water coming through the sides of the brig greet me as a reminder of when I was kept down here. The flickering lantern inside the all-too-familiar darkness washes over me with a sense of familiarity. This is one place I never wanted to come back to. But at least this time, I'm not the one behind those metal bars.

Taking a deep breath, I push the door slowly open and am

met with a sliver of light coming through the wooden panels. I remember the sliver of light. . . At night, it was nothing but darkness unless Gari graced me with his presence. Nkella never even left the door open to allow the lantern light to get through. Okay, here goes nothing.

"Umm. . .I brought you some—"

I'm pulled to my left with incredible force. I try to scream but someone presses a hand against my mouth and jerks my neck backward. The plate drops to the floor with a clatter. Something sharp presses against my throat.

"Do not move. Do not speak," he hisses as he presses his hand over my nose and mouth. My chest pants as I reach for his pinky to pull it down but feel. . .a talon? What the hell?

He moves me back and I backpedal, stumbling over him as he locks me against his chest with his arm.

"Move and I will cut your vein."

I get a better glimpse at his morphed bird-like talon under my chin as the door creaks open, letting in more light.

Scarlet glowing eyes prowl through the door, followed by a menacing growl.

The next thing I know, Iéle lunges at my face.

15

the prisoner's throat. The guy grabs for her snout, releasing his hold on me. The ship sways and my back slams against the wall, toppling me to the ground.

The Ipani man is slammed against the wall as Iéle cuts deep into his neck.

Nkella's husky voice comes from the door. "Enough."

Iéle lets go and Nkella strides over. He picks the man up off the floor and blood drips over his hands. Iéle stays by his feet.

"Hn. I thought you were bound." Nkella's voice is calm and collected.

A sly smile crosses his face. "I am." His hand morphs back to having five fingers.

"Rikorō." Nkella tightens his fist around the man's neck.

"Sometimes it takes a while to work. Lucky me."

I remember them mentioning that word back at the tavern and I want to know what it means but now's not the time to ask him. "How did you get out of the cage?" I ask bird-beak between heavy breaths, clutching my chest.

Nkella's pointy ear twitches but he keeps his gaze on the prisoner.

"I was hungry and desperate. I found an old ipononchi under the metal."

"Gross. It was mush." Yuck.

Nkella huffs.

Yeah, that was my bad. I give him an apologetic look even though he refuses to take his eyes off the prisoner.

"I spared you for one reason only, traitor. Who is in charge of the Ipani trafficking?"

The prisoner chuckles loudly. Speckles in Nkella's eyes give off a glow and I take a step back. He shoves him hard against the wall, lifting him off his feet and hitting his head against the wood. Iéle's growl intensifies and the Ipani's hands morph back into large talons that grip Nkella's hand. His nose morphs into a pointy beak only to fade back to regular size. He already had a bird-like beak, now he has a real one.

Blood drips from his mouth as he coughs. He lifts his chin and squares his eyes to Nkella. "Besēla," he sneers.

Nkella guffaws and I startle. "The rikorō is already killing you. And you are still for the cause? An innocent died for you to use their power."

A grin spreads across the Ipani's face. "The ends justify the means. We will prevail against the Empress as one." He coughs some more, spitting out blood.

Nkella narrows his eyes. "The Empress?"

What's he thinking? I don't understand. . .

Nkella laughs. "Did you think the Empress would come to

bring your death? We are cloaked. You will suffer forever instead, because she will never find you."

"Liar." He coughs. "You are running low on transparency."

I gulp. "Wait. . . Did this jackass board the ship just to die so that the Empress uses her Death Card and finds us?" Hold up. How would the Empress find him? My mind drifts to the throne room on Rutavenye. *No deaths I'm waiting on are present. Let them suffer.* My eyes widen. She knows when people die *because* she has the Death Card.

"Be quiet." Nkella growls at me. My mouth snaps shut. Nkella stays silent for a minute as the man continues to cough.

"Who is in charge of the trafficking?" he snaps.

The Ipani laughs again, and I can tell Nkella is desperately trying to hold it together. If he rages out. . .we're screwed. And I'm the closest in the vicinity. I start moving toward the door. . . And then I remember something the Empress said. Apeiron.

"Nkella?"

He grunts at me, but I ignore him.

"What happens if you throw him overboard?"

This time he cocks his head in my direction. "Daf?" A thin smile spreads on his lips. "Last chance," he says. "Who is in charge?"

The prisoner spits out more blood and his head lowers over Nkella's hand. "You will all perish soon."

Nkella turns his head to me. "Bring me Kaehante."

I bolt up the stairs and up the ramps. Kaehante, rag in hand and scrubbing the ship's rails, stops and stares at me.

"Nkella needs you down there, now," I rasp. He drops the

rag to the floor and leaps down the ramp. Tessa and Harold come from the bow, and AJ emerges shortly after.

Tessa screws up her face. "What happened?"

"Trouble in the brig." I explain what happened the best way I understood it. AJ wipes his face.

Minutes later, Kaehante comes back with the Ipani over his shoulder and Nkella following closely behind, his hat lowered, and Iéle prowling next to him. We all move back, and AJ runs to the side of the ship. I stand by as I watch him lower a plank. My mouth drops. Am I about to witness someone walk the plank?

"Captain. . ." AJ starts. "Are you sure?"

"Daí? You want to defend another prisoner?" Nkella pushes bird-beak onto the plank, and he falls to his knees, blood gushing from his mouth. "I gave him a choice. Tell us who is in charge of the Ipani trafficking or be fed to the sea serpent."

Ah, so my suspicion was correct. Being consumed is a loophole to eternal torture, especially if it's by the Empress's pet.

Bird-beak spits in Nkella's face.

AJ throws his hands up. "All yours."

Nkella scoffs, wipes his face, and grabs the back of the man's neck with one hand and the top of his shorts with the other. In one throw, he tosses him off the ship.

As he flies over, phantom wings spread from his back, and he glides in one last attempt to save himself. As quick as it happens, they diminish, and he plummets to the water with a hard splash. It wasn't exactly walking the plank but. . .close enough.

"No. . ." AJ nearly falls in.

"AJ?" Kaehante grabs him.

"He turned into an eagle. Why an eagle?"

I stare at AJ. His face is pale, and I try to understand what he's talking about.

"Oh, AJ. . ." Tessa starts. "She isn't the only eagle oumala."

"How do you know?" He yells.

Nkella steps up behind him and grabs his shoulders. "It was not her ouma. His beak was black. Lāri's beak is yellow. She still lives."

Panting, AJ snaps himself away from Nkella, then turns back and nods quickly, as if assuring himself Nkella is right.

Kaehante squeezes his shoulder. "The timing would not have been right, AJ. She was being transported when we got to Dempu."

I lean over the rail and watch as the man fights to stay afloat. My stomach is tied in knots. I know he was a traitor to their species and was into some really bad crap, but I've never seen anyone get murdered before.

Something zips through the water.

Tessa reverses her chair. "Everybody get back. Now."

Something below the surface moves under the ship.

Harold grips the rope to his side. "It's the serpent. Can he see us?"

"He shouldn't," AJ responds. I hold my breath.

In one swift motion, the serpent raises its giant head and bites the man's leg clean off. I hear a scream followed by a gurgle as the serpent's next bite covers his entire body. Blood tints the blue waves as the serpent dives under again.

My mouth gapes as the others watch emotionless, apart from Harold, who turns away. My knees buckle, and I walk over to a stool by the barrels and plop down. I stare mindlessly at the floor with my chest heaving. My hands shake.

Nkella flicks his gaze to me and pauses. His lips part, like he's about to say something, and for a moment I think I see a semblance of regret. Then his face hardens, and he stares at the floor as he walks by. I don't know what I thought he'd say to me. I doubt he feels regret for what he just did, and I doubt he was about to console me for witnessing it.

AJ spots me and comes over. He offers me his water canteen and I take it. Even after having the scare of his life, he's still considerate of others.

"I just saw him kill that guy." My voice shakes. "And I'm the one who gave him the idea."

"It isn't your fault." AJ moves my hair from my eyes. "He was dying anyway from eating something he shouldn't have. Take a breather, and then go see Tessa."

My chest heaves as I take a deep breath. Tessa. . . Bomb making. . . Right.

"Are you going to be alright?" He searches my eyes, worry creasing his forehead.

But I know it's not for me. I force a smile and nod.

He thought that Ipani had killed Lāri for her magic and it has something to do with that word Nkella keeps getting worked up over. Dik- dikoro- something. Whatever it's called, it must be some bad stuff.

"Apeiron?"

"Yep."

Harold spins an empty glass bottle on the table. "Is she married to that? Because I kind of already named her Nessie in my head."

I shrug. "Call her what you want. I think it's a boy though."

"A boy serpent."

"Think so. Pretty sure."

"How can you tell?"

My shoulder twitches in a shrug "By his name?"

"Are you two ready to pay attention?" Tessa snaps me and Harold back to her boiling flasks.

I stare at the lemony solution above a blue flame. "Yeah. Sorry. Still shaken up."

Tessa leans back in her chair. "He would have been agonizing in pain forever, otherwise." Although she had just said something impossibly cruel, her voice is kind, as if what happened was the most humane way to kill someone—as oxymoronic as that is.

"Where we come from, that would be impossible," I say.

"Ah, well. . .in this world, suffering is all there is. We suffer in life and then we die and continue to suffer."

"Eternal suffering. I guess having the serpent eat the prisoner was a blessing in disguise."

Silent and pensive, Harold reaches for his potion belt on the back table and unclasps a bottle full of blue liquid. The room is on the same level as our cabins but past the kitchen area. It's a wooden make-shift lab filled with burners, beakers, glass bottles filled with dangerous solutions, and a few of Tessa's belongings. On one of the shelves are drawings of different animals and plants. A wooden figurine of two horses pulling a chariot sits on top of a high shelf overlooking the table.

"Eternal suffering is all part of the curse the Empress cast hundreds of years ago," Tessa says. "Whether you believe it to be true that she is the same one or not, the fact remains that the ones who die in this world still suffer. Their spirits never rest. They live within the deep."

"The deep?"

"Wandering spirits in the ocean, nowhere to go, trapped at sea. Or the forest, or wherever they died."

The flame pops and I jump. Tessa chuckles.

"The flame is at the right temperature now. Harold, you can pour in the *buchiveru*. And thank you again for giving us your supply."

Harold uncorks a small glass vial with blue liquid. "Well, I hope I can make more when I get to Wands—er—Sāgirang."

Tessa reverses to grab something from behind her and circles back to reveal a small glass jar. "You should be able to, I am hoping to get more materials there as well, although, know that some of the plants are endangered now due to over picking and difficult to find. But there are alternatives we can use."

"I did hear about that. It's sad to see plants and animals going extinct in this world too." Harold takes a pipet and fills it up with his blue solution. "Humans ruin everything." He pours it into the yellow solution being heated, and I watch as the liquid quickly turns to a dark green.

Tessa uncorks the small jar in her hand and tips the contents of it inside the mixture. Tiny crystals pour in from the top, changing the shade from dark to lime green. "The crystals make it release the gas."

"What were the other two liquids?"

"The first one is a sleeping potion made from hū raku plants—they grow in the high mountains of Sāgirang. It only enacts the sleeping effects when heated, unless mixed with the crystals I just poured. We call it raku potion, or just raku for short. The blue liquid Harold has stabilizes the potion so that when this becomes a certain temperature, it won't be poisonous for the user."

"It's from a poison berry, though," Harold tells me, "but is used as a moderator in potion making."

"I hated chemistry," I say flatly. "Not sure how I can help here."

"You are going to keep making these so that we have a large supply," Tessa says.

Oh. She needed me for the grunt work. I should have known.

"Take those empty bottles over there, and light up another flame under one of the ceramic pots. We should have enough for thirty, maybe thirty-five small bombs."

"Is that going to be enough for where we're going?" I ask.

She smiles. "I hope so. We have other weapons as well, but these are convenient to take out multiple Arcana soldiers or any nefarious folk who get in our way at the same time."

I get busy preparing another burner and setting up the flask. Harold does the same while Tessa oversees us and makes her own. After a few moments working in silence with only the sounds of the boiling liquids and popping flames, my mind drifts back to the prisoner who was eaten alive by Apeiron.

"Tessa?"

She flicks her eyes up from her flask.

"What is. . . diku. . .dikuro?"

"Rikorō," Tessa says darkly. "Rikorō garisi."

When the Ipani turned into a bird. . .and AJ thought he had killed Lāri. . .what does that mean? How would he have done it? I mean. . . "I heard Nkella say that word a few times, and once at the tavern. But what is it?"

Harold wipes his hands on a cloth and leans over the table. "Remember when you met me at that tavern? I told you some pirates wanted me to make some nasty potions for them? It was rikorō. It means soul-thief. It's a plant that can steal the spirit essence of an oumala, but in this case, an Ipani's ouma. In order to make it, the Ipani is killed and their ouma is transferred into the potion. And garisi just means drinkable potion."

My eyes widen. "What happens when they drink it?"

Tessa eyes me straight in the face. "The potion allows you to have whatever ouma the dead Ipani had. But it is very unstable and not worth killing for. No one has been able to perfect it and usually the person—Ipani or human—who takes it will get very sick and die."

"That's why that Ipani dude was dying—or suffering," I say. "And that's why Nkella said he was a traitor. He killed Ipani people for their ouma to become stronger."

"Yes," Tessa explains. "The prisoner was bound like most Ipani are. Some groups of bad men try to perfect the recipe so that they can create their own army and overtake the Empress. To eventually get their own ouma back—if that's even possible.

Some humans just want ouma of their own, despite the laws against it."

Harold's face turns somber. "The Ipani girl I met when I first got here. . ."

"The one you said who almost killed you? Your lady friend?" I smirk.

"Yeah, she taught me all this." He slants a smile. "I found out she was involved"—he turns to Tessa—"it was a brain-washing situation, she never meant to hurt anyone but. . . She was making rikorō." He sighs deeply. "She was killing herself for 'the cause.'"

Tessa's brows furrow. "Killing herself?"

He nods. "She was testing it on herself in small doses to avoid hurting anyone."

"That is very dangerous. Rikorō is unreliable and unstable."

He sits back and stares blankly at the flames. "She's a great chemist but I'm worried about her. Whatever that prisoner took though was terribly made, given that he could hardly shift into a bird and died quickly."

I stare intently as my solution heats up in the small ceramic bowl. All these magical plants and cookies that can make you invis-ible, and float, and this is what people decide to do? Steal unbound Ipani magic for themselves? Nkella asked bird-beak who is in charge of the trafficking. Now it makes sense. "That's what they want with the traffickers, isn't it? They're all unbound?"

Tessa nods grimly. "That is why we need to get to Lāri before it's too late."

Potion finished, Tessa collects her flask and moves it over to the back table for it to cool. She then collects Harold's and does the same with mine. I grab another, and we each start on a new one.

That night, I stay up on the main deck with AJ, Tessa, and Harold, our backs against the quarterdeck, facing the bow of the ship. I'm mesmerized by the blue and purple swirls making nautilus patterns in the night sky as if someone is painting them with a paintbrush over and over.

Glittering stars twinkle in between them and a cool sea breeze passes through my hair bringing in the smells of the ocean, making me think of the twinkling light bugs and the Louisiana Gulf coast. I wonder what Talia is doing right now.

AJ flips through pages in a leather-bound journal he holds in his hands. As he flips, I catch images of the ocean, the serpent, landscapes, and a bird.

I lean in close to him. "Wow, those are really good. Did you draw those?"

"No, Lāri did."

"Oh, she's an artist?" I ask. AJ gives me a soft smile with a gleam in his eye. "Tell me about her."

"She's talented, for starters." He flips to a page of a mountain range, with a wolf howling at the moon. "And she wasn't born female."

"Oh?"

He shakes his head. "Nope. She's *jelisi*, which means she identifies as female."

"Got it. What else?"

He looks up toward the crow's nest. "That's her favorite spot. She likes to be high up so she can watch our surroundings. . .and draw," he says with a smile.

"I guess it makes sense she likes to be high up. Like a bird."

AJ chuckles, moving his long hair behind his shoulders as he closes the journal. "She's also an oumala animal activist. She's amazing." He smiles sadly.

Heavy boots make me turn to see Kaehante turning from the ramp with a large jug and wooden cups in his hands. He passes the cups to Tessa and starts pouring them one by one, passing them to the rest of us.

"This should be nice," AJ smirks.

"What should be nice?" I ask.

"Have a taste." He hands me two cups and I pass one to my right to give to Harold. I bring the wooden cup to my nose and the sweet aroma of warm vanilla and sugar, mixed with the smokiness of hickory intoxicates my senses.

I stare at the amber liquid suspiciously. "Is this going to. . .do anything weird?"

They laugh, and Harold leans into my ear. "I think this is like their rum."

Oh. "Smells familiar." I take a sip and swallow, coughing shortly after as the drink burns down my throat. Harold stares at me and I scrunch up my face. "What? It's not the first time I've drunk alcohol."

He snorts.

"Yeah, mostly it's Nkella who drinks this stuff. I'm a lightweight," AJ says, taking a gulp.

"He's been drinking a lot more since Ntaoru. . ." Tessa drops her voice. "You know, since it happened."

I flick my eyes to her, the concern on her face bringing me back to my conversation with AJ in the kitchen about the Devil curse making him mad inside; a burning question has been sitting in my core since then. I take another sip and swish the liquid in my mouth before swallowing. Then I clear my throat. "What happens if Nkella loses himself? If he gets too angry, or as you say, enough curse days pass and he becomes more. . .?" I act out horns on my head.

AJ and Kaehante take another swig of their drink, and Harold leans in to listen to Tessa's response.

She glares at the drink in her hand and swishes it around in her cup. "Eventually, it'll take over, and Nkella will be gone forever. Only the Devil will remain." She lets her words linger.

I swallow a gasp.

"Hmm. . ." Harold sits back again. "Why do it, though? Curse him with that, I mean. I get you all betrayed her, and he was the leader, so got cursed and all but. . . when I saw him change. . ." Harold makes a fist. "He was strong and powerful. And I know the Ipani are strong built"—he nods over at Kaehante who smirks back—"but it seems it just makes him even stronger—I mean—not the losing control part but. . . What if he goes after her in that state?"

I take another sip. This time, I feel it in my head. The swirls in the sky continue to spiral and I get lost in the movement and the rocking of the ship as they talk.

Tessa nods. "I think the Empress wants him to turn so that he's no longer in control and she can use him. As long as he's still in there, he can make a choice. What she wasn't expecting was that the Devil curse brings its own magic and is stronger than she thought." She makes a clicking noise with her tongue. "He's so young and has so much to deal with."

Notes of leather and smoked hickory mix with the aromas from my cup and the sea. Everyone stops talking and looks to the right as Nkella comes from the stern and joins us. He takes a seat next to Harold, his flask already in his hand.

I stiffen. I've gotten to the point that I'm more relaxed around the crew, but the moment Nkella walks in, my stomach immediately twists itself into knots.

I don't even know why he came. Well, I guess he wants to hang with his crew. . . I'm the anomaly here. It's funny, I almost forgot that. And he seems to be fine with Harold. His silence is awkward as everyone scrambles to change the subject. I exchange a look with Tessa and AJ.

"Sso, w-what causes the sky to do that?" I slur. Oh man. . .my mouth feels numb.

AJ giggles and I can tell he's feeling it too. He did say he was a lightweight. "It's the ancient Ipani gods putting on a light show for us," he says. "Happens very seldom." I raise my brows in his direction and smile. Someone's already drunk.

"Kh. It is where the ouma inside the Aō meets this plane," Nkella responds in a hoarse whisper. His voice catches me by surprise; I didn't expect him to answer me. I glare at him as he leans back watching the spectacle in the sky. His arm hangs over his raised knee. Twinkling lights dance on his face, highlighting his exotic Ipani features. His high cheekbones, slightly pointed ears, and a brush of the darker shade of stripes are revealed from his open shirt at the collar bone.

My mind goes back to when I snuck into his room and he

stood in front of me, shirtless and warm. My cheeks flush. Now I know I've had too much to drink. I quickly get up and excuse myself, tripping over my foot on the way out. I can feel Nkella's burning stare on my back as Kaehante steadies me, and Harold and AJ giggle out loud. I snort and go to bed.

Yeah, not today, Devil. I'm d-definitely drunk.

16

I BRING IN THE SHORT PORTION OF THE ROPE AND pass it through the small loop. Cinching the knot closed, I secure the bow with the finished loop.

"Good, Soren. You are getting it." Kaehante pats my shoulder and takes the rope from me. "You will become a sailor yet."

"Thanks, Kae."

AJ jumps down from the rail, pulling another rope with his body weight. Kaehante takes it from him and heaves.

I fight my hair back into a tight ponytail. "Those extra sails we added to the stern really helped us pick up speed," I yell as I hold onto the rail against the wind pushing my back. The sun rising beyond the horizon makes me stifle a yawn.

The ship rocks and water splashes over AJ's face, revealing his skull as his skin disappears. He wipes his bones with his shirt and shakes the water off until his face re-materializes to normalcy. I swallow and look away, trying not to be rude. It isn't his fault the Empress cursed him to be undead. And I guess it's better than eternal torment or becoming a masked soldier zombie against his will.

"Sorry, Soren. It's hard to stay dry on a ship."

"It's okay." One thing that's been in the back of my mind though is, what happens if and when they break the undead curse? Will they come back to life? Or will they drop and. . .die?

"The added sails helped us pick up speed but we're still not going as fast as we would be with the potion. We have a little bit left, but after a week's use, we're almost out. Nkella thinks we should save the rest in case of an emergency."

I shake off the image of them all falling to their deaths. I can't believe it's already been a month since we set sail to find the traffickers. "Are we getting close to Wands then?"

AJ nods. "Hopefully, we'll reach it by nightfall."

"AJ, help me with the sail in the back," Kaehante shouts as he jumps down, landing with a thud on the wooden floorboards. His skeletal hands dry off as he walks past.

"I need to go back to the kitchen to prepare breakfast. I'm sure Soren can help." He gives me a nod and a smile.

"Be right there, Kae."

"Want to help me after?" AJ asks me.

I scoff. "I think I'll leave tonight's dinner to you and keep helping Kae today."

"Fair enough," he says, whistling to himself as he goes. I've left the cooking to AJ as all that was left was cured meat and bread and broth to last us for six days. I'll be happy to never taste another piece of dried meat again.

I jog over to the stern to help Kae with the back sails. I've done this so many times already that it feels like it's my job. Like, a real job. Kae normally does all the stuff that requires a lot of strength—the stuff humans need a lot of manpower for. And not the things a potion usually does the work for like carrying heavy sails and moving heavy barrels around. But with everything else, it almost feels like I'm training to do this as a permanent career. I guess life on the *Devil's Gambit* has become easier for me.

Nkella has stopped giving me so much grief as well. . .for the most part. We have our moments. But the last thing I want is to go back to the brig, so I bite my tongue.

Living with the crew has become surprisingly bearable, if not, sometimes, enjoyable. AJ, despite being worried sick over Lāri, is still so attentive and caring. Tessa is a bit stricter but she's older and wiser; I feel like she's the glue that holds the crew together—especially when AJ and Nkella argue, which seems constant.

Kaehante jumps down and wipes his hands. "That should hold. I will get ready for breakfast now."

"And I'll do the same," I tell him, turning to leave.

Back in my small room, as I fold the sheet over my bed and tidy up, I almost feel like it's actually mine. I don't know if it's the normalcy of doing daily chores and being around the same people who don't have ulterior motives for me—well, I'm still talking about the crew, not the captain. But regardless, it feels normal. Unlike temporary rooms with foster parents like the Nelsons who want to use me to make money. Where I always have to keep an eye out for Talia and hide my things from

Bradley's snooping. Or ending up in a worse situation where I have to sleep with one eye open.

Not that it didn't feel this way when I first got here, but it feels different now.

It almost feels strange. . .getting so caught up with sailing and chores that I almost forget, once we get to Wands, I'm on a journey to get home to my sister. But one thing has changed a bit. Being this far away from home and not knowing what's going to happen has changed my perspective. Nkella lost his sister and may never see her again; AJ lost his girlfriend, and as much as no one wants to admit it, we may never rescue her. Life is unpredictable. When I get back, I'm going to prioritize seeing my mom. No more excuses.

I touch my wrist and bite down a sob. I do wish I still had my charm bracelet though.

After changing out of my nightclothes—lent to me by Tessa; I feel weird borrowing anything else from Nkella's sister —I check on the clothes I washed last night to make sure they're dry. I quickly dress, brush my teeth in the communal sink, and head out to the main deck. One thing I still haven't gotten used to is brushing my teeth with powdered charcoal and scented oils. The little bits of powder get stuck between my teeth and drive me nuts. I can't wait to have regular toothpaste again.

Salt and the sea breeze push at my senses as I make my way up.

The others are gathered around Nkella at the wheel, and I fight my anxiety to join the rest standing around him. Hey, I said I bite my tongue around him, not that I feel hunky-dory around my captor.

Grave looks cross their faces, and I already know what the matter is.

Harold wrinkles his forehead as he watches me walk up. "Soren, any luck reaching out to Gari?"

I shake my head. "Sorry guys, I guess drakons can't hear far through the Aō."

"He could be anywhere," Tessa says glumly.

"The cloaking potion is running dangerously low," Harold remarks. "What are we going to do?"

Nkella has one hand on the wheel, the other resting on his lap as he turns to us. "We won't make it close to the Karst Temples, only to the east shore. I have sent Iéle to alert the resistance of our arrival. They, at least, will know we are coming. And in the meantime. . ."

"We do the only thing we can do. We fight," Kaehante says.

Harold lets out a sigh and looks out to sea.

I clear my throat. "I'm sorry but. . .how exactly are we meant to fight off the Wands' Minor Arcana and Prefect? Don't they patrol the area—sky and sea? From what I've heard, if we're not cloaked when reaching the island, they'll obliterate us." I flick my eyes to Kae. "The night Gari brought me back from the Tower, he said they'd shoot him down for his fur. I'd rather not be obliterated."

"We can only fight back," Kaehante says.

"Or jump ship." Nkella's voice is hoarse and low. Everyone stares at him.

AJ leans over the rail next to Harold. "Each choice is a suicide mission."

"And now I've lost my appetite," I say.

AJ glances at me. "You mean you don't want any more delicious dry meat?"

"Very funny."

He snickers.

"Well, Gari, now would be a good time to turn up," I say, even though I know I'm talking to the wind. Bringing us some more invisibility potion from wherever he has his stash would be helpful as heck right now. Not to mention, he could have been helping us find Lāri. But that's assuming he wants to help. He only seemed interested in helping me, and my gut has always told me he's in it for himself—for whatever reason that may be.

By the time the sun starts to die down, we can see Wands—Sāgirang—in the horizon; soon I'll be off this ship and a step closer to finding my way home. After a late lunch, I busy myself with sweeping the main deck while the others have split up different tasks that prepare us to dock. They think that if we can cross while invisible and dock by nightfall, we may just get away with not getting caught.

A shadow eclipses my light as I sweep the ramp that leads to the kitchen. The scent of warm leather and smoked hickory engulfs my senses, and my stomach is already twisting into a knot. I spin around to find Nkella's hard stare burning into my back.

"Follow me," he says. He doesn't have his hat or jacket on, and his black hair is tousled on his head. His lean muscles protrude from his long-sleeved black tunic. The stubble on his chin shows he hasn't shaved for a few days. He looks tired.

I swallow and put the broom aside. He leads me inside his cabin and sits me down at a small round wooden table to the left of the door. Gold light spills across the room, making the shadows of the flickering gas lamps dance across the sharp planes of his cheekbones. He takes a seat in front of me, takes out the World Card, and crosses his arms.

"Time for your training, gembella."

"Really? Now? We're almost at the island." He's kept his distance from me for weeks and now he wants me to practice with the card. Maybe he was afraid that if I got it to work, I'd leave, and he'd lose the ability to get the Ace of Wands. Or his bargaining chip if that failed. I'm not delusional.

"Yes. Now." He moves the card under my nose. I stare at it, now really taking notice of the map of the world that's on it. Ipa, as the Ipani call it. Fateland, as the Empress calls it. I still call it Tarotland—if anything, that carnival was the bridge to get me here. The beautiful gold embellishments reflect off the dim lighting of his room. The familiar shine of purple sweeps the card, and the waves start to move.

My vision zooms in, hypnotizing me, as a serpent pokes its head out of the water and disappears with its tail following behind. I hold my breath. What did Gari say about focusing my intent? He said that about the magical drinks and cookies, but could it be the same with the cards?

"Anything?" Nkella snaps me out of my concentration.

Ignoring him, I keep my focus on the image, which is now refusing to move. And now it feels like a memory or a dream. Was it ever truly moving? I study the intricate design as it only just appears as a card now. Oh, damn him, couldn't he see it? Why had it changed before? What had I done that I didn't realize I was doing? Or better yet, how did it open a portal? My focus changes, *I wish for it to open a portal*. Maybe it *is* all about my intent.

"Comfortable prisoner. Is it working?"

"Koj." I say.

Amusement flickers across his face before it goes back to brooding. I snicker.

"Try harder."

"I don't know how."

"Then you are only good for one thing," he says with grim amusement in his voice. "For trading."

For trading me to the Empress, he means. I sigh deeply. "No. I can use it to get the Ace of Wands. It'll work."

"Kh." He turns the card over and stares at it. "Fate magic is unpredictable."

"That's strange, considering it's meant to be fate. . ."

He taps the edge of the card on the table and narrows his eyes at my arm.

"Unpredictable because only she controls it."

Oh. . .

"Try using your mark." He reaches over the table and traces my mark with his finger. A shiver runs down my spine at his touch, causing my cheeks to burn. I clear my throat and bring my arm back. "Don't touch me."

He lifts his chin and pulls back, fierceness flashes in his eyes.

Right. He threw me in the brig and tortured me. I'm still his prisoner. I can't forget that.

I clear my throat. "Use my mark? How?"

The knob of his cabin door twists open and Kaehante barges in. "We have a problem."

The chair scrapes against the wooden floor as Nkella bolts for the door. I spring up, following suit but he holds his hand back, blocking me in at the door frame. I move to the left, press myself up against the window, and peer outside. A small gasp escapes my lips.

An Arcana soldier is standing on the stern staring down at the floor. I glance around at the windows circling the cabin. Tessa and Harold are coming from a side ramp on the stern, cutting in from her lab and up to the windowpane. There are no signs of another soldier though. Just the one.

AJ peeks from around the corner of the quarterdeck and inches as close as possible to where Nkella and Kae stand. "What do we do?" he whispers.

Kaehante whispers. "Captain, maybe we should capture him. Hold him prisoner."

"Koj. It will alert the others. Or the Empress."

"Or maybe we can figure out how to free him," AJ suggests.

"Koj. Be quiet."

I'm pressed against the glass window watching the masked guard who is looking around the floor of the ship. He can tell something is off. How much do they understand? He's standing on a platform he cannot see, and I'm sure they know about the invisibility potions. . . How common are ships like these that can use potions in their engineering? I tap on the glass. "Harold," I whisper loudly, "how much cloaking potion is left?"

He purses his lips, giving us a warning look and I shrink back. "That's why we need to decide on a plan," Harold whispers back.

The Arcana soldier snaps the depthless sockets where his eyes should be over to where I'm standing. I straighten my back and wince. Nkella and Kaehante take out their swords. The soldier starts to glide over slowly, then stops a few feet away. Kaehante readies himself, but Nkella holds him back.

"Not yet," he whispers.

The Arcana soldier's black robes flare out in the wind, his mother-of-pearl mask reflecting the light. The soldiers with mother-of-pearl masks and shields with tower clasps come from the Tower, meaning the Empress gave them psychic powers. Suitable to be her scouts.

Afraid I might cause a floorboard to creak, I don't budge. It stares right at me. Nkella follows his glare to me and then back to the soldier. I inhale sharply. Can it see me?

To my surprise, it starts to glide back a little, looks around once more, and in a whirl of black smoke, vanishes from the ship. I let out a long breath.

"That was a close one," Harold exhales.

While the rest of us drop our shoulders, I notice Nkella is tense. His eyes narrow, he returns his sword into his sheath, and he spins on his heel returning to the room.

"Captain?" Kaehante says, coming inside.

"Prepare for battle." Nkella walks over to his quiver and straps it over his shoulders. I've never seen him shoot an arrow before. He opens a drawer and takes out what looks like a glass bottle of ink, but something tells me it isn't ink.

Tessa calls from the door, "We are sailing close to *Chong Alēla*. We must be careful about crossing those waters; we don't want to be pulled in with the tortured dead."

"Hn. Prepare either way."

"What's Cho-ng Alē-la mean?" I repeat the word slowly, trying my best to say it correctly.

Tessa starts to back away, but before she leaves, says, "It means Phantom Mists. The area we are avoiding is where trapped souls try to reach the living." She puts her chair into gear and drives off into the dark part of the ship.

The gas lamp flickers outside one of the windows and goose bumps prickle my arms and knees. "Trapped souls?"

Nkella drops a map onto the table, and Kaehante leans in for a close look, leaving my question unanswered and the hairs on my arms standing on end.

A popping sound makes me spin back to face Nkella. He and Kaehante's brows are furrowed down at the table we had been sitting at earlier. A small spider about the size of a quarter with a sapphire blue mosaic body dances on the table by the World Card. I suck in a breath. For a second, I thought it was Philo, but she has a ruby red pattern.

Nkella moves quickly and takes the card, tucking it into his coat; then, in one incredibly fast movement, he picks up the spider between his index finger and his thumb and holds it up to his face, its legs moving frenziedly. Nkella grimaces and presses his fingers together until a squishing splat rings in my ears. Bile rises to my throat as yellow goo stains his fingers. I hold my hands to my mouth.

Kaehante grunts and steps back. "We prepare for battle then."

"Th-at. . ." I swallow. Gross. "That was one of the Empress's. . ."

"Utwa."

I flick my eyes up at him as he wipes his hands on a clean towel. "I'm not—"

"The spider. It was one of the Empress's utwa."

"Oh. . .yes." One of her spider spies. "And you killed it. . ."

"I hate spiders." He ushers me out of his cabin. "Gembella, they are looking for you. Should I make my trade?" He flashes me an impish smile, grim amusement in his voice.

"We have a deal."

"Kh. Go be a comfortable prisoner, daí? Go and hide."

An unsettling feeling resurfaces in my gut with the last look he gives me. "I want to help."

A muscle under his eye twitches and his lips start to form a smirk. I can't tell if it's agitation or amusement. "How will you help? You cannot even fight."

"Give me a weapon then."

He continues to walk, pushing me aside. I follow him down to the main deck, the wind blowing at my hair. "You should hide. They come looking for you. If they see you, we are all in trouble."

"But if they see you, we're all still in trouble. Maybe you should hide."

He stops walking momentarily, his back now to me. "Kh."

"I'm not a coward. I want to help." Not that I'd sit around anyway even if he told me to.

"Go get ready then," he breathes.

Heavy footfalls make me spin around and I catch wind of AJ running to the bow.

Really? "Get ready, how? I don't have a weapon." But he ignores me and steps onto the back stairs that lead to the quarterdeck.

"Soren." Tessa's voice spins me around. She's holding a bandolier with six glass bottles filled with a lime green solution. She holds it up to me.

"For me?"

"Well, you can't just stand around looking pretty. And you don't know how to fight with a sword or shoot arrows, do you?"

I shake my head. "I can hardly even pull a punch," I admit.

"Then here." The bottles clank together as she holds it up for me to take. My muscles constrict as I take it and wrap it around myself. Prepare for battle, he said. Holy cow, this is happening.

"No," she says, pointing to the bottles, "that bit is meant to cross over your chest. Take it off and try again."

"Oh. . . Sorry." I do as she says and hold it in front of me, pulling the part with the bottles over my head. The bottom bit now looks simple enough. I tie it around my waist and buckle it.

"There you go. Go back to the lab and help Harold bring the rest of the raku bombs we made for backup."

I nod and run down the ramps and into the lab. Harold meets me inside and passes me a heavy wooden box with twelve potion bottles, each being held at their base. I take it and head back to the main deck with him. "Where are we meant to put these where they'll be safe and easy for us to access?"

He shakes his head. "My guess is near the cannons where we'll have better cover. I'd rather keep away from the wheel."

Because it's more visible. That makes perfect sense. "Hey, what's this about ghosts and souls?"

He shudders and releases a breath. "Some are split souls

that were wretched from their bodies to become part of the Minor Arcana. Others are half alive, being tortured. . ."

"Why do they go to sea?"

"I think some do because it's where they died. I had to cross a phantom forest in Piupeki. It was terrifying."

"Real ghosts?" I mean, why am I surprised there would be real—

The whistling sound of an airstrike makes me freeze in place. The sound of an explosion makes the walls and the floorboard of the ship quake. My breath leaves my lungs and my blood runs cold.

"The Arcana soldiers," Kaehante shouts from overhead. "They attack from the Tower!"

I gape at him as he runs from behind Nkella at the wheel. A long smoke trail whistles down at us, followed by another.

Harold grabs my arm and starts pushing me toward the ramp.

A blast hits the side of the ship and I am thrown against a barrel. Harold flies down the ramp and hits the back wall full of baskets and carts with a crash.

"What do we do?" I yell. There's nowhere to go; we're stuck on a ship. If we stay on deck, we get blasted. If we go below deck, we still get blasted, and possibly drown even quicker.

"We have to get the raku bombs," Harold says as he scrambles to his feet, stepping over boxes.

Gunfire roars above us as the crew starts firing at the soldiers. Will that do us any good?

AJ's voice cuts through the wind. "Nkella, where are you going?"

My mouth drops. He's leaving?

Another bomb hits and the ship makes a sharp turn to the left.

"No. . ." Harold says, turning to look back up the ramp. "He can't be. . ."

"What is it? What's going on?" I flip around.

Harold makes a beeline up the ramp. I follow as we both struggle against the strong winds and the jerking back and forth of the ship, pushing us down. "Weren't we grabbing more raku?" I call after him.

Another bomb strikes. I hit the floor and cover my head with my arms, squeezing my eyes shut. Gunfire booms all around me and I try to sink into the ramp, feeling for cover with my eyes closed.

"Soren, get up!" Harold's voice sounds distant as a wave hits him and muffles his voice.

Water pours over my head, and I jerk up to find a barrel rolling down the ramp about to crush me. I quickly stand and try to run back up the ramp.

BOOM

My legs topple over to my right, and I hold on to the wall, as the ship speeds quicker to the left. Fire sizzles over the sea, releasing fumes as the bombs hit.

BOOM BOOM

BOOM

Air strikes pour from all directions. I crawl to the edge of the ramp, looking outside. It looks like the skies opened up a heavy fury of fireballs. And we're the only target for miles.

AJ and Kaehante shoot up at the sky, standing back-to-back.

Harold's face pales as he stares up at the wheel. "You're going to waste all the potion. What are you doing, Captain?" he yells through the blasts.

I run up to meet Harold at the ramp and arch my neck to gaze at Nkella. So, he didn't leave. He's just taking us somewhere. He has an intense and determined look on his face as he steers us into a dark, misty area. Christ. He's guiding us right into the Phantom Mists.

AJ's voice booms from behind me. "You're crazy, you know that?" He stands with his gun pointed down. His face is fear stricken but Nkella ignores him.

"It is the only way," Kaehante says.

A bomb flies down and hits the water near the right side of the boat. Waves splash on the deck, and Tessa, Kaehante, and AJ's skeletal bodies flash before my eyes.

My knees shake from being thrown around and catching my balance. A few seconds later, silence is the only sound. The bombings have stopped.

"Is it over?" I ask.

Nkella's eyes darts to us from the quarterdeck. "They cannot see us from Chong Alēla."

"Yeah, but now we have a new problem," AJ says.

"Would you rather have been blown up?" Nkella hisses.

Harold tugs at my sleeve. "Let's go get the rest of the raku bombs."

Right. I nod and follow him to the bottom of the ramp where we left them. We pick them up and carry them to the cannons on the main deck. A light fog covers the floor of the ship. It isn't too thick, but it's cold. Goose bumps prickle my skin and I rub my arms.

Kaehante rubs his chin as he stares up at the sky. "That is new. Them bombing us. Why didn't more soldiers come?"

Tessa drives up to where we are by the rails and looks out. "My guess is the one soldier scout made the Empress realize her best option was to attempt to blow us up and not take any chances of losing us since her army couldn't see through our cloaking. She'd rather we get eaten by her serpent."

"Kh." I turn at Nkella's voice. "Foolish of her to almost kill who she's after."

My stomach turns. He means me.

"Nah, she still could've had them pick up Soren like last time," AJ says. "The soldiers from the Tower are psychic, remember? She knows what she's doing. She wanted to destroy your ship, Cap."

"Hnn, destroy the ship, destroy the cloaking spell," Kaehante adds. "Then our remains are left visible. Good thing our cloaking held up, or they wouldn't have missed."

Nkella doesn't respond. The ship starts to sail slowly through a darker part of the sea. The stars are lost beneath a blanket of deep blue as the moon is eclipsed by a dark cloud. The gas lamp on deck, our only light, flickers.

"So now what?" I whisper.

"Be alert," Kae answers me.

A haunting wail carries through the wind as an icy chill smacks my face. My hair blocks my view as I lean against the rail and feel my way to the closest cannon. I set the box down and move my hair from my eyes.

A translucent head speeds full force my way. It happens so fast I don't even have time to scream.

Its mouth is open wide, and I get a glimpse of its entrails

hanging where its neck should be. Its wind rushes against my face, pushing me back so fast I hit the rail.

Harold pushes me away and in doing so gets hit in the face by the phantom head. His neck snaps back and his body gets flung over the rail. I scream as I reach to grab him. Quickly, Kaehante grabs Harold's foot and pulls him up. Harold grabs onto the rail as Kaehante gently sets his feet down. Harold dry heaves.

"Are you okay?" I ask him.

He reaches for his cheek as he turns to me, I gasp. A swollen red rash is on his forehead and cheek where the flying head hit him. "I'm fine."

The sorrowful wail comes back from the darkness, and I spin around to see the head dive back into the water. My fingers grip the wood and then I make my way to one of the glass bottles.

"Don't," AJ's voice comes from behind me. "The potion will be wasted on souls."

I let go of the glass bottle. "What do we do?"

"Don't let them take you. On any other occasion, sit inside and ride it out." He cranes his neck up to Nkella at the wheel. "But for now, we need to be vigilant. We're about to become visible."

I peer into the deep blue waters. Not even the moonlight reflects upon these waves. Instead, a mist starts to rise from the depths, covering the surface and becoming thicker and thicker as the ship sails. I can understand why Nkella is hoping we'll be able to blend in.

Moans gurgle from below. Hundreds of faces with gaping mouths scream at us from the surface. Somewhere in this strange world are the other halves of their souls. Tortured in two different places. Trapped. And forever wanting to unite.

My nails dig into the wood as I stare at them. I can't tell if their bodies are attached to those heads from below or if they're just floating but given the one soul that came flying at me, I don't want to find out.

The mist rises up over the deck, quickly reaching up to my shins. As we sail deeper into the mist and the more we're consumed by it, the thicker it becomes. I move closer to Harold and AJ, with my hand on a bottle of raku. I know what AJ said about it not working on souls, but it still makes me feel safer. "Guys, you're there, right?"

AJ's voice answers me. "Yeah. We're not going anywhere, Soren. Try to stay calm."

The mist almost covers my head, and I climb to the wall of the ship. I peer across the floor to see if I can make out Tessa or Kaehante, but I can't.

I glance up toward the wheel. The mist hasn't risen there yet and suddenly I regret listening to Harold about preferring to stay low and not visible, although I don't think this is what he meant by it. I hate not being able to see what's out there.

The shape of a large man walks toward us from deep in the mist. At first, I assume it's Kaehante, but then the shape starts to flicker from big to small as it strobes in and out of the mist. A shiver runs down my spine. I blink once and the shape zooms straight at me, flickering as it moves. I let out a scream and duck. I hit someone to my left and jerk back.

"Woah. You okay?"

"Harold?" I mutter.

"Yeah, it's me. It's okay."

"Did you see that?"

"See what?" AJ moves in closer as Harold's voice gets louder. "Did you see an apparition?"

"Why can't we wait this out from inside the cabin?" I ask.

"You don't want to get trapped in the same room with one," AJ says. "It'll only be a matter of time before the psychic soldiers catch up to us anyway. This may be a detour to give us a chance to reach the island, but I want to see around me. We want to be ready for them."

Oh. "I'll stay."

A low moan comes from my right. Some of the mist clears, leaving a small open space illuminated by the gas lamp. The sound comes from a woman; her head hangs low, and her body sways slowly off the ground as if hanging by something invisible.

The sounds of the tortured souls seem to have quieted, giving way to the thrashing of the waves and the creaking of the ship. I spot Kaehante kneeling on the other side, staring intently at the phantom woman. His eyes look heavy and wet. He reaches for her and she disappears. His shoulders drop and a hauntingly tortured moan escapes his lips.

I shudder, take a breath, and drop my shoulders. Something grabs my hair from behind me; I scream and jerk around. Harold and AJ grab whatever it is and pull me away.

As I turn, a rotting arm hangs off the ship. An inaudible screech escapes my throat as Harold kicks it off the ship.

"You okay?" he asks.

I nod rapidly, despite my body involuntarily squirming with feelings of phantom hands grabbing at me. My chest heaves but in a moment the mists start to disperse even more, and soon, it no longer covers us.

"Is it over? Are we through?" I spin around to find Kaehante, his eyes heavy. He nods.

"We are out of the Phantom Mists, but it is not over."

"Kae. . . w-who?" I clear my throat, unsure if I'm prying too much.

"She was my wife."

"Oh. . . I'm so sorry. . .I didn't know." I reach for his arm and squeeze. I had no idea he had a loved one who was being tortured after death. Tessa said suffering after death was eternal in this world, but if the Empress controls death with a Tarot card. . . "Is there a chance. . .?"

His eyes are distant as they fall to my hand on his arm. "To save her?" He purses his lips together and clears his throat. "I took her body back to Danū in the hope that someday. . ." His voice trails off and he clears his throat again.

"Then she's not really dead." As in, she's not disemboweled somewhere. Or eaten by a serpent. "There's hope. And I'll help." I have no idea why I just said that; I don't even know how I can help.

His eyes move to mine and he smiles.

Nkella's voice rings from the wheel. "The cloaking potion is at its last drop—"

Before he can get another word in, a loud whistling sound falls from the sky. My eyes dart up at what looks like a purple bomb is launching right at us.

"It's the Wands' Prefect!" AJ shouts.

My knees buckle and I hit the floor as the bomb drops to the water right beside us, causing the ship to lunge up and down in a giant wave. I slide backward, hitting my back against the ship's wall; my head almost smashes against a cannon.

A loud hissing sound takes off, followed by the same siren type whistling before it smashes against the bow of the ship. We're thrown back and all I see next is a massive wave crashing down on me.

17

THE SHIP SLAMS DOWN; MY BODY LIFTS AND SLAMS with it. Saltwater rushes down my throat and I spit it out. The two boxes of potions that were next to the cannons are now underneath them. I quickly climb off and run back to the bow with my side pressed against the edge.

"Full sail!" Kaehante shouts.

Nkella jumps over the quarterdeck rail with an arrow aimed straight ahead. Kaehante sprints from behind me, carrying the box of raku that I left behind. I follow him. He drops down next to the cannon and starts unlatching the straps that hold the potions in.

"What are you going to do?"

"Quick, open the other box."

I run back to where the other one had slid under and fish it out, unlatching the rest.

"Fill the cannons!" he yells.

My eyes widen as Harold runs up holding two cannonballs in his arms. He sticks one into a cannon.

"What are we doing?" I ask. "We don't have any gunpowder."

"Improvising." Kaehante responds sharply as he chases the cannon with an exploding potion. My eyes widen as the cannon shoots out with a loud blast, hitting something northwest of us.

"Brilliant!" I grab another raku as Harold sticks one in another cannon and we both follow Kae's lead. I glimpse Tessa on the other side of the ship doing the same with AJ and shoot a look at Nkella who is shooting arrows toward the island. Although I can't get a clear view of what he's shooting at from where I'm standing, shouts of an opposing army on the other end grow louder as we approach the island.

Another bomb gets released from their side and it dawns on me that the closer we are to the island, the better their chances of hitting us. We're an easy target.

A bomb hits the water behind the ship sending a tidal wave, which lifts us up. I hold onto a cannon and don't let go. Nkella's body slams against the quarterdeck behind me but gets up immediately, unhurt. As soon as the ship slams down, we release another cannon.

Another blast shoots out from the starboard and I know it was either AJ or Tessa who released it. With no time to check if either of them is okay, I reach for another raku bottle.

Nkella tucks his bow back and takes out his firearm. So does Kaehante. Nkella either ran out of arrows or was waiting for us to get closer. They both edge toward the front of the bow, and I exchange a glance with Harold. I unlatch a raku bomb from my bandolier and duck against the wall, waiting until I can get a good throw. Not that I'm confident in my abilities.

An arrow misses my nose by an inch, and I hit my head against wood.

"They're shooting at us!" Harold bellows.

"And I'm guessing these arrows are poisoned," I shout back, recalling the black liquid Nkella grabbed in his room. I'm sure they have the same stuff.

Harold glances at me, worry smeared across his features.

The wind picks up and it takes me a second to realize the ship is moving faster as the island approaches. "Why are we moving faster? We're going to crash!"

"No one's there to release the sailing potion!" Harold shouts back.

"Go then!" I tell him. "We'll hold them off."

He bolts to the stern, leaving me alone. I inch closer to where he had been and peek through the open space in the cannon hole closest to the bow of the ship.

A row of Arcana soldiers in black robes and purple masks are lined up with bows and arrows aimed directly at us. Walking in front of them is a man dressed in all black. He's not wearing a mask. My guess is he's the Wands' Prefect.

A second later, they release their arrows and Kaehante, AJ, and Nkella start to shoot.

I press my face against the wood and try not to close my eyes. Peeking through, I see two of the soldiers get hit and disappear. A groan comes from the ship, followed by a thud. I gasp and my eyes fling open to Kaehante kneeling on the ground, his arm bleeding.

"Kae!" I scream and crawl over to him but stop as another arrow just misses me.

"Soren, get back!" AJ shouts. Nkella doesn't flinch; he continues to shoot.

Kaehante climbs to his knees and continues fighting. I feel completely useless. We're not close enough for me to make a throw count. It'll hit the water and waste a potion.

A howl cuts through the air. I recognize that sound.

"Iéle," Nkella mutters.

I get up, no longer caring if I'm hit with an arrow. I need to see where the wolf is. The Prefect shouts and kicks something into the air. Iéle is flung to the sand, but spins around and lunges for his neck.

I glance at Nkella who tucks his gun away and nocks one arrow and then another, loosing each with ease and taking out two more Arcana soldiers.

Something zips through the water toward us and I gulp. With everything that's happening, please don't let it be the damn serpent. But then I squint when I see something else zipping through the water beside it. Two serpents?

The one in front has a fin on its back and a grayish-blue tail. The one that follows has shimmery orange and red fish scales.

A man's head pokes from the surface, followed by another man with long, dark brown hair. They have stripes on their necks and subtly pointed ears, like Nkella. Ipani.

"Help us up!" the man shouts. I look around for a rope and grab one on the floor near the quarterdeck. I drop it down and hold on to the end.

"AJ, Kae, I need help!" I call. AJ comes running and grabs

onto the man climbing the rope. I stifle a gasp as I see the end of his body; it looks like a dolphin tail. It morphs into legs as he climbs onboard. He turns and grabs the other man's arm next, his tail is more like a mermaid, or—merman. His tail also transforms to legs as he steps onto the ship, wearing brown shorts like the other, with a utility belt strapped around his waist. He has skin-toned stripes across his stomach as well.

"Iéle told us you were coming," the merman says.

"You got here in the nick of time," AJ slaps his shoulder. The merman unstraps a bottle from his belt and hands it to AJ.

AJ takes it, shares a look with Nkella, and books it to the wheel. Seconds later, Nkella loosens another arrow just as an iridescent film passes over our heads.

"Umm. . . Hi, I'm Soren," I wave.

The mermen squint their eyes at me and exchange glances. "I'm Ānga. This is Loá," the man who just had a dolphin tail responded.

"You've taken a translation potion," Loá says. "You are not from Ipa?"

I shake my head and he beams.

Nkella jumps down from the bow of the ship and runs up, clasping Ānga on the shoulder. Ānga does the same.

"I*á*," Nkella greets them in Ipani.

"Iá."

Tessa drives up and I peer over at the island. The bombs and arrows have subsided, but the Prefect and soldiers are still standing around. One of them shoots an arrow but it lands on the water behind us.

"Is the cloaking back on?" I ask. Tessa nods and AJ runs back down. An involuntary half sigh and laugh escapes my lips.

They can't see us anymore. "They're just shooting aimlessly now."

"They probably won't waste ammunition either," she says. "We hope. But one thing is certain, we don't want the Wands' soldiers to reach us. There is no escaping their power."

I gulp and glance back again. One of the soldiers vanishes in a gust of purple smoke, followed by the others. I can no longer see the Prefect, so I'm guessing they gave up.

"Either way, they'll report to the Empress," Tessa remarks. "That's most likely where the Prefect went."

"The potion should last for a few weeks," Loá says.

"Hate to interrupt"—AJ shoves past—"but we're about to crash."

We all make a run for it and grab onto the ropes. Harold shows up from the stern, holding up the potion bottle. "We've picked up too much speed!" he shouts and grabs onto the rope behind me.

"Heave!" Nkella shouts.

"*Two, six, heave!*" Kaehante takes the lead in pulling the rope.

The ship rumbles underfoot as we barge into the island. I bump Harold behind me and then get squished against him and AJ as the ship hits the island at half force.

Good thing the Prefect left, or we'd be in for a round two. Laughter comes from below as the bow of the ship slips between two trees.

We let go of the rope, and I shake my hands. Ouch.

Nkella straightens his coat and hat and heads for the ramp.

My eyes land on Tessa. She looks over to me and Harold and smiles. "Welcome to Sāgirang. We made it."

18

"ARE WE SURE THEY'RE GONE?" I FOLLOW THE CREW and the two new Ipani mermen to the very tip of the bow and watch as Nkella and Ānga drop an anchor. The fact that I have seen Kaehante do this all by himself is now far more impressive after observing two Ipani men swing it over. I wonder how many humans it would take; that anchor looks heavy.

Crows caw overhead and AJ wraps his girlfriend's scarf around his neck, readying to leave the ship. "We can never be sure the Minor Arcana is gone. They're always watching. That's why we have the cloaking potion."

The metal hits the ground with a hard clank, followed by a crunch as the bow of the ship, which is no longer deep in the water, hits the rocks. I peer down through the darkening night. I guess they wanted to anchor it anyway for good measure.

"But we won't be cloaked by an invisible potion once we get off the ship," Harold chimes in. "This'll be fun."

I bite the inside of my cheek. "That's what worries me."

"This is why we will be quick about getting to camp. We have cloaking there," Loá says, joining Nkella and Ānga by the ropes.

"That does make me feel a bit better."

Nkella grips the rope and jumps down with a few easy slides. I watch as Harold and AJ do the same, and I glance at the two new Ipani. The sound of waves hitting the rocky shore sends a sense of peace over my shoulders but is interjected by the wafting stench of rotting flesh. My nose twitches; I have to hold it to stop myself from gagging. A sea breeze passes by and takes the smell away.

"Go ahead. You first," Loá says.

My eyes fall along the distance from the top of the rope all the way down to the shore. Right. I can do this. I grab onto it with both hands and swing my leg around. Steadying myself carefully, I slide my boots toward the bottom. Torches up ahead dance on the reflective surface of the water and the other's faces as they wait for me to climb down. Easy does it. Using my knees, I grip the rope tightly as I carefully climb down as far as I can until my legs accidentally swing off the rope. I hold my breath as I struggle to grab the rope with my feet and my arms grow tired. I kick with my legs as I try hard to lift my body weight. Heavy wind pushes against my back, and I swing against the ship. A burn starts to hit my palms, but I hold on for dear life. Oh no, I can't do this.

"You have to jump, Soren," AJ says. "I'll catch you." His feet crunch on the gravel.

Heck, no! He's not gonna cat— "Ah!" My hands give in and I involuntarily let go. My breath hitches as AJ catches me. He steadies me. "Thanks." I step back, slip on a round rock, and fall on my ass. A wave hits me from behind; it soaks my pants and lower back.

"Soren, are you alright?"

Cheeks flushed, I scramble to my knees. My fingers fit into holes as I squint at the ground. I gasp, jerking upward as I realize I'm sitting on a pile of skulls; I stand, and then slip backward and land on my ass again. The putrid smell of rotting flesh engulfs my nostrils. A crow caws by my feet and I jerk back in time to see it picking the flesh off some bones.

I let out a shriek as I kick the skulls away, only to pick up another one as I try to stand. AJ lifts me from behind and steadies me as he takes my hand and leads me to where the rest are standing. My eyes are still glued to the ground. On top of a rocky beach, skulls and bones reach the shoreline for as far as I can see in the darkness.

"Kh. This time you will not be so foolish as to try and run away, gembella." Nkella's smooth voice reaches me through the night.

"I wasn't planning to," I hiss. In the corner of my eye, I catch Tessa coming down the ramp with Kaehante. I should have waited and joined them instead of making myself look like a fool. Through Tessa's torch, I can see her chair lift off the ground, and the gears change underneath, allowing her to off-road through the skull landscape. That's cool.

"But *why* are we standing on skulls?" I finally ask.

AJ steadies me at my elbow as I almost topple over again. "The Wand Prefect's sick sense of humor. It's meant to be a warning."

"Great."

Footsteps join us from the forest, and I spin around,

careful not to slip on another skull. A woman wearing a purple dyed leather skirt down to her ankles with slits halfway up her thighs and a strapped brown top walks up to us holding a torch. A beautiful circlet woven out of green leaves and purple flowers decorates her head. As she moves, the light from her torch reveals a mark on the inside of her wrist of a small crown over a wand. Interesting. I wonder what that means. She has long black hair and stripes that meet on her clavicles, arms, and stomach. But no pointed ears.

"It looks like you have your hands full, Prince Nkella."

I snap my gaze to AJ and mouth the word *prince?*

"Just Nkella these days, Princess Soanalo."

"It is good that Iéle came to find us." She motions at the ship.

"Thank you."

As she gets closer, she stops at Nkella, her high cheekbones meeting his. They place a hand across each other's shoulders and say, "*iá.*"

"What does that mean?" I whisper to AJ.

"It means hail. It is a custom Ipani greeting."

I raise my brows in understanding. The mer-Ipani made the same greeting on the ship.

Nkella's brows rise to the top of his head as his gaze pauses on the mark on her wrist. "Should we be addressing you as Queen?"

I gape.

She smiles. "Á?" She holds her mark up for him to see. "This? It's nothing. The Aō thinks I am suitable for the role."

"It's not nothing. If the Aō made you Queen of Wands, then your people willed it." He takes a deep bow. My eyes widen as I see the rest of the crew follow suit. I quickly do a half-bow, unsure of myself. So she isn't a princess, she's a *queen*?

"That isn't necessary. Please, call me Soanalo." She turns to us before returning her gaze back to Nkella. "You know, some of the Ipani still recognize you as the prince of Danū." She smiles. "They see you as hope."

Nkella grimaces. "Kh. Soon I will be unrecognizable." His voice darkens. She peers into his eyes and for a moment their gazes lock. A strange knot twists in my stomach and I start to wonder if there's something between these two. Not that it matters to me. I couldn't care less. But I can be curious.

"Is there no hope of breaking your curse?" Her shoulders slump and a tinge of sadness resonates in her voice.

He doesn't say anything. I part my lips.

I grab AJ's arm and pull him away a few steps. "Okay, Prince? Princess? Care to explain?"

"Nkella doesn't really like people knowing," he mutters under his breath.

"Won't people recognize him anyway if he's a *prince*?"

"Some think his entire family burned in lava."

I swallow a gasp.

"Don't treat him any different though," he says. "Nkella really doesn't like it." I nod.

"Come, I'll show you to our camp," Soanalo says to all of us. A howl comes from the edge of the forest, and Iéle comes out to greet Nkella.

Nkella holds out his hand to us. "We cannot stay, Soanalo. We must keep going."

She cranes her neck. "Nonsense. Stay with us this evening.

I know you must all be hungry after your journey. Leave in the morning."

Nkella doesn't move. Tessa drives up to join him. "The crew needs a safe place to rest and a good meal to eat. It should be okay just one night," she says. "We will continue on our rescue mission once we've rested."

I glance at the crew. AJ leans on one leg with sunken eyes, Harold has decided to sit on the skulls with his head leaning on his hand, and Kaehante's shoulders are slouched yet he is still standing, ready for whatever Nkella decides to do. Nkella sighs.

"One night."

Soanalo nudges his arm. "Don't be such a grump."

"Kh."

She seems nice, why wouldn't he want to stay the night wherever she lives?

I give the ship one last look and almost startle when I don't see it. Now that we've stepped away from the cloaking, all that appears are waves beating against the rocky shore and the odor of death wafting under my nose. I'm glad to be leaving this death beach.

The steady tempo of beating drums greets us as we follow Soanalo up a moss-covered stone path and away from the creepy skull coast of the island. With Nkella walking right behind her, the rest of us follow in a straight line up the narrow path, along with a few others she brought with her, and Ānga and Loá in front of me. I'm in the back with AJ and Harold.

Lime green and aqua-colored lichen cascade down the uphill, moss-heavy path. Large leaves with beautiful blue flowers hang down vines from trees on either side of us. I take in the breathtaking scenery as I follow closely behind while they discuss what we're doing here and how Lāri was captured by traffickers.

"You can stay for as long as you want, and I can send a few of my men to aid you. In return, I hope that you will consider helping with the resistance," Princess Soanalo says.

"Hn. I will consider it," Nkella answers.

I fall back in step with AJ. Harold is just behind us. "What's up with those two?" I ask.

"What do you mean?"

"I don't know. . . They seem. . .interested?"

AJ chuckles. "Why do you ask?"

I snap a glance at him, trying to read his features through the darkness. "No reason. It's just that I've never seen Nkella so. . ." The way he and Soanalo locked eyes earlier emerges in my memory. "I've never seen him act like that. I'm nosy."

"Oh. . . Hmm. . . They've known each other since childhood. They could have united the islands before Danū went under siege. Unfortunately, over the years a lot of the older Ipani generations started to abide by the Empress's rule. Some even agree with her so. . .not sure how much allegiance to the Ipani thrones are left."

My mouth drops open. "Some of them agree to have their ouma bound?"

Loá turns around. "We are all born with different types of ouma, mei? So, some of us, you could say, are more powerful than others. Some would say, even more dangerous."

"And a lot of Ipani have become friends with humans," AJ adds, "like our crew."

"Right." I duck as a thick vine wrapped with a thinner

bioluminescent vine grazes the top of my head. The drumming grows louder as we walk deeper into the forest.

Loá steps over a mossy rock and I follow, careful not to trip in the dark.

"Some believe it's worth the sacrifice to keep everyone, including their mixed children safe," he whispers.

"I see."

"While others grow up mixed and believe that they have a right to the Aō and their ouma," AJ says, "like Princess Soanalo."

"Oh, she's half-human?"

"Yep."

That explains why her ears aren't pointy. I'm learning so much about their customs here, and suddenly, I feel overwhelmed by it all. Nkella is a *prince*. Soanalo is a *princess*—no, a queen. "I've never met a real queen before," I whisper.

"It's rare," AJ tells me. "A lot of the royalty were killed, but there are descendants. Whether they matter or not depends on the allegiance they have to the Empress. Take Oleanu, for instance. There is still a monarchy there, and the Empress pretty much leaves them alone." I take that in. "Apparently, Soanalo taking command of the resistance has made her Queen of Wands."

My eyes widen as I gape at him.

"She should be hiding that," he whispers. "That's going to be dangerous."

Loá laughs. "Soanalo isn't the hiding type."

Laughter and chatter rings through my ears as we hike deeper into the forest. Soon we reach flatter ground. Notes of smoke and some sort of cooked meat assaults my nostrils, and my stomach grumbles. It's been days since I had a real meal that's more than the ship's small rations. What's a girl gotta do for some of whatever they're cooking?

"We're here," Loá says.

"Here where?" I don't see anything. I can sure smell it though.

Soanalo blocks us from walking further into a flat area in the center of the woods and my gaze stops at her.

"We are about to enter our cloaked dome," she says. "The Wands' Prefect doesn't know we are here, so when you depart, do not mention this place to anyone. Do you all agree?"

"Pirate's honor," Nkella smirks and places his hand over his heart.

She scoffs and shoves him a bit. "I am serious."

"Yes, of course. We would not dream of giving up your location," he says.

"I know, but I have to say it anyway. Come in."

19

A THIN PURPLE FILM PASSES OVER ME AS I PASS Soanalo and enter the dome. My surroundings haven't changed color like they did when I ate the cookie on the ship. Come to think of it, they didn't change color when we were sailing under the radar with the cloaking potion either. I guess external uses work differently than ingesting it or maybe it's a different mix of potions all together.

We stand outside a large bonfire with shades of blues and greens dancing in the flames. People gather around on large carpets and pillows, laughing and talking. Moss hangs from large oak trees and bugs that remind me of fireflies dance within them, illuminating the leaves. These are turquoise in color, instead of green or yellow.

Princess Soanalo raises her arm. The drumming stops. "Pr—"

Nkella clears his throat.

"*Captain* Nkella"—she darts a look at him and smiles—

"and his crew are friends of mine. They are staying the night on their way to search for a missing friend who was kidnapped by oumala traffickers. In return, they will help us with the resistance against the Empress."

We will? I flick my eyes to Nkella, whose face is grim.

"Let us feed them and make them feel welcome." She brings her hand down and the Ipani cheer. She turns back to us, "make yourselves comfortable, I have a few rounds to make." She scurries off, and Nkella turns to us.

"We will leave early tomorrow morning." He raises his hat just a little so we can see his face in the light of the flames.

"What's the plan for tracking the traffickers?" AJ asks, his tone serious. The closer we get to finding Lāri, the more anxious he becomes, which is something I'm familiar with. The longer it takes to get home to Talia, the more I fear I'll never see her again.

"We know they are headed to the Temples. Iéle will take care of the rest."

"What about helping them with the resistance?" Kaehante asks and I nod. I was thinking the same thing. I hope it doesn't delay me from finding my way home.

"We've always been in a fight against the Empress anyway," AJ says. "Of course we'll help."

Nkella bows his head, lowering his voice. "We are not joining their fight."

AJ snaps his eyes to him. "What?"

"This dome"—he points around us—"is bancha. She is going to get them all killed. We have our own fight. First Lāri. Then my sister."

"And then the Empress, right?" AJ asks. Tessa reaches for

his arm to hold him back, but AJ pulls away. "This will never stop if we don't do something. What about our curse?"

"Our curse comes after we save Ntaoru. And formulate a strategy. The resistance is chaotic."

"We're stronger in numbers."

"Do not argue with me here, AJ," Nkella growls.

Tessa clears her throat. "That's enough. We will talk about this tomorrow after we leave."

AJ scoffs and goes to sit down by the fire. An Ipani woman joins us holding a plate of food in her hand. She hands one to Nkella and the other to Harold, who she's closest to.

"Come, join us." She beckons for us to follow her and leads us near where AJ is sitting. Over by the other side of the fire is a large pot with some kind of meat stew. "Sit. I will bring you a plate," she tells the rest of us. I find a place next to AJ and Harold plops himself to my left, followed by Tessa and Kaehante. Nkella finds a spot away from us on the other side of the fire. My eyes follow the dancing flames as they appear to almost be moving to the rhythm of the drums.

"If they want to be hidden from the Wands' Prefect, aren't they worried they'd hear the drums?"

"Nah," AJ answers me, "humans make bonfires all the time. That's not illegal. They just don't want anyone else seeing if they use ouma."

"Got it."

The Ipani girl comes back with someone else and hands us all wooden plates of food.

I take one from her and squint at what looks like a piece of chicken on top of tiny yellow balls. "I have no idea what this is, but it smells delicious," I say.

Harold laughs. "I'm so hungry I don't even care what it is." He lowers his eyes to his plate, picking up his fork and takes a bite. I take my fork, realizing it's made out of wood too, and cut off a piece of the meat, scooping up some of the balls with it. I shrug. Maybe it's a type of rice? A smoky honey sauce tickles my taste buds as I stick the forkful in my mouth.

"Mmmm. . . This is so good," I say between chews. "What is it?"

The girl who served us, now sitting to the right of Kaehante flicks her eyes to me. "Roasted seagull with stuffed caterpillar and caterpillar eggs."

Harold and I both stop chewing and glance at each other.

"I'm sorry," I say with food in my mouth, "did you say caterpillar?"

"That's right." Her forehead crinkles.

Harold sticks another forkful in his mouth. "Yep. It's fine. Delicious." Harold smiles with his mouth full.

My eyes fall to my plate. "I think I'm gonna be sick," I mutter to him.

"When in Rome. . ."

"But. . . It's a caterpillar. And its eggs. Not to mention, who eats seagulls?"

AJ chuckles beside me. "I'll eat if you don't want it."

"Just pretend you're eating sushi," Harold tells me.

"But sushi is fish. It's different."

"Some places eat insects on Earth, too, you know," he says matter-of-factly.

My stomach grumbles and I grimace. "No, it's fine. I'll eat it." I take another bite and swallow. "It tastes mostly like the delicious sauce anyway. Good thing I didn't really fall into

Wonderland. I don't think Lewis Carroll would have approved of us eating Absolem."

Harold snorts. "That's grim." And he sticks another piece in his mouth.

"Mm-hmm. . ." I sigh, thinking again of my lost charm bracelet.

AJ leans closer to me. "Many Ipani won't eat animals they or their friends and family can turn into. So it leaves little options for meat."

"Are many Ipani vegetarian? Like, non-meat eaters," I add, in case there isn't a word for vegetarian in the Imboe dictionary.

He nods. "Many on the mainland are."

I swallow a mouthful and scan the Ipani surrounding the circle. Some are human and some are mixed. A much older Ipani man sits on a stump, eating his food; fine lines decorate the corners of his eyes and face and his stripes are prevalent in the firelight.

He looks up at me and raises his chin. I drop my gaze back down at my food.

I've eaten most of the bird and have left a good portion of caterpillar and eggs. There's something about it I just can't get past.

In the corner of my eye, I see Princess Soanalo plop down next to the old man.

I overhear whispers to my left. "It is said that the Empress cursed Tetalla into becoming the Devil himself. And anyone who commits a heinous crime will obtain the threshold of the Devil Card." I dart my eyes to find the person talking but too many others are in the way. Nkella's presence must be making some people nervous.

A pair of crimson eyes stare from across the fire. I snap my eyes to Nkella. Did he hear them?

I don't blame people for talking about his curse; I'm curious too. I still don't understand how he almost slit the Empress's throat. With the Tower being so heavily guarded, how did they manage to get near enough to almost kill her?

Then an image of the Empress's sad green eyes staring back at me from behind her gold mask comes to mind. It must be awful being so alone. And if what they say about her is true—about being so old, immortal even—then how long has she been all alone?

"Why does the Empress wear a mask?" I blurt out. The drumming dies down and people stare at me.

The old man who I spotted earlier leans forward on his stump. "No one knows. They say she was burned long ago from the magma of Danū, before any of us were born. They say it was the fault of the royals from Danū."

"The royals?" I resist my urge to look at Nkella. AJ said he doesn't like the attention.

"Not the present-day royals. The royals from centuries ago," he sings. "The Warrior prince named Tetalla was responsible." He spreads his hand in front of him, facing the sky like a storyteller about to tell a tale.

"Is it true? Is the Empress really that old?" I ask, reverting my eyes back to him.

A few people murmur, others just stare at me. The old man gets up and takes a step toward me, his eyes furrowed. "If the legends are true, then she is." He bows his head to me with a scrutinizing eye. "You used a translation potion."

I nod.

"Where do you come from?" he squints.

I exchange a look with Harold who doesn't seem bothered by the question, then glance back at AJ. "I-I came from a different land."

"A land called Earth," Harold says. "I'm from there too."

I relax my shoulders. Good thing he's here with me.

The storyteller's eyebrows rise as he looks between the two of us, then, with a nod and a smile, he returns to his stump. "In that case," he takes his seat, "everyone calls me Aba. It means 'father' in Ipani. Have you heard of the tale of the *Moera Helāni?*"

Harold and I shake our heads.

"Gather 'round. I will tell it."

The drummers start to lightly tap on their drums, creating a slow tempo as he starts. Loá and Ānga cozy up next to each other close to Aba.

"It has been passed down for many generations." Aba looks at each of us, starting with the princess and making his way around the circle. "Three powerful beings came from another land, long ago. Back when times were simpler, and only Ipani and oumala animals roamed the land."

I lean in as he continues, taking another mouthful of the smoky honey sauce on my plate.

"No one knows why they came, but they brought with them pieces of their world—animals, grain, metals, weapons— and they aimed to conquer."

"Sounds about right," Harold mutters under his breath.

"Sh." I gently shove him.

"But the Ipani were not going to allow themselves to be conquered."

The crowd around the fire cheers, and Soanalo smiles, fist pumping the air. They settle down and Aba keeps going.

"It is said, these three powerful beings were descendants of the Fates of their world. They controlled people's past, present, and future."

Harold and I exchange a glance. *Descendants?*

"But this story is just a myth, mei?" Loá asks.

Soanalo speaks before Aba can answer. "All fables once started with the truth." She smiles.

Aba brings his hands up. "Shall I keep going?"

"Yes, Aba. Sorry." Soanalo winks at the rest of us.

"These sisters were magical, and they were warriors, but they loved each other and were inseparable. It is said they arrived looking for a safe haven for their people. The oldest, who controls people's future, used to travel to the future of her world. The youngest would travel to the past, where she would learn and bring time capsules back to Ipa. The middle sister controlled the present, and she was the weakest for she was trapped in her own present and unable to affect destiny without her two sisters being with her. But she would stay here and make conquests while the others came back with supplies. She trained their army. She also trained her power.

"The sisters of the past and future traveled together and brought back a newfound gift. They drew pictures on what they called cards of Tarot, which they had discovered from their travels. Back then it was no more than just a game, but it became an obsession among the three of them."

My eyes are locked on the flickering flames as I continue listened to Aba's soothing voice. The fire dances, and I swear it takes the shapes of people—three women, dancing within the embers.

"While the sisters were distracted, Ipa was changing, and the Ipani were being affected by the new powers seeping in. Their serpent was eating all the fish, the crops were being cultivated—especially the ouma plants—and battles were breaking out between the new settlers and the natives.

"Danū, Pentacles as the Helāni call it now, was ahead of politics at the time. Their currency ruled Ipa, with its impenetrable resources of ouma fire that could forge the strongest of stones."

My eyes widen as I recall the flattened rubies Nkella had used to pay Demitri.

"Kh. Still is." Nkella's husky voice makes my eyes flick to him. He had been quiet until now. Soanalo giggles at him, and Aba continues.

"While the Helāni built their new empire, Danū trained their strongest—the elite from the volcanic tribes—those with the ouma of heat." He pauses to look between the Ipani sitting close. A man with a sleeve of tattoos on his left arm materializes a fireball in his palm and bounces it in the air. He smirks and one of the guys behind him pats him on the shoulder. It makes me wonder what kind of ouma Nkella had before he was bound.

"One night," Aba continues, "Tetalla traveled far seeking allegiance from the other islands. Sāgirang, which the Helāni call Wands, turned him away, for they wanted war with Danū to claim power. Oleanu, or Cups, did not want to fight at all.

They told him, why shall we fight? We are not affected. We are busy fishing and enjoying the sandy beaches." Aba pauses with a smile. "But Piupeki, always a friend of Danū, shared their best forgers of Piupeki steel, and together they made a sword powerful enough to defeat a divine being from another world.

"Tetalla journeyed to a lonely island where the sisters had taken refuge and built their Tower. Back then it was not called Rutavenye for it still floated in the sea. But Tetalla saw the most beautiful girl he had ever seen, the present Fate. When he laid eyes on her, he dropped his sword. And she saw the bravest, most handsome Ipani warrior she had ever seen as well. And so, they fell in love."

A spiky-haired Ipani guy next to Kaehante interrupts. "Why doesn't Oleanu ever want to fight, hn, Loá?"

"Don't look at me, mei? I am here, fighting the battle like you."

"Silence," Aba booms. The spiky-haired Ipani startles. "In this circle, we do not fight among each other. Where was I? Ah, I remember. When the other sisters came, they all played with their cards of Tarot. Because the name Tetalla means "death bringer," and he had come to kill them, that became his role in their game.

"More and more, it became evident that the younger sister and Tetalla had become smitten with each other. We do not know what happened between Tetalla and the present Fate, but he fell in love again, this time with the sister of the past, making the Empress we know today jealous."

Gasps come from all around the circle. The fire cracks.

"The two sisters fought with magic no Ipani had ever seen, until the Empress killed her. Some said she didn't mean to, that her magic got out of hand, but ever since that day, the Empress has worn a mask."

I flick my eyes up from the fire to see him. She killed her own sister. I recall the Empress talking about her sisters' betrayal.

He leans in and stares at me and Harold. "If you have not yet noticed, the Aō is highly intelligent. Back then, it learned from the new ouma the sisters brought with them; that ouma seeped into the Aō, causing it to learn any intent that was cast. You see, the Aō aims to bring harmony, so instead of fighting it like your body fights a parasite, it embraced it and made it a part of this world. It took their game and made it reality."

My eyebrows rise. "I don't understand. What do you mean by. . .any intent that was cast?"

"You see, when an Ipani reaches puberty, we have the ability to use the ouma, but only by making a sincere connection with the gift of the element it presents to us at puberty."

"A connection? Like with the animals too?"

He nods. "Yes, very good. Just like that. An oumala animal will not communicate with anyone without first creating a bond. The legend the Helāni ancestors told was that the Empress in truth loved her sister. If that were true, the Aō would have grabbed onto whatever the Empress was holding when she cast her spell."

I stare at him. "What was the spell?"

He drops his shoulders and shows me his wrists. "To make us bound. The Empress, they say, tried to control her spell after she cast it, but it became too strong, causing everyone to have a mark, including her."

"Wait," I interrupt. "She can't control it?"

"Maybe. Maybe not." He smiles. "This question is one that conflicts so many Ipani." He leans in and raises his index finger. "The Aō is what commands, not *her*. It is greater than the Empress. It is why it would be impossible to beat the fate of the cards—the Aō and the cards are intertwined."

"But we can still take down the Empress!" Soanalo shouts and the others cheer.

Aba holds up his hand and they quiet down.

"Sorry, Aba. Finish the story." Soanalo smirks and Aba continues.

"Tetalla, having charge of death itself, was locked up for his betrayal. The Empress took his ouma from him, to make him suffer eternally for his betrayal. Later, she made everyone else suffer as well, and the use of ouma became illegal."

I pull down my sleeve to hide my mark.

"You have not been the first voyagers after the Helāni to come," Aba says. "Others have been crossing for hundreds of years. Do they hold the same ouma in your land as they do in ours?"

"Oh. . . we do not have magi—ouma in our world."

His face slackens and murmurs erupt all around me. "No ouma? What do you call your connection to the spirit world? To your Aō?"

Harold shakes his head. "I guess we could call it the fifth dimension in our world, but it's nothing like the Aō. Ouma is not possible at all. The connection you have here with the Aō is fascinating."

"And I thought we had it bad being bound and then stripped of our connection."

"Well, we can't miss what we never had. You did have it," Harold says.

"This is true. And some of us still do," Aba says. "It has not fully left our world."

I let that sink in. Harold had told me before that there is magic on Earth. . . I wonder if it was ever remotely like this. Or if others had just brought it to Earth, like the Tarot. Wait. "But there were three. . . what happened to the other one?"

Aba's eyes light up as he leans in. "The legend says the one who died by the Empress's hand had birthed a child. The oldest sister, and future Fate did what she thought was right and took the baby and fled. No one knows where she went but she hasn't been seen for hundreds of years."

"The Empress cast her spell because she feared your power," I say, a little louder than I expected.

"Yes, it was her fear that caused all of this. But as you can see, many of us have had enough and wish to live freely as we were intended to. With our connection to the Aō."

"As you should," I say, sitting up. Several people stare at me, their faces brightening.

Soanalo stands up beside him. "This is why we must never give up! Why we must fight! And keep on fighting!"

Cheers erupt from all along the circle. It's physically impossible for me not to be fueled with encouragement. Even if I don't know what it's like to be one of them.

My eyes skim to everyone pounding their fists in the air and land on Nkella. He has a bored, grim look on his face. He takes another swig of his flask—lost in thoughts of his own grief as usual.

"I have a question," Harold says. "If the Empress controls the present here, what happens to *the present* if you kill her?"

My gaze lands back on Soanalo. Others await her response; some whisper among themselves.

"We are not tied to her magic," Soanalo says. "We will break her curse and take back the Aō. That is all."

Harold rubs his chin. "But what about—"

"Enough storytelling. It is time to celebrate life. Drummers, drum!" She raises her arms. "Fire dancers, dance!"

"Sounds a little irresponsible," Harold mutters under his breath.

I give him an apologetic shrug and lean back on my elbows to watch the turquoise fireflies zip from moss-covered leaf to moss-covered leaf. I can't imagine killing my own sister. I feel less sorry for her being alone now. My sleeve runs up my arm and I quickly change positions to pull it back down. The last thing I need is for the lot of them to think I'm a spy.

Someone throws something into the fire, making it change colors. The Ipani with the sleeve tattoo holds out his hand to the furious flames. I gasp as a fireball flies from the pit and into his hand like a magnet. The fireball grows, stretching out in size.

A few others cheer as he throws it into the air, and it shifts to resemble a drakon like Gari. My gasp turns into a smile as I stare at the long fiery tail and mustache swishing through the air. It flies around the circle and opens its mouth wide until it dissipates into embers.

I marvel at the Ipani using their ouma for fun. People can turn into birds and fly, while others can manipulate flames. I wish I had some special power like them. Even Harold has a power, even though it's probably subtle and lame because it comes from Earth. But what do I have? Card tricks and the ability to steal—and even that I'm not so great at.

A hauntingly beautiful tune makes me want to lie back while watching the different colors in the flames dance inside the pit. An Ipani man wearing a tan cloth wrapped around his waist down to his knees plucks the chords of a long metallic instrument. It reminds me of a guitar but with fewer strings, a narrower body, and a circular end. Soanalo joins him in song, and my eyes grow heavy from her lullaby.

Around me, people get up and dance to the serenading rhythm of the drums and song:

"Hu'w a isu, hi'r a kong

Heika poé a uro kelante hū nong rō

M'mae e tesī kū yi chī Moera."

A shadow eclipses my view of the fire dancer. "Would you like some garisi?" The young girl who served us food now holds out a tray of small wooden cups with some sort of drink.

"Oh, uh. . . No thanks."

"Are you sure? Everyone else is partaking." Her voice is soft and sweet and it makes me feel bad to tell her no.

Harold and AJ reach over and each grab a cup. "I certainly will." Harold smirks.

I narrow my eyes at them. "What is it?"

She points to the ones on my right and says, "These make you giddy"—she points to the ones on my left—"and those allow you to talk to plants."

My eyes widen. "Wait—what? So, if I drink that, I'll be able to talk to the grass?"

She giggles. "Maybe. If you press your ears down to the

grass, you could hear them. But you will at least be able to talk with the trees and flowers."

Harold grabs one of those too. "What happens if I mix them?"

"You can, most people do."

His smile widens and he chugs the other.

"You'll try everything, won't you?" I jeer.

"At least once." He winks at me. "Before this, I wouldn't dare do anything illegal *because* it could enact my family's curse. But now that I am cursed, what's the worst that can happen to me? If I can't break this damn hex, I'll die anyway so I'm going to live it up. Besides, who doesn't want to talk to plants?" He elbows me. "And find out what they know."

I purse my lips. I'll have to ask him more about his curse when he sobers up later.

"Oh, come on, you're going home. When is the next time you'll get to talk to plants?"

"That's a good point. . ."

"That's the spirit!" With that, he climbs to his feet and takes off to a nearby tree.

What's the worst that can happen that hasn't already happened? I've become invisible, floated away, and then flown on a drakon. Why not talk to plants too while I'm at it?

"Don't go too far. Please stay inside the dome," the girl calls after him.

Harold half turns and does a salute before joining a few others surrounding a big oak tree. I spin to AJ who's lying down on his back with his eyes closed.

"How about you? Don't you want to talk to trees?"

"No. I just want to try and feel happy."

My heart sinks, and I squeeze his wrist. "I understand."

The girl turns to offer the drinks to others, and I call her back. "On second thought, why not?"

Her face lights up. "Each are mixed with spirits. In case, you do not know this. . ."

"Spirits?"

She nods.

"Okay, this might be a stupid question, but by spirits, do you mean. . . alcohol?" Because I'm not drinking ghosts.

Confusion flickers on her face. "Yes. . .with alcohol."

I let out a breath and giggle. Whew. "Okay good. . . In that case, then, hell yes!" I take one of the cups filled with the talking plant enabler and take a sip. The odd mixture of dirt and maybe a mushroomy-type liquid with the spicy essence of rum burns down my throat. I take another sip and a fireball catches my eye as the fire dancer now spins three fireballs in the air. A girl next to him dances to the beat of the music as Soanalo keeps singing her tune.

"Oruoko a pepao n'doá poé Ranū
Onje sehu, ja a asuisi mō."

A pressure weighs down my head, and soon the singing and music fades away.

"*You* shouldn't be here."

"Who said that?" I say.

"Over here."

"Yes, us." Another voice joins in.

I spin around in my spot. AJ cocks his head up from the ground. "Soren, are you okay?"

I flick my eyes down to him. "Did you say something?"

"I said, 'Are you'— Ohh, is the potion working?" He grins.

I gasp and look around.

"Down here!"

I snap my gaze down by my side. Two little purple flowers poke out from the gravel. They have a conical shape with little yellow round tops poking from within them.

"Wow. . . I can hear you! Like, *really* hear you!"

"Well, snap out of it, missy! Get out of here, the lot o' you!"

"Oh. . .!" I gape at them.

"You shouldn't be here," the other says more sternly.

"Why not?"

"Because you'll end up catching us all on fire!"

I gasp. "No, we won't. It's a controlled flame. You'll be fine."

"Oh, we'll be fine, will we? You and your Devils always think you run this land."

"Don't you think you're being a little dramatic?" I ask them.

"Well, we won't talk to you then." The other crosses his branches, fisting his leaves like they're hands.

"You're still talking to me."

"Hmph."

My face deadpans, and I look down at my drink. Maybe I don't want to talk to plants anymore. I shift my gaze back to the fire, and away from the plants. I catch a glimpse of Nkella sitting on his own, staring into the flames. Kaehante and Tessa are mingling with the crowd as well, but this entire time, Nkella hasn't moved from his spot. I would have thought he'd want to talk more to the princess, his childhood friend. He lifts his chin, eyebrows furrowed as he catches me looking at him.

Still, his gaze doesn't falter. A shiver moves up and down my spine. He looks away.

I don't know if it's the ambiance or the liquid courage I have in my hands, but in the spur of the moment, I decide to get up and go sit by him. He flicks his eyes to me as I sit down. His face hardens and he moves his gaze back to the fire. He holds his usual flask in his hand. Notes of hickory and vanilla tickle my nose.

"Don't care for talking to plants, huh?"

"Hnn."

I snort. "Guessing you don't care about laughing either."

He scowls at me. "You should not drink."

I twist my features. "Why not? Everyone else is."

"You are not used to it. We need to be alert early and ready."

"Lighten up a little. When was the last time you had fun?"

No response. I sigh. "Fine." I take another sip and smirk. "So, I bet you enjoyed your meal."

"Daí?" His left brow arches in my direction, but his body remains rigid.

"Finally, being able to eat good food and all. . .or. . .at least something to your liking?"

He grimaces.

"Right?" I press. "I mean. . . I'm sure AJ is a great cook when he's not cursed. They told me your curse is different. You're not undead, right? So, you can taste food?"

He nods.

"That sucks. Not the not-being-undead part. . ."

"That is the true curse."

"Not being undead?"

"Koj. Not being able to eat good food on the ship."

I shoot him a glance. "Did you just make a joke?"

The corner of his lip curls up and he glances at me from the low corner of his eyes. Then he flicks them back to the fire. "It will not last. I will save them. I will unite their spirits with their bodies if it kills me."

I swallow. "Sounds like you have a lot on your shoulders."

"Hn."

"Man of few words." I shake my head.

A girl with short bouncy hair, wearing an overlap skirt, walks over to us holding a tray of drinks.

"Some garisi for the *aovate*?"

I quirk a brow. "Aov—what?"

"Aren't you lovers?" she asks, her face beaming with whatever euphoria she's feeling from her drinks.

My face pales and I quickly notice how close I'm sitting to Nkella. I quickly inch to my left and shake my head at her.

He scoffs. "She is my gembella. And she will not have any more garisi," he says flatly. The girl's eyes widen, and she gives me an apologetic look, backing away. My cheeks flush and I turn my head.

My eyes land on an angry buttercup.

"You need to leave *NOW!*"

Ugh! This thing still hasn't worn off? Ignoring it, I search for Harold and find him leaning against the big oak he had been having a conversation with but now talking to an Ipani girl and laughing. At least he's having fun. I wonder what the tree told him and if it was as annoying as these dumb flowers. I give Nkella a side glance. He hasn't moved.

"So, I'm still your gembella then, huh?"

"You know our agreement. You are my comfortable prisoner."

"Right. . . But you did say for now. . ."

"Hn."

"So. . ." Changing the subject, I nod toward Soanalo who's dancing with Loá and Ānga. "What's the deal with you and the princess over there?"

He quirks a brow. "There is no deal between us. She is the head of the resistance and respects my decision to not take a major role."

"No, I mean. . ." I clear my throat. "Why aren't you two. . . What was the word? Ao—v. . ."

He guffaws. "Aovate? Koj."

"Why not?"

"Our parents would have liked that. But she is more like. . .family to me now. Besides, she likes the same sex."

A girl with long brown hair down to her rear walks up to Soanalo and hugs her from behind. Soanalo arches her neck, and they kiss as they dance together.

"Oh, I see."

"There is no space in my world for aovate," he concludes.

I catch a glimpse of Ānga and Loá enthusiastically embracing each other, their mouths locking. My cheeks burn, so I dart my eyes back to the flames. I didn't realize those two were a couple, but I guess they were pretty cozy while Aba was telling his story.

A popping sound goes off in my ear and a tickle on my hand makes me drop my gaze. I gasp. "Philo!"

"*Muse*," Nkella hisses darkly.

The glare from the fire reflects off her red mosaic pattern as she dances on the back of my hand. He reaches over and I pull back.

"Wait!"

"That is an utwa. Like you if you are defending it."

"No. . .you don't understand." I stammer. "I know this one from my world. . . But I didn't know she was from here." I don't even know why I care so much about defending a spider, but I feel like I know this one. . . And she's Madame Asteria's. "She is afraid of the Empress," I spew out.

"Dai? How can you tell?"

"I don't know. . ." I move Philo away from him, so he can't get her. I don't want him to squish her like he did that other one. "I felt like she was trying to warn me away from her when I was at the Tower."

"Hnn. Oumala animals do not trust loosely. I would find out what it wants. Unless, you do know and are lying to me again."

"I'm not lying," I sigh.

"Hn."

My eyes drop to Philo who is waving her two front legs at me as if they're arms, her eyes staring at me intently. "What's the matter with you, Philo?"

She stills and then disappears with a pop. Huh. That was weird.

"They're coming."

I look down to the buttercup. "Who's coming?"

"You've doomed us all. . ." The buttercup hides her eyes with her leaves as she tries to duck in place.

Nkella squints his eyes and looks at me. "Who are you talking to?"

"The plants," I sigh again. "They won't shut up, and honestly, they're kind of downers! I thought this would—"

"What are they saying, daí?" His brows furrow as he starts to get up.

"Um. . .that we've doomed them all and that someone is coming."

"Why did you not say something?" He takes out his bow, and I gasp.

"What? Because they weren't making sense. They said they were afraid of burning. I thought they meant the bonfire."

He stares at me, and a fiery glow flickers behind his irises. I gulp. "I thought we were invisible here. What's the problem?"

The music stops playing and several people pause to look at us.

He grunts. "This was reckless."

Soanalo takes a few steps toward us. "What is going on?"

A warm wind brushes against my cheek. I rub my arms and dart a look around, locking eyes with Harold who wrinkles his nose at me. Nkella nocks his arrow and my eyes widen.

A loud whistling like the sound of an airstrike siren drops down from the sky. My stomach plummets as I arch my neck. Dark purple fumes zip down from the sky.

"Doomed!"

I glance down at the buttercup. The flowers were right. But how did they find us? More purple fumes fall from the sky. This time, they start to drop right inside the circle! I duck close to the ground.

Nkella yells something inaudible as he aims his bow. Everyone now stumbles to their feet; more than few, drunk and disoriented.

"They found us!" Soanalo yells.

"But that's impossible!" Ānga says from behind her. "How'd they get past our cloaking?"

Nkella flicks his eyes to me, and I shrink. "I had nothing to do with this. There's no way I could have!"

He presses his lips together but snaps his head to face Kaehante who's running toward us.

"Captain, they must have been following us."

A large purple spark ignites on one end, and in a flash, the entire invisibility dome is caught in a purple flame. I shield my face from the heat and a minute later, the flames dissipate, leaving ash where flower beds had been. Oh no. . .the buttercups. I back up behind Nkella as a circle of Arcana soldiers blocks anyone from leaving.

20

THE FOLIAGE AROUND ME CRINKLES, TURNING FROM luscious green to brown, until it becomes ash—not from the fire, that would have been expected, but from the Arcana soldiers. I don't know how they did it, but the moment they fell from the sky, every fruit hanging from the trees and every plant within the dome's vicinity died.

The poor buttercups. The fire was the least of their worries. Their harrowing screams will forever haunt me; I wish I had never drunk that garisi. The nearby trees are also dead, their leaves lying singed on the ground, and the turquoise fireflies are gone. The Minor Arcana encircles us dressed in their black robes clasped with metallic purple emblems displaying a wand on a shield and their metallic purple masks over blank faces.

The Hierophant, Demitri, steps out from between the soldiers; he is wearing his long black robes and black and gold hat. The Wands' Prefect steps up beside him, followed by an

Arcana soldier. This soldier has a chrome mask with a yellow sheen and his metal emblem reveals a yellow sword on a chrome shield. I flick my gaze to Nkella who has an arrow nocked and ready in his bow.

Demitri walks along the inner circle, carefully eyeing each of us. My eyes land on the Empress's spiderweb clasp on his robes, which reminds me to pull my sleeve down, even though he's already met me. Maybe he won't recognize me. But then his gaze meets mine and lingers on my face, a smirk curling on his lips. So much for hoping he doesn't recognize me.

"How did you find us?" Soanalo speaks first. Ānga and Loá back her from both shoulders, holding sharp spears. Soanalo grips a spear firmly in her hand as well.

"I have my ways. Did you think the Prefect wouldn't report a pirate ship making port on the island? My scouts sensed ouma in use." My gaze snaps to the soldier with the chrome mask. "The Empress wouldn't be pleased about that, you know."

"Then why have you come and not her?"

"I wouldn't dream of disturbing Her Divinity for someone as"—he crinkles his nose, making a face of disgust—"as trivial as you."

Ānga points the tip of his spear at Demitri's face. In one swift motion, one of the purple masked soldiers closest to Demitri grabs Ānga's neck. I hold my breath. Loá runs to his side, his eyes wide and full of fear. Ānga's skin turns a dark purple, and his eyes bulge. The soldier drops him to the ground. We all gape as his skin wrinkles and he gasps for air. Loá mutters Ānga's name in a muffed cry as he takes his head and sits it on his lap, everyone watching. Demitri's expression doesn't change; it's as if he's watching a show, bored out of his mind.

Ānga's arms shrivel up but his skin doesn't return to his natural olive color. Instead, it swells up, then quickly shrinks down in size. Within seconds, his body decomposes, releasing gasses. Loá's hands shake as he watches his lover crumble in front of him.

I stumble back, holding my nose, but a soldier steps up behind me and I freeze, terrified of him touching me. I don't even look at the soldier behind me, afraid that even glaring at him will have a deadly effect on me.

Whatever power they've been imbued with, it rots living things. Impossibly fast.

Loá jumps up and grabs his spear, but Soanalo grabs his arm and shoves him behind her. He fights her off. Two more Ipani grab him to try to keep him back. My throat constricts, and I narrow my eyes at Demitri. I'd want to kill him too, but it isn't safe to attempt that right now. Not after witnessing what just happened to Ānga.

Demitri winces but quickly rights his posture, repositioning his clasp. He turns to the chrome-masked soldier. "Take them alive. We'll sort out the bound ones later. Leave the humans." He backs away, his gaze falling to me. I gulp.

The Arcana soldiers start advancing toward every human and Ipani in the circle. My breath catches. I stumble forward, almost walking into Nkella.

Soanalo releases a loud scream from the back of her throat sounding like a war cry. Others join in. Nkella loosens an arrow, hitting a soldier in their eye. The soldier disappears, and then reappears. All around me, people draw their weapons; those with ouma use it.

The Ipani with the sleeve tattoo throws a fireball at one of the soldiers. The soldier disappears and reappears right in front of him, grabbing the man before he can run and taking off in a gust of smoke.

"Protect Aba!" someone's voice booms from within the chaos.

Aba is backed against a dead tree. One of the purple masks appears next to him and grabs him with a robed arm. Nkella nocks an arrow, immediately letting it loose. My heart hammers in my chest as I watch it aim straight for the soldier. The arrow hits the tree right as the soldier disappears, with Aba in his clutches.

I choke on a scream.

A swarm of Ipani and soldiers fight to the death. Powers are shooting out from unbound Ipani, while arrows are being shot and spears and swords are being swung from those who are bound. And I'm standing here useless. The Ipani who was behind me has moved away since Demitri gave the order to leave the humans, but that doesn't stop AJ or Tessa from fighting. I grab one of the raku potions in my bandolier and tug it loose. My crew is in trouble, so I have to try and help. When I glance up, I spot Demitri standing on the opposite end of the circle. For a moment, I catch his gaze. My eyes narrow. He inches toward the Prefect and whispers something to him. The Prefect stares at me, his brow arched.

See you soon.

He's going to try and take me. And honestly? This isn't even my fight. I'm no warrior, and I'm gonna get myself caught by Demitri if I stay. Or worse, a soldier will make me rot from the inside out.

This is the perfect opportunity for me to run away. I can run to a village. Get myself situated and find out where the Ace of Wands is by myself. I don't need Nkella or that stupid World Card.

I duck my head and lower myself to the ground, turning slowly to sneak away. I spot a nearby tree and bushes that didn't die when the Arcana soldiers landed. I run and take cover behind the bush, my heart hammering hard in my chest. All I have to do is run to the next cover, then the next, until I'm far enough away from the fight that I can keep running for miles. Nkella's too preoccupied to notice me gone.

I take another second to catch my breath before looking for the next place to take cover. A tree with a large trunk blocks my view of the path. Perfect. I give myself to the count of three before making my next sprint when AJ's voice makes me pause. He calls for Tessa, desperation sounding in his voice. My mouth dries.

He'll be fine. They'll all be fine. They can take care of themselves.

What can *I* do? I'm no fighter, and I need to get home to my sister.

I sprint to the tree and hide behind the trunk. My back leans against it while I catch my breath.

Tessa screams, and my blood runs cold. Tessa's never screamed like that before. I look over my shoulder just to make sure she's okay. Damnit, the shrubs and dead trees are in the way. I'll have to get closer and risk getting caught.

Memories of me, Tessa, Kae, and AJ around the barrel

where we eat fill my mind. Memories of the full week at sea, getting to know the crew, becoming one of their crewmates. AJ's laugh as I show him a card trick rings through my memories. Memories of how he opened up to me about Lāri, of Tessa lending me clothes, and caring enough to buy me a toothbrush, of showing me how to make raku bombs, of Kae covering for me about the powder and teaching me how to tie knots, and of Harold being silly on the ship with his stories about Frost Giants. Even Nkella comes to mind. I may hate him for being such a jerk to me, but I know it's because he's overprotective of his crew—and his sister. I swallow. His sister who's imprisoned by the Empress. And I never told him I saw her. This entire time he's kept me as a prisoner because he's been looking out for his family. And now I'm running to save myself while they need me.

If I'm honest, my time spent with them is the first I've ever felt like I belonged. And neither AJ, nor Tessa, nor Kae has ever made me feel less than or asked me to do anything I was uncomfortable with. Whether I like it or not, this crew became my family, and I'm not sure I'll ever find anyone like them again. My chest tightens and I pull myself off the tree. I can't leave them. I have a bandolier full of raku, and maybe I'll suck at fighting, but they need me. I have to at least try.

I run back and stop where I had stood before. Across the circle, soldiers grab hold of four Ipani women. Tessa launches a raku potion at them, spilling out a lime green gas. I let out a sigh of relief seeing that she's okay. The girls scatter and the soldiers disappear. They each reappear in different locations, but AJ and Harold intercept two of them. Even if it's for a moment, the women have a chance at getting away.

One of the purple masks grabs AJ. I quickly unclasp a raku bottle from the metal bearing and throw. It hits the ground right at his feet. The green gas fumes out and the soldiers stall. AJ jumps free, turns around with a handgun, and takes one shot at the first soldier and another at the one about to grab Harold. Yes! I even remembered to hold onto my intent to keep AJ and Harold safe from the effects of the raku. I unlatch another raku from my belt when I catch the Prefect walking toward me and I take a careful step back.

A soldier grabs me from behind, and I jerk forward, letting out a scream and dropping the raku to the floor. Lime green smoke sizzles out into the air as the glass shatters and I hold my breath. No!

Nkella spins around and releases his arrow into the soldier's deep eye socket.

The soldier lets me go as he smokes out. Nkella grabs my arm and pushes me into a tree.

"Hide."

"But. . ." I hold up a new raku potion from the bandolier.

An amber glow flares behind his dark pupils, and I retreat. He nocks another arrow and turns back to the fight.

I huff to myself and lean against the tree. I'm not hiding, I came back to fight and that's what I'm going to do. I search for the Prefect, as I seem to have lost sight of him, but then catch him back by Demitri's side. They've walked away from the battle and seem to be having a private discussion. Demitri scans the field, probably looking for me. I can tell he doesn't like to get his hands dirty. After all, he sent the Prefect after me instead of crossing the battle himself. The Prefect grabs his arm, says something, and another soldier appears next to them —the chrome-masked soldier.

I spot AJ pointing his gun at the chrome-masked soldier, but then he lowers the gun. Why doesn't he shoot? AJ shuffles back, running toward Kaehante and Tessa.

The chrome-masked soldier disappears and reappears behind Loá. AJ whips around and screams, running toward them just as they disappear. My hands shake as I grip the glass bottle of raku. I wasn't fast enough. How am I going to help anyone if I'm not fast enough?

The chrome-masked soldier reappears, and AJ runs toward him at full speed. My gut drops. What the hell kinda tactic is that?

The soldier grabs onto him and I throw the raku. Before it splatters on the ground, inches from where they are, the chrome mask disappears with AJ.

Fear freezes me in place. I grab onto my head and spin around. More and more Ipani are missing. They took AJ.

Oh my God. They took AJ.

My heart hammers in my throat as I furiously look for the rest of the crew.

Nkella, bow and quiver now hanging on his back, fights the Arcana soldiers with his sword. They smoke out, he bypasses them, and then he meets another soldier on his other side.

Kaehante steps next to him with a sword in his hand. A sigh of relief leaves me. I pull another raku bottle free and prepare to throw it.

I run a bit closer and duck behind someone's rucksack. Out from the corner of my eye, the chrome-masked soldier takes another Ipani, but I yelp when I see Tessa swinging her arms from her chair and grab *on to* him! What is she doing? Did she run out of raku, so she thought she'd fight them off with her fists? Nkella and Kaehante flick their gaze to me.

Kaehante runs back for her, only to be met with the same soldier. Nkella yells out something in Ipani, his face distraught, but then he is met with a different soldier—one of the purple masks.

The Wands' Prefect starts advancing toward me. Thanks to my yelp, I'm sure. I take my raku and shoot it straight at him.

The Perfect grabs the raku bottle from the air with one hand and stares at me. I still. The Prefect bounces the glass bottle on the palm of his hand and throws it at the group of Ipani struggling to fight off the soldiers. I just armed him with my own explosive, I'm so stupid!

The Perfect turns to face me, and I inch back. I take another raku, and this time, throw it hard next to him. The grenade splatters on a rock, sizzling with its lime-green smoke. He wavers in place, then drops to the floor, hitting his head on the ground. Booyah!

An Arcana soldier appears over the Prefect and takes him away in a cloud of smoke.

All at once, the soldiers stop and move back into formation. The Ipani who remain hold their ground. I search for Kaehante or Harold but don't see them anywhere. My eyes land on Nkella, an arrow nocked in his bow, his face rigid and unmoving. They've taken the whole crew, all except the captain. I quickly make my way over to him, his gaze remaining past me.

"Well, well, well." The familiar voice sends a chill down my spine. "My soldiers have been busy."

I slowly turn around, stepping behind Nkella. In the center of the circle, standing next to Soanalo, is a woman wearing a black decorative spiderweb outfit and a gold mask with a laurel leaf crown. The Empress is here.

"YOUR DIVINITY," DEMITRI SAYS AS HE STEPS OUT from the shadows. "I was just getting ready to tell you the news. I've found the resistance."

Without looking at him, she answers, "And why wasn't I made aware the moment you found them?" She looks around. "You've almost wiped them all out. Did you not think I'd hear their deaths calling?"

"I didn't think you'd want to be disturbed over common news, Your Greatness. You can trust me with these matters, I wouldn't expect a supreme being such as your divine self would want to step foot on this dirty island."

Panic pounds through my veins. I hope *their* deaths" does not include the crew. Where did Demitri send everyone? I push the crew to the back of my mind as I try to stay calm.

"Oh, but I do want to question their leader," she sings. "There may be more of them, you fool."

Demitri shifts uncomfortably. "Apologies, Your Divinity. I will do better."

"Hmm." She eyes him from the corner of her mask. "Very well. You are dismissed."

He stands there for another awkward moment, then backs away, walking toward a purple-masked soldier. I do a quick sweep and no longer see the chrome-masked soldier.

"Oh, Hierophant?" the Empress calls. Demitri pauses. "Collect the dead and tortured. Take them to my Tower to feed the animals."

"Yes, Your Greatness." He turns to two soldiers and snaps his fingers, motioning to the slain on the ground. An Arcana soldier picks up the now-tortured corpse and disappears in a gust of smoke.

Demitri starts to walk to another soldier with a purple mask but glances up at me. We lock eyes. I avert my gaze, and he leaves with the soldier in a gust of smoke.

The Empress sweeps the area, her eyes landing briefly on Nkella, then back to Soanalo. "The rest will become part of my army." I shrink behind Nkella, not wanting her to see me.

The Empress fixes her gaze on Princess Soanalo. "You must be the one leading the resistance. Did you think you could hide from me? *Resistance*," she repeats slowly, like venom leaving her lips behind her mask. "I see you've taken matters into your own hands." She takes a step toward the princess, who doesn't move a muscle. "And led unbound Ipani to their demise."

Soanalo raises her chin. "Toward their *salvation*."

No one moves as we watch the Empress size Soanalo up and down. "Half human, half Ipani. And"—she nudges the mark on her wrist—"*Queen of Wands?*" She laughs. "Tell me,

Your *Highness*, now that you hold the fate of your people in your hands, how will you save them?" She whispers that last part loud enough for all to hear.

Soanalo lifts her chin higher. "We have been waiting. And now we will kill you."

Nkella groans, and I flick my eyes to him. He still has his arrow pointed to the ground. No wonder he is taking so long to shoot; one wrong move, and he'll be animal fodder.

"The only thing you've been resisting is your future."

"You will never defeat us," Soanalo spits.

The Empress gives off a deep chuckle, as she elegantly places a gloved finger on her mask's bottom lip. "Listen closely, all who remain," she commands. Her voice is clear and steady, her eyes remain fixed on Soanalo. Ipani and humans, all with weapons in their hands, stare at the Empress, fearful of what she's about to say. "This is what will befall anyone who challenges my reign."

The Empress raises her hand and Soanalo's chin rises, her back straightens, and her entire body levitates off the ground. Her spear drops to the sand with a thud.

Nkella nocks his arrow and releases it but it dissipates into black smoke mid-flight as the Empress blocks her face with one hand. She snaps her gaze straight to Nkella and I gasp. Her eyes move over to me as well, and I take a step back. Does she recognize me? I tug down on my sleeve, making sure my mark is covered.

"Tsk-tsk-tsk." She shakes her finger. "You tried that once and failed. You should know better. An arrow cannot kill me."

"It can hurt you. And that brings me pleasure." Nkella

nocks another arrow and points it back at her. Yep. He's completely insane.

I glance at Soanalo who surprisingly has a wicked smile pasted on her face. The ground rumbles, and vines start growing from the ash, wrapping themselves around the Empress's ankles. Sharp black thorns grow from their stalks. My mouth hangs open.

"Despite your power, I also have mine as *Queen* of Wands." Although constrained, Soanalo still manages to make herself sound regal. "Even bound, I was born anew."

It's impossible to guess the Empress's expression behind her mask. Is she afraid? Is she unfazed? An Arcana soldier advances toward the Empress. As he holds out a gloved hand, the vines that constrict wither away, quickly turning to ash. The flowers that were sprouting die before reaching full bloom. Soanalo's smile fades but she doesn't look weak or scared. Even with her life threatened, she keeps her composure.

The Empress steps from the ash, pushing it away with her boot. "That just made me get creative, stupid girl. You forget, I have nothing better to do than stand here all day and have fun with you."

Nkella draws his sword and points it at her. I didn't even see him put away his bow and arrows.

The Empress laughs. "My boy," she says. "You just won't give up. I let you go once, why don't you leave now before I do what I've kept myself from doing all these years? I never wished you any harm."

This throws me. What does she mean by that?

"Release Soanalo. Release everyone. Release my crew."

"Your crew?"

"Yes. Where is my crew?" His voice is calm, collected. I can't see his face from behind him but I can tell he's trying hard not to let his rage out.

"Perhaps they were sent to be animal fodder. Why don't you ask your sister?"

With a wave of her hand, red smoke forms next to the Empress, revealing a masked soldier wearing black with a pearly white mask. She wears clasps with a silver shield and tower on the top of her robe—the Empress's Tower. Nkella's lips part and he almost drops his sword but quickly steadies his arm.

The Empress tilts her head toward Nkella. "She's been quite the entertainment, but I admit, I have been saving her special powers for something else."

Soanalo tries to squirm free as the Empress turns to face her.

I stay behind Nkella, even though her attention isn't on me. Nkella looks unsure of what to do, like he wants to run toward his sister or run to Soanalo, even though she's being held by the Empress's magic.

"Your resistance won't be able to save you," she tells Soanalo. "You aren't worth keeping for my Minor Arcana. I suppose the only thing left to do with you is. . .eternal torment. Ntaoru, burn her alive."

Nkella runs toward his sister and I gasp. The Empress holds up a hand and freezes Nkella on the spot.

"Silly boy, did you forget I control everyone's present?"

Ntaoru holds up a hand. Soanalo spits at the ground but then her breathing grows heavy. An agonizing moan escapes her lips and boiling blood sizzles out her eyes. My blood grows cold.

Screams erupt from her friends around us, those who weren't taken yet. I look around, there are only about a dozen left. They stare at Soanalo, unsure of what to do. If they move, surely a soldier will grab them and whisk them away. Likely, the only reason they remain is that the Empress wanted them to watch.

"Let them go," Nkella says.

"As I said, I cannot have a Queen of Wands leading a resistance. How does that saying go? Kill the leader, and you dismantle the army?"

Ntaoru continues using her ouma on Soanalo. The princess's skin is burning off, her face transforming into hot, oozing boils as Ntaoru smolders her from the inside out. The volcanic ouma. The pretty flower crown that sat on her head has burned to a crisp.

I grab my last raku bottle and aim it toward the Empress. Nkella locks eyes with me but he doesn't say anything. I throw, aiming the bomb straight at her. Please, hit her.

The raku lands on the ground right by the Empress's dress and starts to release its gas. The Empress laughs as she steps on the liquid grenade with her foot.

Soanalo hits the gravel sounding like a bag of potatoes. Ntaoru turns her unsmiling mask to look at the Empress.

"Ntaoru?" Nkella asks, his voice quivering. He holds out a hand to her but she doesn't respond. Would she even remember her name?

With a wave of the Empress's hand, Ntaoru disappears in a cloud of red smoke, leaving me standing in front of the Empress, and Nkella frozen at her side. Orangey-amber light burns behind his irises.

The Empress fixes her eyes on me, and I look away from Nkella. I gasp.

"You. . ."

I take a step back.

"You're the girl from the Tower. Soren, is it?"

"Me? I—I don't think so. . ."

"Yes. You are the Fool I've been searching for."

Something crunches next to me, and I snap my gaze toward a moving bush. Blond hair pokes out from the leaves. A soldier appears over the bush and drags Harold out, kicking and screaming.

The Empress tilts her head and stares at him. "Why if it isn't the brave Magician. Come back for these?" She takes out a small pouch from her belt and holds it over her palm.

Harold struggles to pull free from the masked soldier's hold. "Give those back."

The Empress raises her voice an octave, amusement tinging her words. "You were meant to show me how to use them," the Empress continues. "Oh well, I have no use for you then. Hold him there. I'll deal with him next."

A groan rips from Nkella's lips. I snap my attention back to him. His eyes blaze, and his veins pop out in a glowing orange light, releasing him from the Empress's hold. I suck in a breath. What's happening? Is he. . .turning? His hat falls from his head and two horns protrude from his hair. His chest heaves as he turns his attention to the Empress.

The Empress lifts her chin, but her gold mask covers any fear in her face. . .if she has any. "How are you doing this?" she demands. She must mean, how can he free himself from her powers? She raises two fingers and two large spiders with reflective bodies slide down from the trees, dropping a thick web over Nkella. He swings his sword, slicing the webs in half as more spiders pour from their dimension. He jerks harder, but they cling to his skin. One crawls inside his mouth, and he bites down, showing his sharp teeth as he spits it at the Empress. Bile reaches my throat, but I swallow it.

More spiders swing down, some large, some small. There're too many of them for him to fight off. They quickly wrap their sticky web around him, cocooning him until I can no longer see him.

Some of the people who witnessed Soanalo's cruel death have run to hide, but more soldiers are appearing in the perimeter. I wonder if the rebels were caught when they ran. Others are still crouching down on the floor, with weapons in their hands, waiting to strike.

Panic runs down my spine. I lock eyes with the Empress who's striding straight toward me. I dash to where Harold is hiding when a soldier grabs me from behind, his ghostly arms solidifying as they squeeze me in place. I start to kick but his grasp grows stronger. The Empress nears me, her icy stare boring into me, studying me. My sleeve moves up as I fight to get away, revealing my mark. I turn my arm to hide it.

"You *are* that girl, aren't you?"

"N-no." I jerk hard but the soldier grabs my hair and pulls it back so I'm facing the Empress. I swallow.

"You were part of the captain's crew the entire time. You saw his sister in that arena. You're quite the liar. Tsk-tsk."

I stifle a gasp. A fierce glow emanates from where Nkella was being held by the spiders. Did he hear her? Why do I care about that right now? Neither one of us is going to make it out of this alive. I shake my head despite her truthful revelation. "I still cannot read you." She steps closer.

This is it. She's going to find out I have the same mark as her, and then she's going to kill me like she killed her own sister.

No one other than myself is worthy of this mark. Anyone who has it should be dead.

"Such a Fool to continue on your quest with pirates who betrayed their Empress." She raises her hand, and I flinch. "Anyone with them now is my enemy. Perhaps your fate should match the rest of your captain's crew for your treason." Her tongue lingers on the *n* of treason.

The blood drains from my face. I picture myself becoming skeletal like AJ when ocean water hits me. I jerk from side to side, trying to escape, but the more I fight, the stronger the soldier becomes. The Empress moves her hand up, and she lifts her chin. My face snaps to look at her. I swallow.

Magic sparks from her fingers. I brace myself for the impact. My whole body vibrates, and a reverberating white film shakes my bones. The soldier who was holding me lets go and gets blasted away from me. I clutch at the ground, waiting to be turned into a skeleton, when something across from me grabs my attention.

Harold's body floats upward. The soldier who had been holding him has been blasted backward, too, just like mine had. My mouth drops as Harold's body becomes a skeleton from head to foot. And in a flash, reverts back, only to drop unconscious to the ground.

I don't understand. I start to move toward him but the Empress points at me so I still.

Her green eyes lock on mine. "How did you do this?"

"Me? I didn't do anything."

"My magic ricocheted off you and hit the Magician."

I blink a few times. Her magic bounced off me and hit Harold? "But I didn't do anything." I stare at Harold's immobile body, then back at the Empress. I really wish I could see behind that mask right now, to glimpse at her expression. She readies her hand again and takes a step closer. I straighten my back and inch away from her.

She's about to try again when she lets out a hiccup as a sword impales her midriff, slicing right through her. A sharp breath leaves her as she stumbles, revealing Nkella holding a bloody sword behind her. His chest heaves, his eyes are glowing, and a menacing smirk smears his face.

My knees weaken, and I stumble back.

Nkella's eyes move to mine. I gape at him as he spins the bloody blade around his wrist. I crawl back an inch.

A soldier appears to tend to the Empress, but she stands upright. The blood stains on her dark dress are nothing more than a wet puddle. She seems completely unharmed.

She stretches her neck. "It's foul play to stab someone in their back."

"You see everything, daf? So it is not the same."

And yet, she didn't see that coming.

"I let you leave me. And after everything, you still hate me that much?" Her voice quivers. After everything?

As Nkella bows his head, an amber vein appears like lightning in his right eye. "I *will* kill you."

"And just how many times are you going to try?"

A hoard of Arcana soldiers appear around us. Nkella raises

his sword, the veins in his protruding muscles letting off a searing glow.

Just then, Iéle jumps from the Aō dimension straight at us. Nkella gets shoved right into me, and we both land with a hard thud on the grass, his elbow jerked into my gut. "Ow!"

He scrambles off me, and whips over to Iéle.

"Iéle, koj!"

The wolf lowers her head and whimpers. My surroundings are grayed out. She brought us into the Aō. I climb to my feet, ready to run. I face the Empress, who stares right past me. She balls her fists and lets out a frustrated wail.

I jump at the sound of her cry, ready to run or to fight soldiers, but none of them can see us.

Two people materialize behind the Empress and I have to do a double take. The girl has wavy red hair, pale skin, and is wearing a bandolier across her chest. It's me. And beside me is Nkella. "What—"

Nkella cuts me off and holds his hand out to me to keep me from running. I don't think I can run from the dome Iéle just draped over us. If I do, I might escape it and get caught.

The Empress spins around and sees us running. Iéle takes a small step forward and I realize what's happening. The wolf has the power to make things appear that aren't there. When Nkella had tied me to the chair in the ship, Iéle had made me see things that weren't there; it had felt so real, like it was more than a hallucination. I could feel the pain.

Our avatars turn and run. A soldier spots them and I gape as the two people who look like us run faster and disappear into the woods. The soldier disappears to reappear farther ahead, in search for where we—*they* escaped to.

The Empress balls her fists. "Alert all of Arcana. The captain and the Fool are now Enemies of the Tower. I want them alive." She whips her head around to see her Arcana soldiers with their pearly white masks closing in. She points to Harold's body, and I stifle a gasp. "Take him to my Tower." A soldier appears next to Harold and wraps his ghostly arms around him. "Take the rest," she directs the remaining soldiers. They grab the remaining Ipani who are wounded and still weeping after watching Soanalo's demise.

The Empress's eyes do one last sweep of the forest, searching for us, and I duck close to the ashen ground. She's not stupid. One minute we were in front of her; the next, we were behind her running away. She knows ouma was involved. A loud hiss escapes her lips right before she vanishes in a cloud of red smoke. Seconds later, the rest of the soldiers disappear as well, leaving the area empty.

22

Enemy of the Tower? I've only ever received a summons with my name v. the State of Louisiana on it. I've never even been an enemy of the state.

Shadows move among the trees; I know there are soldiers lingering, searching for us. I shift my gaze toward Nkella who seems unbothered by the shadows and runs to the princess. Cupping her in his arms, he brings her close to his chest. Iéle follows, keeping us in her Aō demesne.

A deep, sorrowful groan escapes Soanalo's burned lips. Smoke leaves her mouth and nose; her eyes are shut. At least, I think they are as I approach cautiously. Two red-broiled scabs replace of eyes.

"Nalo. . . Can you hear me?" Nkella whispers.

No answer.

"Soanalo?"

Nothing.

He places his fingers on her neck to check her pulse and lets out a low quivering breath. Almost like he's crying. My gut clenches.

"M-maybe you can still save her?" I ask weakly, my mind struggling to focus on one thing at a time. The crew vanishing, Harold being cursed. . . because of me, Soanalo being boiled from the inside out.

He doesn't look up. His hands tighten around her as he bows his head low. Iéle approaches with her tail between her legs, head bowing low as well.

"The souls. . .they're being tortured but. . .maybe there's still hope?" My voice shakes, unsure if this is too private and I should go away. Her head arches back as he tries to pick her up and her neck snaps, hanging by the thread of her skin from the back of her neck.

My breath escapes me fully, and my hands shake.

He lets out a ground-shattering wail as he lowers her body to the sand. He gets up, walks out of the area that had been cloaked—the area that is now filled with dead foliage, and starts beating a tree with his fists. Iéle follows him, forcing me to follow, too, so I don't leave her demesne.

With each punch he throws, flickers of flame ignite from his knuckles. Branches break off and fall to the ground. The tree groans with each blow to its bark and I wince. I can still hear them from the garisi I drank.

"Noooo. Don't let the Devil hurt him, miss."

I gasp and jump away from the tree next to me.

"Nkella?" My voice is barely a whisper. I take a few steps back and look at the firepit that had been a lively place a few hours ago. Instruments lay on the ground next to the belongings of those who had been taken. The poor plants that had tried to warn me, singed. All these people thought they were safe here. They had just been celebrating their plans to bring down the Empress. And now their only hope lies disemboweled on the ground, still feeling pain. . .and she forever will, with no way of bringing her back. My eyes fall toward the empty spaces where we had all been sitting.

"Th-they're gone. All of them," I mutter under my breath. Poor AJ. Who's going to save his girlfriend now?

The tree breaks in half as Nkella throws a powerful blow. It tumbles down, shaking the ground, nearly hitting Soanalo. I jump back to avoid getting hurt. He stills, with his fist against the ground and half the tree on his shoulders. His shirt is slightly torn at the collar and his muscles protrude from his tunic. His eyes emit a darker-than-usual glow, almost crimson. His head is slightly bowed as he breathes deeply, showing the two Devil stumps on his head. He grimaces, revealing his sharp incisors, and his attention snaps to my direction.

I swallow. His eyes narrow.

The Devil inside him is trying to break free. And I'm the only one in the vicinity. My stomach twists into a knot. The crew isn't here. I'm left to travel with Nkella. Alone. Oh no.

No no no no. I can't travel alone with him.

I'd rather be all alone in this world than travel with someone who psychologically tortured me. Not to mention, we hate each other. And if he loses control, he'll kill me if he sees me as his enemy.

What if I can make it to the Ace of Wands on my own? Then I can still save the crew and return home. I start to back away slowly, creating distance between us as he heaves beneath the fallen tree. He lifts himself up, picks up the branch and throws it behind him, letting out a hoarse yell.

Yep, time to bolt.

A growl comes from beside my leg, followed by a nip.

"Iéle!" I sputter.

Nkella turns to me and points at my face. "You *will not* run. We still have a deal."

I swallow hard.

"The only way to save them now is the Ace of Wands, and you are going to get it for me."

"Are you sure you need me for that? You know where it is. I haven't been able to use the World Card. I'm useless." I'm not lying; I have no idea how to open a portal.

"Ah, but you"—he quickens his steps toward me, and I back up—"are the only one who can use it, daí?"

"We tried and I failed, remember? How do we know I'm the only one who can anyway?" I know I'm going back on the deal I made with him on the ship, but back then, I was just trying to stay alive and out of the brig. I'm not on the ship anymore. What if I never get the World Card to work for me again?

He searches my features. "I have tried. You have mark of the Helāni Moera. Not me. If the Hierophant wants you, it is not clear he will succeed without you."

"Speculation." I cross my arms.

"Either he kills more Ipani for the strength to take it. Or, as you said when we made this deal, he uses you instead. I cannot use the Ace. You *will* learn to use it."

"Well, I don't want to go anywhere with you," I hiss.

A painful look flashes across his eyes but then vanishes.

"How do you expect to go home without it? Or without the Ace of Wands now that the Magician is gone, too, hn?" The leaves of the trees make the shadows dance on his face against the grayed-out dome. The amber glow behind his pupils flashes as he corners me against a tree. "And at night"—he exaggerates the *t*—"you will never survive the island."

"What do you know about me and what I can survive?"

"Kh." He tilts his head and quickly draws his hand behind my neck, pushing me forward. "Or maybe I just cut off your arm and learn to use your mark myself, daí?"

"Oh. . .! Stop! Let me go!" I grasp at my hair, trying to pull free from his grip, but he shoves me to the sandy gravel. I quickly back crawl, trying to get out of his reach. "Or, I can have Iéle make you think you cannot move so I can carry you the rest of the way."

Vines crawl from the ground around me and wrap themselves around my legs and arms. My vision narrows as a dark shadow circumvents my sight, and suddenly, I can't see anything around me. A vine scratches at my skin as it wraps around my neck and torso quicker than I can move, binding me in place. Soon my entire body is covered. I can't move. I can't see. I open my mouth to scream and bite down on the bitter taste of a vine entering my mouth. My chest heaves. Tears form at the corners of my eyes.

Then it all disappears. I sit up, looking at my hands and legs, then up at his face, tears stinging my eyes. Iéle growls beside me.

Nkella towers over me, his face grimacing. He lets out a huff. The fiery glow in his irises dim as he turns and leaves me on the ground. I clutch at my chest, trying to steady my breath and keep a safe distance from the wolf.

"You don't have to be so cruel." I pick myself up off the ground and rub the phantom memory of the vines away. He walks back to where we had been standing with the Empress and picks up his hat.

He puts it on and turns back to me. "You lied."

"I—" I sigh. "I didn't tell you everything. It's different."

"It is still lying."

"I didn't lie about not being a spy. You see that now, don't you?"

His voice lowers and I can sense his pain. "You didn't tell me you saw my sister."

"I told you Arcana soldiers were alive though, didn't I?"

He quiets, holding his hand up to his eyes as he looks away. "You could have told me you saw her. How she was being used. Her ouma, stolen for evil like mine was." His voice trails off.

"And why should I have?" I begin to walk and Iéle growls. I raise my hands in surrender as I follow him back to Soanalo. "I'm your prisoner. Your gembella, remember? I didn't know how you would react to that piece of information. I was told not to tell you in case you. . .transformed."

His face snaps back to me. "Who told you?"

"I-it doesn't matter."

He raises his chin and takes a slow step toward me. "If we are meant to abide by our deal, there needs to be some trust, daí?"

"Oh, now you want trust?"

"Who told you not to tell me about my sister?"

"How would that have changed anything?"

"Who told you?" His eyes are angry as he stares at me.

I cross my arms and raise my chin. I'm no snitch.

He huffs. "I have no energy left in me to argue." He turns to walk away but then pauses to look at me. "I need Iéle to follow the crew's scent and keep them safe. It doesn't matter if she is not here. If you try to run, I will catch you." A flare of amber illuminates the back of his pupils. I gulp. "Do you understand?"

I nod.

Nkella turns back to Iéle and crouches down to her level.

The wolf sits with her head against his. Nkella places his hand on the back of her neck and closes his eyes.

He has a point. What am I going to do? Hide somewhere until a drakon appears? How would I even reach Gari? My translation potion will run out if I'm out here long enough, and then I'll really be in trouble. The Minor Arcana might catch me, I could be eaten. . . I ball my fist. He's my only chance of surviving the island.

I glance over to where he left Soanalo. I admit I'd been avoiding looking in her direction. The soldiers took everyone else, even the tortured dead to feed to the Empress's animals, but they didn't take her. I'm guessing that was intentional—to torment Nkella.

I take a few steps toward her body and squint. It looks like someone has started pouring sand over her—which isn't possible because we've been here this whole time. My eyes widen. Wait, no. . .there's more than that. Vines are closing in around her. I dart a look to Iéle who's still busy with Nkella. These are real vines, not a hallucination.

"Nkella?" I take another step toward Soanalo's body, and another vine pops up. "Nkella!"

He turns his gaze to me. Iéle takes off, running toward the entry path; then she pops out of this dimension. Her protection dome diminishes and we're left blanketed by the dark of night. Nkella turns to Soanalo.

I point to her body. "Is that supposed to happen?"

His eyes widen and he drops to the ground beside her. I'm guessing that's a no.

Vines wrap around her neck and tighten. Nkella takes out a carving knife from his belt and starts cutting them off. He leans over her neck. Right when I think he's about to kiss her, he speaks. "Her neck is reattaching."

"What? How is that possible?" Why do I keep asking these impossible questions as if I'm going to get a possible answer? My mind drifts back to when the Ace of Wands appeared on the World Card. It was a wand with a purple stone at the top, and vines climbing from top to bottom.

He shakes his head. "I don't know. It could be because of her mark."

"Her Queen of Wands mark?"

"It is not fully healed," he says, inspecting her closely. "She is still in torment."

Carefully, he picks Soanalo up, his hand under her broken neck to keep it secured. The vines that were growing around her snap off.

I consider what it means to be Queen of Wands and connected to the Aō. My gaze flicks up at him as he stands, cradling her in his arms like a baby. "So, now what? Where do we go from here?"

He starts walking toward the trees.

"Okaay. . ."

"I am not leaving her here."

"I get that. . .but. . .where are we going?"

"Stop talking."

I sigh and follow him through the forest, trying to tune out the chatter of the trees and plants whispering around us. I could swear I heard one calling me a lanky daffodil.

"Ow! Watch where you step, missy!"

I wince.

We walk in silence for about an hour until the chirping of crickets and croaking of frogs grow louder. Twinkling lights illuminate a grassy area before a large lake. As we step closer, I can see they are lanterns hanging from multiple-story tree houses above pathways created by hanging rope bridges from tree house to tree house. "What is this place?" A cool breeze passes through my hair.

He sighs deeply.

Someone calls something out in Ipani, and I turn to see a young boy running toward us. Nkella stiffens; his face grows pale.

"Stop," Nkella says.

The boy stops running and backs away slowly.

"Go get your mother."

The boy nods and runs off to a tree house. A few moments later, several people walk out.

An old lady runs out among them and stops. "Who is that you carry?"

"It's Soanalo. . ." Nkella's voice cracks. My chest tightens and suddenly I regret trying to run. He has a lot on his shoulders, and I'm only making it harder for him. Can I really be blamed though? He scares the hell out of me.

A haunting cry escapes her throat as she reaches for Soanalo. Nkella drops to his knees and places her on the ground.

"What happened?" the woman's voice shakes.

"The Empress found us."

People gather around, tears rolling down their faces. Nkella cranes his head to look at me. "Hide your mark," he says in a hoarse whisper.

Oh, right. I pull my sleeve down to make sure it's fully covered. A large man comes over and picks Soanalo up. Nkella holds her head, "Watch her head."

The man takes her gently, passes me a look and squints before returning to the tree houses. The old lady takes Nkella's hand and pulls him close, she reaches for me, too, but another woman stops her.

"No, Mama. They cannot stay here."

"They brought back Soanalo."

"And what if there are soldiers looking for them? If they come back, the Empress will doom us all."

The old lady lets go of our hands and looks up at us, grief stricken.

A tiny voice comes by my feet. *"You can't leave. The Empress has scouts."*

I gasp and try to determine which plant is talking but it's too dark to tell.

Nkella's eyes grow somber as he nods.

"Wait," I say.

They turn to look at me.

"We can save her."

Nkella's face grows rigid. "Gembella," he warns in a low growl.

"We're going to go steal the Ace of Wands and save everyone." I blurt. Another promise? First Kaehante, and now this?

Nkella's eyes widen. "What are you doing?"

Yes, what *am* I doing?

"The plants," I whisper. "I can still hear them. One told me there are scouts looking for us."

"We know this. We cannot risk their lives," he says flatly.

"So we're just going to go out there on our own? In the dark?"

The old lady speaks up. "We will hide you until morning, but then you must go."

Nkella sighs heavily and shoots me a menacing stare. I sink into my chest and shrug.

"Come," she says and glances at me. "I'm Chumi."

I wave to her but put my hand down when she squints at it, confusion flickering across her face. Chumi turns for us to follow.

Nkella hesitates but then also follows, placing his hand on my shoulder and squeezing so that I follow closely behind.

I shrug him off. "I have nowhere to go, remember?"

He releases me and we quietly follow the lady to a dark tree house with a single lantern at the bottom.

"Is that Soanalo's mother?" I ask.

"Koj, she is the village mother," he says just above a whisper. "She took care of the princess after her parent's death."

"You can each take one room or share," Chumi says.

"Different rooms," he says. I grimace.

Chumi clasps her hands together. "I will send someone to bring you food."

Nkella nods and they exchange words in Ipani. He smiles at her as she begins to walk away.

"Thank you. . ." I call after her, but she doesn't respond. Dropping my shoulders, I look up at the tree house. "Do you think we'll really be safe here?"

"What were you thinking? Making such a promise, daí? Bancha!" He drops to sit on the stump of the tree and buries his head in his hands.

"I was thinking the last time we didn't listen to the plants, we got raided. Hopefully, we'll be safe."

He wipes his face. "You were thinking you just need to get far away. I am the one who has to live with the promise you made."

I swallow. He's not wrong. . . Once I get that card, I'll have my ticket home. "But maybe we can bring her back from her. . .eternal torment."

"Who told you this, daí? They cannot be put together. It depends how they die. She is disemboweled. Saving her will be to send her spirit to peace. We cannot put her back together." His voice shakes.

My chest tightens and I grip my hands together, looking down at the ground, and then back to him. "It's just. . . She looked like she was healing. Maybe she will and all we'll have to do is use the Ace of Wands to bring her spirit back."

His face blanks and then he groans. "Go to sleep. We have a long journey ahead of us."

"Look. . ." I say.

A muscle in his jaw jumps.

"The drakon said the card could do anything. There's magic here. Ouma! Maybe it will fix things. Maybe it will bring them all back. Maybe only in Wands, right? It's the Ace of Wands after all. . ."

"Kh. Maybies."

I sigh. "Good night, then."

I reach the bark of the large tree and start to climb the ladder, thankful that it isn't talking to me. When I reach the small tree house porch, I push the door open to find a small room with a gas lamp on a bedside stump for a table and a hammock hanging from wall to wall. No bed. I look down at Nkella who still sits with his head against his fists. When I met him, I knew he had experienced loss and betrayal. That much was obvious. But for the first time since meeting the captain, he actually looks. . .afraid.

23

Light trickles in from the windowsill and the dampness from the room comforts me in a cocoon of warmth. I slowly blink myself awake. It takes me a moment to realize where I am. I had gotten used to the rocking back and forth of the ship and the uncertainty of wondering if a cannon would fire at us and the ship would go down and cause me to drown in my sleep. I thought that uncertainty would go away after being on land but I was wrong—especially after last night's raid.

Last night's raid.

Soanalo's tortured cries still ring in my ears as Ntaoru burned her alive under the Empress's control.

The fear in Nkella's eyes left a lingering feeling of dread in my stomach. If he's scared, we must be beyond saving. And with the crew gone—I swallow. Demitri's instructions to the soldiers were to leave the humans. I think that was because he wanted the Prefect to take me somewhere. Which means, he still wants me for himself, and to not be taken to the Tower dungeons. I trace my fingers over the web insignia of my mark. A bad feeling settles over the pit of my stomach. If Demitri is truly after the Ace of Wands, and I'm really the only one who can use it, then Nkella and I are heading straight toward the lion's den.

I hope Harold will be okay. His body turning skeletal and then dropping to the ground unconscious makes me want to shut my eyes and go back to sleep. Pretend it was a bad dream for a bit longer. But no, that happened too. The Empress tried to curse me. And her curse bounced off me and hit him instead. I got my only friend from Earth cursed. I guess I'll add it to the tab of people to save. The only thing left to do is find that Ace of Wands Card and hope I can figure out how to use it without getting caught by Demitri.

Uncertainty boils in my stomach as my own words attack my thoughts.

We can save her.

I'm such a jerk. Why would I promise that? I don't even know if the Ace of Wands can do anything at all. I'm going on a hunch a drakon gave me, a drakon who could very well have made that up.

I let out a shuddering breath and swing my legs over the hammock, planting my feet on the steady wooden floors of the tree house. Here's to hoping the Ace of Wands can actually help, and this isn't all for nothing.

Wiping my face, I yawn into my hand, trying my best to shake the memories away. I spot a jug sitting inside a wide bowl on a table stump and make my way over.

I'm not sure if this is a guest house or if I'm borrowing

someone's room. I hadn't gotten a chance to take a good look when we arrived last night. The moment I lay my head down, I passed out, but it doesn't look like anyone's been occupying it. The jug is filled to the brim with water, so I assume it's for me and use it to wash my face, neck, and underarms.

After making sure I still have my belongings in my pocket, and my empty bandolier, I step out of the tree house and into the misty morning dew of the day. I wonder how early it is.

Dense trees block my view of the entrance to the sea by this small village, but I don't see any signs of Nkella. I wonder if he's still in his room.

I knock on his door. "Nkella?"

No answer.

Water droplets sparkle on the tree and sprinkle my skin as I carefully step down the trunk ladder.

The peace of the air unsettles my stomach. I'm not sure if it's because I'm not used to having peace, or if I'm afraid something's happened.

"Good, you're awake."

I jump and spin around to see Nkella standing there, shirtless with his tattoos and stripes on full display, and holding a net full of fish. His hat is still on his head, hiding his horns.

"Kh. Always be ready, gembella."

I bite back a snarky remark in return for him calling me gembella and clear my throat. "I am. It's just so quiet." I step back, letting him pass. "I see you went fishing."

"Good observation."

Rolling my eyes, I strut after him. "Is that breakfast?"

"We will eat before we set off. The rest is for the village, for letting us stay the night."

He leads us to a circle of tree houses where Chumi, the lady from last night sits by a firepit. There are heavy bags under her eyes and deep worry lines creasing her face; I can tell she's been up crying all night. Her eyes skim to Nkella, who sets the fish next to the pit. She doesn't give him thanks, only stares at the fish.

"We will be on our way after this," he tells her.

She stares back up at us and nods. Her eyes fall to mine, then down to my arm. It takes me a second too long to see what she's looking at and pull down my sleeve. Nkella narrows his eyes at me, and I wince.

"Sorry. . ." I whisper.

"Helāni *gichachi*?" She raises her brows as she looks from me to him.

Nkella lets out a low sigh. "It is the mark of the Empress, yes. But she is not on the Empress's side." He looks down at me. "She wants to help," he adds between gritted teeth.

"It's true," I say, ignoring Nkella's hard stare. It's best if I don't try to explain how I got here and all that. "I want to help."

A young man jumps down from a large oak and helps a small girl down; I assume she is his daughter. The little girl wears a quiver full of arrows while her dad holds a small bow fit for a child in his hand. He glances at us and shares a sharp-toothed grin as he eyes the fish. He says something in Ipani and Nkella reaches in to open the netting.

The little girl gives Chumi a tight hug before sitting next to the firepit while her dad and Nkella start cooking the catch. Chumi locks eyes with me again.

"In the next town, you should buy different clothes," she

says. "You must take care to conceal that mark or it will become very dangerous for you to move around."

I tug on my sleeve. "Thanks. . . I'll be more careful. I don't have any money."

Her forehead wrinkles. "Well, I'm sure your captain will supply you. No matter how young he is," she smiles toward him. "I know who he is, and he has gichang. The village of Jōtenko is on the way to Eyuo Sāgirang, the Karst Temples."

I give her a half smile and stifle a scoff. Nkella buy me clothes? My smile grows involuntarily wider. This lady has no idea I'm his prisoner, but I guess he isn't exactly acting like I am at the moment.

"Kh," Nkella mutters. Even though he's cooking fish, he's still paying attention.

"Hnnn. . ." she hums while eyeing the two of us. "Be careful. It is the bancha mistakes in life that end up getting us killed. And you are already being hunted."

Nkella's frown deepens but he doesn't look up. What's he thinking? Bancha means stupid, I remember that much. I place my hand over my mark. She's right and it really doesn't help that the sleeves only cover half my forearm. Too many people have taken notice of it.

Chumi looks at Nkella and smiles. "Such a pretty girl, *á*?" My eyes widen. Does she mean me? She turns back to me. "There are a lot of nice clothes in the Jōtenko markets. A pretty girl like you should be wearing something more flattering." She gives me a toothy grin, and I can feel my whole face growing hot.

Nkella grimaces and turns his face. He doesn't respond to her as he continues cooking. I avert my gaze completely.

Chumi chuckles.

More people climb down from the trees as the mist settles and the sun rises. I take a seat next to Nkella and eat the fish he caught for breakfast. Not exactly a breakfast item in my books, but then again nothing I've eaten in this world has been anything I'm used to.

When we're done, we get up to leave. Chumi gives us two canteens full of water and I gratefully take them. Nkella takes his and wraps it in the inside of his coat. I guess I'll carry mine in my hand the whole way.

He lowers his head at Chumi's forehead, his eyes grow sullen, and he swallows. "Be safe."

She holds her hand to her chest and squeezes. "Thank you for bringing Soanalo back to us. I wish you success on your journey."

His brows rise as he lets out a deep sigh. I wonder if he's thinking about the promise I made them last night.

"Whatever happens," she says, "there will be nothing we can do anyway. If there is a chance she will survive her eternal torment, then we will be forever in your debt. But if not, nothing will change."

He nods and turns to me to leave. His eyes flick to the hand holding my canteen, and he takes it from me.

Before I can ask him what he's doing, he hooks his hand on the inside of my bandolier along my waist and pulls me close to him. I almost yelp but then ease as he undoes the bottom of the belt and feeds it through the loop at the back of the canteen. His breath is warm and steady as he works. My cheeks burn red at our sudden closeness and his impulse to reach for my waist.

"Oh." I take an unsteady step back.

"Keep your hands free on our journey, daí?"

"You could have just said so. Jeez."

"Hn." His dark eyes glance down at me and narrow. "Let's go."

He sets off at a fast pace and I quickly follow him through the dense yellowing trees of the forest.

The deeper we go, the more he strays away from the main path. I understand why—we can't afford to get caught by the Minor Arcana. I struggle to lift myself over a fallen tree. I just wish it wasn't so dense. Nkella is a few feet in front of me, not bothering to check behind him to make sure I'm still here. Iéle isn't even here to nip me in the butt and keep me in line as if I were a sheep. Not that I would hide at this point.

But I'm still mad about having to be stuck with him. I need the World Card or the Ace of Wands to get back, and he needs me to use the Ace of Wands to save his crew—however that's going to happen. And I do want to keep the promises I've made.

I still don't know what he meant by "use your mark." How am I supposed to do that?

Long vines brush against my hair as I hop over some lifted roots and foliage. My heart pants in my chest. Every jump I take, it seems like his strides grow longer.

"How far is it to the Karst Temples?"

"A week if we hike all the way."

I gasp. "A whole week? What if something happens to the crew during that time?"

"Do you think I don't know this?"

"Isn't there a faster way? Horses? Anything?" My memory drifts to the time I rode on Gari's back from the Tower to the ship, and almost got shot down by soldiers and swallowed by the sea serpent.

"Yes, finding horses is a priority on my list. Until then, hurry up. You're too slow."

I ball my fist. "Sorry for being human!" He scoffs and picks up his pace, leaving me to jog after him. I don't know how long I can keep this up. "Are we hiking at night too?" I say between panted breaths.

"Koj. You will collapse before sundown, listen to your breathing. Kh. Pathetic, daí?"

I stop walking. "Okay, that's it. If you're going to insult me the whole way, you'll have to figure it out on your own. I'll get myself out of here."

He guffaws and stops walking. "Daí? How? You would not even make it out alive after one day."

"I'm resourceful." I cross my arms.

"Let's go, gembella. Stop wasting time."

"I'm not your prisoner anymore, so stop calling me that."

He lets out a husky laugh, drawing out my goose bumps. "You *are* my prisoner," he turns and strides over to me, his face inches from mine. "You never stopped being my prisoner."

I swallow but force myself to hold my ground and raise a brow. "I don't see any shackles on my wrists."

A wicked smile slides on his face. My own stupidity dawns on me. I search his body, no way, he can't be hiding them on him! He reaches up on a branch and yanks a thick vine twining around a thicker vine. He takes out his carving knife from his belt and cuts a long strip.

"No... Don't." I back away.

"But, gembella," he reaches for my arm, and I pull away,

tripping over a lifted root and falling on my rear. "You said you wanted shackles. As your captain, I will supply them for you."

"No. . . please, that's okay." I try to back away from him but he's too quick as he leaps over me, his chest close to my midriff as he grabs one arm. I struggle to pull free and spin myself around. Only to make it worse as he now grabs my other arm and ties them together behind my back. "Stop! Get off! Let me go!"

Hoarse chuckles escape his lips as he pulls himself up, leaving me tied and down on my stomach like a hunted swine.

"You jerk."

He lifts me up from my shirt and I grunt.

"How can I hike like this? You said I needed my hands free."

"And that is why you were not wearing shackles, daí? But if you are going to be slowing me down on purpose, it is better to walk slow, than for you to run away. Now, stop *wasting time.*" He turns to walk.

"Hey! Cut me loose!"

He guffaws again but keeps walking. I lift my knees over the dense forest floor, now more difficult for me to keep myself from falling over. "I only meant, why am I still your prisoner? You saw for yourself the Empress didn't know me. You know I'm not from here. Admit it! You know I've been telling you the truth."

He stops, spins around, and stares at me. "And yet you still lied to me. About my sister. You broke into my cabin to steal. And just because you do not know what your mark means, that doesn't mean you won't switch sides once you learn what it does."

"And what does it do?" I hiss. "Do you even know? Or are you judging like you always do?"

"Ko kuela mū."

Ko kwela mū. It doesn't make a difference.

"What doesn't make a difference? Whether you should trust me, or whether I'm your enemy or not?" His face grows rigid as he stares down at me. I'm fully aware I'm yelling in the forest while we're meant to be quietly hiking.

"Or that I don't make a difference? As in my mark and my existence doesn't matter to you either way."

A few beats of silence pass between us and I feel like he's searching for the right words. Why is he so stubborn? He saw that the Empress didn't know me, that I'm just a prisoner on the island, that now she's after me, and that I don't mean any harm.

"Look. . ." I start, lowering my voice. "I really am sorry I didn't tell you about your sister. I was just. . .scared."

"Of me turning into the Devil?"

I nod, wincing.

"The Empress made it my fate. It will happen inevitably." He adjusts his hat, his black curls tumbling out at the sides.

"I understand that now, but even so. . . I didn't know what you would do. And I snuck into your cabin because I didn't want to stay a prisoner on your ship and wait to be killed. I just wanted to go home."

His rigid stare remains fixed. I don't think he didn't know any of that, and I don't think he cares.

"I cannot risk you getting away and not using your mark."

"I don't know how to use it," I say again for the gazillionth time.

He reaches behind me and takes out his knife. "You need your hands, and I cannot protect you if they are tied. But"—his eyes flick up at me—"we are not friends. And you will still be my comfortable gembella." He releases my wrists and I rotate them.

Whatever. I don't care that we're not friends. Once I'm out of here, I'm gone from this place forever. But until then, "I'm not going to leave, you know."

He flashes a grin at me. "How many times have you thought about leaving since we got here?"

I huff. "Fair point."

"Kh. Let's go."

24

THE DAY GROWS HOTTER AS WE CONTINUE OUR HIKE
in silence, stopping only briefly at a narrow stream for Nkella
to splash water over his head. He takes off his coat and shirt,
hanging the shirt from a belt loop, and swinging his coat over
his shoulder. I on the other hand keep my shirt right on, but I
do splash water on my face and hair. I steal a peek at him as he
splashes more water over his head, shaking his head furiously.

Droplets sparkle on the sharp curves of his pecs and arms.
He stops to look at me and I dart my eyes down, cheeks
burning.

"What are you looking at, gembella?"

Oh my god.

"Hn?"

"Nothing. I was just waiting for you to be done."

He hides a smirk behind his hat as he puts it back on.
"Good, keep up this time, daí?"

He takes my canteen and refills it and we're back on our

way. We've been walking for hours. According to him, we can make it to Jōtenko by sundown. I continue following him; his pace is a tad slower this time so I can keep up.

There's something that's been on my mind I've been meaning to ask but I don't want to upset him. Still, I can't help but wonder. . . "What will happen to the people of Wands without their Queen? Or Princess?" I ask.

He pauses and squeezes his eyes shut. After a breath he tells me, "The monarchy here died long ago. The resistance that made her Queen was dismantled last night. They lost their leader."

"So, people here only follow the Empress," I say as more of a statement than a question. "And the Hierophant, it seems." I take his silence as confirmation. I wonder how it works in Oleanu. AJ said there was still a monarchy there. Or on the other islands. I mean, I know it's dismantled in Danū. That's evident with it being under siege. Nkella being the prince and a pirate makes it seem like there's no king or queen there. Oh, and his parents are dead. There's always that.

"When do you think Iéle will be back?"

"You cannot be quiet for longer than five breaths, daí?"

"Sorry. I can't help it. I'm bored."

"I do not know when or if she will be back. It is best not to think of matters we cannot control. It holds us back."

"Insightful," I mutter under my breath. He quirks a brow and grimaces. We walk for what feels like an hour but is probably only twenty minutes and I start humming to myself. That tune Soanalo had sung last night before all hell broke loose has been repeating in my head like a broken record.

"Hmmmhmmhmm. . .lala la. . .hei. . .e. . .a. . .urooo ke. . .hmmhmm rooo."

"Hn?" Nkella cranes his neck. "What are you doing now?"

"Singing. What? I can't sing? You said you didn't want me talking to you."

He wipes his face and looks up toward the sky. "You make so much noise, gembella. Did you forget, we are hiding?"

"Fine, sorry."

We walk in silence for a few moments before he asks, "What song were you singing?"

"That song from the camp. . . The one Soanalo sang."

He guffaws.

"What? Don't like my singing?" I keep singing as we walk along a less dense path. My legs are finally happy to not have to step over so many logs and roots.

"That is not how that song goes."

"Well, I obviously don't know the lyrics. But it's stuck in my head. What's it mean anyway?"

He pauses. "She sang that song because I was there. It's an old lullaby from Danū."

"The island you're from."

"Yes."

"What does the song mean?"

He sighs behind gritted teeth and shakes his head. Some of his dark curls fall from his hat, cupping the high cheekbones of his flawless skin.

"What?" I press. "We have a long walk. You might as well tell me."

"It starts off in Danū, years before the siege: Hu'w a isu,

hi'r a kong. That means the air was hot, and the sand was red." He glances down at me. "That is what Danū looks like and feels." I give him a nod to let him know I'm listening.

"Heika poé a uro kelante hū nong rō. That means the warriors were strong with the spirits of air and fire."

Nkella's voice grows solemn as he recalls the lyrics to the song, singing it in tune, and finds the right words to translate them. His voice is alarmingly beautiful. I don't dare to interrupt.

"M'mae e tesī kū yi chī Moera." He glances down at me. "That means to guide them to the Moirai battles." He grimaces.

"The battles against the Empress?"

"Back then, it was the battles against the Empress and her two sisters, along with the warriors they brought from their world."

"Oh." A cotton ball grows in my throat.

"There are many stories from my island like that one."

I walk in contemplation as I follow him up a steep path of dense forest. The upside is the trees are blocking the hot sun; the downside is, my legs are killing me, and the terrain just became an uphill climb for who knows how long. At least I'm getting a workout, eh?

"Quiet, daí. You are too noisy."

"What? I didn't say anything."

"You make too much noise when you walk."

I press my lips together as branches crunch underfoot with my next step. I glance over to my right; he is smooth, quiet, and calculating in every step he takes. How is it that he does that?

"Be quieter, gembella. Do you want to let every predator out here know we are coming?"

"Stop calling me that. And I'm trying." I sigh. "I don't know how to walk quieter. Sorry."

He lowers his eyes at me from the side and stops.

"What's up?"

"Walk."

"Huh?"

"Walk, gembella."

"Alright, alright. . ." I start walking, cautious that he's behind me. What is he doing?

"Stop walking."

I pause. "I don't understand—"

"This is your problem. He quickens his pace, "you walk like this." Stomping on the ground with each heel, his arms moving wildly beside him. I snort.

"No, I don't. You're exaggerating."

"Daí? I do not know this word. It doesn't translate with the potion. . ."

"It isn't true. I do not walk like that."

He scoffs. "I am not lying, gembella. This is you." He continues his long strides, stomping on the ground. My cheeks flush and I jog to catch up to him. He glances back at me and guffaws.

I scowl. "What is it?"

"You are mad at me, daí?"

"I don't walk like that."

He laughs harder. Great, so the only time I ever get to see him laughing this hard is when he's making fun of me.

"Keep it down. Do you want to 'let all the predators know that we are here?'" I repeat in his voice. He straightens his face, keeping a sly smirk on his lips.

"Gembella."

"I thought you were going to stop calling me that."

"Koj. It suits you."

I do a double take and narrow my eyes at him. A hint of humor hits his dark amber eyes.

"It suits me being your prisoner? You're such a jerk." I fold my arms and keep walking.

"Gembella, stop."

"What is it?" I ask, snapping my head to face him.

"Come, I will show you how to be more quiet."

My brow furrows as he circles around me, inspecting my body. Umm. . . I draw my arms up. "What are you. . ." My voice trails off as he grabs my shoulders from behind me and squeezes, loosening me up.

"Too tense, daí? Relax your muscles." I let him loosen my shoulders and then almost fall over when he presses behind my knees with his knee. "Bend your knees."

My thighs ache as I hold myself up with bent knees. "Pretty sure you don't bend your knees this much."

"Not so *much*, gembella." He puts emphasis on the last word and curls his lips. "Only a little. Stand up more."

I do as he says, and he presses his lips as he quirks a brow. "The more tense you are, the harder your steps. Relax more, daí?"

"That's so easy to do, considering we're on the run."

"Be serious. Try to walk."

I wait for him to call me gembella but it doesn't come. Keeping the stance he left me in, I take a few steps.

He laughs. "Not like this." He strides over, his knees exaggeratedly bent, and his arms swinging beside him.

"I'm not even swinging my arms."

"Kh." He turns to me. "Try again. This time, no swinging. Legs less bent."

"Fine." I bend my knees slightly, this time I do not swing my arms at all. I keep them straight by my side.

He pinches the bridge of his nose and guffaws. I clench my fists. "Now you walk like this." He proceeds to strut with his arms unmoving by his sides.

"You said no swinging!"

"A little is okay, gembella. Be natural."

"Ugh, forget it. Can we just go?"

Nkella straightens his face. "You need to learn to fight. But you cannot learn if you first cannot be quiet when you walk."

"Why do I need to learn to fight? I'm leaving, remember?"

"Daí? And what are you going to do when we get to the Temples? Stand and look pretty?"

My cheeks flush.

"Can you shoot an arrow? Koj. You can't. How will you protect yourself from the traffickers? What if I am captured? And is there no danger in your world?"

"Fair enough. I get it. But it's not like I'm going to learn to fight in a few days."

"Try one more time."

I sigh. This time, I bend my legs slightly, trying to keep a light foot. I keep my arms at my side, conscious about swinging them too hard or not at all. "I still don't see how this helps me be quieter. I can still hear my feet crunching the rocks and leaves."

"Shhh," he says. "Keep walking like that and listen."

I stare at him, then turn back in the direction we're headed, trying to maintain my posture. I guess I'm not crunching as much gravel as I was. A soft wind blows through my hair and sounds of leaves rustle in the distance. The cawing of a bird to my right disrupts my thoughts, but I keep walking, taking in every sound of the forest. I listen for Nkella's steps behind me, but I don't hear any.

Wait—did he stay behind? I spin around to find myself alone. What the hell? "Nkella?" I spin around again and take a few steps forward. He said to keep walking, but where did he go? I take a few extra steps, in case I didn't see him pass me. But how would I have missed him? My feet crunch some leaves, and I kick a rock.

Something leaps at me from the trees, and I scream.

"Gembella!"

Nkella leaps and pins me to the ground. My chest feels like it's about to burst open.

"Why did you do that?" I rasp, my heart stuck in my throat. Suddenly, I'm hyper-aware that his body is literally on top of me, our faces so close together, I can smell his breath. "Get off me."

His face straightens. "You are still too noisy."

I start to squirm from under him and he starts to laugh, getting up and letting me go. I pull myself off the gravel and wipe dirt off my legs and arms. "Why did you do that?"

"To prove you are unaware of everything around you. You are going to get us killed."

I huff. "You're the one who's going to get us killed if you don't stop laughing."

"Next time, block me like this." He steps behind me and I tense.

"Relax, gembella. I am not going to hurt you." He grabs my left arm. "If you heard something coming from there, then anticipate the move, daí?" He places his hands on my hips and applies pressure, directing me into foundational stance with my knees bent and hips forward. Then, he moves my arm in a circular block. "If they come fast, use their force against them. Like this."

He makes us both sidestep and block at the same time. He does it a few times as we walk farther up the path.

"What if nothing happens?"

"Daí?"

"You said to anticipate the move. What if nothing happens?"

"The point is to always be ready. Now, try it on me." He lets me go and hides in the trees. "Walk, gembella. Keep walking."

I swallow and start walking. I don't like this. He's going to jump at me again.

"Bend your knees, gembella!"

Ugh. I pause. Okay, knees bent, arms not swinging, shoulders relaxed. I ease into a slow pace and then quicken my step, trying to listen for Nkella. The ground becomes more level, making it a little easier on my knees. Trying to keep his blocking instructions in my mind, I attempt to copy what he showed me with my left arm. Then with my right. Leaves rustle to my left and I move to my right, anticipating the attack to come at any second.

Nkella leaps down from a tree to my right and lands right in front of me. I gasp and shuffle back, falling on my rear.

"H-how did you get up there? When you were over there?" I point to the left, confused as hell.

He lets out three slow laughs and steps back to let me pick myself up.

"No seriously. I did what you said and heard leaves rustling to my left. Where you were!"

"Kh. Why would I attack you from the same place you saw me hide?"

My jaw drops. "You did that on purpose!"

"Of course. To trick you so that you will learn."

"How did you get over there so quickly? That's not fair, you cheated."

"You think a captor will be fair to you?"

I part my lips then close them. "No. You weren't." I fold my arms. "And this isn't exactly helping my trust issues."

"Kh. That is for the best. Let's go. We will practice more later."

We hike up the mountain in silence, the trees becoming denser as Nkella leads us off the path. I think about what he said about self-defense. I've always been resourceful, and I'm not afraid to kick or bite. I can and have done what I need to do to survive. But seeing how Nkella fights makes me wish I knew a martial art.

He pauses to collect some berries on a nearby bush. He cocks his head to the side. "I hear a stream. We are getting close."

"Who taught you to fight?" I finally ask.

"Hn. . . In Danū, Kae and I learned together. My parents died when I was young, they refused to have me bound when they realized my power. The Empress killed them when they tried to save me."

"Wow. . . That's. . .really tough. I'm sorry." Not what you'd expect to happen to a prince, but I keep that to myself. It looks like things are worse for royalty in this world.

"The Empress kidnapped me instead of having me bound. She wanted my power to mature so that she could take it."

I start walking in silence, letting him talk.

"Men who still respected my family's honor prepared a heist to save me. These included Kae's parents."

"How long were you kept at the Tower?"

"She raised me until I was eight years old. They could not figure out how to make it to the Tower. But, they must have somehow."

"Oh my god, the Empress raised you?" That's why she said what she said after he stabbed her through her chest with his sword. *I let you leave me. And after everything, you still hate me that much?*

"Kh. My parent's legion and Kae's parents raised me."

"I understand. And your sister?"

"She was older than I was when the Empress took me. They had kept her in hiding, so the Empress didn't know of her power until. . .much later. But. . . It was all for nothing. She took Ntaoru's power, as well as mine.

"And now the Minor Arcana that guards Danū uses my power to intimidate my people." He swallows as his voice cracks. It sends a sinking feeling to the pit of my stomach. "She tortures my people with my power."

I let that sink in. The Empress said Ntaoru's power was unique. I hadn't considered Nkella's power because of his Devil curse. But, it's true—he's bound. "What was your power before?"

"My connection to the Aō is through the spirits of air. I never thought it was much. Ntaoru's power is fierce. Volcanic, like the wrath of Danū." The memory of Ntaoru boiling Soanalo's blood from the inside surfaces in my mind. I shake it away.

"I wondered how she did that. . .like. . .where did the fire come from?"

"Hn. It does not work like. . .creating fire, daí? Oumala connection to the Aō is through the spirits of the elements. When our powers emerge, we learn to use them by forging a connection. At first, you learn to ask as a whisper, then. . .it happens out of trust. But the Aō is confused. It has been for a very long time. There is no balance anymore."

My brows furrow, trying to understand what he means.

"I never thought of anything bad happening with wind. Except, a storm, daí?"

I nod.

"But she used it to stop people from breathing."

I gulp. "Oh. . ."

"I should have been bound before she learned what I could do."

I stifle a gasp and pause. "Nkella. . ." I grab his shoulder and he turns. "The way the Empress uses your power is not your fault."

"Kh," he sighs.

"No, it isn't. Look, she has some serious, serious issues. She kidnapped you when you were a baby, then she stole your power. The fact that she can do what she does with it—expand it for her army—is insane and an abuse of her power. But you? You did nothing wrong. Don't blame yourself."

His eyes soften and his lips part. I smile at him, and we keep walking. As strange as it sounds—because we were just fighting a little while ago, I'm actually enjoying his company right now.

"What was it like living with the Empress? Do you remember?"

"I was too young. But. . . I remember she was very nice. I didn't know back then what she had done to my family." He chuckles. "When my people rescued me, I thought I was being kidnapped. I was so confused. But then I learned. Not at first, but eventually, I saw the betrayal that was done to me."

"Is that why it's hard for you to trust?"

"Hn."

"Yeah. . .I get it."

"Daí? And what about you? Why is it difficult for you to trust?"

I glue my eyes to the narrow path. "I thought my father would always be there for me, but he wasn't. He let me fall into the system—basically let other people adopt me, bad people. . .and now I'm almost an adult and he still never came back for me." Tears start to sting the back of my eyes, but I bite them back.

"Maybe it is better that way."

I glance at him from the side; his expression is pensive and serious. "Maybe," I say.

"Sh." He holds out his hand and stops at a clearing.

"What's wrong?" I look out to see where he's staring. It's just a plain patch of dried grass and sand that goes on for miles.

"Over-cultivated land. Ouma plants no longer grow here. We are close to Jōtenko. No more talking beyond this point, daí?"

I nod. He cuts back toward the shaded forest, and I almost think he's turning back around but then he jumps down into a depression in the land. I search for how to get myself down as I'm not going to make that but am taken aback as he holds his hands out for me. I pause.

"Daí? What's wrong? Don't trust me?" He smirks.

"You know I don't."

"Don't worry. I don't want to care for a wounded gembella."

Fair enough. I turn around and grip on tightly to a patch of grass on the ground. I take a deep breath and let go. A shriek escapes my lips as I fall and he wraps one arm effortlessly around my waist as his other hand covers my mouth. I suck in a breath and squirm to get free.

"Sh."

"Sorry," I say as he sets me down. "How do you know your way to the village anyway?"

"I have been here before when I was a child."

"You have a good memory."

"This way," he turns toward a half-shaded, narrow path with beams of sunlight cutting through the trees. It's vineless and reminds me of Earth. We trod along this path for a few more hours, keeping hidden from the traveled path. My canteen is empty, and my feet are sore from walking; I'm also famished, but I don't complain. He already thinks I'm weak and useless.

We reach the top of the hill, and the sounds of chickens and babies crying in the near distance carry in the wind.

"We are here," he says.

25

A SMALL FARM VILLAGE IS BEING CRANKED WITH steam engine technology. A large waterwheel sticks out of a stream as gears turn to keep it moving. A horse whinnies from the farm just below it and I snap a look to Nkella. "They have horses. Do you think they'll sell you one?"

"We will see." He starts descending the steep hill. "Hn. . .it looks like the Hermit has been through here."

"Who's the Hermit?"

"A friend of Tessa's."

"Oh right. . ." He's the one who taught her steam engineering. He must get around. Maybe that's how he makes his living just on his own. Nkella takes off down the steep path, and I watch my footing, careful not to fall.

As we reach level ground, cries from babies grow into screams. Nkella holds his hand out and I pause. A long line of Ipani women with their children wrap around a brick tower-hut with a red roof right outside the village gates.

"What's going on?"

"The Prefect's men are here, binding the Ipani children at *Ruta Helāni*." He points at the tower-hut. "The Prefect's Tower."

I gasp. "The Prefect's men? Is the Prefect *here*?"

"That, I do not know. We will have to be careful. Usually, he doesn't do the binding himself, but we can't be too sure." He walks off toward a denser area with trees; I follow close behind.

"I expected there to be more of a fight," I whisper behind him as he peers from around a tree.

"A fight?"

"From the Ipani. They're just willingly letting their children be bound like that?"

"Some generations believe it is the right way, safer than being on the run. Many Ipani have never seen ouma being used by each other and feel it is unsafe—or even deadly—especially with the oumala traffickers stealing Ipani."

I squint at the line of mothers struggling with their toddlers and babies and recall Loá telling me that some think it is safer to be bound. I guess I didn't expect it to be so voluntary.

"I don't see the Prefect. Let's go."

We walk along the side of the farm town, keeping an eye on the Prefect's men from the tower-hut. They seem busy enough, and the line of people waiting to have their children bound are covering the door. It makes sense that the Prefect's Tower is at the village gates, but I wonder why they bind children there. I guess I expected it to be done at some kind of hospital or something. I glance at the tall village gates with two men in uniform standing on either side. At least it isn't guarded by Arcana soldiers.

An ear-shattering cry erupts from inside the hut and a little boy around two years old jumps out of his mother's grasp. She calls his name as he beelines toward us. In one giant leap, he crashes into Nkella's leg, falls back, and starts to wail.

Nkella's face pales, and I almost burst out laughing. To my surprise, he squats down and holds out his arms. Rivers of tears fall from the child's face, and my gut twists. Poor little guy was probably just frightened by the baby screaming.

"Is it painful? When they bind the children?" I ask him.

His forehead wrinkles and he nods, sadly.

Oh.

The mother of the child breaks out of the line to run up to us. She attempts to grab her child, but instead, the boy sniffles and climbs into Nkella's arms. My jaw drops, as Nkella stands up and cradles him. The boy starts to calm down as he hugs Nkella's neck.

The mother says something in Ipani, and I remember to keep quiet. I don't need her realizing I'm not from here. I just smile and shrug.

"Don't you worry, little one. It won't be that bad," he says in Imboe so I can understand. He walks toward the hut. A man dressed in the Wands' purple garb greets us.

Umm. . .Nkella, what are you doing? But I say nothing, as the boy's mother is following close. So much for being inconspicuous.

The guard at the entrance squints at us and I pull my marked arm behind me. A second later, he leads us inside to a small table in the center of a round room. An older man sits at the table with a bored look on his face, and waves us in. Nkella sets the boy on the table, but he starts to whimper and kick.

"Sh sh sh. . ." Nkella says and starts to hum a tune. The boy calms and lets Nkella set him down. Huh. Who would have thought Captain Devilface would be good with kids. He holds the boy's right hand, as his mother holds the other. The man doing the binding puts one hand on the boy's head, and the other on his chest. The boy starts to whimper, and his whimper turns into cries. Then a quaking scream erupts from the boy's lungs as a purple light sweeps his body.

Once finished, the man nods at us in casual dismissal. The mother of the boy says something in Ipani which I can only assume is a thank you. The child waves at us and Nkella bows his head, hiding a smile before taking off in the direction of the village gates.

I smile to myself and follow after him.

As the village gates greet us up ahead, notices begin to appear on the trees. I remember the poster attached to the tree at Dempu Yuni that read *If you see something, say something,* with Ipani graffiti on it. But these are different. Newer. Nkella steals one and holds it up.

Imboe letters dance as they switch to English, courtesy of the language potion still in my system. Up at the top it reads *Enemies of the Tower.* Two perfectly drawn photos are underneath it.

I gasp. "That's you! Wait—That's us! How did they get a picture of me?"

"The Empress's magic." He tosses the thick sheet to the ground and looks up at the village gates.

"Are we still going in?"

He nods. "It is getting late, and the next village is too far. Staying in the next forest is too dangerous."

Something about that last part makes me take notice. "Why is the next forest in particular more dangerous than the last one?"

"It is haunted."

I gulp. "Like the waters we passed?"

"Yes, it is called *Ahan Alēla*, Spirit Forest."

"Great." I straighten my belt and head toward the village. "Let's take our chances then."

We reach the gates, and he stares at me.

"What's wrong?"

"We need to find you some new clothes."

"I can't pay for anything though."

"Kh. Of course not."

"I thought my captain would provide," I say with a sly smile, repeating what Chumi said this morning.

He smirks and walks past. "We need to blend in. I'll talk. You *keep quiet.*"

"Got it." It makes sense since Ipani people can tell I'm not from here, and we don't know who might be around.

We enter the gates and walk up the stone steps into the town. An interesting mix of Ipani and ancient Greek huts and buildings decorate the way. Vines grow along the side of white buildings with columns and straw and foliage covered roofs. We stop outside one of the open-air clothing shop huts. The shopkeeper comes out to greet us, speaking in Imboe. He wears a brown leather vest over a loose shirt.

The man squints his eyes at us, deep crow's feet hinting at his age. "What can I get for you?"

I look over the small store while Nkella talks to the store clerk. Wooden tree branches hold articles of clothing in no particular order in front of a single off-white plastered wall. Small cropped-leather tops, with their matching bottoms like the Ipani women were wearing at camp are extended out on a bark against the wall. Yeah, that wouldn't cover much, let alone my mark. Handmade jewelry decorates the counter in front of us, hanging from a small decorative tree stump and branches. Curiosity piques my interest and I go to inspect it. Bracelets and necklaces decorate the stump, some made from wood, others made from white and blue stone. I reach over to pick up a piece and startle.

"Soren."

I blink and stare back at him. That's the first time he's ever called me by my name. It makes sense he would here. . . the moment he calls me gembella, it will raise eyebrows. Nkella points at a long-sleeved, forest green tunic, belted at the waist. Two others of the same style but in red and white hang next to it. The salesman takes it off the branch.

Nkella reaches into his pouch, taking out two flat red rubies with the tree carving on them. The salesman takes it, and flicks his eyes up to Nkella, then at me. Nkella's face remains serious and unflinching.

The man pushes the rubies back. "We do not take this currency here."

My eyes bulge. I stare at Nkella but he still has his gaze glued to the salesman.

"Daí? Why not? Gichang rīrō still runs Ipa."

Wrinkles crease on the salesman's forehead, and his heel starts to tap. A lady comes from the corner and folds her arms, staring at us. She mentions something in Ipani, and the man purses his lips. "Such rubies have not made way here in a long time."

"And one of those could afford you an entire stock of fabric."

"Which would raise eyebrows." He raises his own. "Your face does not go unnoticed with me, Prince Nkella of the Mikiroro family."

Nkella shuts his eyes and gives off a sighing hiss. "What do you want for this tunic?"

"What else do you have to offer?"

Nkella narrows his eyes, and I check my pockets. Do I have anything to offer? I grip my box of cards. Showing this right now will probably get us both in trouble. Nkella reaches behind him and pulls out two arrows.

"I carved these myself."

The clerk takes them and inspects them. "Very nice handi-work, but this is not enough."

"Daí? Why not?"

"I will need them all. And the bow and quiver."

"Kh." He looks off to the side and does a double take. "For one tunic?"

"One tunic for a wanted man and woman, á?" He grins, showing a missing tooth.

Nkella takes a step closer to the salesman, and his eyes give off a flash of amber. His muscles protrude from his sleeve as he smiles menacingly. "Or I can take what I want, and you can take the rīrō. Then we go our separate ways."

The salesman doesn't flinch. Instead, he crosses his arms

and leans to one side. "Maybe you want us to call the guards, á? Either way, more gichang for us."

Nkella passes me a disgruntled look and takes off his quiver.

"No, wait," I say.

He flicks his eyes at me.

"You can't. . . . You made that and. . .and how will you fight?"

He smirks as he jumps at me, and I flinch. "With my fist, gembella, daí?" he whispers at me. I open my eyes to see him smiling.

"Whatever." I cross my arms.

He hands his weapon to the man in exchange for the shirt. My stomach twists. One, I'm not used to people buying me things. In fact, I don't think anyone has ever bought me anything before, apart from my parents when I was little and a few foster parents. And two, my stupid mark has made him trade away his bow and arrows and that makes me feel terrible.

The salesman points to a small, canopied corner inside the tent with a thick wool sheet for a door. "You can go in there to try it on."

Nkella hands me the shirt, and I make my way over to the changing room. Once inside, I close the flap behind me. A tall mirror and a small cushion on the floor decorate the space. It reminds me of the changing rooms back home. I pull Ntaoru's shirt off me and slip on the new shirt. The sleeves reach my wrist, fully hiding my mark. The material is a lightweight cloth of forest green. It shows a little bit of cleavage, and the form of it gives me a waist, a lot more than Ntaoru's shirt did. While I'm in here, I pull my hair free and brush it a bit with my hand, then wipe the sweat from my face with Ntaoru's shirt. That's better.

I grab the bandolier in my hand and step back out of the market tent to find Nkella waiting for me by the edge, away from the salesman. His eyes flick up at me and suddenly there's a sharp look in his eyes. He stares at me, his features alarmed.

"Is there something wrong?" I ask, looking down at my new shirt.

He shakes his head but keeps his eyes on me for a moment longer before looking back down. My cheeks burn. I hand him Ntaoru's old shirt. "I guess you can have this back."

He takes it from me, rolls it up, and stuffs it in his coat pocket. "Let's go now." He steers me away from the market.

"Thanks," I tell him, tying the bandolier back on the way Tessa showed me. "But, what are you going to do now?"

"I still have a sword. And I can fight." He pushes past me.

"But your bow and—"

"I will make another."

"That easy, huh?"

"I enjoy it."

"When are you going to have time to make another—?"

"Not here."

"No kidding." My eyes widen. "You carved that wooden figurine of the two horses pulling a chariot in Tessa's lab, didn't you? Wow! You're actually pretty talented, Nkella. . ."

He walks off with me talking to myself. I roll my eyes and follow him down a narrow stone walkway.

The sun is starting to set in the horizon and gas lamps start to light the cobblestone path.

Screaming echoes disrupt the evening as we get close to a

plain white building with more of the same texture on the walls. "What is that?"

"Let's keep moving."

I glance at him. His voice quivered. Why did his voice quiver? "Is that a hospital or something?"

"Koj. Not an infirmary."

"Then what?" As we get closer, I realize the screams sound like they're coming from children. . . Or younger. "Is someone torturing babies?"

Nkella's eyes go distant as he starts to walk away.

"Wait. . . Are they?"

He continues his walk in the other direction.

"Can't we help them?"

"Help them how? Those children are casualties of war. Eternal suffering, remember?"

My mouth hangs open. I walk over, ignoring his warnings, and peer into a carved out open window. Rows of beds are lined up in a rectangular room, filled with children. Some quiver and shake, not speaking. Others have a hoarse cry like they've been crying for years. My jaw shakes. I can't bear to look, but I can't look away. There has to be some way to put a stop to this. A head of brown curly hair catches my eye. A little girl has her eyes wide open; scabs burn her cheeks. An image of Talia flashes in my mind.

What kind of a cruel, demented person would do this? The Empress can't get away with this. "What's the Empress's purpose for leaving children to suffer? Just because their parents weren't on her side? If they die, just let them be dead."

A few seconds of silence pass when I feel a light brush on my arm. "Come."

I don't argue this time. He was right. There's no point in seeing tortured infants, or children of any age. Eternally suffering. I once thought death was the worst thing that could happen. The thought of that building filled with suffering children, and nothing anyone can do about it, makes me sick to my stomach. That look the Empress gave me when I thought she was desperate for a friend. . . I almost felt bad for her. No, I did. I did feel bad for her. I thought, no one deserves to be alone for as long as she has. But you know what? I've changed my mind. After seeing this, she is irredeemable. She deserves everything that has happened to her.

I walk past Nkella, and he grabs my arm. I startle and stare at him, tears forming at the corners of my eyes. I shudder and wipe my face.

"Do you see why we hate her so much?" he asks me.

I nod.

"The only thing that keeps me going is knowing that one day I will put an end to her. Not now, not soon. But one day, I will."

"I hope that you do."

He gives me a scrutinizing stare. Then leads the way for me to follow. I start walking but then pause and take a look back at the building. Their tortured cries will stay with me forever.

"Gembella?" Nkella looks over his shoulder at me.

"Sorry. I'm coming." We walk in silence down a stone pathway until we reach a corner lodge and pause at a purple door with a sign at the top that says Traveler's Welcome.

"What if they don't take your rīrō?" I ask, remembering the word for his money.

His lip curls upward. "Then I guess I will have to sell you for the night."

Is he trying to make a joke now? I should tell him that sort of thing isn't funny where I come from. "Shut up. That's not funny, and I know you're lying."

"Daí? How come?"

"Tessa and AJ told me you never would have sold me, that you don't believe in that." I take a step forward. "You can be mean and threatening all you want to me, but I know the truth about you."

He quirks a brow. "And what is that?"

I point to his chest, and he deadpans. "You, Captain, have morals."

His eyes narrow but then he smirks. "Hn, be careful, daí? Selling people is very common here." He opens the door and lets me walk in first.

My stomach dips when he says that. Not that I haven't noticed that about this world, but it is depressing. I step into the warmly lit foyer and pause. "Nkella, look."

He's already staring at them. The wanted posters titled *Enemies of the Tower* on the top with our faces on them are pasted to the wall next to the concierge corner. Or what I assume is a concierge corner. There's no desk, only a small metal table next to a chair.

An older lady with curly brown hair talks to a few people, then turns to hand them a heavy iron ring, which I assume is a type of key.

"Maybe they won't notice?" I say.

He tenses up and pushes me toward the lady as the others

disappear through an open archway. The room is dark, apart from a few lanterns and the setting sun outside.

"Well, this is cozy," I mutter.

"Sh."

Oh, right…I keep forgetting not to talk in front of people here.

Nkella steps forward, "I would like to book a room for me and my"—his eyes lower to me—"sister." He grimaces as he says the word. "So, two hammocks or beds." Something about him calling me his sister bothers me. I couldn't begin to imagine being related to Nkella, but I keep my mouth shut.

The lady looks over to me and then up at him. Her eyes narrow. "I only have one bed available."

Oh, hell no.

"How much is it?"

My eyes widen and I glare daggers at him. Is he crazy?

"Two-hundred gichang *riwao* for the night."

"Listen." He closes in on her. "We were robbed on the way here. I do not have any more riwao." Oh, that sly bastard. This was his plan? To tell her we were robbed? Alright, I can dig it. I'm not sleeping on the floor though.

"What kind of currency do you have? We do not take any from Piupeki. Only Oleanu."

Nkella places his hand on the back of his neck. "Do you need any work? I can offer you a trade."

"I have enough workers. But a trade?" Her eyes fall down to mine, and I shrink in my neck. "Does your sister work?"

"Koj." His tone turns deep and hoarse.

"Yeah, koj," I repeat.

"Sh."

I wince. *Sorry,* I mouth.

The lady squints at me, then looks over at the posters on the wall. I bite my tongue. We're in trouble. I take a small step back.

The lady arches her neck, peering over her shoulder.

"Wait. . . I have gichang rīrō, you can still use it," he says.

She calls someone's name, and Nkella curses under his breath. He tugs on my arm, and I take it as a cue to leave. A tall man pokes his head from the corner of the back entryway, and Nkella and I make a dash for the door. With only small lanterns to light up a yellow glow on the stones, the alleyway is dark enough to maybe get away without getting caught.

"We should not have come in," he says as we briskly walk down an alley.

A bright light zaps my left wrist and I yelp. Nkella gets pushed into the wall. My skin burns, and I stare down at it. The light twists around my wrist like a rope, causing it to swell. "It's leaving a rash. Take it off!" I glance at Nkella who's staring at his wrist as well.

Five Ipani men meet us from the opposite side, and I stumble back.

"What is this, daí?" Nkella demands.

The Ipani look rugged, with torn jackets, each holding weapons. One has a shaved head and two earrings in each of his pointy ears, another has a single, long braid. A third is husky, wearing a purple vest. They get closer, and Nkella and I inch back. Can he take all of them?

"Cuffs enchanted with rikorō in order to track prey." The man's voice causes us to spin around; a graying man stands at the entrance of the inn. "The Ipani who died for this potion must have been a great tracker. We paid good gichang for it." He waves us back. "We will make a deal with you."

I glance up at Nkella. He narrows his eyes and yanks at the lighted string on his wrist. It zaps him as he tugs.

He laughs. "The harder you try to cut that off, the more you will bleed."

My wrists burn from it just being on me. I glimpse at Nkella's hands which are already bleeding from him tugging on it.

"What kind of deal?" Nkella's voice is deep and hoarse as we take a few steps back toward the door.

"Aside from this inn, we have a small farm around back," the man says. "Our farm has suffered a great loss. We had a dozen goats that supplied the entire village. They were stolen about ten nights ago." The man takes a few steps forward, scratching the back of his head. "But we are a small village with sick elders and children. Many of our youths have fallen, and just two days ago, we lost one of our bravest as he was trying to steal back our herd."

I want to give them my condolences, but given he just pulled something shady, I keep my mouth shut.

"And you want us to steal them back."

My eyes widen, and I glance at him. *Us?*

"You have a sword and are big and strong. I am too old, and if I go and lose my life, who will care for my wife and children?" He pauses, and Nkella nods. "If you are up for the task, we will let you go, and will not speak of this to anyone."

"Why not have them do it?" He nods to the five Ipani who block our exit. They stand with their arms crossed, smirks across their faces.

"I would rather risk your lives than theirs." The old man

grins. "If you try to run, the tracker will tell us. My boys will hunt you down and turn you in. Do we have a deal?"

"Sounds more like a threat than a deal," I hiss. Nkella glares in my direction, and I huff.

"Or we tell the guards you are using rikorō."

"You can do that," the man says. "But word is you are worth more than that. Don't you know rikorō is becoming a commodity to the guards?"

My brows furrow. The deadly rikorō potion the traffickers make is a commodity among the guards? The Arcana soldier from Swords who was taking orders from Demitri comes to mind. I have a feeling this inn owner knows something we don't.

A muscle twitches under Nkella's eye and he stares at the five Ipani, as if daring them to fight him.

"You can try to fight us," one of the thugs says, "but you'll never find the counter potion if you do." He grins.

Nkella grunts and turns to face the owner of the inn. "Do you know who stole your herd?"

"In the East, there is a desert village, a place called *Bilu Laoguro*. It was a lake before, but now it is a dry desert. The people there are fierce and will kill without mercy. You must be careful."

"Aw, nice of you to care," I say.

"And we have your word that you will keep your silence?" Nkella asks.

The old man nods. "You have my word as long as you come back with my herd before daybreak."

I gulp and stare at the setting sun.

Nkella tries to yank on his tracking shackle again, but

blood stains his fingers. "I will bring back your herd," he says behind gritted teeth.

I don't take my wide eyes off Nkella. Talk about making promises. . . Just how does he think the two of us are going to take on a fierce village of robbers to get a dozen goats back? I bite my tongue.

"I'm Lgao," the old man says. "May the spirits of the Aō guide you."

I clear my throat, and Nkella flicks a stare at me.

Lgao eyes the group of thugs beside us. "Come inside, let them be for now." He takes a few steps back, eyeing us before turning to walk back inside the inn. The one with the long single braid gives us one last look, and winks at me before they go in.

I intercept Nkella as he tries to head out the stone path. "Why don't we just run?" I whisper.

"It doesn't look like we have a choice." He narrows his eyes at me. "Why? Are you scared, gembella? Maybe you should have kept your mouth closed like I told you to."

"Scared? Me? Of what? Raiding an Ipani village and facing those who kill without mercy to bring back a herd of goats? No, not at all. I herd goats all the time. It's a piece of cake."

"Kh."

"In my sleep, maybe," I finish. "Nkella, how are we going to do this?"

"It should be easy for you, rikwa. Or are you not a thief?"

I want to object but I'd be lying, and he knows it. "Not at that magnitude. And if you haven't noticed"—I lift my empty bandolier—"I'm empty and have no other weapon. We're going to get killed."

"We are not." He walks past me, leaving me open-mouthed. I can't believe he's considering this.

"We can just run and stay hidden." I trot after him. "Let him think we're bringing his herd back."

He stops and turns to me, moving up his wrist. "We cannot remove this without a counter potion."

"Can't we just buy it from some other shady people? We're on our way to the traffickers, aren't we?"

He groans into his hand. "It doesn't work that way, daí? Each rikorō potion is unique to whoever's ouma they stole and killed them for. And this?" He tugs on his rope more, causing a red rash under his fingertips. "I have never seen this before. They are enchanting objects now. What will be next?" His voice is somber as he walks away from me.

I bite my lip. Ipani are being trafficked and killed for their ouma. It is either taken for the traffickers or used to make things like this. This is a setback, but he's right. We'd never be able to get this rope off us, and they'll track us faster than we can run. By the sound of it, he has Demitri's number on speed dial. . .or the Ipani equivalent of it for that matter. My stomach turns. This is more reason to need to hurry and get to the Temples. I hope the crew is okay. "So, these goat thieves. They live on a dried-up lake? Is it far?"

"It is just over the mountain. Like the dead forest, it must have been used up and dried out for its ouma. If they are stealing, they are hungry. I do not plan on fighting them."

"Glad you have a plan then. Care to share?"

"End their misery."

My lips part. "What exactly do you mean by that?"

His lip curls upward.

"Nkella?" Just when I thought he wasn't so bad. "Don't go all Devil berserk, okay?"

He stares at me darkly. "I cannot afford that to happen. I am too close."

I shudder at the thought of Nkella losing himself completely to the Devil inside him.

I follow Nkella deeper into the village, passing families and smaller farms. I stare up at the rising moon. Not sure which way the moon rises in this world, but it feels like we're going deeper into the village instead of heading outside of it and toward the mountain. "Where are we going?"

"To get supplies."

"Oh. Am I getting a weapon?"

"Kh. Koj."

"Still don't trust me? That's fine."

Passing the last hut of the village, I realize we're not going shopping. Instead, he leads us into a small lake where he removes his coat and shirt. He rolls up his pants but leaves on his pirate hat as he dips his feet and sinks to his knees.

I stand on level ground, not wanting to get my pants wet. "What are you doing?"

"Fishing." He hovers over the water, and reaches in and grabs a fish, throwing it by my feet, the water splashing on my knees. I gasp and jump back.

"I can see that, but why? I thought—"

He grabs another and throws it next to the other fish, still seizing on the ground. "I do not plan to fight them. I plan to distract them. Maybe make a barter between villages."

My eyes light up. "Do you think they'd go for a barter?

Like, these people offer them fish in exchange for. . .for what? To not rob or kill them? That doesn't seem fair."

He throws another fish my way. Then another. Wow, he's good at that. And once again, I feel useless. He glances up. "If nothing else, a distraction will allow us to steal back the herd."

"Okay, so like a goat heist." I chuckle. "I can get on board with that. But how are we going to herd goats? Have you ever done that before?"

He ignores me, and I take it as a no. This isn't going to be so simple.

After he's grabbed about a dozen fish, he finds a long stick and pierces each one through, carrying it over his shoulder. Their acrid stench assaults my nostrils but I don't complain.

"Is there something I can carry?" I ask.

"Daf? You want to help?"

"Don't sound so surprised. There's not much I can do."

"You will have your use soon."

"What the hell is that supposed to mean?"

I can see a smirk creep across his lips even from behind him. I run to catch up. "Hey, what do you mean by that?"

"You talk a lot. Use that."

"Oh, that's my special skill, huh?"

He chuckles.

"I might need you to help with the distraction of this. . . 'Goat heist.'"

My brows furrow as I contemplate how I could help. I guess I still have my cards, but would that just piss them off if they think it's the Empress's magic? "I thought I shouldn't talk, in case they realize I'm different."

"Hn. Try not to speak."

"You love contradicting yourself, you know that?"

He snorts. I think he likes messing with me on purpose. Pretty sure of it.

As we make our way down the mountain, trees and shrubs become scarce. He was right about one thing. This is no desert. The sand is dark gray, like ash. This area is dead. Thorny branches reach from beneath the surface, much like in the dead forest.

"What happened here?" I ask him.

"Overcropping of ouma plants and war. Always war."

"That's sad."

"Hn."

Moonlight lights our path as Nkella struts into the center of their town and sets the fish down next to an empty hearth. He begins to collect kindling for a fire, and I start to help him. First, a young Ipani man comes out, being pushed aside by a little boy, curious to see what we're doing. The man calls to us, but Nkella ignores him. More people come out from their huts and a knot twists in my stomach. The people who come out are scrawny and starving. I also don't hear any goats.

"Nkella?" I whisper.

He turns to me just as a spark ignites over the hearth.

"Where are the goats?"

He shakes his head and reaches for the fish, propping it over the now open flame. A tall Ipani woman points a spear at us. Nkella smiles without taking his eyes off the fish.

"Are you hungry?" he asks her in Imboe. Interesting. He's still choosing to speak Imboe.

She grunts and pushes the spear closer to him. He doesn't flinch.

"You wouldn't happen to know where a herd of goats went, do you?" he asks, still calm and relaxed, completely unfazed by the crowd now forming around us with pointed spear. I inch closer to him.

She steps forward, this time pricking Nkella's coat with the tip of her weapon.

He cuts off a piece of fish and hands it to her. She gapes, but doesn't lower her spear.

He pushes the fish forward. "Take it."

I keep my eye on a guy with his spear pointed at me as he starts to edge closer. I raise my hands slowly as the lady, still holding her spear in one hand, takes the fish with the other. She chews slowly at first and then sticks the rest in her mouth, lowering her weapon. Nkella stands and offers the rest to everyone else. Slowly, they start lowering their spears. Within minutes, they swarm around the hearth and Nkella feeds them fish, except, there are more Ipani and only twelve fish.

"Now what?" I ask.

Nkella walks over to the lady who first threatened us. "We are looking for a herd of goats. Have you seen them?"

She shakes her head and smiles at him. She either can't speak Imboe or is refusing to, but it seems like she does understand.

Nkella's shoulders drop. "Are you sure? An entire herd of goats came through here. I know they did."

She whistles. A young man pops up from the hearth pile and struts over. She says something to him in Ipani, and he glances at us and smiles, showing us his sharp teeth. Something about this doesn't feel right

The man sticks his arms on his head and makes a "bah"

sound.

Nkella nods. "Yes. The goats. I know you know. Where are they?"

Why doesn't he just talk to them in Ipani? Who cares if I'm here?

The man takes his spear, points it to the ground and stabs the air. Then he acts like he's breaking off a piece of something and takes a bite. Then he smiles.

My stomach sinks, and Nkella and I exchange a glance.

"You ate the goats?" Nkella asks.

Well, there goes our plan.

The two villagers smile at us and exchange a glance with each other. They say a few words in Ipani, and Nkella steps back, drawing his sword. Uh-oh.

In a matter of seconds, the entire village has their spears pointed at us again, and this time they're advancing quickly. I steal a glance at Nkella's face, but he's still calm.

One of the men jumps toward Nkella, while another pokes me in my back. I side sweep and grab the spear with my left arm. Holy shit, did I just block him? I grab the spear and pull him toward me, tripping him with my leg.

Another Ipani grabs me by force, and I kick furiously. Nkella doesn't notice as he's now in spear-to-sword combat with what feels like the entire village.

The female Ipani from earlier drops her spear and everyone moves back. Wait, what's going on? The ground starts to rumble around us and I steady my footing.

Nkella pushes on my arm as he yells, "Run!"

I turn to sprint, but a pointy boulder emerges from the sand in front of me, and I stop in my tracks, choking on a gasp.

He grabs my arm and spins me around. We make a dash to get away, but another boulder appears from the ashes. The ground quakes beneath our feet. I can't even see the other Ipani who were around us. We spin around again and now we're trapped. Suddenly, the ground starts to shake more, and a deafening crack roars beneath our feet. Then we plummet below the surface.

Nkella breaks my landing as I fall on top of him with a loud thud.

"Oof." He lets out air as dark sand falls over us. I wipe my eyes and cough. It takes me a moment to realize I'm cradling his waist with my legs.

"Gembella," he says. "Get off."

"Sorry!" I scurry off him and land on my back beside him. The Ipani woman looms over us on top of the crater she created to trap us in.

"Thank you for the meal," she says and my jaw drops.

She speaks Imboe? What a sly son of a b—

"Now we will prepare an even greater hearth. The spirits of the Aō thank you for your sacrifice." Laughter erupts from behind her as she steps away.

I prop myself up and stare at Nkella. "Did you know they were unbound?"

He wipes his face with his hand. "I had my suspicions."

"Great. How do we get out of this one? All part of your plan?"

He grimaces.

"What are they going to do to us?" I demand.

He stares at me with his dark, fierce eyes. "They plan to eat us."

26

I SEARCH HIS FACE FOR A HINT OF HUMOR BUT THERE is none. "Is that what they meant by sacrifice?"

"It is the loophole to escape the torture. To consume in order to send back to the Aō. If they are who I think they are, then this is their practice."

Their practice? Like, their *religion?* My heart starts to hammer so fast in my chest I can hear it in my ears. "Ipani people are cannibals?" I yell.

"Shhh. . . Keep it down, gembella. That is not helping. No, not all. This is rare."

"Great," my voice squeaks. "Glad it's rare. How do we get out of here?"

He stands up and digs his fingers into the sand wall. Some sand from the top starts caving in and he stops. "We will be buried alive if we try to climb out."

I bang my head back against the sand wall. All because I

couldn't keep my mouth shut at the inn. "We're not getting out of this, are we?"

"You are pessimistic, gembella."

"So what do we do? Our options are get buried alive, get eaten, or get out empty-handed because they ate the goats."

He plops himself down on the sand. "Let me think."

"You don't always have a perfect plan, do you?" I spit out. Despite the moonlight above, I'm sweating bullets down in this hole.

"Kh. And you are so resourceful, daí? Come up with something."

I fold my arms in front of me and bring my legs up. "Looks like we're both prisoners together, for once."

He squeezes his eyes shut. "Please, gembella, I am thinking."

"Fine. But you're gembella here too."

A smirk dances across his lips for a split second.

I look at my arm and rub the gray sand off my mark. Nkella quirks a brow at me.

"What are you thinking, gembella?" He disrupts my train of thought.

I shake my head. "Nothing I know how to do." If only I knew what this mark meant, maybe I could use it to help us get out of here. "What do we do?"

"Fight."

"That's your answer for everything."

"Hn." He wipes his eyes. "Iéle will sense I am in danger and come find me."

"If she comes," I say. She usually appears right away to feed him information. Whether she found the crew or not, she should have been back by now.

He shakes his head and looks away.

A few minutes pass as we sit in silence. I try not to stare at him, but I can't help noticing the worried look in his eyes. I doubt it's because of our current situation. . . I know he's been in worse trouble. He knows he'll think of something. The fact that Iéle hasn't reported back though. . . That even worries me, and I hate the dumb wolf. "I'm sorry I said that."

He looks over, curiosity in his face.

"About Iéle. I'm sure she'll come."

"Hn."

"So what was your reason for not speaking Ipani to them?"

He quirks a brow in question.

"You keep talking in Imboe. Wouldn't it have been faster for you to—"

He chuckles. "I do not need them to pick up on my Danū accent. If the Minor Arcana comes by asking, they can't say for certain they saw me."

"That's smart. You think of everything."

He lays his head back.

A few Ipani chatter overhead, and I arch my head back but don't see anyone. Nkella brings his legs in and stands. More chatter comes, but no one appears.

Okay, Soren, think. There has to be a way out of this hole. I need to get home, and to do that, I need the Ace Card. Wait— the cards. . . My eyes fall to his coat. "Nkella?"

"Shh." He holds a finger up behind him.

I huff. "Let me see the World Card."

He spins around and frowns at me.

"Maybe I can get it to work this time. Open a portal and get us out of here."

"You have practiced many times on my ship. Why do you think you can use it now?"

"Well, we don't have much else to try here, do we?"

He frowns, contemplating my words.

"What's there to think about?" I reach over to his coat and open it up. In an instant, Nkella is on top of me. My hand was already on the inside of the pocket, I could feel the card in hand. "Hey, what are you doing?"

He whips my hand back and I try to push him off. "What is it? Why don't you want me to use it now?"

"And if you open a portal, daí? What then? You get yourself out and leave me here?"

My mouth drops. "Are you kidding me? That's what you're afraid of?"

"Of being eaten alive by these Ipani?" he demands.

I almost felt like asking what kind of Ipani he would feel like being eaten alive by, but I bite it back. "I thought we'd both be able to go. . .you and me."

He narrows his eyes.

"It might be our only chance." I swallow. "You'll just have to trust me."

He sighs, shaking his head.

"Listen, I get it." I lock eyes with him but then he looks away. "I have a hard time trusting, too, but right now, I don't see any other options. And—"I can't believe I'm about to say this but—"I've trusted you this far."

He snaps his gaze to me, confusion flickering his face. He gives me a half smirk and scoffs. "How?"

"I've trusted you to keep me safe, remember? Every time we're in danger, you've always protected me. For selfish reasons, I'm sure, but you have." Hey, I'm not saying I trust him fully, only that I know he won't get me killed. I still have the bruise from him saving me from that cannon to prove it.

He lets out a sigh as he reaches into his coat pocket, revealing the World Card. He hands it to me, and I take it. He grips it harder, and I flick my eyes to his.

"I promise, if I can get it to work, I will not leave you here to die," I say. "I probably still don't know how to use it."

His face hardens, but then his eyes relax. After a deep sigh, he lets go of the card.

The moonlight beams overhead. Sitting back on the gray sand, I study the card. The intricate designs of the waves in the strange world of Ipa. Five major islands with one floating along the top and smaller ones circling them. I squint at it, thinking hard, trying to recollect what could have made it work before. "What did Gari mean by it's a Quartermaster Card?" I say out loud, mostly to myself.

"On a ship, the Quartermaster knows how to do everything. That was my sister's role, in case someone went missing, she could take over."

I vaguely remember AJ saying they need a new one and Nkella getting mad. "You guys seem to manage."

"Hn." He leans in for a better look at the card. "The drakon is Gari, daí?"

"Yes."

"He called the World Card a Quartermaster?"

"Mhmm. . ." I stare harder at the image, waiting, hoping for it to move again like it has before.

"Then, maybe, it can transport you anywhere in this world."

"And into this world, so also, maybe out of it." In truth, if I can get this to work, I no longer need the Ace Card, I can just go home, right? I mean, not without getting us both out of here first, because I'm sure as hell not taking him back to Louisiana with me.

"What were you doing the day the World Card brought you here?" he asks.

"I was just lying in bed." A prison bed, but I'll keep that part to myself.

"What were you thinking? What emotions were you having?"

I take a deep breath and swallow. My eyes drift to the side as I remember. "I was thinking I had failed." I clear my throat. "I was feeling desperate, like I needed to escape my reality. I was wishing for an answer to change the situation for me and my sister."

"It changed because you were in need."

"Yeah. . . I guess that's right." I flip the card around, still nothing. "To think I'm in need now."

A popping sound comes from above, and Nkella and I rush to our feet. A flutter of excitement buzzes in my stomach, just hoping Iéle is here to save us.

A bird's cry erupts from right above us, and a hawk pops into the hole. I jump back against the sand wall, and some sand pours down on my face from the top. The card falls out of my hand, and just as I fall to find it, the hawk grabs onto Nkella's shoulders, piercing his skin. He lets out a pained yell, and I run and grab his arm, trying to yank him free.

Whipping around, Nkella grabs onto his sword, pulling it from his sheath. The hawk lets go as he swings his sword around.

An arrow hits him in the arm, and he drops his sword. Before I can grab it, a villager jumps down and lands with his feet on the blade. He picks it up and pops into the Aō. I don't know what kind of oumala shifter he was, but I was too slow.

Another arrow flies past my nose and hits Nkella in his shoulder blade. His knees weaken as he reaches for the arrow, letting the hawk regain its clutches.

The Ipani woman we met when we arrived holds her bow in her hand at the edge of the hole. "The boy comes first. Then the girl."

"Nk—" I stammer as I run to him. "I'll get the card to work. I will come back for you!"

His face hardens, and the hawk pops out of the hole with Nkella under its talons. I try to reach for him but grab air.

In an instant, he's gone. And I'm left in this hole alone with a card I'm unable to use. I reach down to the ground and pick it up. I let myself fall to the floor, landing on his coat.

My throat dries up, and I choke on a sob. Forget getting this stupid tracker off us, they're going to throw him in a firepit. A village full of oumala animals and Ipani, against one bound captain with a Devil curse he can't control. And then, they'll eat me next. And I'm nothing here. Let's face it, I'm nothing anywhere. I can't even get this stupid card to work when I need it the most.

I grip it in my hand and a tear rolls down my face. "Why couldn't it show me what I needed the most to go home when I tried it on the ship?" Another sob leaves my lips and I squeeze my eyes shut. "Then none of this would have happened." A soft purple hue emerges over my closed eyes. I open them to find that soft hue emanating from between my fingers. I gape at the ocean waves moving in the image. A purple glare sweeps across the card face as a serpent whips its tail from under the water. I gasp. The image of the world map starts to fade, replaced with the image of the Devil in chains. Nkella? A memory of his fierce eyes from when the card first showed me a vision in Madame Asteria's tent rushes back to me, and I feel a wave of excitement.

The card starts to shake, and I drop it just as it lets out a flash of light and the hole starts to spin. It's working! Quickly, I spin around, grab his coat, and put it on. This time, instead of a hole on the ground, the card has opened a portal on the side of one of the sand walls. I bend down, pick the card up, and without a minute to lose, step inside.

27

My surroundings merge as I step behind one of the boulders that had erupted from the ground. I take the card and tuck it back into Nkella's inner coat pocket and press my hands against the solid rock. Peeking around the corner, I spot him. Nkella, who looks like he put up a fight with a few blows to the head, hangs his head down as he's pinned up against a post over an unlit hearth. Ipani villagers surround him as they gather purple crystal rocks and set them in a wide circle around him.

Back at the tavern, I saw his curse take over and he fought four thugs at once. But could he take on an entire village full of unbound Ipani?

Something "bahs" behind me, but I ignore it. How the hell am I going to get him down without being seen? At this point, I wish he would get angry and break away from those ropes. But I guess if he does, they'll just use more of their ouma and kill him on the spot. Knowing Nkella, he's probably trying hard not to give in to his curse, so that he dies as himself, and not as the Devil inside him.

"Baaah."

What the hell? I spin around and my eyes fall on a small goat looking up at me with its creepy rectangular eyes. "I thought you were eaten!" Or maybe this one just got away. The goat has beige stripes across its white fur. With a loud pop, it disappears into the Aō. An oumala goat? It must have saved itself from being eaten by popping out before. I wonder if the others were oumala and managed to escape, or if they were all captured and eaten.

The goat reappears and bahs at me again. I shake my head and focus back on Nkella. "Go away, goat. I can't deal with you right now. I have to save my captain first." The goat grabs onto Nkella's coat sleeve and I jerk my arm back.

"No, don't eat that!" I whisper loudly. It grabs on tighter as I try to pull my arm away, so I grab its horn with my other hand. Suddenly, a big pop sounds off in my ears, and everything turns gray. I let go and gasp. "You brought me into the Aō?"

The goat baahs at me and I laugh. I peer at Nkella tied up over the hearth. A few villagers pour a bucket of what appears to be crushed purple stones inside the hearth. One of them ignites a flame with his hands and catches the crushed stones on fire. The fire doesn't get large, but the stones glow like they're burning coal. Nkella still doesn't wake.

A pop sounds off in my ear, and color returns around me. I stare at the goat who just brought us out of the Aō. A memory of Nkella talking to Iéle head-to-head resurfaces in my mind.

I have an idea.

I crouch low to the ground and tilt my head forward. The goat charges at me and bumps me in the head, offsetting my balance so I fall on my rear. Ow. No, that's not what I wanted. Dumb goat. I rub my forehead. How do I get her to do what I ask like Nkella does with Iéle? Something about forming a bond with an ouma animal. . . I reach into my pants pocket and take out my cards.

The goat reaches down and grabs them, a few of the cards fall out of the box and onto the ashen ground. "No!" Quickly, I gather them up, but she manages to grab one and gobbles it up. "Oh no! My cards," I groan. Ugh, I don't have time for this, Nkella is about to be eaten alive!

I hold my hand out under her nose, and she immediately starts to lick my palm. As she does, I start to gently stroke her nose.

"Baaah."

"It's okay. . . I'm not going to hurt you." I close my eyes and visualize what I need the goat to do. A wet spot hits my cheek and I open my eyes to her wet tongue licking my cheek. I pull back and wipe my face. Yuck. This is useless. "Please? Don't you want to go back to your farm?" I visualize the farm we came from, the one we want to return her to. When I don't hear a bah, I open my eyes to see the goat staring me down.

Here's to hoping she got the image. "Are you ready?"

"Baaah." The goat takes a step forward, and I grab onto its horn. A second later, a giant pop rings in my ears. I'm standing inside the gray Aō dimension. Still gripping her horns, I turn to walk her toward the fire so that it shrouds over Nkella as well. I mean, that's what I'm hoping for. These oumala animals seem to walk among us, without any of us knowing. But I've at least communicated the intent of me wanting to shroud him as well. I think that's how Nkella does it with Iéle.

"Nkella?" I poke his arm and spin around to see villagers walking around, building more crystal towers around the fire, and not seeming to notice me standing here.

He raises his head. "Soren?" His voice is hoarse. "You did it. You. . .came back."

I blink my eyes. He didn't call me gembella. He called me by my name again and this time no one's around to hear it. "I told you I would."

He eyes the goat.

"It's oumala," I say.

"Be careful. . ."

"I know, we have to hurry before it pops out and leaves us here." I run up and start tugging on his ties but they're too strong and heavy.

"Get my sword."

I search behind me. An Ipani woman piles a couple of crystals around the hearth, while another carries a heavier one over and places it to her side. To the left of a boulder is Nkella's sword and hat.

"This is going to be tricky." I stare at his head hanging low. A black and blue bruise covers the top right of his forehead. They beat him to a pulp. A flash of red glows in his eyes but flickers out nearly as soon as it starts. Fear pulses in my veins. I'm not used to seeing him lose a fight. . . Or seeing him weak.

If he couldn't take them with his rising Devil curse, how are we going to get out of this if they catch me stealing back his sword?

I lower myself to the ground and rub the goat's snout.

"Please don't pop out yet," I whisper. I get up slowly, with my hand cupped around her horns and carefully tiptoe toward his belongings.

A few Ipani villagers pass me carrying crystals, and I hold my breath. The goat trots a bit faster, making me jog beside her. I kick up some dirt as I reach his sword and hat, pausing momentarily to make sure no one noticed.

An Ipani girl stares in my direction. The area is grayed out so I know she can't see me, but I've made enough of a ruckus to arouse attention. They're unbound; they're aware of ouma being used. As well as I'm sure they're aware of a missing oumala goat. The goat jerks from my hand and yanks me toward her, almost making me let go of her horn, but I hold on tight.

The girl shouts something in Ipani, calling a group to congregate and look in my direction. My heart hammers in my chest, and I stare down at the goat. She stares back with her rectangular eyes, completely unaware that she's about to get me killed. The Ipani girl takes a few steps forward, with one of the guys close behind her. They hold up their spears, and I inch back. Behind them, Nkella stares at me, his eyes wide. He yanks on his restraints, and an Ipani runs at him, striking him against his face.

I bite down a scream and bring my attention back to the villagers pointing their spears at me. *They can't see me.* I loosen my grip on the goat so she doesn't fight me and take a long stride backward and toward the sword, holding my breath, not making a sound.

The villagers jab the air with the pointy ends of their spears, missing me by an inch. I take another step back, and they take another jab. I keep holding my breath until I'm blue in the face. The guy swings his hand out in front of me, trying to see if I'm there. I inch my face back.

The girl says something to him, and he darts his gaze to a spot by my feet. Now he's yelling, and they're calling out to someone. I follow their gazes, wondering what they're looking at. The hat and sword, or absence of them. They can't see them because the goat brought me into her demesne, and now the items aren't visible because I'm focusing on them with my mind, just like Gari told me to do.

They scatter as more come our way, leaving the crystals and their posts. My guess is they think I got out of their trap and stole the items already.

I grab the sword and stick the hat on my head, making a dash for Nkella. The goat bahs loudly, alarmed by the sudden outburst and pops us back out of the Aō. Villagers are running in all directions. Some stop to stare at me and point at me with their spears. I ignore them and sprint with the sword in my hand, sliding to a stop at the base of Nkella's post.

"Hold on." I swing the sword up, and he closes his eyes. Slicing down, the rope drops to his feet, setting him free. His mouth parts as he stares at me, like he's about to say something.

"Save it," I say. "We have to go."

"Hurry," he nods. "They have oumala animals too."

The hawk flies over our heads and the villagers circle around us, their spears pointed, anger across their faces. My eyes skim over them as I feel inside Nkella's coat that I'm still wearing. No sign of the goat. One of the men lets out a war cry. I whip out the card as my mind scrambles for what to do. How did I get it to open before?

The rest of them join in the cries of war and raise their spears. The hawk swoops down to attack. Adrenaline pounds in my ear.

Home.

Nkella.

Safety.

A bright light spins off the card, opening a portal. I stifle a gasp. The villagers, however, do gasp and jump back. Nkella's mouth hangs open. I grab him, and we both enter into the light.

My heart is in my throat, and bile rises in my chest. I grip the gravel ground, my chest heaving as I stare down a cliff. We're on top of the mountain, and far away from that cannibalistic Ipani village. I can hardly see what they're doing, but they look like ants running around mad. I gape at them.

Nkella catches his footing as he almost topples over. I grab onto his muscular arms as he unsteadies my balance. His breath is deep and steady, his eyes tired as he stares at me, lips parting. "You got the card to work. And. . .you saved me."

"I saved us both." My voice cracks as I stare at my wrist and his. "But I lost the goat."

He comes closer, his features awestruck as he doesn't move his gaze from mine. "We almost did not make it out alive," he says. "You did what you had to. I failed."

I stare into his dark eyes, mesmerized by the way he's looking at me. "You did not fail. It was you against an entire village of cannibals. The last thing I would have wanted was for your Devil curse to overtake you completely." I glance at the nasty bruise on his head, and without thinking about it, I reach over and touch it. He sucks in a sharp breath at my touch. "We need to clean this up," I say.

"Soren. . ." My name is like a whisper on his lips and my heart flutters. "I—"

"Not gembella?"

He shuts his mouth and looks down. "What you did was *neyuro*. Brave. You risked your life for mine."

"Again."

His gaze flicks back up to me. "What?"

"I believe I risked my life for yours *again*. I did it twice. The first time was when I jumped off the ship after you."

"Kh. I still don't know why you did that."

I smirk but his eyes stay steady on mine. I swallow. "So, I'm not your prisoner anymore?" I ask.

He tilts his chin and smirks. "Kh."

I roll my eyes but don't miss the amber flakes lighting up his eyes.

He takes his pirate hat off my head and sets it on his. "How did you get the card to work?"

"Um," I whisper, studying the amber flakes inside his dark eyes. "I thought about what I needed to get home. I was desperate. And the card showed me. . .you."

I blink a few times. Does this mean I've always needed him to get home?

Confusion flickers in his face as he continues to stare at me with such intensity. My throat dries as I stare into those dark fierce eyes of his. He moves his gaze down to my lips and my breathing grows rapidly.

"Baah."

I let go of him and glare at the goat. "You're back!"

"Baah."

A hawk cries overhead.

Nkella peers at the cloudless night sky. "Can you make the card work again?"

I take it out and stare at it, focusing like I did before. A few moments pass but nothing happens. The light from the moon reflects off the gold trim of the card. "Maybe it needs to recharge?" I ask. "Sorry, I'm not too sure how I got it to work in the first place."

"It's okay, neyuro. Let's go get these tracking ropes off."

"Is that what you're going to call me now?"

"Would you prefer gembella?"

"Nope." I grab onto the goat's horns and with a pop, we enter the Aō dimension, keeping us shrouded from danger as we make our way back to the inn.

28

NKELLA PULLS THE HANDLE OF THE INN, BUT IT'S locked.

"How can they lock an inn?" I knock on the door but no one answers. I peer in through the window, but the lights are off.

"They won't answer." A voice comes from around the corner, and I turn around. A young Ipani wearing a vest and medium-sized braids in his hair nears us.

"Where is Lgao?" Nkella asks.

"I don't know. I'm just here to collect the goats." His eyes drop down to the one by my feet. "Only one?"

I pat the goat on the head, and she licks my hand. "Just the one," I say. Nkella gives me a hard stare, and the guy squints his eyes at me. I let out a low sigh. I keep forgetting to keep my mouth shut. Even though they promised not to turn us over to the Empress, Demitri still wanted me for himself, and Lgao did mention something about rikorō being a commodity among the guards. If they can reach Demitri, would they rather turn me over to him or to the Empress?

Braids takes his eyes off me and walks toward the goat. The goat backs into me and I crouch down to meet her face to face. "It's going to be okay," I tell her. "You're back home with your owners." She bites on Nkella's jacket that I still haven't returned and pull my arm back as Braids takes hold of her horns. If I could keep her, I'd call her Sally. "Bye, goat," I say.

"Wait." Nkella intercepts, grabbing the goat by her horns with force. "Take our trackers off first."

"I can't." He lets go of Sally's horns. "My job is only to collect the goats."

"Then we wait here until whoever can remove them comes."

"The goat will come with me," Braids insists.

Nkella chuckles. "Lgao never intended to let us go, daí? My friend here has bonded with this goat. Unless she says it is okay, you cannot have her."

"I too have bonded with all the goats, and they all went missing. Goats are fickle creatures." He bows his head to Sally and clicks his tongue, taking out something from his pocket. He holds it out to her, and she's instantly pulling away from me to eat what's in his hand. A second later, both Sally and Braids pop into the Aō dimension. Leaving me and Nkella behind.

Nkella cusses under his breath.

"This isn't going to plan." I glance at Nkella. He's still wounded from being shot by an arrow and a blow to his head. Plus, we haven't slept nor had anything to eat in ages.

Nkella pushes me back toward the path we came from. "Start walking."

"Where are we going?"

"I'll figure it out later. But now we must move," he says, urgency in his voice. I look around us.

"Why?"

"Kh. Neyuro, do you think they are just letting us go? We are being watched, daí?"

I chew my cheek. He's right. This whole thing was a setup. We make a few turns, heading toward the exit, each alleyway becoming more crooked and more narrow.

"What do we do?" I ask.

"We walk toward the forest. I doubt they'll follow us there."

"But you said it's too dangerous to stay in the Spirit Forest."

"We are going to have to now."

I gulp.

Two men come from around the corner, and we pause. They pick up speed in our direction, so we turn around and keep going.

Three more men turn the corner. We skid to a stop, turn, and quicken to a sprint in the opposite direction. I notice that they're the Ipani from the inn before we left to rescue the goat.

We sprint to another corner and reach a dead end, a tall, plastered wall fencing the village.

Five against two, and I'm hardly a fighter. They each reveal swords. Nkella takes his out. I place my hand on my empty bandolier out of habit, because I've got nothing.

The five of them start ascending toward us at the same

time, their sharp fangs showing from their wicked smiles, ready to capture us and turn us in. How long before the Arcana soldiers get here?

I snap my gaze at Nkella. He hasn't budged. The five Ipani keep walking toward us. My feet automatically move me back against the wall.

The Ipani start to run straight for us, and my chest starts to heave as I grab onto the wall, waiting for impact. Nkella doesn't flinch. His eyes burn amber and a sinister smile spreads over his face.

29

He can't possibly want to fight them. He's still injured from the arrows and the blow to his head. Not to mention neither of us have eaten or slept in ages.

Nkella unsheathes his sword.

The first Ipani has a long single braid down past his butt. He holds up his sword, steps forward, and swings down. Nkella blocks it with his own. When he does, an amber glow illuminates the veins in his arms, and in one immeasurably strong blow, he pushes forward with the center of the blade, jolting the man back against his cohort. Nkella swings around and slices his cohort through his midriff, cutting him in half.

I shriek as the man's upper body falls clean off. I force myself to pull my eyes away from the sight.

A third Ipani with a shaved head and two earrings swings at Nkella from behind, clocking him on the side of the head and catching him off guard. Nkella's feet wobble from the blow he took, but he grips his sword and swings, missing the guy completely. The hit to his head disoriented him. A shriek escapes my lips as the long braid Ipani joins his buddy, forcing Nkella to fight them both at the same time.

With a swift move of his own sword, the bald Ipani knocks Nkella's sword out of his hand. He holds his sword to Nkella's neck, forcing him to move back with his chin up. He almost trips over the disemboweled body he had sliced but catches his balance.

I jump to the side as they back in my direction, hitting my shoulder against the rough wall. The fourth Ipani is big—like Kaehante big. I glance down at where Nkella's sword had fallen and look back up at the big guy. I leap to grab the sword, but he rushes toward me.

As he reaches to grab me, I swing with my right arm and punch him hard in the nose. He yells and holds his face, so I kick him in the balls. He hovers over, lets out a hoarse yell, and in one swift motion, grabs my hair.

I fiercely jerk my body in all directions, trying my hardest to get free as he wraps his arm around my chest. His hold on me is strong.

A bright glow illuminates the space around me. I startle and turn my head enough to glimpse Nkella ripping the sword away from the bald guy's grip. Blood stains his hand, and glowing veins reach his neck. I gasp as I witness him bashing the bald guy against the stone floor. Then he gets up and rushes toward my assailant. I squeeze my eyes shut, and the next thing I know, I hear a horrible cracking sound, and I'm released. The Ipani falls dead on the cobblestone.

Not a second later, Nkella turns to sprint after the last

Ipani sucker who decided he didn't want to join his buddies as one of the tortured dead.

I don't know if it's that he's better trained, or if it's his Devil curse, or a combination of both, but Nkella is faster than our assailants. Him against a village of unbound cannibals? Maybe not. But him against five regular dudes? He's terrifying.

I hold my hand to my mouth as Nkella reaches the last of them. He sticks his foot out and sweeps his leg from under him. The guy falls hard on the ground. Nkella picks him up with both hands and holds him up.

The glow emanates from his eyes and the man starts to kick. Nkella spins him around and bangs him against the wall. Then he smashes his head six more times. The man's body drops to the ground, motionless.

My eyes fall to the dead on the ground. I'm shaking.

I still have my hands cupped over my mouth when he turns to look in my direction. He walks briskly toward me, and I back against the wall.

"Grab onto my back," he says, not making eye contact.

"What?"

"We cannot walk out through the village. We have to jump. Now do it."

I glance to the height of the wall. There's no way he can jump that with me on him. "B-but. . ."

"Now, before the Arcana soldiers get here, daí?"

Purple smoke whips through the darkness and starts landing within the village. It could be seconds before they find us.

Hesitantly, I grab onto his shoulders. He lifts me with ease. I wrap my legs around his waist and grab onto his collar.

Suddenly, he doesn't feel the least bit injured. He leaps up and clutches the top of the wall with his left hand.

I shut my eyes, afraid we won't make it, but open them when we didn't plummet to the ground. He holds onto the top with his right arm and in one swing of his legs, stands on top of the wall. I peek down at the ground and nearly jump out of my skin.

"Nkella. . ."

He springs to the ground before I can finish my thought. I bite down a squeal as he effortlessly lands on two feet. My chest heaves as he lets me down.

"Holy sh—"

"Let's move."

"Right."

He sprints toward the dark, dense forest and I almost halt. "The Spirit Forest." I pant as I jog, still wrapping my head around running straight to danger.

"No choice, neyuro. Move."

Looking over my shoulder, I catch sight of a few more dark purple fumes zooming down right outside the wall. They're gaining on us. I pick up speed and dash after Nkella as fast as my legs can take me. Will they enter the Spirit Forest? Would they be able to find us there? No idea. Just run. We make it to the wooded entrance, and Nkella beelines to a denser area, outside of any spotted path.

I trip over a root and catch my footing. The area surrounding us is pitch black. "I can't see."

"Follow me."

"That's not helping."

Someone grabs my arms, and I startle. "Nkella?"

"Sh. Stay close." He lets go of my arms, and I relax my shoulders. I touch the back of his shirt with my fingers to feel my way through.

"How can you see?" I ask.

"We can see in the dark."

Jeez, they're not only stronger, have great hearing, but can also see in the dark? Humans really got the short end of the stick. He slows his pace to make sure I can keep up, but I can feel the urgency in the way he moves. Every time I catch the glow of his eyes, I can assume that's what he's doing. Constantly pausing to look over his shoulder. I wish I was faster.

As we advance into the thickest part of the forest, the trees become drier. . .or dead. And the moonlight breaks through the empty branches, lighting our path. Their roots become larger, twining up and down with terribly sharp thorns. I glance behind us.

"Was that it? The Spirit Forest? I didn't see any ghosts. . ."

"Because we moved quick. It's not over." He stills, extending his neck to see which direction to go. Pointing his nose up, he sniffs the air.

"What are you doing?"

"That village is as far as I have ever gone in Sāgirang."

"So you don't know where you're going?"

"Koj."

I squint in the direction we came from. "It sounds quiet, and I don't see any more falling Arcana soldiers." I slow my breath a little. "Maybe we're safe now?" I snap my gaze at him. "So, now what?"

"We make camp until morning, but not here." He points

to more dead forest. "Past this area there is more woods. Once there, we will be safer."

I squint my eyes through the dead of night. "How do you know? I can't see anything with all these giant thorns blocking the path."

"I can smell it in the air. Here, the air is dry, dead. But I can smell the dampness of the forest east of here."

Great sense of smell too. Wow.

Something moves within the shadows, and I crinkle my forehead. Nkella's ear twitches.

A howls makes me gasp. "Is that Iéle?"

He holds a finger up to his lips and scans the area with his eyes, bending his knees slightly. He grabs my hand and urges me to keep moving through the dense thorns.

"No," he whispers, "that is not Iéle."

My heart sinks to the pit of my stomach. "As in. . .there are wolves we have to watch out for now?"

"Be very quiet."

I wince as I follow him through the pathless density, ducking under large thorn roots, stepping over shorter ones, trying not to catch my leg on one of them, or worse—get impaled. Nkella walks in a slow but smooth manner, eloquently cautious with every step he takes and watching me at the same time. He doesn't make a sound, unlike me; I make noise when I step. I don't know how he does it.

A popping sound makes me jump, and a growl spins us around.

A gray wolf with its head lowered snarls at us. I back into Nkella. Another popping sound, followed by a wolf appearing next to what I assume is the alpha. Two more pops come from behind us. Four wolves surround any escape. With our backs together, we face them off.

"What do we do?"

"Look away. Do not stare at their faces."

I gulp. "Do we play dead?"

"Koj," he hisses. "Do not turn your back on them."

Don't look at them but don't turn away? Right, makes perfect sense.

A loud growl-turned-roar comes from behind me. At first I thought it was the wolf, but then I realize it's Nkella. I side-step to see what's going on, careful not to turn my back away from the two that are watching me. He raises his arms above his head and jumps at them. I jump back, but luckily, the two wolves that are keeping their eyes on me are too consumed by Nkella's movements to care. The wolves skid back, all but the alpha cowering in place. He jumps forward again. Three of them get close to each other and act like they're about to scurry off. The alpha holds its ground, sniffs the air, and takes a step forward. One of the wolves behind him howls.

The alpha jumps at Nkella's face. He blocks it with one arm, and flings it off to the side. Another jumps at him, while one switches its attention to me.

Despite him telling me not to move, my instincts kick in, and I start to run. The wolf leaps in my direction, and I cower to the floor, raising my arm as a shield. As it lands on me, I don't know why I do it, but I spin myself downward, using my back as a catapult. The inertia of the wolf's fall plus my movement launches the wolf over my head. My chest heaves.

The wolf lands on its feet, its head low, but it isn't looking at me.

I steal a glimpse at Nkella who has done something similar, except the wolf flies over his head and lands on a long, sharp branch sticking up. A shriek escapes the wolf as blood protrudes from its body. I gasp in horror. Despite the wolves attacking us, I don't like to see an animal hurt. And by the horrified expression on Nkella's face, neither does he. One of the wolves starts to howl. Nkella's ear twitches as he surveys the grounds.

"More will come," he says.

A shiver runs through me as my eyes dart around us.

He advances toward the wolf and places a hand on the thick branch impaling its midriff. He takes hold of it and breaks it in two, catching the wolf with one arm. He slowly sets it to the ground. The wolf closes its eyes, letting out a whimper. He takes his knife out and cuts the branch closer to the wound.

"What are you doing?"

Worry lines crease his forehead. "It was not my intention to kill their alpha," a hint of irritation tinges his words.

I swallow and look at the other three wolves closing in on their alpha. "Does death here mean the same to animals as it does to people?"

He ignores my question as he removes his sister's shirt from his pockets and with one strong rip creates one long piece of fabric. He wraps it around the wolf's wound, tying the ends together. "It is only their nature to hunt," he says as he places his hand on the wolf's head.

"I know," I whisper. I wonder how he became familiar with Iéle.

His back is toward the shadows of the woods, his body still

open to the wolves. They have stopped attacking us, instead watching Nkella's movements with their alpha.

"What are they doing?" I whisper. "How come they're not attacking?"

Nkella bows his head at them. "Because I wounded their alpha. Oumala wolves are sentient beings." The smallest of the wolves, with brownish red hair, lets out a soft whimper. He looks to the other two in his pack and then back at his alpha, lying in a growing pool of blood under Nkella's hand, his breathing becoming fainter by the second. A puncture wound like that would surely kill him. The other two keep their eyes on Nkella.

What does that mean to them? My eyes widen and I gasp. "Does that mean you're their alpha now?"

At my words, the white wolf in the middle gives a low growl. Nkella moves to the side, lifting his hand off the alpha. He is steady and doesn't make any quick movements.

"Take him home," Nkella tells them. "I am not yours to follow. Your leader still lives."

"Will he, though?"

"Quiet. I cannot be their alpha."

Right.

The middle one steps forward, leading the other two. Nkella steps aside. A violent scream cuts through the air, and I still, my eyes darting to Nkella.

More will come.

But those weren't wolves. . .were they? "We have to get out of here," I remind him. A distant howl makes the white wolf sniff the air.

Nkella's looking out to the beaten path of the Spirit Forest. "They're scared."

The wolves close in around their alpha. And with one last hesitant look at Nkella and me, they all disappear into their dome inside the Aō. Their popping sounds make me jump. They're finally gone, but now we have bigger problems than wolves.

Nkella looks at the blood in his hands and wipes them on the ground. A hint of a glow hits Nkella's eyes and now I back away.

"It wasn't your fault," I say. "I could have done the same with the one I flung off me."

"Kh. You did not fling him off you. It was distracted by its alpha being hurt."

"Oh. . ." I ignore his snark implication of me being weak and useless. I know he's agitated. "So I wasn't strong enough to catapult the wolf. It sensed his alpha in danger and got distracted."

"Hn."

"Even still, it's not your fault. What could you have done? We were being hunted."

"We would not have been here at night." His voice is accusatory as he stares into the space where the wolves popped into the Aō.

I blink rapidly. "What are you getting at?"

He turns to face me. "Why did you speak at the inn?"

My brows rise. Is he serious? "Are we really doing this now?" I look around, expecting a ghost to pop out at any second. "I said I was sorry."

"You are sorry, daí?" He wipes his face. "You cannot keep quiet for two breaths."

"Are you saying this whole chase was my fault?"

"Was it mine?"

"This is all really new to me still," I say. "I messed up. I shouldn't have talked. Quite frankly, I can't tell who is Ipani or human at times because sometimes they're mixed."

"And what is wrong with that, daí?"

"What? Oh my god, nothing! I'm just saying I can't tell sometimes, so I don't know if the potion will work. That's all." I have to keep reminding myself that Ipani people can tell if I've drunk a translation potion.

He pushes himself toward me, forcing me to step back. "That is why you needed to follow my simple instructions. Can you not even do that? Do *not* speak. And you spoke. Who cares if you cannot tell the difference between people, daí? That is why you should not speak!"

I glance behind me, making sure I don't end up impaled on a stupid thorn. "Is this your intimidation tactic? To push me back? Or do you just like to tower over people?"

His face darkens, but his posture doesn't waver.

I ball my fist but try to hold my ground. This isn't helping. We had just been getting along a few hours ago. I saved him. He started calling me neyuro. He's not okay. "Nkella? Something is obviously going on with you. It's probably your curse acting up. We've both been through a lot, and you almost got killed." I'm out of breath as I speak. An amber glow flickers in his eyes. "They recognized us from the posters. They would have put trackers on us anyway."

He squares his jaw as he searches my face, trying to read

me. "Since day one of you landing on my ship, you have caused us problems. We were hunted, Lāri got captured, and then we were chased, all because of you and your mark," he hisses.

A cotton ball grows in my throat. AJ's girlfriend was captured because of me. I knew he was holding onto that. I don't even know the girl, but I messed everything up for AJ and the crew.

A shivering breath escapes my throat. He narrows his eyes and lifts his chin.

"My being here is not my fault, and AJ said you were being tracked anyway because of curse day. . ."

He starts to say something, but I cut him off, holding my hand up to his chest. He stares at it and shrugs me off. "You're right. I shouldn't have spoken at the inn. But you freaking out right now isn't helping anything."

"It is the bancha mistakes that get us killed."

"That's what the old lady at the first village said," I recall.

"Yes. Remember it."

I nod once. "Got it."

A distant scream makes my hairs stand on end. His chest rises up and down as he tries to calm himself. He stares at me for a second longer before turning to head out of this dead forest. I follow him with my gaze. Something moves within the shadows again.

"Nkella?" I whisper.

He pauses, but his ear had already twitched. He takes out his sword and jumps at the shadowed area. A man blocks his face as Nkella drags him out.

I gasp as recognition hits me. Braids, the guy from the inn who took the goat.

"No no, please!" The guy yells, moving his hands up to his face. "I didn't see you. I saw nothing."

Nkella holds his blade up to the man's neck. "Lies. You followed us."

"N-no. I live behind the thicket. I swear." The man tries to scramble from Nkella's grasp, but he isn't strong enough.

I arch a brow. "Yeah, right."

"I'm telling the truth. My house is back there. I heard a nose and came to see what it was, that's all."

"You are one of Lgao's sons. You tracked us." Nkella holds up his wrist, showing his tracker.

"I didn't. I swear, but—"

Nkella moves his sword back as if he's going to jab him in the chest. I jump toward him.

"No, wait!" I can't let him kill this guy. "You already killed enough people today. You need to stop." Or the curse is going to take over. A shiver runs down my spine. I think it is taking over.

"Give me one good reason why I shouldn't kill you."

"I can remove your tracker."

I roll my eyes. "After he said he couldn't?"

Nkella lowers his sword. "Prove it."

"In my pocket. I have the counter-potion."

Nkella nods at me. I run to the guy's side and search his pocket. Sure enough, I find a small vial with a glowing grayish solution.

I uncork the top and flick my eyes to Braids. "How do I use this?"

"Please—let me go first. I will do it."

"Koj. Tell her or I kill you now."

The man's breath shudders. "You'll kill me anyway. I'm useful. I know these parts. I can guarantee your safety outside the Spirit Forest."

"Kh. How?"

"I have something to ward away the spirits," he says.

"More rikorō?" Nkella's face darkens.

"Nkella?" I step closer to him. "Don't kill him. He can get us out of here safely."

Nkella grimaces and puts his sword away. He grabs two fistfuls of fabric from the man's tunic and lifts him inches off the ground. "How do we remove the trackers?"

"It's easy. Just pour a drop of the potion on them and they will deactivate."

I hold my wrist out and pour a drop of the counter-potion onto the glowing rope. The light emanating from it diminishes, and it snaps easily off. Nkella holds his wrist out next, still gripping Braids with the other. I pour a drop of the potion onto his tracker and its light flickers off, falling off his wrist.

A heavy sigh leaves my breath.

A shriek shatters my eardrums, and I scream. Nkella holds out his hand to keep me still.

Braid's eyes widen.

We cannot catch a break. I slowly turn around.

"Be still," Braids says.

Some kind of creature stands ten feet before us.

Wait, not a creature. A person?

It has pointy ears. There are Ipani stripes on its bare, scrawny chest. Its legs are tall and skinny. Its large eyes are mostly white with tiny pupils as it stares down and screams an anguished cry. Its skin looks wrinkled—leathery—with patches of stringy hair on its mostly bald head. It starts to shake as it gapes at us, eyes bulging and widening its mouth, showing us long pencil-like teeth.

"Don't move." Braids takes out a small lantern from his pouch and holds it up.

A harrowing scream erupts from the creature's mouth, and it charges at us. Fast. And vibrating. I shield my face, but just as I do, Braids gets in front of me and holds up his lantern. The creature bursts into a gust of ash.

Once again, I'm shaking.

Nkella grabs Braids by the neck and urges him forward, his hand still gripping onto him from behind. "You will secure our way."

"And you won't kill me?"

"Koj."

We set off into the dense forest, my heart lunging in my throat the whole way. Something screams right in my ear—I shriek as it touches my hair—and grabs at me from a tree. My skin crawls as I punch the air, scurrying behind Nkella as he whips around with Braids, the lantern shining in my direction.

Haunting and torturous howls come from all directions as we walk.

I tread cautiously with my arms wrapped tightly around me, forcing myself to keep my eyes locked in front of me, and not on the red eyes on either side of us, following our moves up the path.

Eventually, the screams become distant. The farther we go, the farther we are from the agonizing screams of whatever dead Ipani we leave behind.

"The ones in this forest are left vengeful," Braids says. "Not knowing who to be vengeful with, so they go after anyone."

"And they can't be killed," I say. I'm starting to see why this island is so dangerous.

As we hike the rest of the way, the ground becomes more elevated and darker; this new part of the forest is dense with trees again. The farther we walk, the colder the air grows, and soft misty rain starts to sprinkle.

Nkella starts to slow down. "Can you smell that?" he asks.

"What?"

"The air. It is damp here."

"Oh. . ." I smell the air. "Yeah, I do. . .it's cold though." Overhead, moonlight shines through thick purple clouds.

"It is safer now."

He has no idea how glad that makes me.

"We will make camp outside this stretch of forest."

Just then, Braids slams his hand down on Nkella's elbow, releasing himself from his grasp. He takes off in a full sprint toward the forest. Nkella takes after him in a full leap. He pins the guy down on the grass with a loud grunt.

"No no, please!" The guy yells, moving his hands up to his face. "I just want to live. Please. I won't tell anyone."

"Kh." Nkella aims his fist, and the guy screws up his face, bringing his arms up in defense. Nkella stands him up and clocks him right on the nose. Blood smears his face as he struggles back, trying his hardest to block Nkella's blows.

He isn't fighting back.

Nkella swings again, and the guy yells something muffled.

"Wait," I say, running toward them.

"Neyuro, stand back."

"Stop!" I grab at his arm and pull it back. An amber glow flashes in his eyes as he yanks his arm back from me and I almost lose my footing. He's going to kill this guy and lose himself completely. "Nkella, wait."

"Please," the guy spits blood out his mouth. "I won't say anything, I swear."

"Lies. How big is the reward for me, daí?"

The guy shrugs and shakes his head. "I don't know. I know nothing. Let me go, I won't say anything. Please, I have a family." He holds his hands up higher to his face.

"Think about this," I say. "You can knock him out instead. By the time he wakes up, we'll be long gone."

Nkella narrows his eyes at me, hopefully, considering it.

"He took off our trackers. He gave us safe passage out of the Spirit Forest. You don't have to kill him. And—"

Nkella stops to stare at me, expectantly. Braid's gaze shifts from Nkella's to mine as I lock eyes with him.

I take a deep breath hoping this will buy Nkella enough time to calm down. "Back at the inn. . . Lgao said something about rikorō being a commodity among the guards." It doesn't seem likely that unbound Ipani would give up their lives for its creation, so maybe there's a connection between them and the traffickers.

A flare reaches Nkella's eyes, and he pulls Braids up by his shirt with his fist. "I am only going to ask this once. Do you know who is leading the traffickers?"

My breath hitches. If he helps, Nkella will surely let him go.

Braids nods.

"Who is it?" Nkella's voice comes out like a growl.

"I-if I tell you, will you let me go?"

"Depends."

"The Empress's Hierophant."

Nkella searches the man's face. "Brave assumption, daf?" he hisses his words close to his face.

"Demitri?" So he isn't only after the Ace of Wands, he's in charge of the whole kidnapping unbound Ipani operation. I gasp. How many people has he killed for their ouma?

"I've never seen him, but everybody knows the Hierophant is friends with the Swords' Prefect more than Wands. People have seen the Arcana soldiers from Swords around town, doing his bidding. Only one or two ever show up, never causing much commotion. . ."

Nkella narrows his eyes and slowly lowers him. The farmer readjusts his tunic and shares a nervous smile.

Nkella smirks but then does something strange. He runs his fingers down the man's arm; the guy does a double take and steps back, but Nkella grabs his wrist. At first I startle, but then realize what he's looking for.

I squint to try and make out the mark, but before I can tell what it is, Braid's eyes grow wide.

Something sinister flashes in Nkella's eyes, the crimson glow flickering once. Before I can process what's happening, a hideous crack rips from Braid's neck, and he drops to the ground.

My hands shake, and I backpedal.

Speechless, and with my heart throbbing in my throat, I gape at the lifeless body who had just begged for his life. Harrowing sounds of agony and despair come from his lips. This close, I feel like it comes from a deeper place than his throat, like it's coming from the lingering parts of his pained soul. The eternal suffering has started. I step back with blurred vision and move my gaze to Nkella. "W-why?"

"He had mark of a *Page*."

"So what?"

"So he is a messenger. He would have spoken."

"But you could have just knocked him out! You didn't know for certain he would have given us up!"

"Kh. You are naive. He would have woken up and called a guard. He is a *Page*," he repeats.

"He was obviously a *farmer*!" My voice shakes. "He tended goats. Who knows why he had that mark? And he was helping us!"

"I cannot take a chance!" he shouts at me, and I shake. "I will not risk the lives of my crew, or of my sister in the hope that a potential threat is benign!" His irises grow bright as a vein in his neck bulges.

My throat constricts as I stare at the guy's lifeless body. His glossy eyes stare at me as blood continues to flow out of his mouth.

"Move, neyuro. It's time to go."

I flick my eyes to him, and a spark of amber dances in his irises. I turn to look away. "You didn't have to kill him. He was innocent."

"You would have preferred to be taken by the guards, daí?"

Not even a hint of remorse in his voice. My jaw aches from how tense I am right now. "You were more bent up about killing a wolf than a human."

"The wolves weren't going to turn us in."

"You're hopeless. Maybe you want the curse of the Devil

Card to take you. And you know what? Maybe you should be cursed. Maybe the Empress was right about you all along."

A muscle under his eye twitches as he gives me a hard stare. "Maybe you are nothing but my prisoner, gembella. Afraid to kill, always trying to run away and getting caught. The only place you will ever be is inside a metal cage."

My breathing shakes. "The only one here stuck inside their metal cage is you." I take off his coat and drop it at his feet. A flare of amber ignites in his eyes, his irritation soaring, his anger banked but not gone.

I walk past him, left of the clearing, toward the wooded path. So much for progress. He hasn't corrected me, so I assume it's the safest path in the right direction. There's no point in talking with him. He's a murderer. I knew this on the ship when he threw that prisoner overboard to his death. Just when I thought he wasn't that bad, having a soft heart for wolves, caring for his crew and his sister. Being there for a child he didn't know. He only cares when it directly benefits him. He could have chosen to knock Braid out, but he decided to kill him. If he wants to be consumed by the curse of the Devil Card, then so be it. I just want to go home.

I need to remember that. Everything I'm doing is to go home to my sister. He can save his own crew. Remember your instincts, Soren. Stay focused, and don't trust anyone. Especially not a murderous pirate.

His footsteps crinkle on the dead grass some paces away from me, so I assume I took off in the right direction. Good. He can keep his distance from me.

We walk in silence until he stops. I assume we've reached the safer forest he talked about. I still refuse to look at him. I topple down to my knees and stretch my legs; every muscle and fiber of my body aches. I want to ask him if he's sure we'll be safe here, if the guards can scope us out in this forest. The Arcana soldiers from the Tower are psychic, aren't they? How does he know we're safe?

But I keep my mouth shut. The image of the guy's glossy stare as blood pools from his lips keeps flashing through my mind.

Nkella drops his coat on the ground. "Sit there while I go find us some supplies."

I stand right back up. "Stop telling me what to do." My eyes bore into the back of his head, and he stops walking.

"Fine," he says without turning around. "Come collect blackberries. I will collect firewood."

"Fine." I take off in the other direction. After a few steps, he calls after me.

"Where are you going?"

"To collect blackberries. You literally just told me to."

"Not over there. With me. So I can keep an eye on you, daf?"

"Yeah, I don't think so. I need to be as far away from you as possible."

"Kh. So you can escape?"

"And go where?" I turn to face him and place my hands on my hips. "To go to the same Temples you're going to? You'll catch up to me before I find out how to get there, and it would make no sense for me to run. We both want me to use the Ace, don't we?"

He raises his chin and stares down at me with those unforgiving eyes. "It is the stupid mistakes that will get you killed, *gembella*. Remember."

I resist the urge to roll my eyes. "If a guard shows up, I'll scream, 'kay?" I turn on my heel and take off before he says another word.

The moonlight lights my path through the trees, reflecting on the dry leaves. A bird caws over my head and goose bumps break out on my skin. Maybe this was a stupid idea.

No.

It'll be fine. I'll just collect the stupid berries and head back. I can't stand to even look at him. I near a luscious bush with what looks like raspberries and blackberries and pick one out to inspect it. Assuming they're the same kind as on Earth, I start plucking them from their branches and filling my loose pockets, hoping they won't squish.

Did he kill Braids just to spite me? To prove a point because I begged him not to? He's so confusing. Sometimes there's a semblance of kindness, and other times. . .he's a brute. I shake my head. Stop it. He's a heartless pirate, and I can't get out of here fast enough.

I pop a few berries in my mouth as my stomach grumbles, while mindlessly filling my pockets with the rest.

"Enjoying my berries, Fool?"

I gasp and spin around, dropping the berries I had in my hand to the ground. I blink as the Empress's golden mask appears to glow under the moonlight, adding to her divine essence. She wears a black corset, tight black pants, and boots with a spiderweb lace cloak. No laurel leaf crown this time.

"Do you know why the Fool is called the Fool?" Her sharp voice makes me jump. I shake my head and feel the tip of my new shirt's sleeve right at my wrist, fully covering my real mark. She still thinks I have the Fool's mark.

"It is because when one embarks on a new journey, they do so with the foolishness of a child. Are you sure those berries are edible?"

My eyes widen as I take a few out of my pocket to inspect them again.

"Things are different here than they are in other worlds."

I pour the berries out of my pocket and open my mouth to make myself gag.

The Empress guffaws. "Relax. Those are indeed safe. But I am right, aren't I? When I saw you together with the Magician, it hit me that my sister must be alive. I know now you're from Earth. So, which are you? A spy? An assassin?"

She takes a step forward and I take a step back.

I open my mouth to speak but then close it.

"Be careful with your words, Fool. Why else would you be here? Why else would you be on a Fool's Journey and the Magician have magic? I knew your dimension long ago—magic does not come easy to mortals. Only one can open that portal, and it is my sister."

I swallow. I have to play my cards right here. I'm not about to start arguing or begging for her to believe me. I won't win. But if I pretend, she might kill me or curse me like she did to Harold.

"Are you going to try and curse me again?" I ask, avoiding her question.

She chuckles. "That question is one I've kept turning over in my head. Why didn't my curse work on you? The only answer is my sister sent you and protected you with a guise." She taps her chin with her index finger. "You were able to get close to me in my Tower. What information did you plan to give my sister?"

She actually thinks one of the Fates came to me and sent me here to spy on her. Or kill her. Her curse mustn't have worked because of whatever my mark means. What if I tell her about it now? How do I know she'd really kill me? The screams of the tortured children infiltrate my memories. Her heart is black and cold. Do I really want to take that chance?

No one other than myself is worthy of this mark. Anyone who has it should be dead.

That's what she said while we were sitting at her arena. She'd absolutely kill me. "I didn't find anything," I say. "I failed."

She narrows her piercing green eyes at me. "Then why are you still here? And hanging with those pirates."

"I'm stuck here. I can't get back."

She gives me a scrutinizing stare. "She must have the World Card to open the portal. She'd be keeping tabs on you to bring you back. Unless. . ." She taps the chin of her mask with her index finger. "I did sense great energy earlier which is how I found you. Have you seen the card?"

My throat dries. "I—she may have tried to contact me but. . .the connection was bad." I quickly lie. The connection was bad? That probably made no sense to her.

She tilts her head. "My sister tried to come through?"

"She—"

"Tell me the truth so I can help you." Her voice softens. Can she really help me?

"I thought it was valuable so I stole it from her. I thought it would ensure my way back, but it's been no use."

She laughs. "Silly girl. Only a fate can use it. She must have tried to reach you. That must be what I felt."

Only a fate can use it.

I can use it.

I'll think on that later.

"She can do that?" I ask.

"With a familiar, she could," she says. My mind drifts to Philo.

The Empress lifts her chin. "If you have it, let me see it."

"What do you want with it?"

"Allow me to help you. If you give it to me, I will send you home."

My eyes widen. "You can help me get back?"

"Of course I can."

"Just like that?"

"In fact, that is why I am here. To give you a choice. Since I could not curse you"—a small bottle materializes in her palm in a gust of red smoke—"I can send you home. Drink this and your body will immaterialize to appear back where you came."

I stare at it. It looks like a small wine bottle closed with a cork. It's too dark to tell the color of the liquid but it looks almost blue or dark purple.

"What's wrong? Don't you want to go home?"

"I do—"

"Worried about your pirate friends?"

More like I don't trust this. An ominous potion from the Empress who had previously tried to kill me? And yet, she seems to want me out of this world as badly as I want to get home. The last thing I want is to look at Nkella's stupid face again. "Why not just open the portal with the World Card?"

"If I do it that way, my sister will know I have it. No. You'll go back a different way. I've spent the ages perfecting this transport potion. Take it."

With a potion here for almost anything, I guess I could believe one will immaterialize me and send me back home. I reach for it, but she pulls it away.

"The World Card first," she says.

I swallow. I'd be leaving them all behind. Harold, who's now cursed because of me. AJ, who I promised I'd help find his girlfriend. Tessa and Kae who looked out for me on the ship. And the promise I made to Chumi about Soanalo. Nkella was right. It was a promise I couldn't keep.

The sound Braid's neck made when Nkella mercilessly killed him lives inside me as an earworm. None of those things are my responsibility. I reach into my pocket and take out the World Card. She snaps it from my fingers.

"Go on, drink it." She holds out the bottle and I take it, moving my eyes to her expressionless mask. Here's to taking a leap of faith.

I uncork the top and a cold smoke comes out from it. This is it. I can finally go home. My pulse quickens as I imagine seeing Talia again and getting back to my life. I'll never have to deal with being Nkella's gembella again. I'm no one's prisoner. All this, so he can use me. My breathing becomes shallow as all the times he's upset me come rushing forward.

Too slow, gembella.

"Shut up." I lift the bottle and pour it down my throat. A sour-yet-bitter taste assaults my taste buds, and I gag.

"Good girl." The Empress waves her hand and smoke starts to materialize at her feet. "I liked you, Soren. You would have fit right in my castle." And with that, she leaves in her gust of red smoke.

I find myself alone, half expecting to see a gust of smoke appear around me, to take me away, but instead I get a cramp in my stomach. I groan and everything around me starts to spin. I stumble back and accidentally lean on the bushes, making me fall to the ground.

Suddenly, the temperature drops around me, and I start to shiver. My shivers become shakes, and my shakes become convulsions. The next thing I know, Nkella is leaning over me. He mutters something in Ipani that sounds like a cuss.

I think he's propping me up, but my vision goes in and out of focus. Something metallic tasting builds in my throat. I lose control of my body. I lose focus completely. And all I feel is the ground shaking around me. Nkella calls out to me, but his voice sounds distant.

I feel like I'm slipping. Fading away. And then there's nothing.

30

My eyes fly open, and I gasp for air. Nkella's lips are on mine and I freeze. He jumps back and it takes me a moment to realize what was happening. He was doing CPR. They do CPR here? Well, I guess so! My chest heaves as I gape at him.

His coat and hat are off, and he lets himself lie back as he wipes his face, a nervous laugh escapes him. He reaches for his flask and takes a gulp of his rum.

My throat and mouth are dry. "Water?" I mutter, too weak to speak. He lunges up and grabs my canteen, pressing it up to my lips. I take a few sips and stare at him. "Thanks."

He responds with a sigh and reaches for something next to the tree bark. "You are too weak. Eat." He sets a large leaf down in front of me with some fruits, berries, and nuts.

"What happened?" I ask. My head weighs me down, and I blink through long branches of a willow tree. "Where are we?"

I struggle to prop myself up on my elbow and look out to a lake.

"You were taking long. I thought you were being slow. Careless."

I cringe.

"But then I went to find you, and you were unconscious on the ground. What happened to you, daí?"

"I—Ow!" I grab for my stomach as sharp needles feel like they're ripping me apart. I lift up my shirt a little and gasp. Black gooey veins are spidering out from a dark spot on my abdomen. I blink rapidly, and an image of the Empress's mask reflecting off the moon emerges in my mind. The bottle. Smoke. And then. . .

The pain subsides, and my chest heaves. "I don't understand," I say. "She said it would take me home."

His gaze intensifies. "What are you talking about?"

"She said to drink from a potion, and it would take me home."

"Who said this?"

"The Empress."

The blood drains from his face, and he pulls away. "The Empress was here?"

I nod weakly.

He shakes his head, his forehead wrinkling. "You don't trust anyone." His voice is soft; it almost sounds hurt. "Why would you trust her, daí?"

"I'm an idiot. I shouldn't have believed her. I was just so mad at you, and she offered me a way home." I gasp. "She took the World Card. I'm so stupid."

His eyes squeeze shut for a moment. "What did she give you?"

He doesn't even sound upset. That worries me. "I don't know. It was a dark potion in a corked bottle."

"What did it taste like?"

"Mostly bitter. . .and sour."

His eyes widen. *"Itachi."*

"What?"

"It is a poisonous elderberry. She meant to kill you."

My mouth gapes. "I'm going to die?"

"Koj." He starts to get up. "Itachi grows in Ahan Alēla. There might be someone in the next village who can make a detox."

"How long do I have?" I look down at the spidery veins.

He shakes his head. "I don't know." His voice is stern and dark. "I will find the detox while you rest."

I nod, and the realization that Nkella just saved my life through CPR sinks in. "You saved me. . ."

"Hn."

"Why?"

His eyes meet mine; worry lines crease his forehead. Then he eases, and his features form into a smirk. "Gembella. Kh. I need you alive, daí?"

"Right." Of course. He's a killer. Everyone in this world is a killer. I lean my head back against the tree.

While he's gone, I let myself fall back to sleep. I wake up after what seems like hours; Nkella is still gone. Light trickles in from between the long willow branches. I reach for my canteen and drink some water. I'm so thirsty. My stomach roars, and I find a large leaf with nuts and berries he left me.

What time did Nkella leave? Another wave of nausea overwhelms my head. I close my eyes again.

Hours later, I wake up in a full sweat. I blink awake, and Nkella is there with a large leaf in his hand that he presses against my forehead. Sweat trickles down his torso as his shirt is wrapped around his head. Pain in my abdomen strikes me again, and I focus on his tattoos as he pours water over another leaf and presses it to my neck and chest. Large markings, which I can only assume are Ipani scriptures, blend with the Ipani stripes over his pecs.

"It's so hot. How long was I out?" I ask.

"We have lost half the day."

I gasp and try to sit up, but my head is too heavy, and now I have a shooting pain at my temples. "Ow. . .migraine."

"Koj, koj, don't move."

"But we need to go. We're wasting time."

He nods. "I will have to carry you to the next town. I found the berries."

I shake my head and try to stand, "I can walk." He takes my hand and steadies me. The ground moves below me and I feel another wave of nausea coming.

I fall back down, and he breaks my fall, helping me down slowly.

"This won't work. I will have to carry you."

"I'm sorry," I say.

He doesn't respond; instead, he puts on his coat and lifts me from my arms and legs, cradling me like a baby. I grab onto his chest and close my eyes, laying my head against the nook of his neck. Tones of leather and hickory engulf my memory of him as I take him in. The sunlight hits against my eyelids as he steps out of the willow tree. Memories from when I first met him surface in my mind. He was cruel. Psychologically cruel. And now he's carrying me to try and find a healer. Strange odds in this Tarot deck.

Bile rises up my throat. Uh-oh. . . "Nkella. . ." I muff my mouth with my hand.

"Daí?"

"Put me down."

He quirks a brow, and I start to wiggle free. He sets me down and my body starts to convulse as my chest heaves. My body lifts me up uncontrollably as it forces out the berries, fruits, and nuts I ate. I could taste the fish from yesterday morning too. I barely notice him picking up my hair as every-thing leaves my system. As my body settles down, I lie down on my back, facing the hot sun against my face. He squats down and hands me my canteen. I take it and take a sip.

"This won't work," he says.

I don't respond. The ground is still moving. I'm afraid that if I speak, I'll vomit again.

"You are changing colors, gembella. Let's go." He lifts me up again and takes me back to the willow tree and sets me down.

"Changing colors?"

"Your complexion. You are very sick. We cannot go to the village like this." He sets me back down in the spot where I awoke.

"What do we do then? We can't stay here. . . Is it safe to be here for another day?"

He wipes his face. "Bancha."

I sigh. "Yes, I'm stupid. I know I'm stupid. I should have known better." I dig my fingers into the dirt beside me.

"No, not you. Me. I was stupid. I should not have let you go on your own. Her psychic soldiers must have had eyes on us. I should have known this. I should have done better."

His voice sounds like he's in agony. Is he. . .apologizing to me? My throat tightens, and I clear it. "Umm. . . It's okay. I shouldn't have taken off by myself. This world is different. Even though you shouldn't have killed that guy."

"Kh."

I ignore him and try sitting up on my elbows. I know he won't apologize for killing him, so why bother? I tug on my shirt. "How bad is it?"

His eyes fall to my throat, and he shakes his head. I touch the place on my skin where he's looking and feel something sticky. "It's spreading, isn't it? So her plan was to give me a slow and painful death. How fitting for her. What's the point of that?"

"Hnn. I thought this too. But then I remembered what happened when she tried to curse you."

"Harold. . ." I say. "What are you getting at?"

"You drank a whole bottle, daí? A potion from the Empress won't be weak. It should have taken you quickly. The fact that it hasn't is suspicious." He narrows his eyes. "Maybe your mark makes it hard for her to kill you. Just like she couldn't curse you."

"She thinks I have the Fool's mark, thanks to AJ." I smile. "She wouldn't have known it wouldn't kill me quickly." The image of Harold getting hit and being cursed like the crew flashes through my mind. I push it out of my thoughts. "How much do you know about this poisonous plant?"

He studies me with deep set eyes.

"What is it?"

"Some Ipani take it in small doses. It is too dangerous for humans. Many have died trying to see what it's like. If taken properly, you can speak with the dead. But if it enters your blood, it will capture your soul. With time, you will forget who you are, until you are taken by eternal torment."

I gape at the oozing, black spidery veins spreading to my legs and take in what he just said to me. I'll forget who I am. . .like my mom. After all this time, in another world, I still end up like her. My pulse quickens as panic courses through my veins.

My mom. I never got to see her again. I kept putting it off, waiting until I was an adult, waiting until I had money for a flight. Waiting. And waiting. Making excuses. Ignoring the real reason I never went, which was. . . I'm scared. So scared she'll look at me and not recognize who I am. And now. . . I'm going to lose my mind in this strange Tarotland, never getting to tell her that I still love her. And care about her. To at least let her know that I'm okay. . .that her sickness didn't ruin her kid's life.

But it found me in a different way. I shudder, my breath catching. I guess you really can't escape fate. "Oh no. . . I never made it back to my sister. She'll think I abandoned her forever." Tears start to stream down my face.

"Shhh. . .gembella. Do not upset yourself right now. You will make it worse."

Gembella. "And I'm dying as a prisoner. I always knew. . .I would die as one." Tears roll down harder now, my cries breaking up my words as I shake.

"No. Not a gembella."

"What?"

"I will call you neyuro like I did when you saved me in Jōtenko. Because you are brave. I called you gembella again out of anger."

"You're only saying that because you know I'm dying."

He doesn't say anything; instead, he looks away. My head spins again, and I feel that overwhelming weight drag my head down. He's worried—that much I can tell. But it isn't for me. Every minute wasted is a minute Lāri could be dead, the crew could be killed, and the further Nkella gets from saving his sister.

His voice darkens. "There is another way, but I am not sure it will work." He takes out a small branch of red berries from his coat pocket.

"What are those?"

"Itachi berries."

"The poison, itachi?"

"Eating them could help."

"How would me eating poison berries stop the poison from spreading?"

"Not you. I will eat them."

My brows furrow. "I don't understand."

"I've heard stories of it helping, but it is dangerous. It can also do the same to me."

"Sounds stupid. Then we'll both lose our minds until eternal torment takes us." I raise my head to look at him, and place my hand on his chest. Curiosity flashes in his eyes, and his lips part.

"Go," I say.

He stares at me.

"Leave me here. Save your crew. Save your sister."

"What are you talking about, neyuro? Kh. You are not making sense."

"I am. I'm dying. I'm too weak to keep up when I'm not ill, and now I'll only hold you back. You're wasting time because of me." I cough. "Go save them. I didn't help you use the World Card. I hope you believe me now that I didn't know how." I push his chest harder, but he doesn't budge. His face is serious, and his eyes search mine. I push at him again, but this time he grabs my wrist and I startle.

"What are you doing?" I ask. "Just leave me here. You have a much more important task. You have to save everyone. Not just your sister, but your island. Go. Maybe I'll get lucky and some healer will pass by." I try to grin but cough again.

"Koj."

"What?"

"I won't leave you here to die."

"Now you're not making any sense."

"Sh." He helps me lie on my back, and my eyes close as I drift off to a dreamless sleep.

I wake, alarmed to feel him stroking my hair, but I don't bother to pull away.

"Soren," he whispers, almost inaudibly. "I do not think you are weak."

I don't remember ever telling him my thoughts of what he thinks of me.

"You had guts sneaking into my room."

I snort, and he stops stroking my hair. Did he not know I was awake? "It almost sounds like you don't hate me," I say.

"Kh."

A smile curls on my lips.

After a few moments, he says, "I admire you for caring for your sister."

"I can say the same about you." I prop myself up and stare at his features. His black hair pours over his cheekbones, outlining his soft skin. His dark eyes stare back at me with a softness in them I've never seen before.

We need to at least make it to the next town if we're going to find someone who can heal me. We can't stay here until I die. It's been a whole five minutes since I felt dizzy.

"Should we get going?" I whisper. I sit up, but still as an immobilizing pain seers down into my bones, this time spreading from my legs to my hips. My head bobs to the side, the whole world spins, and I drop back down.

"Neyuro? Neyuro!" Nkella's voice grows distant as a whirlwind of nausea spins me like a tornado. I shut my eyes, but that doesn't stop the spinning. All I see is color until a loud popping sound erupts inside my head, and I burst into a million pieces.

31

TICK-TOCK. TICK-TOCK. TICK-TOCK.

The spinning stops, and my nausea goes away with it. Heat from the yellow sun warms the top of my head; the smell reminds me of being a little girl playing in the backyard of my parent's house during Louisiana summers. Back then, everything was as it should be. My mother was watering her new garden of tomatoes, southern peas, and eggplants. My father was indoors in his study. A cooling breeze brings a tinge of honeysuckle.

The sound of the ticking clock grows louder, snapping me back to the present. I gaze around me, expecting to see a standing grandfather clock, but instead, I find that I'm standing on a cobblestone path on a meadow of wildflowers.

Despite the bright sun, a hazy purple dew glistens over the grass, trees, and flowers. My arms also glisten with the purple dew. I smile. It's so pretty.

Tick-tock. Tick-tock.

Tick-tock. Tick-tock.

Tick-tock.

Wasn't I supposed to be somewhere right now?

Up ahead is a large clock tower. But when I say large, I mean it's much *much* taller than me. How lovely would it be to climb up it and sit on top? I bet I could see for miles from up there!

Skittering toward the clock tower, I stop as something brushes past me. My eyes widen as a rabbit, unusually large, stands on hind legs, wearing a waistcoat and a black top hat. It thumps its foot once in my direction and pulls out a pocket watch.

"The ticking! Was that you all along?" I ask him.

He wiggles his nose and eyes me with large red eyes. "Goodness me, you're late! Time's almost out. Come on. Follow me, Soren."

I gasp. "How do you know who I am?" I ask, ignoring the fact that a rabbit just talked. I feel like I've seen and experienced many strange things lately, although. . . I can't place where I've seen them. . .

"You really have a knack for keeping me waiting, don't you? Of course I know who you are! We all do!"

"Who's we?"

The rabbit sighs and thumps its foot on the ground, shaking his head.

I narrow my eyes. "Where am I?"

"Please, tell me you're joking. I won't merit that with a response, Soren. I won't. Hurry up, will you?"

I part my lips and stare at him.

"Well, don't just stand there. Come along!"

"Wait!" I start to follow him down the cobblestone path, through the meadow of wildflowers. "Where are we going?"

"To your party, of course!" he calls out.

"My party?"

"You're the guest of honor!"

I am? "But I'm not dressed for a—" I stop running and look down at what I'm wearing. A light blue dress with white frills. Hmm. I guess I am. "But rabbit, I don't remember ever owning a blue dress. . . Rabbit?" Looks like he ran off ahead of me. That's rude. I thought I was the guest of honor.

I take a few steps, and the flowers start to get taller. I pause as it's only been a few steps. I walk back three steps, and the flowers get smaller. This isn't right. The hazy purple dew shimmers over my face; I shrug it off as some sort of optical illusion and keep walking. As the stems get to be my height, little faces start to poke out of the flowers. Snapdragons with long noses, roses with puckered lips, daisies with chubby cheeks. They all stare at me as I walk past them.

My cheeks burn. Why are they staring? A daisy as tall as my waist starts to laugh, pointing at me with her leafy stem. I pause and drop my jaw. "What's so funny?"

A rosebud behind me spins me around as she too starts to laugh. Soon, all the flowers in the meadow are crying in laughter.

"Stop it!" I ball my fist. "Tell me what's funny!"

A foxglove with a button nose and long petals for eyebrows points at me while giggling. "She has her head inside out!"

I gasp and touch my face.

A group of daisies practically shrivel to the ground with laughter. "Her head's on the outside!"

"What are you talking about?" I say as I pass my hands over my ears and lips. "Everything's all there." I take a strand of my red hair and hold it out. "See?"

The purple hue sweeps over me once more and their laughter rings through my ears even louder. A giggle escapes my lips. Then another. Soon, I'm laughing hysterically, and I can't stop. Maybe my head *is* inside out.

"I wish my head was a flower, like yours." I say. "You're all so pretty."

"Maybe you can turn into one!" One of the chubby cheek daisies says.

"Really? How?"

The laughter roars all around me, and I join in again with them. What a funny thought. Me, turning into a flower and being planted in the ground. Forever to laugh at passersby. "It is lovely here, though. I probably wouldn't mind living here forever."

Tick-tock. Tick-tock.

"There's that ticking sound again," I say between laughs.

"That's the doom clock!" a monkey orchid shouts.

The daisies cry out in unison, "Stay away! Stay away!"

"Doom clock?" I stop laughing. What does that remind me of?

You've doomed us all!

I gasp and stumble back. The buttercups from. . . The memory gets lost again.

"There you are! Wasting time *again*?"

I spin around to find the white rabbit with his hands on his hips.

"Opps, sorry!" I turn back to the wildflowers. "I guess I have to go."

"We're not going anywhere!" a rose says.

"Yeah," adds in a daisy with chubby cheeks, "we'll be here when you get back, you know!"

I start to laugh again but the rabbit pulls at my skirt, moving me into motion. Soon, I'm following the rabbit back down the cobblestone path. The giant clock tower is at the far end, except the closer I get, the farther away it seems.

"Soren!"

A voice calls from behind me so I stop to see who it is. Far away among the flowers is a tall guy wearing a pirate hat and coat. I know him. He's running down the cobblestone as the flowers lay down on his path. He trips, and I can hear their laughter from here. He stands and pulls out a sword from his sheath.

"We really must be going," the white rabbit says. I ignore him as the pirate swings his sword and slices the flowers in half. I shriek as their screams ring down the meadow. "No!" I cry, "he's killing them all!"

The pirate snaps his head up and stares at me, his eyes emanate an amber glow, and I take a step back. I do know him. The captain of the *Devil's Gambit*. I remember now. He had me thrown in the brig.

Nkella starts to run down the cobblestone path.

"I won't be his prisoner anymore." I take a step back. "I won't."

"Then, hurry!" The white rabbit rushes off with a hop, and I sprint after him.

Tick-tock. Tick-tock.

"Soren," Nkella yells after me. "Don't go farther, neyuro. It's too dangerous!"

What's he talking about? He's never cared about me being in danger. He's only ever put me in danger.

I follow the white rabbit farther into the meadow, ignoring Nkella's warning as his voice grows farther away until I can't hear him at all. We pass large mushrooms with twisted tops, and smaller ones that look like inverted umbrellas. A large cloud in the shape of a cat with a wide menacing grin floats past; only this cat has gills and fins and seems to be swimming in the sky.

I pause as a feeling of déjà vu sweeps over me, but I can't put my finger on what it is. In fact, I've lost all sense of why I was running. But it doesn't matter, does it? This place is so lovely.

Tick-tock. Tick-tock. Tick-tock.

The sound of the ticking clock. I've grown to expect it, and to be quite honest, I've come to like it. It's soothing. I think I'd feel off without it.

"Sorry, we're late!" The white rabbit hops down a small hill toward a beautiful picnic area with a wooden table dressed in a white fabric. Spread on top are three different three-level tiers of muffins, cupcakes, and little sandwiches. Teacups and plates are placed at every seat. At the far end sits a woman with wavy red hair wearing a bright purple and green jacket. She takes a sip of her tea when her eyes snap up to look at me.

She nearly drops her tea and stands. My throat dries as recognition hits me.

Mom.

"But. . .how are you here?" I mutter, making my way down

the hill. She meets me at the bottom and takes my hand, pulling me in for a tight hug. Tears wet the corners of my eyes. There's so much I want to say to her, but I don't know how I'm going to get the words out.

I'm sorry for not visiting you.

I've missed you so much.

I'm okay.

I love you.

But all I can do is stare into her brown eyes, so alert and alive.

"I've been waiting for you," she says. "Come, sit with me."

I do as she says and take a seat next to hers at the far end. I still can't believe this is happening.

"Tea?" My mom takes the kettle as I hold my teacup. The scent of carrot cake tickles my nostrils as my cup fills.

The top of the sugar bowl jumps off as a dormouse pops out. I giggle.

"While I've been waiting for you, I've been thinking of words starting with the letter *M*..."

Where have I heard that before? It sounds awfully familiar.

"The word *memory* comes to mind when I think of you," my mom says.

"It's funny, ever since I got here, I haven't been able to remember much. But I do remember you."

She takes a sip of her tea and I do the same, taking in the hot carrot-cake-flavored beverage. "Remembering before you got here doesn't matter now that you are here with me. Drink, eat, and enjoy yourself. I'll tell you your favorite story."

"My favorite story?"

"Why yes, *Alice's Adventures in Wonderland*! Do you want me to tell it to you?"

I beam at her. "Of course! Just like when I was little."

I don't remember how I got here. But it doesn't matter.

She begins with Alice following the white rabbit down the rabbit hole and I rest my head on my hand.

"Soren!"

I startle and spill my tea. My mom stops storytelling and I turn to see who just called my name.

Nkella stands at the edge of the hill with his pirate hat on his head. How did he find me?

"Wonderful! A Hatter!" My mom waves him over. "Come, sit for some tea. I was just getting to the good part."

Nkella squints at her, then at me. "Let's go, neyuro. Before it is too late."

I grab onto the table. "No."

"No? But you have to, or—"

"Everything is perfect here. Why would I ever want to leave?"

Nkella blinks and then takes his first steps toward the table. "Neyuro. . . None of this is real. It is in your mind, daí?"

"In my mind?" I start to laugh. Then, my mom bursts into giggles. The white rabbit comes from the corner and starts laughing too, as does the dormouse from the sugar cup.

The seat on the other end of the table pulls away by itself and my mother holds out her hand. "Come, take a seat."

Nkella narrows his eyes at the seat as if it's going to turn into a snake and bite him if he sits. "Soren, we don't have time. You will lose your mind. And then so will I if I stay here longer."

I open my mouth to speak, but my mom interrupts. "Oh, shush now," she says. "Have some tea."

The white rabbit runs and lifts the kettle, nearly spilling some on him as he runs to pour it into Nkella's teacup.

"Soren," he asks, "why does this rabbit wear clothes?"

"Because he's from the story *Alice in Wonderland*," I say with a roll of my eyes. I gasp. That's true, isn't it? A fuzzy memory overcomes me. This is the first time I've realized it. I look at my mom. "Am I stuck in the story?"

She pats my hand and smiles. "Doesn't that make you happy, dear?"

The purple hue sweeps over my head, and I blink. "Yes, so happy."

"Soren," Nkella's voice is rigid. I snap my gaze at him, and an amber glow surfaces behind his pupils. He lifts the tea to his nose. "This smells like itachi. Do not drink anymore."

I shake my head. "Stop being silly. It smells like carrot cake."

"It smells however your mind wants it to smell." He sets the cup down, now taking the seat beside me. "You are poisoned from the potion you drank. You need to remember."

"If this is all in my mind, then how are you here? Everything was wonderful until you came in. Maybe you're made up too."

"Koj. I am really here. I ate the itachi to come find you."

"Yes," I scratch my head. "I think I did make you up. If this is all pretend, I want you to go."

"It is fake, but I am not." He now stands next to me and tugs at my arm.

My mom taps my hand again. "Soren, I am not fake, honey. You know that."

I stare at Nkella. "My mom isn't fake."

"Let's all calm down and have some cake. More tea!" My mom taps on her teacup with her fingers.

The dormouse pops up from the sugar bowl. "More tea! More tea!"

I giggle. "Yes. More please."

"Soren." Nkella comes closer, trying to make eye contact, but I avert my eyes. "Stop. Look around you. This is not real, neyuro."

A fly buzzes past me and lands on a biscuit.

"See?" he says. "Not perfect."

"Flies are normal," I say.

"Neyuro. . .if we do not go now, you will lose your mind."

"Will that be so bad? My mom lost hers, and she's here with me."

"She has a point, you know," my mom says.

"Neyuro. . ." He lowers his voice. "What about your sister?"

"Soren doesn't have a sister," my mom says in a matter-of-fact tone. "I knew a Hatter almost as mad as you. Shall I tell you about him?"

"Koj," Nkella doesn't look her in the eye. He keeps his gaze fixed on me. "How will you go back home to her if you stay here?"

"Didn't you hear my mother? I don't have a sister."

Nkella sighs and stands. He points over to the ground. "Look at the flowers. They are dying."

"That's normal. Flowers die."

"Here? So fast?"

I take another sip of my tea, and he smacks it from my hand. I yelp.

"Why did you do that?"

"Soren, last chance. I will not die from itachi. Come with me, or stay a gembella to your own mind until you suffer eternal torment."

Gembella.

I gasp.

Nkella's eyes widen. "Neyuro. . ." He drops to his knees, searching my eyes. "What is your sister's name?"

My pulse quickens. "Talia." I raise my hand to my lips. "Nkella. . .I. . ."

"Look around now."

Flies buzz all around us, maggots eat at the cake, and the tea smells like. . .death. I turn to look at my mother and scream. Her corpse is rotten, her head leaning back. Her mouth gapes open, and maggots crawl from the inside out.

I jump up from my seat and scream, bumping into Nkella behind me. He grabs my arms and spins me around, hugging me tight. I shudder into his chest.

"She wasn't real, neyuro. It was the itachi making you want to stay."

My chest heaves as I try to gather my thoughts. I drank a potion from the Empress. None of this was real. Of course, my brain would choose *Alice in Wonderland* as a setting to lure me into permanent delirium. My mom isn't really dead behind me. She's safe in a hospital bed. And I need to leave here to finally be able to see her again. . .and to see Talia. I nod to myself. "Thank you. . ." I say to Nkella. "Wait. How did you find me?"

"I ate the itachi, then I focused my intent on finding you."

I look up at him. "Why would you do that?"

His eyes are gentle as they sweep my face. His lips part, but he doesn't say anything, as if searching for the right words.

Tick-tock. Tick-tock. Tick-tock.

We pull away from each other, and he looks past me.

"We must leave before it starts again," he says.

"How do we get out of here?"

"I hoped you would wake up when you remembered."

The ticking grows louder, and I spin around, spotting the clock on the hill at the far end of the cobblestone path. It seemed to get farther the closer I got. Something tells me that's on purpose. The flowers warned about it being a doom clock. "I think I know how." I point to the clock tower.

We start making our way up the hill when the grass and flowers die under our feet at an impossible speed. We both stop to look at each other and then I dare look behind me. Even though I know she isn't real, I don't want to see her dead rotting corpse being eaten by maggots.

Everything is just as we left it. Except, the white rabbit is now rabid, with strands of dirty twine-like hair as he digs his teeth into the dormouse. All around the table, the color is changing from vibrant pinks and purple hues to dark blacks and grays. The plants and trees, although dying, pull their roots up from the ground, reaching out toward us, growing thorns in their wake.

All around us, it's as if the tea party is spreading its mark of death. Nkella tugs at my arm, and I start to move. Dark clouds loom over us as the Wonderland my mind created becomes a nightmare—soon to be one I won't be able to wake from. Then, my mother's corpse starts to move.

I swallow a gasp as she shakily stands. Her head snaps in my direction; a bug crawls out of her right eye. She starts to advance toward us.

And we run.

We run fast, side by side. I won't look back. Can't look back

Just run.

The clock tower's loud ticking reverberates in my ear, and my mother's ghastly cries no longer sound like her. I pass a look over my shoulder and almost stumble on my own feet as I see my mother's bones crack and bend, lengthening in size until she is three stories tall. Her hair darkens into strands of hay as her nose morphs into a snout. Fins grow from her cheeks and her body elongates to form the long slithering body of a drakon.

Red and orange stripes run from her nose to the tip of a barbed tail. She opens her mouth to reveal a mouth full of needles instead of teeth and roars. My knees buckle, and I stumble back.

Nkella pulls at my shoulder. "Keep moving!" I let him pull me away and I start to run, refusing to look behind me.

The clock tower is just up ahead, no longer moving away as I near it. I'm not sure what changed, but I'll wonder about that later.

The red and orange drakon looms overhead as we make a dash up the hill, for the clock.

I pick my knees up as fast as I can as fire roars overhead. Nkella pushes me to the side, making me sidestep away from getting burned. My heart feels like it's going to burst out of my chest, but I ignore it and keep going.

Just a few more steps.

The clock tower, intricate with wooden spirals and gold dials, casts a shadow across the hill, until we reach the top. I groan as I now cast a shadow over the clock tower. Nkella gives me a double take and stares down at the clock.

"What are we supposed to do with this, daí?"

"You're asking me?"

"It's your mind."

I drop to my knees and lower my head to the tiny clock. A small door is at the bottom of the Tower with a tiny keyhole.

From either side of us, card warriors appear, and I jump to my feet. They're not regular playing cards like in *Alice and Wonderland*; they're Tarot cards—the Minor Arcana from the Empress's army but in actual paper card form, holding spears in their gloved hands. All at once, they jump toward us, closing in with their sharp spears against our necks. Masked faces with hollowed eyes bore into me from the top center of their card-like bodies.

Nkella unsheathes his sword, our backs pressed against each other. I square off with three cards in front of me, all of them from the Wands Arcana: a three, a six, and a nine. They charge at me, and I duck, swinging my arms up to block my head from the attack. A second later, they've dispersed around me, and I'm left in a dark room.

Everyone is gone. The cards. Nkella. A shiver runs down my spine.

I spin around. "Nkella?"

My voice echoes, and I kick something that makes a clattering sound. Squinting at it, fire illuminates from behind me and reflects on the blade of a long sword. My eyes widen and I quickly grab the hilt to turn and face the drakon.

The blood drains from my face as I stare at the red and orange fur, her eyes menacing, her teeth barred.

She isn't your mom.

Nkella's voice rings through my memory. He's right. She wasn't really here. And although I'm stuck in my mind, it is the itachi poison trying to trap me here, until it takes every bit of my memory and disperses it into the Aō in million bits of me. Until my body is left suffering eternally.

Yet somehow, a sword appeared. My mind is trying to preserve itself. The only way out of here is to go through it. Gripping the hilt of the sword tightly, I jump forward and swing down.

The drakon arches her body to avoid my blow but follows through with a quick snap of her mouth. I sidestep, slashing the sword to my left, cutting her on the cheek.

It doesn't seem to faze her as she attacks, moving her body swiftly and swimming through the air. She snaps at me again, and I jump to the side, only to meet her barbed tail to my right. I instinctively block it with the sword and am surprised by my actions. Sparks fly as metal hits metal. As she swings back to hit me again, I strike at her body, cutting her in her midriff.

The drakon squeals and swings her barbed tail like a sling-shot in my direction. I jump back, but she gets me across my knees, and I fall on my rear, dropping my sword.

An icy pain stings my skin. I bite it down and reach for the sword. The drakon swings her tail again. This time, I roll quickly, avoiding it as it hits the ground hard, its bottom spike sticking in the ground. She lets out a fiery roar, but I'm already lunging for the sword.

Got it.

I swing it over my head just as the drakon pulls her tail free. She opens her mouth to let out another surge of fire when I stuff the tip of the blade down her throat. Fire blazes from her throat, and I shut my eyes, keeping the sword lodged in the roof of her mouth, between her needle teeth. She swings her body violently, but I hold on with both hands. Spit sprays my face.

With one sharp jerk, the drakon releases herself from my blade; blood spurts from her mouth, spraying on my skin. I hurt her. Good.

She squares her eyes at me, her posture winding back like a snake about to strike. I swing my sword from side to side, making her follow my movements. Without warning, her barbed tail whips at me and I slice down hard, this time splitting it in half. Blood sprays from her entrails, and I resist the urge to celebrate. Not yet.

The drakon lets out a furious roar, and the heat of the flames pushes me back. Her body, in attack position, strikes at me fast; I jump back but topple to the floor. I try to stand, but the drakon's face is inches from mine. I still hold the sword, but her body closes in on me, the bloody length of her wrapping herself around me, like a constrictor squeezing her prey. I try squirming free as she studies me, taking her time to revel in her glory. She knows she has me. One final tight squeeze and she can snap me in half.

Her eyes dilate, and I watch my own reflection in her dark pupils. The fear in my own eyes stares back at me. This drakon is about to eat me and disperse my remains into the Aō, where I'll live in agony for all of existence. I can't let that happen.

I squeeze the hilt, and with all of my strength, I twist my arm up.

For my sister.

Her head snaps back in shock, releasing her hold a bit as I know I cut her with my blade. But I don't stop slicing.

For my mom.

I dig the blade in deeper until she's reeling back. I finally squirm free and climb to my feet, while keeping the end of the blade inside her.

For myself.

As I step over her body, I raise the sword high, and I stab her in the throat. And then I stab her again. And again. And again. Until I fall to my knees.

I'm going home.

My heart beats hard, and I drop the sword. The drakon disappears in a gust of red smoke to reveal a small bottle on the dark ground. I lift it up. Around the cork is a card that says, "Drink me," and a little key hanging off its neck. As I inspect the blue drink inside, the darkness around me is replaced by the warming sun from before. Grass covers the endless black void I was standing on. I'm back in Wonderland. Or, my version of it at least. I look around me. The Tarot cards are gone.

To my left is the tiny clock tower, but beside it, Nkella's body is lying cold on the ground with one hand on his chest and the other flat on the grass. My heart skips a beat as I run to him.

"Nkella!" I drop beside him. What do I do? I only have one drink.

Tick-tick-tock.

The ticking clock still sounds, but it's different. I spin the bottle in my hand. I have to drink it and hope he's there when I wake up. I'm in my mind now. I can't reach him from here. I uncork the bottle, letting loose white smoke. Bottoms up.

32

My eyes blink open, and I spring to my knees. The gooey spiderweb veins that had taken over my legs are gone. Nkella lies on his back, his eyes closed and unmoving.

He came to save me. He ate the itachi berries and came for me. Why, I have no idea, but he did. "Nkella? Nkella!" I press my ear to his chest. A slow and soft thumping tells me his heart still beats. He's alive.

I pick up a small branch clutched in his hand, careful not to prick myself on its thorns. This must be the itachi. He ate them all, leaving no berries. How am I meant to wake him? My pulse quickens. The entire time he was trying to wake me from my hallucinations, he was getting closer to the itachi taking him over. But now, I can't enter his mind to save him. I wouldn't even know where to search for the plant.

I look around at the forest surrounding us. Berries like these aren't in the immediate vicinity. Before blacking out, I remember him saying he had searched the whole day for them.

I don't have that kind of time, nor would I be able to identify them.

I wish there was a way to reach him without the itachi. If only I could see inside his head and pull him from where he is.

Nkella's lips start to turn purple, and I gasp. I place my hand on his cheek and start to lean close to his face to check his breathing when a soft glow comes from my arm. I startle. A white light illuminates through the spiraled web of my mark, and a strong magnetism forces my mind into Nkella's.

My vision blurs and is replaced with firelight coming from a bonfire. I'm standing on sand, and high pointed mountains shadow the distance.

A little boy between eight and ten years old sits barefoot on the sand, holding a carving knife and a piece of wood. Subtly pointed ears peek through tousled black hair. Ipani stripes decorate his collarbone, going all the way down to his arms. His dark eyes and high cheekbones are familiar. Could this be Nkella when he was a young boy? Beside him is a young girl around three or four years older. Straight black strands sit neatly behind her pointy ears. She has his high cheekbones and chin. Could this be his sister, Ntaoru? She takes the knife from him and shows him how to hold it, slicing thin slivers of wood outward from her body. Her little fangs gleam in the firelight as she smiles at him and hands it back.

Nkella mimics what she did, but his sister leans in and corrects his finger placements. Nkella tries again but accidently chops the arrow in half. His eyes get wet and he throws the stick into the fire, causing the embers to flare. Ntaoru laughs and hands him a different stick. She says something in Ipani, but I imagine it's her telling him not to put so much pressure on the knife as she pulls at his thumb and wiggles her fingers in demonstration. Nkella—still with a pouty face—continues to try again and the memory fades.

The sand is replaced by black rock; Nkella is balancing on a high boulder, just a few feet shy of lava. His arrow is aimed straight at what appears to be a hanging fruit on a black palm on the other side of a river of lava. Even though I'm fully aware this is just a memory, I still hold my breath.

He lets the arrow loose, and it pierces the fruit. Just as the fruit falls, a gust of wind holds it up. Nkella holds his hand up, as if suspending the fruit in air. The fruit slowly glides over the lava river, starting to drop at one point, and Nkella steadies his ouma along the way. His hand shakes as he does so, and it's obvious to me he's still getting used to his power. I remember him telling me he was a late bloomer, and that the Empress hadn't taken his power until he became a teen.

The fruit lands in his hand, and Nkella beams, showing a sharp toothy grin. He bounces it once in his hand, proud of himself, when some sort of sandy whip flies past me and knocks it out of his hand. The whip retracts back to a kid about his age, with long brown hair. I blink as the whip turns into sand, as it retracts back to his hand. Ouma that can turn into sand whips? The kid grabs his stolen fruit and gives Nkella a smug smile. Before leaving, he sends a sand whip back to Nkella, hitting him hard on his back, throwing him off balance. I yelp as Nkella plummets toward the lava.

"Use your ouma!" I shout, but he can't hear me.

The rock he fell from extends its black slate, forming a slide and catching him right before he hits the lava. It grows, making him slide all the way to this end, letting him land on his feet. I squint at him and then turn as I hear a girl's voice.

Ntaoru stands with her hands on her hips. The sand whip boy backs up but the ground quakes as a rumble makes him topple forward. She reaches out and grabs his collar. He drops the fruit on the ground. With his shirt clutched in her hand, she rushes him forward to the river of lava and shoves his head down to where he's almost touching it. The lava bubbles, and the boy shuts his eyes as she leans in and whispers something in his ear; her eyes are menacing. She holds him there for a second longer and then pulls him back, releasing him. The boy takes off running.

Ntaoru bends down to pick up the fruit and hands it to Nkella who takes it but then throws his arms around his big sister.

The memory fades, and then I'm standing on the black and white checkered floor of the Empress's Tower. An Arcana soldier holds Nkella in place; Ntaoru is also being held by an Arcana soldier. They're older now. Nkella must be around my age and Ntaoru around twenty-one. A violent cry escapes her lips as she tries to get free. The Empress holds up her hand and what looks like a scarlet red spirit leaves Ntaoru's mouth. Nkella screams a hoarse cry, as he attempts to twist out of the soldier's impossible strength. Soon, Ntaoru goes limp and a gust of smoke cocoons her, dispersing to reveal her wearing black robes and a white expressionless mask. Smoke oozes from inside her mask, so we cannot see her eyes or any semblance of the person who was.

The Empress lets out a shrill laugh.

"Ntaoru. . ." Nkella's face pales as he stills. The soldier lets him go, and he runs toward his sister. He begs for a response from her, but she stares past him with the dark, smoke-filled sockets of the mask. Desperation reaches his voice. He lost his parents when he was an infant, and now he had lost his sister. The one who not only cared for him and taught him things but protected him.

"Nkella?" My voice rings through his memory, and he snaps his gaze to me. Wait—can he see me?

Recognition flashes in his eyes, and our surroundings dissipate, the grassy area under the willow tree coming into focus.

His face comes into focus, and he takes a deep breath. I gasp.

"Nkella?"

He blinks and stares at me, confusion sprawled across his face. "Neyuro. . ." He sits up, his brows furrowed.

"Are you okay?" I ask. He stares at the ground with his arms over his knees. A distant, haunted look lingers in his eyes. I give him a few moments to process what he just saw so I sit across from him in silence.

Finally, he speaks. "She was the only person in this world who understood me."

"That can't be true. What about Kae?"

"Not like her. I never met my parents. She took it upon herself to take care of me. Even more so than Kae's parents. She made me her responsibility. She followed me in my stupid plan to kill the Empress. And I failed to protect her back."

I swallow. "You still can. . ."

His eyes move to mine, and he squints. "How were you there, daí? I was in an imaginary land. . . happy, with my sister. And then I was pulled into my memories."

"I—" I don't know how to answer that. My eyes move down to my mark, a subtle glow still emanating from the webbed lines.

Nkella jumps to his feet, his eyes glued to my mark. "You used your power."

"I guess I did. But I don't know how." I get up, too, and he steps away from me. Fear flashes in his eyes, but only for a moment.

"That is the Empress's magic," he says.

My breathing grows shallow, and I stare at my mark as the glow dies down. I shake my head. I know I have the Empress's mark, but. . . "I don't know how it's possible. I really don't know why I have it. Nkella. . ." I step forward. He takes another step back as if I'm going to suddenly turn into the Empress and turn him into a masked soldier. "Nkella, I don't even know what this means. I thought you were going to die. . .and it would have been my fault. You ate the itachi. At least that's what you told me in my dream. Did that really happen?"

He nods his head. "Yes. It happened."

"Why would you do that?"

One ear twitches, and his brows furrow.

"Risk your life for mine, I mean. You could have just revealed my mark to the Empress if I was dead. Whatever threat she'd think I was, she'd have given you back your sister."

He chose to save me over saving his sister. Over saving Lāri and the trafficked Ipani. Over finding his crew. Leaving behind his ambition to trade me for his sister or getting me to use the Ace of Wands. It doesn't make sense. Why did he do it?

"Kh. Neyuro." His voice is low. "I can't be certain the Empress will take you dead, daí?"

"Uh-huh." I can't stop a smirk from appearing on my lips. "You're not fooling anyone."

"Why did you save me?" he asks. "I took you prisoner. You could have run. You could have found the drakon and asked for help."

I give him a modest shrug. "Maybe I saved you for the same reason you saved me."

"And what reason is that, daí?"

"Neither of us can fully betray someone we care about."

His eyes soften, and he parts his lips. "Hn."

33

Dusk settles in the forest as a mist starts to rise between the trees, covering the entire ground up to our knees. Because of our voyages within the depths of the other's mind, we wanted to hike up the mountain as far as possible while there was still daylight.

We've been walking for hours. And we're both practically on the brink of death.

Not literally, but we're both exhausted.

Nkella, likely concerned about his crew and how long we've taken, has been quiet most of the way. We've only stopped to forage once, and he did most of the fishing in a stream. Okay, he did all the fishing. But even then, he's barely spoken a word. Maybe he's thinking about what I said earlier.

Neither of us can fully betray someone we care about.

My cheeks flush. I'm not sure if I'm more stunned about admitting I care about him to him or to myself. He didn't exactly deny caring about me either. But still, I shouldn't have said it.

Mix that with having my heart lodged in my throat all day. My stupidity in trusting the Empress put us further behind than we already were. All because I got mad at Nkella killing an innocent man.

Okay, it wasn't a stupid reason to be mad, but I also can't imagine what it's like to have a raging Devil inside me trying to break free.

I can't believe I willingly handed the Empress the World Card. Gari warned me not to let her have it. And what do I do? Trust her enough to let her have it. I'm so mad at myself, I don't want to think about Tarot cards anymore.

I step over a densely rooted area right behind Nkella and take a deep breath before asking, "Will we make it to the Karst Temples in time?"

He waits a few moments before responding. "There is no way to know if they are safe," he says, semi-avoiding my question. "We will move until the next stretch of forest, but we will have to stop before the Crystal Forest. If the farmer was right and Demitri is running the trafficking, he will have the Crystal Forest guarded with his own soldiers."

"If he was able to breech one of the Empress's Arcana soldiers, he might have more." I don't want to think about the possibility of us being too late either.

"Hn." He stops and looks at me. "We should stop and rest."

My shoulders relax. I'm glad he's the one saying it because I don't want to be the cause for stopping again.

"I won't be able to fight like this." He still has blood smeared on his face, and neither of us have slept.

"I agree." I smile. "Let's stop."

He leads us down a path, following the sound of a flowing stream until we come to a nice, shaded area. We choose a nice tree by the water, and he removes his hat and cloak, and his shirt.

I lean over and pick up his coat, searching for the remnants of his sister's now-ripped shirt he had cut in half to help the wolf. There's nothing else I can use to wipe things off, so it will have to do. I take his hand, and he startles.

"Come on."

I lead him to the edge of the stream, and we both sit down. I take a corner of the shirt and dip it into the water, trying my best to clean it off first before dipping it again.

"What are you doing, neyuro?"

"Helping." I lean in and dab his wound with the damp edge of the shirt. He hisses. I shush him. I gently blot away the dried blood under his eye and his cheekbones, stopping only to dip the shirt back into the stream. He follows my movements with his eyes as I work.

The entire time, he doesn't say a word. I lick my lips in concentration, which draws his attention to my mouth. I suck in a breath and swallow, aware at how close our faces are.

He looks to the side. "We will sleep for a few hours only," he says. "Then we will have to hurry."

I nod in agreement. I finish with his face and pick up his hands. Blood is smeared on his knuckles. I lift the sleeve of his shirt and run my fingers over tiny bumps—the pointy ends resembling metal. It looks like they reach up to his elbows. I hadn't noticed them before.

"What's up with your arms? Did you brush up against a poison plant or something?"

He shakes his head. "Koj. It is the curse. It appeared after my fight in Jōtenko. Each time, I lose a piece of myself."

My eyes meet his. "It happens that fast?"

"No. Not fast. Very slow."

"Okay. . .you need to stay calm then."

He stares at me and the little amber flakes in his eyes send off a crimson glow.

"I'm just saying. . .handle your anger better."

He shakes his head and wipes his face.

"I'm sorry. . . Do you know what else will happen?"

"Before I lose myself?" He presses his lips together and stares off into the dipping sun. Orange and pink glistens off the water. "I don't know what to expect. Each time I experience a change, it is slow and different."

I stare at my mark, tracing the web design with my left hand. And then, I notice something strange. On my left. I quickly pull my left sleeve up and do a double take. What the hell? Another mark has appeared! My mouth splits open.

"Neyuro? What is it?"

A tiny sword with the roman numerals VI above it stains my pale skin in a darker birthmark tone.

"I think I have a problem."

He quirks a brow. "A new one?"

I sit closer to him, and he pulls back. "Let me see your mark," I ask him. "You have two, don't you?" I remember seeing it on him in his bedroom on the ship, and AJ told me it was possible to acquire a second mark.

"Why?"

"Just let me see it."

He shows me his other wrist, pulling hesitantly as I grip it to inspect the "0." The Fool. It makes sense. He's on a journey to find his sister, among other things for his Island.

"This just appeared on my left wrist!" I push my mark to his face. "What does it mean?"

He takes my wrist in his and squints at it. "I do not know."

"You don't?" I take my wrist back. "But I thought you knew these things."

"Kh. I do not know all of the Empress's magic cards. Every time I think I do, a different one shows up."

Well, that's comforting. "Something doesn't make sense to me. On the ship, you told me to use my mark. Can you use your Devil mark? Or your Fool's mark?"

"Hn. . ." He twists his features. "Koj, it only affects me."

"But I can use mine? How did you know to tell me to use my mark?"

"Because you are the only one with the *Helāni* symbol— the Empress's mark." He points to the web insignia on my inner forearm. "I thought you would know how." He leans his head back. "Not everyone knows how to use their marks."

There are seventy-eight Tarot cards in a deck. What does the Six of Swords mean? I wish I knew. . . If only I had learned the Tarot for the carnival instead of my dumb magic tricks.

"Is there anyone you know who would know what the Six of Swords Card means?"

"Maybe. If we save them." He eyes me from the corner of his eye.

"Right." There's nothing I can do about this now.

I wipe away the blood from his arms. He offers me a soft smile and pulls his hands back.

"All done," I say, dipping the shirt in the water and rinsing it off. He wipes his face, and we sit in silence for a few moments, staring at the stream. A few times he's moved like he's wanted to say something but doesn't. So, I decide to break the silence.

"Nkella," I mutter.

He flicks me a gaze. "Daí?"

"Oh, just thinking. . . that's an unusual name. I like it."

After a few moments, he furrows his brows. "You have an unusual name. Soorren. What is the meaning?"

"Oh, I hate my name but thanks. And. . . I actually don't know what it means."

"Daí? How come you don't know what it means? Everyone here knows what their names mean. It is part of Ipani."

"Well, I guess at some point we did, or still do depending on what language we speak. My name is French, but I'm mixed. My mom is Greek, and my dad is Cajun."

"These are places in. . .Earth?"

I nod. "I guess I never thought of what my name meant. I don't really like it. Kids would make fun of me."

"Hn." He moves closer to the fire and to me and lays his head back. "I don't like my name either."

"Nkella? Why not? I've never heard of it before, but it sounds nice."

"Hn."

"What does it mean?"

He twists his face. "It's bancha."

"No, tell me. It can't be that stupid."

"It means Hope." He grows silent. Looks like his parents had high expectations.

"What about your last name?"

"Mikiroro means Black Palm tree. It is Danū's symbol." He takes his pendant from around his neck and shows me. "It is this symbol here."

I lean in for a closer look, taking the pendant in my fingers. I remember this from when I snuck into his room and he was shirtless. Hints of leather and hickory tease my nostrils, and I let the pendant go. "That's a strong name. So do they ever call you Nick?"

He grunts and takes out his rum, taking a swig. "Koj. Not Nick." He stretches the way I pronounced his name in my accent. I cringe. "Nyko."

"Okay, fine, Nyko." I mimic him.

His eyes narrow at me. "You will not call me that."

"Fine, fine." I smirk. "Your money has a symbol on it too, right? Gichang rīrō?" If I recall correctly.

He nods and takes out his pouch of rubies, reaching in and taking one out. He hands one to me. I hold it up so that the light from the blaze illuminates through the opulent red gem. An etching of a curved palm tree is at its center, with gold flakes surrounding it. "Your money is pretty," I say, handing it back to him. "Back in my world, it's just paper. I bet one of your rubies would be enough to bail my sister out and buy me a flight to see my mom."

He drops the flat ruby back in his pouch and ties it back to his belt. "Danū's currency powered Ipa. But ever since it went under siege, Sāgirang is trying to take over. You know, Wands.

"I remember. But it seems to be more valuable since it's a ruby, right? What's the currency for Wands?"

"They are like mine, but amethysts. I have yet to trade them. I should have done that at Cerberus, but I did not have time. Danū is the only currency that kept my family's crest. The rest of the islands have adapted to the Helāni symbols."

"Of the Tarot?"

"Hn." He nods. "Danū's currency is still strong, but because they look for us, it makes us a target."

"Because of me."

"And because of me," he says. "I need to find my crew and save them from the traffickers before it is too late."

"We will," I tell him. "Nkella?"

"Hn?"

I swallow. "Why do you hate being called a prince?"

A flare ignites in his irises, and I'm taken aback. "Kh. Neyuro. You ask too many questions." He stands and walks over to his coat. "I will make a fire," he says.

We collect firewood, and Nkella starts to build the fire. As he does that, I sweep the rocks and brambles away with my feet, clearing the area to sleep in. I pile together some soft moss he said was safe for beds.

When he's finished, I sit close to the flames as he goes off to hunt for some food. When he comes back, he carries a small furry body over his shoulders.

"What's that?" I ask.

"White rabbit." He grins.

". . .Oumala?"

"Koj."

"Okay, good." Not that regular rabbits aren't sentient but. . . I don't know. Eating an oumala anything feels weird to me. He sits down next to me. I watch as he skins it and cooks it over the fire. We must have been starving because once it's cooked, Nkella splits it in half, and we scarf down our food.

After eating, we both sit by the flames.

"It gets so cold here at night," I say.

"Are you cold?" He gets up and hands me his coat.

"Are you sure?"

"Take it."

"Thank you." I take the coat and drape it over my legs. He reaches over my legs and digs into one of the side pockets, bringing out a knife.

"What are you doing?"

He grabs a long piece of wood from the pile he collected and starts to carve.

"Carving arrows."

"Are you going to make a bow too?"

"Not tonight, but I can still use these as weapons. Get some rest, daí?"

I yawn and stretch my aching legs.

I turn on my side and stare at the dancing flames cracking against the sounds of Nkella's knife splitting wood.

Soon, I'll be back with my sister, and I'll never see Nkella or the crew again. I bite my nail, pushing back all my worries about something going wrong at the temple. If the Ace of Wands isn't what we hoped it would be. If only I still had the World Card. I was able to get it to work. . . except, it took me to Nkella when I asked what I needed to get home.

Why couldn't it show me what I most needed to take me home when I tried it on the ship?

My stomach twists. That was strange. . .wasn't it? Why did it do that? I mean, I'm not complaining. I wanted to find him. To save him. . .although I'm having trouble wrapping my head around why.

What if the card had taken me back home? What would I have done? Would I have come back to help him? I swallow. I don't think I would have because my sister is more important and Nkella held me captive. But would I be okay knowing he was being eaten by cannibalistic villagers? No, I wouldn't, but I would have had to live with it. If I get out of here, I'm never coming back.

Nkella puts down his knife and half-carved arrow and lies down next to me. I turn around to face him, staring at his features and watching the flames dance on his face. He turns his head to stare at me.

I never in a million years thought I'd find myself in a situation where I was running from harm with my pirate captor. And a prince.

He blinks a few times, then moves his body a bit closer.

I hold my breath, unsure about his sudden desire to be so close to me.

His hand moves up to my face, and he tucks a strand of hair away from my eyes.

I blink at his action. I don't know why I do it, but I lift my hand as well. Not sure what I'm doing. Curiosity, maybe. My fingers wander across his cheekbone and over his lips. He closes his eyes at my touch. I move my fingers up to his hair, the tip of my index finger brushing against a small stump—his devil horns. His eyes fling open at my touch, but he doesn't move away. I hadn't seen them, since they aren't visible through his curls.

The fire crackles behind me, and the shadows of the flames dance over his fierce features.

He really is brutally handsome.

He brushes his thumb over my bottom lip, and now I close my eyes. I want him to kiss me. I want to feel his lips against mine.

Admitting that steals some of the oxygen from my lungs.

My eyes flutter open. His eyes are lingering on my mouth, and I can tell he's thinking the same thing. I bite my lower lip and push myself against him, our legs now touching. I take in his leather and hickory scent.

Speckles of amber illuminate his pupils like fire in his eyes, and a shiver shakes through my shoulders.

Then he kisses me, long and deep.

A mixture of both excitement and fear crashes through my veins.

His lips move hungrily over mine, our tongues meet, and my hands wander up his chest. He gently pushes me back so that I'm lying on the ground. The warm press of his body makes my skin tingle, drawing out every craving I've ever had of him yet conflicted over the hatred he's made me feel. And it makes me want him even more.

Then he pulls his lips away, his eyes staring at me with a gentleness he's never shone toward me before. I stare back at him, wondering why he pulled away. What is he thinking? He caresses my face with the back of his hand. I pass my fingers over his parted lips, the tips of my thumb feeling his incisor. He closes his eyes and kisses my thumb.

With fire in his eyes, he leans down and kisses me again. I take in his warm lips, his scent. Instinctively, I arch into him. A deep growl sounds in his chest as he holds me close. I kiss him back furiously. He stops and pushes away.

Why does he stop?

"I can't," he breathes.

My heart pounds in my eardrums. I reach for him, but he moves away. My chest aches for him. Yesterday, I hated him. And today I want him.

What is wrong with me?

He lies back down. Still close to me as his eyes don't leave mine. The fiery specks in his eyes flare, but then slowly die down. Is he afraid he'll hurt me?

Or is it because he knows I'm leaving?

He's right. When this is over, I'll never see him again. But I ask anyway, "Why not?"

His breathing is deep. His gaze still lingers.

"Because I am not a nice man. And I am a worse prince."

34

SOMETIME DURING THE NIGHT, I WAKE TO THE SOUND
of a howl. I bring Nkella's coat up to my chin and blink my
eyes open as a chill in the air makes me shiver. A low growl
makes me sit up. The fire is out and Nkella is gone. I gasp,
bringing my legs up to my chest. I think I see two glowing red
eyes somewhere between the trees but then they're gone.

A cool wind blows through my hair, and with it I think I
hear voices, the sound of a man talking. It sounds like there's
more than one, but I'm not sure.

*"What are you doing, Mikiroro? You know no one breaks
deals with her."*

"Nkella?" I ask.

*"Who said anything about breaking deals? Besides, I am not
the only one with secrets, daí?"*

A shiver skitters down my spine. I grip Nkella's coat. Who
is he talking to? I push myself to my feet then wince as small
rocks pierce the skin under my foot. The familiar deep popping

sound of an oumala animal goes off and the voices disappear. I hold my breath. Iéle is definitely here, and now it sounds like Nkella and whoever he was talking to have disappeared into the Aō.

I lie back down in my spot and rest my head, unease settling in my stomach. My eyelids grow heavy again and I urge myself back to sleep.

After a restless night wondering if Nkella has come back, I wake to find him still gone. I climb to my feet, my hands now feeling clammy.

He wouldn't have just left me here, would he? If Iéle came back and said his crew needed him?

Pebbles and brambles crunch underfoot as I walk through the trees. "Nkella?" I look both ways, making sure I'm not in the way of any wolves or anything that could eat me. Where could he have gone?

"Nkella?" I call again. Morning light stretches through the trees.

A branch breaks as I take another step into the dense forest.

Something jumps at me and before I can see what or who it is, I fall backward and land over a tree stump. It all happens so fast, my heart lunges to my throat. My eyes widen as Nkella steps over me.

"That is no good, neyuro. I could have killed you."

My mouth gapes.

He holds his hand out to me, and I take it, letting him help me up.

"That wasn't fair," I say. "I didn't know you were going to do that."

"Neyuro, you need to be more prepared. And make less

noise, daí?" He rushes past me. "An ambush doesn't warn before it attacks." He sighs again. "You are not ready for where we are going, neyuro."

My frown deepens, and I rub the scrapes on the back of my legs.

He offers me an oval yellow fruit. "Breakfast?"

"Thanks. What is it?"

He picks up the pace and doesn't answer me. I take a bite out of the fruit and my eyes light up. A sweet buttery custard that tastes like lemon mixed with vanilla, and a piece of cloud, if that were possible, tingles my taste buds. "Mmm." This is so good.

Nkella's ear twitches but he stays quiet. We reach the firepit we slept next to and he bends down to pick up his coat and hat. His silence is unsettling. He's refusing to look at me. My mind drifts to our kiss last night, and my cheeks warm.

"We have to talk," he finally says.

My stomach jumps. "Look. . .about last night."

He flicks his eyes at me. "Koj. Forget it. It never happened." He turns to leave and starts walking. "Let's go."

"Right. Never happened." My chest tightens. "Where did you go last night?" I ask.

"Why?"

"I woke up several times, and you were gone. Also, I heard a howl. . .and a growl. And voices. Was someone else here?"

He doesn't respond.

I fall into step beside him. "Well?"

"Hn. Iéle was here."

"It was her? She came?"

He pauses. "Yes."

"And?"

"And what?" Annoyance tinges his voice, making me pause.

"Really? What did she tell you? Is the crew safe?"

Nkella sighs and walks away, leaving me to follow. "AJ got captured on purpose."

"He did what!"

"Sh. Neyuro, keep it down."

"Why did he do that? And what about Tessa and Kae?"

"They are together. Tessa did what AJ did and Kaehante followed. Iéle showed me that AJ noticed an exchange between the Prefect and Demitri and an unbound Ipani. He saw the same chrome-masked Arcana soldier reappear behind a different one. Being selective in his taking. I do not know how the Hierophant and Prefect managed to infiltrate an Arcana soldier, but they took the unbound ones to the Temples—not to the Empress's prison."

A memory of AJ charging at the chrome-masked soldier from Swords resurfaces in my mind. I had wondered why he had done that—only to be taken. I was confused when Tessa had done the same. Now it makes sense. AJ made a spur of the moment decision and went for it.

My eyes widen. "So, Demitri is part of the traffickers. This confirms it."

"Hn."

"And the Wands' Prefect?"

Nkella nods and then he snorts. "Iéle made a connection with AJ so that she could learn what he sees, but knowing her, it will be only temporary. She is not the most sensitive oumala wolf. She did not seem happy about it." He laughs again.

I frown. "They could have told us their plan."

"There was no time. Demitri has them now."

"Why is Demitri doing this?" I ask.

"You remember the prisoner from my ship, daí?"

"Yeah, what about him?"

"Did you see what was happening to him when he shifted?"

The memory of the prisoner becoming a bird rises in my mind. "Didn't you say he knew he was dying anyway?"

"Yes. He was a bound Ipani who drank the rikorō. Drinking that potion gives you the ouma of the Ipani who was killed for it. The traffickers are trying to perfect it."

"What's the end goal?"

"I imagine it is to become strong enough to defeat the Empress. That is why that Ipani pirate said he does it for our kind."

"To kill your own people to gain strength in order to defeat a divine being? That's no means to an end. It's suicide."

"Now you see why I fight them. Why Lāri and now the crew are in so much danger."

I swallow.

He turns at a tree to the right and huffs under his breath.

"So who else was with you last night?" I walk after him. "Did you go somewhere else?"

"Too much talking, daí? Mind your own business." The corner of his lips lifts into a smirk. But I don't smile back.

The leaves around us start to change color as we make it to an even steeper climb.

Nkella stops walking and turns to me. "Neyuro."

"Yes?"

A soft morning breeze ruffles my hair. He reaches over and pulls a strand back behind my ear, releasing a swarm of butterflies in my stomach. What is he doing? We agreed we'd forget about last night—his soft lips running over mine flashes through my memory.

He lowers his eyes at me, and my breath escapes me.

Finally, he says, "Do you trust me?"

I blink. My throat dries. "I—" Do I? Trust never came easy for me. My whole life I've had to protect me and what's mine from strangers pretending to be my caretakers.

Before I can decide on an answer, a purple lights glows over my head. I don't think much at first but then I spin around to find Gari's sharp teeth grinning down at us. Nkella already has his sword drawn and pointed up in his direction.

I almost can't believe my eyes. I quickly lower Nkella's arm. "It's okay. He's a friend." I whip toward Gari. "Where have you been?" I can hardly hold the excitement in my voice even though I want to demand to know why he hadn't come around in so long. "Do you have any idea how many times we've needed you? How many times *I've* needed you?"

Gari's large purple eyes widen as his tail slithers back in the air, then he disappears.

"Gari?"

He reappears behind me, his tail trailing around my shoulders. "I'm not omnipotent, you know." He gurgles as he floats on his back. "I went to check on you but couldn't find you anywhere. Then I followed the posters with your faces on them." He comes close to me, then swings his head to be close to Nkella's nose. "And then I saw a scrumptious looking oumala wolf and I thought, the Devil is near." He giggles.

Nkella raises his sword again.

"Don't worry," Gari says, pressing his face close to Nkella's. "I didn't hurt a hair on your familiar."

I relax my shoulders. "Do you think you can give us both a ride to the Karst Temples?"

"To find the Ace of Wands Card, I presume?"

"Yes. It is what you suggested I do, right?"

"Did I?"

"Gari..."

He laughs, and Nkella keeps his hand on the hilt of his sword.

I ball my fist. "Katergaris..."

"I just came from there," he gurgles, lengthening his sinewing body. "Looking for you. I couldn't get in. There are guards surrounding the area and keeping an eye for oumala animals and drakons."

He told me once before he avoids Wands because of their oumala guards. He's risked his fur trying to find me.

"But we need to get there before it's too late to save the crew," I say.

"I flew high enough to see the girl on wheels and the large bald Ipani. The one with long hair was there too."

"That's my crew," Nkella says, a tinge of relief in his voice.

Gari bows his head. "You need to get there before the Hierophant steals enough ouma to pick up the Ace of Wands." Gari's gurgles become a bit hoarse; it sends a shiver down my spine. "You don't want him to get his hands on that card."

Getting his hands on the Ace of Wands could mean Dimitri using it against the Empress. If he kills her, will that make him Emperor? Given the ways he's going about it, trafficking unbound Ipani and killing them for power, I can't imagine he'd be any better than her.

I stare at Nkella whose face has gone pale. With our plan, this just got riskier. But if I can grab it before he's powerful enough to, I can make sure he never succeeds.

"Gari," I start, "how long have you known about Demitri?"

"Through the grapevines, but only recently. Are you hopping on?"

Gari's body has now extended long enough to carry us both. "I thought you said you couldn't get in," I say.

"I can't." The fins on the sides of his face move as if he's under water. "But I can get you close enough."

I share a look with Nkella, and he nods. I grab onto Gari's hair, swing my leg over his body, and hold onto his neck. Nkella climbs on behind me, his warm body pressing against mine.

Ignoring his closeness, I ask, "How long until we get there?"

"A couple of hours," Gari gurgles as he sways his tail behind us.

I turn my head back to Nkella. "How long would it take us to walk there?"

"This saves us a few days walking and camping."

Gari lifts us higher off the ground, and in a sway of his body, we pop into the Aō dimension. The pink and orange waters that shone in the distance become a slightly softer color, while mostly everything else turns gray. He doesn't want to be seen and shot down. Good thinking.

A buzz of excitement mixed with nerves swarms in my

stomach. I didn't want to admit to myself, but I was starting to lose hope. At least now we know the crew is alive and kicking. As far as we know, Demitri doesn't have the card yet. I'll be home soon.

I decide to forget about what I heard last night; whatever it was about, I'm sure it's part of Nkella's plan to save the crew. He's not a complete ass hat.

Goose bumps prickle across my arms and legs as the temperature drops, in contrast to the warmth emanating from Nkella's body sitting close behind me. I refuse to warm my arms though as that would require me to let go of Gari's hair.

I gaze down at the trees and lakes as Gari flies us over them, his body gliding easily through the air. It's serenading. The quiet of it makes my mind drift to other places I had been avoiding thinking about. Getting poisoned and almost dying made me acutely aware that if I have another brush with death, I may not be so lucky and get out, and I might never make it home. Talia probably already thinks I ditched her, but if I die and never tell her what happened to me, she might live with abandonment issues for the rest of her life.

But beside that, there's one thing that's been stabbing at my heart. The one thing I've forced myself to leave behind on the back burner. . .seeing my mom. Having seen her in that horrible hallucination gave me a sense of urgency—I needed to see her now. Even though it wasn't my real mom in that strange dream, there must be a reason my mind chose her to be the thing that would make me want to stay in fake Wonderland. I swallow a ball in my throat.

"Neyuro, you are quiet."

Nkella's breath brushes against my neck, and I'm suddenly transported to last night and our kiss. "Yeah," I say.

"You are never quiet. What's on your mind?"

"Oh, umm. . ." I shake the memory of his lips away.

Gari twitches one of his gills at the sound of our voices. Why shouldn't I tell him? I just saw pieces of his past with his sister. "I was just thinking about my mom."

"Hnn."

"She's. . .sick."

Wind passes through my hair, and he leans in closer. "How is she sick?"

"She has something called early Alzheimer's and dementia. She doesn't even remember who I am." My voice cracks. "And the biggest thing is she's so young. It's so rare that this happens to someone so young." Nkella remains quiet as I go into a full-blown explanation that I had been keeping in for so long. "I guess I've been afraid to go see her and. . .and confront the fact that she doesn't know who I am." A few moments of silence pass, and I regret talking about it out loud. He has his own problems; why should he care to listen to mine?

"Sometimes," Nkella starts and I startle, "it doesn't matter if they don't remember us. Sometimes, what matters is being there for them anyway."

Sometimes, what matters is being there for them anyway. I consider this a little longer. It must resonate with him because his sister has had her agency taken from her. He doesn't know if she's there at all, or if she's witnessing herself doing horrible things for the Empress. And yet, he doesn't lose hope. But do I have any hope that my mother will be cured? No. There is no cure for what she has.

"Will you visit your mother when you go home?" he asks.

"Yes. Now I want to, more than ever." I lift my empty wrist, still holding on to Gari with my other hand. "I had a charm that she gave me, but I lost it in the water, when I was trying to rescue you."

"Kh. I still do not know why you saved me."

I ignore him. I already explained it to him, but he didn't get it.

"What was your charm?"

"It was a little teacup from a story she used to read me."

"Daí? What kind of story?"

"You've seen some of the images from the playing cards I carry. And also, the made-up world you were just in when you came to save me from the poison. It's called *Alice in Wonderland.*"

"The one with the rabbit wearing a coat?" He chuckles. "We have a long ride. Tell it to me."

"Really? You want to hear it?"

Wind whips around us, making me raise my voice a little. So far, Gari is flying smooth and high. I expected it to be loud but it isn't. A caveat I've noticed while being in the Aō. I can still hear sound, but they sound a bit distant. Touch stays the same.

"I told you one from Danū. It is your turn now." He moves his hands up to my waist and leans in.

"There was a little girl named Alice," I begin. "She followed a white rabbit down a rabbit hole."

"Daí? Why would someone follow a rabbit down their hole? How would they fit?"

"This is fantasy. . .a lot like your mythology."

"Hn."

Gari swooshes to the right, and Nkella's grip becomes tighter. I grab onto his hand, afraid to fall off, but then Gari levels out again.

I start again. "When she fell, she entered into a whole different world. There was a talking door knob and—"

"Kh. That is bancha."

I half turn to gape at him. "What's bancha?"

"Doorknobs don't talk."

"Well, in this story they do!"

"Hn. Keep going."

I sigh and continue. "In order to get through the door, she needed to eat a cookie to get smaller."

"Why to get smaller?"

"Oh, because the door was tiny, and she was too big."

"Bancha. There is no iponnchi to make you small."

Oh my god, I'm about to push him off Gari's back. Gari lets out a giggle. I wonder what he's thinking. "Well, in this story there is," I say behind gritted teeth. I steal a glance at him and glimpse a curled lip behind me. "You're messing with me, aren't you?"

He chuckles.

"Wow. Do you want me to keep telling it? Or not?"

"Yes, sorry. I will be quiet."

I fight a smile trying to creep on my own face and tell him the rest of the story, wondering if he's enjoying it or just using me to ease the silence. Then again, he usually hates it when I talk, so maybe he does like it.

An hour later, the sun is completely gone, and the only things lighting our path through the mist are the bioluminescent purple lichens growing on the large leaves and moss on the ground. I haven't finished telling the entire story due to him constantly interrupting me, but I get to the part about the tea party and stop.

"Neyuro, why did you stop? Was that the end?"

"Oh, I wasn't sure if you wanted to hear more."

"Yes, I was listening. I remember the cups on the table. There was rotting food when I got there."

"Yeah. . . I hadn't noticed it until you made me aware of it."

A biting cold wind passes through, and I bravely let go of Gari's hair to rub my arms. My teeth start to chatter as I keep on with the story.

"You are cold," he says.

"Aren't you?"

"Koj. My temperature runs hot."

Gari tilts his head up. "Get ready for landing."

"Already?" I ask.

Nkella points to what looks like a castle carved out of rock. Rows of arched open windows align a great space of Karst Mountain, some forming what looks like half towers, with rounded half circles coming out of the front. "Those are the Karst Temples," he says.

"They're beautiful." My eyes linger on them until an Arcana soldier comes into view. Three vultures circle over the ground, midway from the top of the Temples, traces of shimmering gray trails behind them. That's not something I've noticed before. Maybe it's visible because we're in the Aō.

"I'm landing in the forest below," Gari says. "Any closer and we'll be visible to their ouma animal guards."

"Is it safe?"

"Safer than the dead forest," the drakon responds.

Gari makes a sharp swoop, and I gasp, grabbing tight around his neck as Nkella grips my stomach. I don't know why, but his touch makes my stomach flip. It could just be the swooping down making my stomach flip. Yep. That's it.

Gari slithers through the trees, and I briefly close my eyes, thinking for a second we might crash into one. He finds us a shallow concave and lands gently next to a tree. I let out a long breath and move my hair from my face.

Nkella lets go and jumps down. He holds his arms out for me. His face looks serious. Pensive.

I take his hand and let him help me down. Large roots creating a small cavern spider out toward the large ditch we're in.

Gari is already shrinking in size as I turn to face him. "Thanks, Gari. Where will you be?"

"I'll be poking my head around, trying to get in." He smiles. "I may just have some oumala vultures for dinner, but I'll have to do it without setting off the alarms."

"Drakons eat anything," I say.

He winks and pops back into the Aō.

35

"So how far until we reach the Temple gates?"

"Not far."

"If Gari wasn't able to get in because they have the Aō guarded, how are we going to get in?" This must be why Iéle took so long to get back to him.

A sly smile spreads across his face. "With the element of surprise."

I narrow my eyes at him. "Glad you have a plan. Care to share?"

"Koj. Let's go."

I start walking after him. "You're really not going to tell me?" My stomach turns. We're about to walk into the lion's den, and I have no idea how we're going to do it. He has a sword, an arrow he carved last night but didn't finish. And I have nothing but an empty bandolier. Oh, and a deck of ordinary playing cards.

"There is nothing you can do now to prepare yourself for

the fight we are going to encounter. Stay low. Find the Ace. Let me do the rest, daí?"

I purse my lips together. Before Gari appeared, he had asked me if I trusted him, and I didn't answer. I guess this is part of that trust.

I don't like it.

This entire time, I've only been able to see half of a plan, but I knew my end game was going back home. Now that we're closing in on the heavily guarded Temples—guarded by Ipani traffickers no less—I'm afraid.

Demitri had infiltrated the Empress's army, and we don't know how many he has on his side. He has the crew. We don't have backup. And it's all of them against two of us.

I wish I had never given the Word Card to the Empress.

"Neyuro."

I gasp. "Huh?"

"I sense you are troubled."

"You think?"

He looks down at me. "Tell me the rest of the story."

"Now?"

"I want to know the end."

"So, you don't want me to keep quiet and mind my own business?" I hiss.

"Neyuro. . ."

I arch a brow.

"Yes, I want you to mind your own business," he says slowly, "but I also want to know the rest of the story."

"You are unbelievable."

He doesn't say anything.

"Okay, fine." Where did we leave off? Oh, yeah. "Alice was at the Mad Hatter's tea party when—"

"Why is he mad, this Hatter?"

"Oh, well, it's more like he's insane. . .not actually angry. . ."

"Hn."

Not unlike Nkella, though he's more mad *and* angry.

I keep on telling him the story and he listens intently only to interrupt to ask:

"Why are the Mad Hatter and the hare so rude to that mouse? I thought the Hatter was supposed to be good."

I curl my lip upward. "I'm not sure. I guess I never thought about it."

"It is not like the mouse is their gembella, daí?" He chuckles.

I ignore him and keep on with the story as the foliage becomes sparser, and the trees become more spread out. I get to the part of the story where Alice faces the Red Queen in her court and is sentenced to death. "'Off with her head,' the Queen shouts."

I smile to myself, realizing what he did. He wanted me to get my mind off what we were about to do. It worked for a bit.

A purple glare shimmers off the ground and I stop talking, paying close attention to our location. Clusters of purple crystals reflect from the sunlight. As we go deeper into the forest, the crystals get taller, some even growing with the trees.

"What forest is this?" I ask.

"Ahan Rī. The Crystal Forest"

"It's beautiful."

"A lot of ouma is here. That is why the Ancients built their temple on top of this mountain. Any kind of ouma made here will be stronger."

"And that's why the traffickers picked this location," I say in contemplation.

Clouds form overhead, and rain starts to patter down in a light sprinkle. The sunlight is dim between the clouds and mist of the Crystal Forest. Pebbles crunch underfoot as the height of the Karst Temples greet us over the hill.

Three swirls of smoke shoot down from the sky, and I pause.

The smoke dissipates to reveal Demitri, the Wands' Prefect, and the chrome-masked soldier from the Isle of Swords.

Nkella draws out his sword. Here we go.

Demitri walks toward us, the pointy gold hat snug on his head, his long black robes almost touching the ground. The Prefect has on a black suit with a purple sash across his chest, and a sword at his waist.

"Wonderful," Demitri says. "I was afraid I'd have to send my troops after you."

I scoff. He almost sounds like he was expecting us. Like he was wanting us to come. I glance at Nkella, whose face is hardened.

"Hand over the girl."

"Like hell." I resist the urge to laugh at his face.

Nkella puts away his sword. He turns to me, his eyes looking down at my feet, avoiding eye contact. "Let's go, gembella," he says.

Gembella? The blood drains from my face. "What are you doing?"

He grabs my arm and pushes me toward Demitri. I resist

and stumble over my feet. He grips me harder and shoves me in front of him, not letting me go.

"Nkella," I whisper. "Is this part of your plan?"

"Move." he says. I search his eyes. He finally glances at me but there is no hint of a shared plan in them. He has a clinical look in his eyes, as if I'm just some cattle he's trading, or a goat.

"Nkella?" My voice cracks.

Demitri steps toward us. "Not very clever, is she?"

My lips part, and I snap my gaze to Nkella. "What is he talking about?"

Nkella frowns and pushes me forward with two fingers on my back.

And now my heart is hammering in my chest. "No. . ." I start to back away, pulling away from him, but he strengthens his grip on me. Tears well in my eyes as my heart feels like it's being stabbed by the six swords on my new mark. "Please no. . . Nkella. . . what are you doing? You're not handing me over to them, no. I won't believe that. You wouldn't do that."

"Quiet, gembella," he snaps. My throat closes up.

"Have her come quietly, or the deal is off," Demitri says. The Wands' Prefect stands behind him with a sneer pasted on his face.

I crane my neck to face Nkella but his eyes are glued to Demitri.

"Why?" I ask, with a shaky voice.

His eyes fix past me, all emotion devoid on his face. "My crew comes first." He pushes me toward Demitri who grabs me and lifts my arm up, revealing my mark. I squirm, trying to free myself, but he grips me stronger and throws me to the chrome-masked Arcana soldier.

Tears sting at the corners of my eyes as I scream and try to get away, but the soldier doesn't budge. He's a robotic tower of a man, with no emotion, and no shaking him. I give one last look at Nkella. He refuses to look at me. This shouldn't surprise me. I knew he would never see me as part of his crew. I was always just a gembella to him. I was never anything more.

The memory of the voices I heard last night before the popping sound resurfaces in my mind. Two men speaking. It was them; he was making a deal to trade me in.

He always meant to turn me into the Empress in exchange for his sister. I thought something had changed between us, but at least that I could understand. But this?

"You said you didn't believe in selling people!" I scream.

His frown deepens, but he looks straight at Demitri. "Now let my crew go."

"Already done, as requested."

"Lāri too."

"Lāri? Name doesn't ring a bell."

A flare of bright crimson flashes in his eyes.

"If she was captured before your crew got themselves caught, then make sure you rescue her on your way out."

"You will give me safe passage there then."

"Done."

"Wait," I say. Nkella turns, his eyes narrowed.

"Did I really mean nothing to you?"

"Ko kuela mū," is all he says and he continues to walk toward the Temple gates.

I choke on a sob. *Ko kuela mū.* It never made a difference whether he started to care for me. Or whether I was part of the crew, no matter if I saved him, or if he started to trust me.

He needed to save his family, and that came first.

Just like I've always put Talia first. It doesn't matter that he betrayed me. That I trusted him, and he still betrayed me.

It doesn't make a difference.

"You son of a bitch!" My throat hurts from my sudden outburst. Rain starts to patter on my face.

Nkella pauses and looks over his shoulder. "Kh."

Demitri turns to the Arcana soldier holding me and snaps his fingers. Then, I'm blinded by smoke.

The smoke whirls away and I fall to the ground. Demitri lifts me from the back of my shirt. A disgusting look is smeared on his face.

Metal cages line the side of a shaded area covered by massively large pointed rock formations, filled with caves and crevices. I'm inside the Karst Temples.

"Soren, is it?"

I grunt and jerk my arm away from his hold.

"Oh, come now. You won't be here long. I have big plans for you."

"Bite me." I turn to run but come face to face with the chrome-masked soldier.

"There's nowhere to run. Your friends betrayed you. The only option left for you is helping me."

"And why would I do that?"

"Because I know what you want—to go home. And because you don't have a choice. Because if you don't, all these people will die. I will get what I want, one way or the other. But you have the power to make that happen, Soren."

"I have no idea how to do what you want me to do."

"Oh, you'll figure it out. Come quietly, help me, and I'll let everyone else go."

I choke on a laugh. "You expect me to believe that after all this"—I wave my hand toward the cages—"you'll just let them all go because I helped you? Please." I roll my eyes. I may have been a fool with Nkella, but I'm never trusting anyone else's word for as long as I live.

"My only end game was to gain enough power to hold the Ace of Wands. You can just wish the Empress dead and make me Emperor. Then you can use the card to go home."

I narrow my eyes at him.

"There'll be no one to rule if they're all dead. You can rest assured, I will let them go."

One thing's for sure, I'm going to use the card to get myself home. I cross my arms. "Fine. Let's go."

"That's a good girl." He waves at the soldier still holding me. "I'll take her from here."

As I turn, I catch a glimpse of some pirates. The Wands' Prefect is there along with two pirates I recognize from the fight at the tavern. One of them is the man who had grabbed me and who I then kicked in the balls.

Nkella stands with his arms crossed as a few men bring out AJ, Kaehante, and Tessa from the Karst Temples all the way to the left. A cotton ball gets wedged in my throat. They enter the crowded area of the court. I only see them. Did they not find Lāri? AJ has a serious look on his face, so I don't think they did.

He yells something at Nkella, who yells something inaudible back. It's not my problem.

Demitri pulls at my arm and leads me through tall double doors made of stone within the Karst Mountain.

Inside, he leads me up a tall staircase. Around me are more cages with Ipani inside them.

I hear Kaehante's voice booming down below, and I pause. "Go! Run, run, run!" Kaehante screams.

Confusion flickers through my mind, but I'm not asking any questions.

A bomb hits somewhere outside, and I grip the sandstone ground. I crane my neck to look out the window. Demitri does the same. Tessa had released a bomb, opening a ton of cages. Ipani run out of their cages, and I see Nkella throw a few punches at the pirates who are running after us.

Four loud popping sounds make me do a double take. Iéle's large black coat is recognizable, but three other wolves stand guard around Nkella. My mouth drops open. The three wolves from the dead forest. They're back. . .and helping Nkella?

As if Nkella could get any scarier—and now he has a pack of wolves.

"I don't have time for this," Demitri growls. He pushes me toward the right of a long hall, speeding up.

I struggle to keep going despite the sounds of crying and agonizing pain. We pass cages upon cages of Ipani, dead— except, not. They're stuck in their pain forever.

Demitri grimaces as his robes billow behind him, pushing me further down the hall. A set of stairs comes into view.

As we near it, I hear AJ's voice among the sounds of rain and fighting outside.

I start up the stairs. I'm sorry I won't see AJ's face when he sees Lāri is free. But soon, I'm going home. Here's to hoping this Ace of Wands Card works faster than the World Card did for me.

I climb up the narrow winding sandstone steps with Demitri too close for comfort behind me. At the top is an open round room with no windows.

The air in here is musky, the walls thick. I can hardly hear any of the commotion going on outside. There, at the opposite end of the room, is a sandstone podium, attached to the wall with candlelight sconces illuminating the circumference of the room. On top of the podium is a card. There it is. The Ace of Wands.

"Hurry up." Demitri is breathing down my neck. I can sense the urgency in his voice, his desperation to become Emperor.

It's not going to happen.

I reach the podium, my footsteps silent against the dense sandstone flooring. A purple glare sweeps over the card just as it does with the World Card. A beautiful amethyst sits on top of a stick with vines spiraling from top to bottom. It moves with the glare on the face of the card. It so vibrantly sticks out; I can almost pick it up and lift it out of the card itself. Slowly, I reach for it with my hand.

"That's right," Demitri says. "Take it. Make your wish."

A popping sound startles me, and I feel the tingling sense of tiny legs walking down my arm.

"Philo!" I gasp. "Where have you been?" I lift my hand, and she sits on my skin.

"Get rid of the spider," he snaps.

Philo jumps to the podium, and I follow her with my gaze, not wanting to lose her. Whenever she's appeared, it's been for a reason. I ignore Demitri's hard stare as Philo walks over some words engraved on the wood of the podium, right above the Ace of Wands.

Greek morphs to English:

A single spark to change a path. A single spark to die within.

"What the hell does that mean?" Suddenly, a weight pulls down on me. My head starts to spin and the colors from Philo's reflective body meshes with the heaviness of the room. What's happening?

Demitri flicks Philo off the podium. She grabs onto the edge, and he goes to smack her.

"Wait," I tell him. "I think she's showing me how to use the card."

Philo jumps back to me and dances on my hand. I peer down to her. My surroundings keep spinning as my focus is drawn only to the spider. Her large eyes captivate me in a hypnotic trance; her reflective body of black and red mirrors mesmerizes me with her moves, drawing me in even more. Like a magnetic pull I don't want to be freed from.

Black and red hues reveal an image of a woman at the center of my mind. She sits at the center of a large web as she pulls on a thread. The lady has fair skin and red curly hair. She pulls the string long, keeps pulling, and keeps pulling. Suddenly, she fades from view and is replaced by an older woman with graying hair. She cuts the string in one loud snap of her fingers. Her eyes flick to mine.

The ground shakes under my feet, and the red and black hues dissipate from my mind, breaking my focus with Philo. Then she pops out of this dimension.

"What did the spider tell you?" Demitri demands.

"I—I'm not sure. . ." But I think I understand the meaning of this sentence.

A single spark.

I can only use the Ace of Wands once.

I keep that to myself. That drakon tricked me. He didn't tell me the card could only be used once. He said it could be used for anything. I ball my fist.

"Take the card."

Looks like I have a choice to make. An easy one. I'm going home.

I reach out and take the card. The ground below me starts to rumble. I steady my footing.

The vibration stops, and I'm left with the thunderous sounds of my beating heart in my ears.

"Enough procrastinating," Demitri snaps. "Wish for me to become Emperor. Do it now. Or everyone you know will die."

I am not a good man. I am a worse prince.

I shake Nkella's voice away. All I can think about is how he betrayed me. That entire time. Our kiss. The passionate way he held me. It was all a lie.

"What are you waiting for?" Demitri steps up and snaps his fingers at my face. I blink. He then takes a knife and holds it to my throat. "Perhaps you need some more incentive."

The knife gets knocked out of his hand and I jump back. Demitri wails as an arrow sticks out of his hand.

"Daí?" Nkella's voice cuts through the room, and I freeze. "Tell me how you want to incentivize her."

I spin around to find Nkella standing at the doorway, his pirate hat snug on his head. A bow lowered by his side. Not his bow. He must have stolen that one. Beside him is the Empress.

A golden eye-mask embellishes the top half of a mother-of-pearl mask. Her military-fashioned spiderweb garments cover her neck.

"Well, well," her high-pitched voice reverberates through the height of the Tower. "The pirate was telling the truth. My Hierophant works to overthrow me." Her piercing green eyes fall on me. "And you. . ."

I stand back.

"She was a pawn," Nkella says. "Let her go. Release my sister, like we agreed."

I blink, not sure I understand what he's saying. He didn't betray me?

Confusion swarms my chest as the Empress advances toward us. She snaps her fingers and white and purple masked soldiers fill the room with smoke. We're surrounded. Soldiers wearing the shield with tower emblems from Rutavenye stand side by side with Arcana soldiers wearing the emblems from Wands.

Demitri does the same and his chrome-masked soldier appears behind him.

I grip the card tight in my hand.

"Why the girl?" The Empress stares at me through her gold mask. "I thought she was dead."

"Your Divinity. . ." Demitri cups his hands and takes a step toward the Empress.

She flicks her gaze to Demitri. "And what are you all waiting for? Seize him!"

"Don't come any closer, or she dies!" Demitri grabs at my throat and pulls me close to his chest. Nkella knocks another arrow and points it at him.

"Why should I care if she dies? She's nothing but a Fool."

"Take a closer look, Your Divinity. I was only bringing her here to you."

"Liar," I say. "He was trying to get me to use the Ace of Wands to make him Emperor."

Demitri shoves my head down and grabs my arm, pulling up my sleeve to reveal the spiderweb mark I share with the Empress. I try to pull away, but it's too late; her eyes are fixed on my mark.

I struggle to break free from his grasp, my hair covering my face.

"That is curious," she says, tapping her fingers on the chin of her mask. "So, you lied to me, Soren. Fine, then. Hand her over. She clearly belongs with me." Her eyes fall to my hand holding the card. "Take her! And bring me that card!"

Although she yelled for a soldier to grab me, she, too, is advancing toward me. I walk back, hitting my back against the wall. A white-masked soldier appears in front of me.

Nkella shoots an arrow, and it lands on the back of the soldier's head. The soldier disappears, and I stand gaping at Nkella.

Another soldier appears in front of me, but this time, I hold up the Ace of Wands.

"Wait. If you want this, keep your hands off me. Or I'll break it."

The Empress's eyes widen. "Clever girl. My sister cast a spell so I could never take it from the podium. But you did. . ."

Demitri takes a step back toward his masked soldier.

"Enough of this," she says. "Seize him now." Two white-masked soldiers appear in front of Demitri, but he backs into the chrome soldier. His soldier grabs him from behind, and they both disappear in a gray swirl of smoke.

"After them!" she yells. Several white and purple masked soldiers leave as soon as she demands it.

"Neyuro, come here," Nkella says.

I make a run toward him, but I'm intercepted by one of the Empress's Arcana soldiers.

"Let her go, Empress. She has nothing to do with this."

"I beg to differ," she says. "She has my mark. She belongs with me."

"I don't belong with anyone," I snap.

She glues her eyes on me and takes another step. I inch back.

"Empress," Nkella hisses with urgency in his voice. "You promised me my sister. Forget Soren."

"Not likely. But as for my promise," with a swirl of her hand, red smoke swooshes down from the ether, landing on the floor. "There, your sister." A white-masked soldier, looking like the others stands in front of Nkella.

He drops his bow. "Ntaoru?"

The soldier doesn't say anything.

Nkella faces the Empress. "Make her whole."

"That wasn't part of our deal."

Nkella's face darkens, his eyes flashing an angry crimson glow.

The Empress laughs. "Care to try and hurt me again? Devil?"

"You test me, Helāni witch. I am getting stronger. Return my sister the way she was."

The amethyst reflects from the Ace of Wands in my hand. I turn it over. It almost looks 3D, like it's ready for me to pluck right off. *One wish.*

Kaehante barges through the door followed by Tessa, AJ, and Lāri.

Gari slithers through, unnoticed by most. He spots me and disappears. A second later, a tiny voice comes from my shoulder.

"Soren, down here."

"Gari?" I whisper.

"The one and only," he sings.

"What took you so long?" I ask.

Gari giggles, and I grimace. It's hardly the time for jokes. "I decided to take a detour to the Tower."

I'm about to ask him why he'd waste that sort of time when the crew takes out their weapons. I stare at Nkella who's facing off with the Empress. I shake my head at them and mouth the word "no." If they try anything again, she'll do worse than an undead curse.

Kae locks eyes with me. *"Reverse the tortured, dai?"* He mouths.

I suck in a gasp. I'm never coming back here. I have unfinished business back home. Besides, I'm not like the rest of them. I can't follow the fate of Ipa. Or Tarotland as I call it.

"The agreement was your sister for what I wanted," the Empress says, "not that I'd rebind her soul. Besides, my Hierophant has fled."

"That is not my problem. I brought you to him."

I take the card out and flip it around, the wand glaring at me. *A single spark.*

I wish. . .

Talia's face sitting in jail emerges in my memories.

Be brave, I tell her. *Like Alice.*

My mother lying in the hospital bed infiltrates my mind next.

My chest tightens.

I need to go to her.

Nkella unsheathes his sword and points it at the Empress. The Empress recoils, snaps her fingers, and makes Ntaoru disappear. All around me, Arcana soldiers grab at the crew, who fight back in hand-to-hand combat.

My heart beats loudly in my chest.

Gari disappears.

I stare at the wand in the card. It practically sticks out. I reach for it with my thumb and index fingers and feel the wand between my fingertips. As I pull the wand out of the card, a purple glare sweeps over my hand and my mark begins to glow.

The Empress uses her magic to fling Nkella across the room. Then her gaze snaps to me. "What are you doing?"

The wand has now grown to be the length of my forearm and I can wrap my hand around its center. The purple amethyst glows beautifully in the dimly lit room.

Everyone stops and stares.

The Empress stalks toward me.

Gari pops over my head. "Even in a land governed by fate, destiny isn't absolute," he sings. His eyes change from yellow to a dark purple as I stare at him floating above me.

Destiney isn't absolute. "I wish. . ."

"Stupid girl, be careful with that." The Empress is three feet away. "That card can only be used once."

Nkella picks himself up, his eyes glued on me, his mouth parted.

I step back.

As I focus my intent, an icy, sizzling feeling envelops the top of my head and shoots down the length of the wand, the tip of the amethyst glowing bright.

"I wish the Ipani will never be bound again."

The Empress stops in her tracks, and I gasp. The vine that's wrapped around the wand in my hand withers and rots. The light from the tip of the amethyst flickers, until it no longer shines. The wand crumbles in the palm of my hand and turns to dust. I clean off my hands and tuck the card away.

Nkella gasps; his sword shatters to the floor. Strong winds pick up inside the room and it feels like a tornado formed all around us. I buckle to the ground. Through the winds, I catch a glimpse of AJ holding on to Lāri as she turns into a bird. She had been bound, and now she's not. Despite the winds pulling at me, I smile.

White and purple light swirls around the Empress's hands and up her arm. "No! What did you do?"

Metallic-looking bony plates rapidly tile up Kaehante's arms in an armadillo-esque body armor. My eyes widen.

The winds whip my hair over my eyes, and I struggle to see. The moment they calm, Nkella gets blasted against the wall.

His arms spread, his mouth opens, and I think I hear him scream, but it's masked by the howling wind as it shoots through every orifice, his eyes blazing red.

The winds stop, and he drops to the ground. His chest heaves. His fists touch the floor.

The room is silent. AJ picks himself off the sandstone, and he gapes at me. Lāri changes back from a bird and runs over to hug him.

"Stupid girl," the Empress rasps, her eyes now on me. "You wasted the Ace of Wands."

"I didn't waste it," I say, out of breath. I stare her right in the eyes. "Now you will never be able to bind another Ipani's ouma again. And the ones who were bound, now are not. Because *they can never be bound again.*"

The Empress gasps sharply behind her mask. She pivots, bringing her arms up, and turns to face Kaehante at random. He stills, as a red smoke appears in the palm of her hand. She throws it at him, and he braces himself but just as the fume reaches him, it dissipates.

A shrieking gasp comes from behind Kae; I think it came from Lāri. AJ's mouth is agape. Everyone is stunned and staring at the Empress. And at me.

"I may not be able to bind, but I can still send you to your fated torture." She whips around to the soldiers. "Get them!"

Fighting breaks out among the soldiers, but each time they grab a member of the crew, either Lāri shifts to a bird to evade their reach, or AJ and Tessa shoot them.

The Empress faces me, and I step back. "You. . . You did this to me." She raises her arms, and a gust of red smoke circles around me. "To the Tower."

I feel myself lifting when a gust of wind blows the Empress against the wall. Nkella stands a few feet away, the winds, *his winds,* calming around him. His ouma is the element of air. He rushes to her side, pointing his sword at her.

"Soren!" Gari reappears beside me, now larger than when he was on my shoulder. "Look what I found in the Tower." His tail uncurls around a black and gold card. The World Card.

"How'd you get this?"

"In her Tower, of course! I know where she keeps all her little trinkets."

I take the card from him, turning the card over to face the image of Ipa. Next to me, the Empress is getting up from the floor. Quickly, I stick my hand in my pocket, feeling my deck of playing cards in their box.

Can I get the card to work again? I did it before. All I did was think about going home, and the card led me to Nkella. I'll do it again.

I focus on the World Card. The waves on the sea start to move; the serpent sticks his head up and dunks himself below. A ship appears headed north. It's working. "Get us out of here." I say out loud, visualizing the "death beach" we docked in.

The ground rumbles, and a bright white light emanates from the card. An open doorframe shines out of it like it did when I was stuck in the ditch. The ocean waves crash outside of it; the seawater tickles my nose.

"You did it!" Gari says.

I turn to face the crew and yell, "Hurry!"

The crew stops fighting and races toward the portal. I spot Nkella facing off with the Empress. She snaps her face to look at me and then at the portal. I grab Nkella's arm and pull him in with me. Gari flies over my head just before the portal closes.

As the portal starts to shut, red smoke spews in every direction. Nkella pulls my shoulder, but the Empress grabs my arm, jerking me forward.

Her sharp green eyes emerge behind her gold mask. I choke on a gasp and pull my arm back, but she digs her nails into my skin, clawing for the card in my hand.

"The World Card is mine," she growls. "Let it go."

I grin. "You want it? You can have it!"

Nkella roars from behind me. "What are you doing?"

I let go of the card.

The Empress releases me just as the portal closes, her expressionless mask the last thing I see. I step onto the sand and glimpse my empty hand. The card is gone.

"You let her keep it?" Nkella's voice is barely a whisper, disbelief tinging his words.

I laugh and hold up the World Card. "The Empress has the Queen of Hearts from my *Alice in Wonderland* playing cards."

His eyes widen, and a smirk twists his face.

"And all it took was a sleight of hand."

36

As I step onto the skull beach, strong winds slap my face, and I find my balance over the broken bones and cracked skulls. The stench of death wafts under my nose.

AJ runs up to us, followed by Lāri. "Soren, you're okay!"

"Yeah," I smile and glimpse Nkella. He frowns out to sea.

"Someone finally realized he's being an asshole," AJ says, nose pointing to Nkella.

Nkella ignores him, and Lāri smacks AJ on the arm.

I chuckle. "It's been a long journey," I say.

AJ squeezes my shoulder and brings me in for a hug. "You kicked ass up there. And you got the World Card to work."

I smile into his shoulder. "Finally, huh?" I chuckle.

Tessa drives up with Kaehante walking beside her. "It won't be long before they find us. We need to make haste." I frown and walk over to meet them. My eyes fall to Iéle who sniffs the air. She must have just popped in from the Aō. Everyone's here and in one piece—everyone except for Harold.

A heavy sigh escapes my breath as I stare at Kaehante. "Kae, I—" My voice shakes. "I'm so sorry. . ."

Wrinkles crease his forehead. "Why? You could have gone home but you stayed for us."

"I wanted to bring back your wife. . .a-and Soanalo. . .and—"

"Koj, Soren." Kae shakes his head. "You made the right choice. The Empress still lives but the war isn't over. You returned our ouma and now we are stronger than ever and will be able to fight her."

A sigh of relief leaves me, and I spin to find Gari but he's already gone. Fickle little guy. I won't get to say goodbye. He had gone to steal the World Card back without knowing if I could use it. I had no idea. I made the choice to save them instead without a plan to get back home.

Kae grins, bringing his arm down as the armor that appeared before starts to climb up his knuckles to the top of his shoulder. "We have powers to connect with now."

"I did it so that you would have a chance at saving your family. I thought that if I brought everyone back instead, the Empress would just kill them again and you'd be in the same position you are now."

Kae smiles down at me. "Thank you," he says.

"Do you think Demitri got away?"

AJ shrugs, and I glance at Kaehante who has now turned to find Nkella. "He won't be able to go far."

"I don't know," I say. "He appears to be well connected."

AJ smiles. "Don't worry. We'll get 'em."

I smile but then frown. "AJ. . .and the rest of you. . . I wanted to break your curse."

Tessa shakes her head, her wheelchair hovering over the skull-ridden sand. "Don't even think about it. Our curse is ours to bear. We will fight it. You did the right thing."

I nod and then turn to Nkella who started walking away from us. "What's he doing?" Then I squint out to the distance as the waves crash against skull and rock.

And more skull and rock. . . "Hey guys. . .?"

AJ quirks a brow.

"Where's the ship?"

The crew exchange glances.

"Did I bring us to the wrong spot?" I say.

Lāri laughs. "Uh-oh."

AJ scratches his head and looks out to where the ship had been. "What the hell? Where's the *Gambit*?"

I glimpse Nkella rubbing his unshaved chin.

"Captain," Kaehante booms, "it appears the *Gambit* has been taken." He brings up a piece of torn cloth. "This was left where we docked."

Tessa circles around. "The cloaking potion must have run out."

Nkella balls his fist, and an unsettling glow passes through his irises. I take a step back, cautious he might flip out. But the glow fades. His anger has banked, but as usual, it's still there.

Tessa hovers over the skulls on the shore and drives toward the sea. Kaehante follows her, his face serious.

AJ runs after them, and I follow. "Those slimy scumbag pirates! How'd they get here before us?"

"How can you be sure it was them?" Lāri says.

"Who?" I ask. "The traffickers?"

"Who else could it have been?" he yells, his hair whipping around behind him.

Nkella turns to Iéle who's walking in step by his side. He squats down next to her and says, "Go find my ship." In a pop, she disappears into the Aō.

"There's only one thing we can do now," AJ declares.

I raise my brows. "What's that?"

"We're going to have to commandeer another ship to get ours back!"

A soft chuckle escapes my lips.

"Well, they're not getting away with this!" AJ swings his fist. "The *Devil's Gambit* is our ship! To think some creep is sleeping on my bed! Or on your bed, Captain!"

"Yep. It's definitely gone," Tessa says as she and Kaehante come back.

I cup my eyes, looking out to sea. "They couldn't have gone far, right?"

"Those slimy bastards," AJ repeats, shaking his head.

A popping sound makes me jump. Nkella spins to communicate with Iéle.

"That was quick," AJ says.

Nkella stands straight. "Iéle has reported. Our ship is on the way to Piupeki. They must be heading for the Ace of Swords."

"Who?" AJ asks. "Who's captaining the *Gambit*?"

Nkella winces. "You won't like this, AJ. Your exboyfriend."

AJ grabs his head, muttering profanities under his breath.

"Do we have a heading then, Captain?" Kaehante asks.

"Hn." He nods. "We are going to the Isle of Swords."

"To Piupeki it is then!" AJ jumps. "I'm gonna freeze my balls off. My coat's on the ship!" He slaps his forehead.

I rub my right arm and steal a glance at Nkella who returns my gaze.

"Well, let's get a move on then, dammit!" AJ yells. "They're not stealing from this crew!" he turns to me. "This time around, we're definitely going to need to forage some hū raku to make more raku potions."

"AJ. . ." Nkella says.

AJ ignores him or doesn't hear him. "Get ready for a whole lot of mixing, Soren."

I chuckle.

"AJ," Nkella says louder.

AJ looks at him. "What?"

"Wait. . ."

"Wait?" a brow raises to the top of his head. "For what? The longer we wait the—" AJ wrinkles his forehead as he stares at Nkella. "What's the matter?"

Nkella's face is serious, his eyes sad. "Soren has to go home."

AJ's lips part and his brows rise. "Oh. . .crumbs. I almost forgot."

I stare at Nkella who gives me a nod and a small smile. I look at the others.

"As much as it sounds badass to go steal a ship and see more of this world, I have some things I need to do back home."

"Say no more, Soren." AJ crunches on some bones as he approaches me with open arms. He takes me into his embrace, and I hug him back. "It's been a pleasure."

Tears sting the back of my eyes as I squeeze him harder. "Thank you for always being on my side."

"Hey, thanks for helping us get Lāri back. I'll never forget it."

We let go, and I turn to Tessa. I reach down and give her a hug. "You too. . . thank you for believing me when I said I wasn't a spy." I look up at AJ as well. "Both of you."

He returns the smile.

Tessa grabs my hand. "Go do what you need to do, but don't forget about us, you hear?"

"Never." I smile. I turn to Kaehante.

"Hug?" I say.

He shrugs and widens his arms. I give him a tight squeeze. "You guys are the coolest crew of pirates I've ever heard of."

Someone taps me on the shoulder, I turn to face Lāri.

"It was nice meeting you, Soren. I'm just sorry it was under these circumstances."

"I'm just glad you're safe," I say.

That just leaves. . . I glance up to find Nkella standing on his own next to Iéle. I take a deep breath and walk over to him.

"I guess this is goodbye," I say.

He glances up at me. "Hn."

"I thought you had betrayed me." My voice quivers a little at the end.

"I would never betray my crew."

I swallow and force a smile. "Why didn't you tell me about your plan?"

"Kh. Neyuro. You should know I would never risk a chance."

"You could have trusted me," I hear myself say.

"And you?" He touches my cheek with the back of his hand. "Do you trust me?"

I lean into his touch. I want to say yes, so badly. But I can't let myself fall for someone. Especially now that I'm leaving. I'm never going to see him again and admitting that to him is admitting it to myself.

I gently pull away and stare down at the World Card in my hand. I'm starting to finally get a feel for how this works. It tells me what I need, but I need more than one thing. So, here's to redirecting it.

"Neyuro."

I glance up at him. He reaches into his belt and unhooks his pouch. He pours a few gichang into his hand and reaches for my palm.

"What's this for?" I ask.

"You said these are worth a lot in your world. Go help your sister. See your mother."

My chest tightens. "Are you sure?"

"Yes." He pours them into my palm and closes my hand.

"Thank you." I tuck them away in my pocket and stare into his dark eyes. The speckles of amber dance in his darkness, and for a second, I allow myself to get lost in them.

"Listen. . ." I say, pulling my hand back. He frowns. "I guess I should leave this with you." I hand him the World Card. "I'm not going to need it."

He takes my hand in both of his and gently pushes the card back to me. "It would be safer with you. I cannot use it."

"I don't think that's true."

"Daí?"

As we've seen, marks can change."

"Yes, they change."

"Well, one thing I know about the Tarot is it tells you about your life and gives you guidance. With the right moves, I think you can change your mark to move past the Fool. And the higher you go in the Tarot hierarchy. . ."

He quirks a brow. "Then maybe I can control the World Card?"

"Bingo." I smile at him. "So, you keep it after I leave. Keep it away from the Empress, and go save your sister."

I let go of him and take a lasting look at the World Card. "Take me to my world so that I can see my mom." The card changes to show the six of swords and then shows me the carnival. "Why the carnival and not my mom's hospital?" I roll my eyes. "This card can be so cryptic sometimes. . ."

This time, instead of throwing it down on the ground, I hold it out to the sea. A purple light emanates from the card in the palm of my hand, and a spinning vortex appears in front of us. It grows wider to show the jester-like grin of Tarotland Circus. I think I'm finally getting the hang of this, right before giving the card away forever.

Strong winds push at my hair, and I take a small step forward.

"Neyuro. . ."

I flick my eyes to him, lift the flap of his coat, and slip the card in his inside pocket. His chest moves up with each inhale, and he places his hand on mine. A sly smile spreads over his lips. He takes a step forward.

I clear my throat. "You said you were a bad man. And a worse prince."

His eyes grow heavy.

"It isn't true," I say. "Oh, and by the way, I saw all those little wooden figurines on the ship. Don't stop creating. You're so much more than a mean captain, Nkella Mikiroro."

The winds from the portal hit me from behind.

"Kh. I always knew you were a spy."

I smile, and he steps closer. His gaze lingers between my eyes and my lips. My heart starts to hammer in my chest.

The magnetic pull of the portal starts to tug at me. Nkella moves a loose strand of my hair behind my ear and brushes my cheek with the back of his hand. He lowers his head, his fingers lifting my chin.

I close my eyes, waiting for the touch of his lips, but it doesn't come. I reach out and feel nothing there. I open my eyes, and the winds have stopped. The magnetic pull of the portal has caused a motionless distance between us.

The memory of Nkella from a second ago feels like a dream. I place my hand on my lips and swallow.

The skull shore is replaced with carpet. I blink a few times before realizing that I'm facing a closet full of purple and gold robes.

"I was wondering when you'd be back."

I gasp and spin around to face Madame Asteria, standing arms folded, and staring right at me. She widens her smile. "I want you to tell me all about it."

37

I BLINK, DUMBFOUNDED, AND STAND WITH MY MOUTH open. Just a second ago, I was standing on skulls on the island of Sāgirang, also known as Wands, saying goodbye to a crew of pirates who had become the closest family I've ever had. And. . .I was about to kiss their captain. Again.

Now I'm back in Madame Asteria's tent, wearing the green tunic Nkella had bought me and an empty bandolier. The smell of incense and old books engulfs my senses, a stark contrast to the salt water and occasional wafts of rotten corpses.

Hold on. Why am I in the fortune teller's tent?

Asteria's long curly brown hair frames her face as she stares at me behind purple framed glasses. "Don't just stand there, I want to hear how it went." She takes a seat behind her and crosses her legs.

My eyes widen as I stare at her. "You knew?"

"Knew that you had stolen my World Card and taken it for a joy ride? Why, yes."

Philo pops onto her hand.

"Philo!" A little burst of excitement buzzes through my veins. Maybe it's from seeing a friend after having gone through an extraordinary journey together, or from having real proof that all of this happened.

"Philo showed me plenty. You have been busy."

I step away from her open closet of costumes. "Yeah, I am sorry. . .I guess I should explain."

She smiles at me expectantly, folding her hands together.

"At first, I wanted it to pawn so that I could move out of the Nelsons' home." I twirl my hair between my fingers and flick my eyes at her. She's listening intently, not surprised by anything I'm saying at all. "Wait—Philo showed you?" Duh, it's her spider, and she had the card. Now I cross my arms. "Who are you?"

She laughs. "My dear, melting that card for its gold would have been impossible. Its gold is special, and it never would have allowed itself to be melted. Now, as for who I am, I am but a Greek fortune teller. A traveler. And by the looks of it"—she motions to my mark on my right arm, and I instinctively cover it up with my sleeve—"you are a descendant. Or that card never would have caught your eye, let alone allowed you to use it."

My eyes narrow at her. "A traveler? Bullshit. You're from there." I've been through way too much for formalities. "Cut the act. Who are you really? An oumala animal won't bond with just anyone. And how did you have the World Card anyway?"

Madame Asteria's eyes sparkle. She's enjoying my annoyance.

"You act just like someone I used to know." Her voice cracks at the end. Philo moves about her arm, her little glass mosaic pattern dancing in the light. "I appreciate that you have so many questions, and I promise I will answer them all for you, but I know you have a mission of your own to handle first," she motions to my other mark, The Six of Swords. "Those marks won't last long here, by the way. They'll be gone by the end of the day."

I stifle a gasp and peer at my two marks. A day ago, I would have been happy to be rid of this stupid mark of the Empress, but now? I almost feel like it's a reminder of Ipa. Philo jumps from her to me, and I catch her in my hand. I smile down at her.

"She's taken a liking to you, hasn't she?" Asteria says.

"Yeah. . .she followed me through the portal and kept me company sometimes." I bring my attention back to Asteria. "Who do I remind you of?"

"All in due time, child. First, where is it?"

Child. I study her features. The way she just said child. . .

"Where is what?"

"The World Card. You did bring it back, didn't you?"

"Oh. . .umm. . ." I twine my fingers together. "You see, what had happened was. . ."

"Oh, dear. You left it."

Here we go. I cross my arms over my stomach.

"Who did you leave it with?" she demands, her voice rising an octave.

"With friends. I felt they needed it more than we do on

Earth, where it doesn't even belong." I bite my lip. Asteria sits back in her seat, bringing her finger to her bottom lip. "The friends I left it with. . .they need it to save their family."

"They won't be able to use it. Only ones—"

"Only ones with this mark can, I know. But I don't think that's entirely true."

She quirks a brow. "You did learn a ton, didn't you? Clever girl. It won't be easy for them, you know."

"I know."

"The important thing is that the Empress doesn't get her hands on it."

I'm alarmed at the mention of the Empress from her lips. "She won't. The people who have it will protect it with their lives. I can promise you that."

"Yes, well, that is what I am afraid of."

I gulp. Did I make the wrong choice? Did I just endanger the crew by leaving the World Card with them? I drop my hand to the side of my pocket and feel something inside. The empty Ace of Wands Card. Completely useless now. But I can live in solace knowing I returned ouma to the bound Ipani. And took away the Empress's ability to bind them. All with one wish.

"Is something the matter?" Asteria asks.

"Not anymore. I just remembered I really need to get to my sister."

"Ah yes, I haven't seen her in a while. The Nelsons haven't brought her back since you've been away."

"How much time has passed?"

"Time here is parallel, with a subtle time difference." I glance out of the tent where the sun sets. Before I left the island, the sun was rising. That's both good and bad. At least it's not like the real Wonderland where I would just come back to before I left. Although, a tiny part of me wishes that were true. How long have I been in Ipa? Six, seven, eight weeks? Where would I even find Talia now?

I better bolt. "I have to go."

"You come back when you have more time. We have a lot of catching up to do."

I look over my shoulder. "Oh, you can bet on it," I say and walk out of the tent.

Outside, the streetlights around Tarotland Circus light up my way, along with Asteria's dim lighting from the tent. I pick up my pace and sprint to the Nelsons' trailer. Part of me knows Talia won't be there. But another part of me hopes to God they at least bailed her out. Please, please, please. If anything, they can tell me where she is. I jump over a few tent stakes as I cut through the grass and into the trailer parking area.

I reach the front door and knock. It can't be too late because the kitchen light is on. Someone peeks through the curtain and a second later, unlatches the lock and opens the door.

Bradley's chubby figure silhouettes the kitchen light. His eyes widen. "What are *you* doing here?" He eyes me up and down. "And dressed as a pirate?" He laughs. "Hey, Mom, Dad! Sore loser is back from joining the Rennies!"

"Yeah, no thanks to you!" Might as well go with it. "Listen, I know you don't like me or Talia being here, but it isn't forever. Trust me, we'll get out of your hair in no time."

"Talia's already out of my hair," he snickers.

My stomach drops. "Where is she?"

Sonja approaches the door wearing a robe and curlers in her hair. "Where have you been?"

"Uhh. . .hi. Can I come in?"

"No," Bradley says.

Sonja snags her attention to him. "Bradley, go to your room."

"But. . ."

"Now."

He rolls his eyes and shuffles from the doorway. Sonja opens the door wider for me to step inside. The aroma of sautéed onions and sausages hits my face and my stomach grumbles. She must have been cooking gumbo tonight.

"We looked everywhere for you. The police were searching for you all over the city! If Talia hadn't told them they had already called your name and let you go—"

"Talia covered for me?"

"That's what their report said, but they didn't believe her at first." She folds her arms. "Your disappearance caused quite a stir."

"I know, I'm sorry. . .I got. . ." Taken? Kidnapped? Thrown into the brig of a pirate ship? I take a deep breath and let it out slowly. "I was let go and then got into some trouble." Might as well stick with Talia's story. "Are they still looking for me?" Please don't tell me I'm now a fugitive here too. . .

"What kind of trouble? You've been gone for over two months! They searched for you for weeks but since there were no signs of an escape, they assumed they made an error, and that Talia was telling the truth. That guard was probably fired."

I gasp. "Oh God, I'm so sorry. I didn't mean for this to happen."

"Well, you're back now but we thought you weren't coming back. You'll have to tell the police where you were."

I purse my lips and nod. I'll have to make something up. Although, saying I joined the Renaissance festival would track. "Where's Talia?" I ask.

"By now, you should know where she is." Sonja's wrinkles crease on her forehead. "You knew our deal."

I gulp. "Back at the group center. . . or?"

"I have no idea if she's been fostered yet but yes, she went straight back to the group home. But Soren, we thought you left, so we got rid of all your things."

I rub my forehead. Ugh. "My phone too?"

"No, that we kept. Figured we could use it. You can have it back."

"Thank you. Just tell me where she is so I can go see her."

"You can't go tonight, it's late. You know they have curfew. Go tomorrow."

I nod. "Fair enough. . . look, I know I disappeared on you but I'm willing to make it up. Could I stay here? Just for a little while?"

Sonja nods. "I'll make a few calls."

After indulging in the longest shower in the history of showers, I sit alone in my room. I take the set of pants Tessa let me borrow and the green tunic Nkella bought me in Jōtenko. As I carefully feel the fabric in my fingers, my heart grows heavy. I bring it up to my nose and smell it, taking in the exotic aroma of Sāgirang, Wands, of Ipa, of Nkella.

Neyuro.

A lump form at my throat. His amber speckles sparking in his dark eyes stare at me when I close my eyes. His smirk teases me. I push it out of my mind and lie down on the bed. Sonja lends me a pair of old pajamas to sleep in, and luckily, she kept a few sets of my clothes to have handy for new fosters.

The next day, I'm up early and out the door to catch a bus to the other side of town. I get off at my stop and add a pep to my step, nervous to finally see Talia after so long. She's going to be so mad, but I'll make her understand—I have to. I reach a pink two story building with white trim and a white picket fence and take a deep breath before knocking on the door. I bounce on my knees, jittery with anticipation.

A short girl with curly black hair opens it. I ask for Talia.

After a few minutes, Talia approaches the door. My eyes light up, and I reach to hug her. She moves her shoulder to keep me from touching her. My stomach sinks.

"Talia. . . I am so sorry." I start.

"Save it." She starts to close the door.

"Wait! Please, hear me out."

She crosses her arms. "This better be good. I woke up and you were gone." Her voice cracks. "You left me there. I covered for you. I thought you had a plan, and I didn't want you to get in trouble, but you *actually left me there.*"

"No, I didn't mean to. Something happened."

She leans to her side. "What happened?"

I sigh and look around. People are staring at us. A few notice me looking and walk off. "You wouldn't believe me if I told you."

"Great." She rolls her eyes. "You better make this good."

"Talia, please," I stammer. "I don't want to lie to you. But this, it's hard to explain."

"Just go home, Soren."

"Home? No, I'll stay here with you. The Nelsons got rid of all my stuff anyway. I have nothing."

"You haven't been with them?"

I shake my head. She drops her arms.

"Okay, then. . . Guess you can sign in and tell me what happened."

I take a step back. "I will. I promise. But I have something to do first."

Her head tilts to the side. "Soren. . . "

"I know, but this time I will come back. I'm going to go see my mom first. I just wanted to come see you before I did, to tell you I was sorry and that I haven't abandoned you."

"Isn't your mom in Florida?" Her brows furrow. "How are you getting there?"

"I have my ways." I give her a smile.

"Fine. I didn't like the Nelsons anyway. Promise you'll come back though."

"Cross my heart."

"Pinky swear." She sticks out her pinky and I take it in mine.

"Pinky swear."

She shuts the door and I dash out of the neighborhood to make it to the next bus for the next thing on my list. Get money, buy my plane ticket. My first stop is Caco's Stash—24 Hour Pawn shop.

Once there, I swing the door open.

A medium-sized burly man with Valkyrie wing tattoos on each arm stands behind a glass divider. The name tag on his shirt reads "Caco." He stares at me as I reach the counter. "Can I help you?"

I take out my pouch full of gichang Nkella gave me and pour it into the window box. His eyes light up.

"Where'd you come across these?" he asks, picking one up and inspecting it.

"My grandma?" I lie.

"Fine. It's better that I don't know." He pulls them out to inspect them and checks them under a magnifying glass. "Nice."

"So how much for them?"

He peers closely with his scope. "Well, the insignia makes them a little too unique to do anything with."

My stomach sinks.

"I'll give you two thousand for them," he says. "I have a buyer who's into this sort of thing."

My jaw slackens. That's a lot more than I expected. Enough for a plane ticket and then some.

"Great, deal. But give me one back." As a keepsake.

"Done deal."

In the bus, I sit with my legs crossed and a wad of money in my pocket. I lay my head back. This day is going just as I had hoped it would. Talia doesn't hate me, the pawning of the currency worked. And, now I am going to purchase a plane ticket to see my mom. Will she remember me at all?

Sometimes it does not matter if they remember us. What matters is us being there for them.

Wise words from a pirate. I chuckle to myself.

The bus pulls up to my stop; I hop off, walk to the trailer, and prepare myself to ask to use their laptop so that I can purchase my plane tickets.

Sonja and Albert stand at the door.

"What's going on?" I ask.

"Soren, we tried to call you, but you didn't answer."

"Oh?" I look at my phone. Four missed calls. "Oops. Sorry, I had it on silent mode by mistake. What's up?"

"Well, after making some calls about fostering you again, they called your dad. He had apparently been calling."

My heart takes a leap. "My *father*?"

"He's here."

I pause and stare at them blankly. "I'm sorry what?" Did they just say what I thought they said?"

Albert moves from the doorway, letting me through. "We just thought we'd give you a little warning before you came inside."

I stare at him, open-mouthed, and push my way in. No way. My dad can't really be here. It has to be someone else. My dad hasn't tried to reach me in like ten years, give or take.

"Through the kitchen," Sonja whispers.

I walk down the hall and stop at the kitchen's neon lights. Sure enough, my dad sits at the small breakfast table wearing a pin striped shirt, his ashy hair combed back.

His eyes light up when he sees me, and he stands up. Tears form at my throat but I fight them back.

"Wow. . .look at you. . .you're all grown up," he says.

I want to run into his arms and cry. I want to ask him what took him so long. And say that I missed him every day. But instead, "What are you doing here?" is all I can manage to say.

"Uhh. . ." He frowns and looks down to the floor. "Maybe we should sit."

I hold my ground. "Are you picking me up?"

He puts his hand behind his head. . . "I uhh. . ."

"Right. That's cool."

Sonja peeks her head in. "We'll just give you some privacy, but we'll be in the other room if you need anything."

"I came here to see you. . . but I can't pick you up. I'm just not fit to be a parent right now."

"I mean. . .I'm seventeen. You don't really have to be my parent at this point. You could have at least called sometime, you know."

"I know, and. . .yes, I do. But that's beside the point."

"Besides the point of what?"

"I really think you should take a seat."

"Okaay. . ." I pull up a kitchen chair and sit. "What's this about?"

His eyes grow red, and he brings his hand up to his mouth. "It's your mom. . ."

My mouth dries and my heart starts to beat loudly. He wouldn't have come all the way over here if. . .

"She passed away three nights ago in her sleep. I thought I should tell you in person."

My face blanks, and I swallow. I don't even know how I'm

supposed to feel. Sadness would be a good start. Is numbness normal?

"Did you hear me?"

"I-I'm sorry. Yes, I did. . .I just. . ." My voice trails off. I hardly knew her. But I still have the memory of her when I was little. I never went to see her. The corners of my eyes and nose start to itch.

"I'm sorry it took me so long to tell you. The foster home gave me the Nelsons' number, but when they told me you were missing, I took the first Greyhound out to find you."

"Oh, sorry, Dad. No, I'm not missing. I just got caught up somewhere. . ." I let my voice trail off again. I don't know how to handle this.

He smiles at me. "I'm glad you're okay. You look good."

"Thanks." I gaze upon his graying hair and crow's feet. Time hasn't been kind to him. I stare at the white linen cloth of the kitchen table in silence for a few minutes, my mind blanking.

He reaches into his backpack on the floor and opens it up to reveal a small wooden jewelry box. "This was in her belongings. I thought you should have it."

He sets it on the table, and I place my hand on it. "Thanks." A few moments pass with my eyes glued to the box. I know I should open it, but right now I can't even move. My dad checks the time on his phone, pushes his chair back, and starts to get up.

"Wait, you're leaving?" I start to get up too. "Didn't you just get here?"

"Do you want me to stay?"

I pause.

"I can book a hotel for longer." His voice sounds hopeful. "I'd love to catch up some more."

I shrug. "Me too. Just not tonight. It's a lot." I haven't seen him in years, but I don't know if I can handle the news he just brought me, not with how angry I've been at him for most of my life.

"I understand," he says. "But do you mind if we stay in contact this time?"

I nod.

"I'm sorry, pumpkin." He kisses me on the head. "She loved you very much."

Maybe when she remembered me.

I hold my tears until he's out the door. Sobs form in my mouth, and I let them out. I hardly knew her. But I'm still sad. And angry with myself.

I gaze down at the jewelry box and pass my hand over the carved sunflower etchings on the top. I open the tiny brass clasp and open it up to a few trinkets.

I pick up an *Alice in Wonderland* charm of a little key and giggle through my sobs. She kept hers. Of course, she did. I put it on, remembering how I had lost mine. I bite back a memory of him.

Gembella.

I shake it away and look back at what else is in the box. Then I pause. Something red and round sticks out from one of the inner pockets. I do a double take—the object that comes to mind would be out of place. I laugh at myself. I've been in Ipa for too long. I take the red, reflective object out and gasp as I pull out a necklace.

The Mikiroro crest is carved at the center. A curved black

palm tree, with the Danū insignia surrounding it, similar to the dark disk Nkella wears around his neck. But in this case, a coin had been made into a necklace. How would my mother have this?

My pulse thunders in my ears as I hold it up for inspection. This doesn't make any sense. . .because this would only mean. . .that my mother had held the World Card and gone through the portal too. That my mother had lived in Ipa. More than that, she had lived in Danū.

THANK YOU

Thank you so much for reading *Lost In Tarotland!* I hope you enjoyed Soren's adventure into Tarotland as much as I loved writing it. Watch out for book two of *Chronicles of Tarotland,* coming out in 2023.

If you would like to receive updates on all my new releases, please join my mailing list at http://killianwolf.com/. You will also get access to my books at a discounted launch price when they first come out, along with an exclusive sneak peek or short story just for you.

GET IN TOUCH!

Come say hi in my Facebook Reader group. In there, every day is Halloween!

facebook.com/groups/killianwolf

Please feel free to get in touch with me.

Website: http://killianwolf.com/

FREE BOOK

Scan to get this free book and sign up for my mailing list.

"Don't kill" is a no-brainer. But what if it's for a good reason?

My name is Harold and my family is cursed. When my aunt made the tough call to pull my mother from life support, she enacted the curse of the Frost Giants, freezing herself from the inside.

To save her, all I had to do was step through the portal, but one wrong move sent me flying off to Tarotland, a place where the tarot cards have come to life. The good news is I still have my runes. The bad news? Magicians are illegal here. Not to mention, I haven't exactly come into my powers yet. . . and I can't get the portal to reopen.

My salvation is a breathtaking native. She makes me act like a Fool, but she also told me about a sword that cuts through any doorway.

Power doesn't come without sacrifice, though. With a mysterious predator out for blood, and my name on every wanted poster, who knows if we'll make it before my aunt breathes her final breath?

ACKNOWLEDGMENTS

Some book ideas come like a spark, others develop and change over time, like this one. But the moment I heard the voices of my characters in my head, they didn't let me sleep until I met their demands. This book is the product of many sleepless nights and feverish writing. But despite my enthusiasm, it wouldn't be what it is without the help of some exceptional individuals.

A special thanks to Christian Thalmann. Language and culture are so heavily intertwined, that without your creation of the Ipani conlang, Captain Nkella Mikiroro wouldn't be the character he is. I look forward to working with you for the rest of the series and any future projects.

To my critique partners Christina, Emily, and Shermon, this book would not be what it is if it wasn't for you three. Thank you for being brutally honest, and making me rewrite scenes until my fingers bled. Our group is the ultimate writer's guild any author could ever dream of being a part of. You guys rock.

Logan, your feedback has been invaluable, to say the least. Your critiques made the world of difference. From the bottom of my heart, thank you.

To my Developmental editor Claerie, you're my sanity.

Even when I thought everything was wrong, you made me realize why it worked. Thank you.

A special thanks to Malachi. As my old coworker and friend in archaeology, who else could I have asked as one of my sources for making sure my fantasy world feels as real as it can be? I'm lucky to have you as a friend.

To Meryl and Hunter, AJ is who he is because of your advice. He's one of my favorites, so thank you.

A heartwarming thanks to my mom, for having my room-themed Alice in Wonderland when I was little, and for teaching me how to escape to other dimensions by showing me a love for books. And for inspiring me to write.

To my husband, your patience and support means more to me than you could ever know. I promise, one day this will all be worth it.

Lastly, a huge thanks to my readers, especially the ones making it all the way here. I hope you enjoyed reading these characters as much as I loved writing them.

ABOUT THE AUTHOR

Killian Wolf is a Miami, Florida, native who enjoys pirates, rum, and skulls as much as she loves writing about dark magick and sorcerers. She holds a Bachelor of Arts degree in Cultural Anthropology and Sociology and a Master of Science in Environmental Archaeology and Palaeoeconomy.

Killian writes books about obtaining magickal powers and stepping into other dimensions. She lives in Florida with her husband, a tornado of a cat, and the most timid snake you'd ever meet. When she isn't writing, you might find her at an archaeological dig, rock climbing, or sipping on dark spiced rum while working on a painting.

GLOSSARY

IPANI VOCABULARY

á: Sound often used by natives of Sāgirang, used to represent a sound made in speech in a variety of situations, often used to ask for something to be repeated or explained or to elicit agreement.

Aō: [a.ˈo] world spirit

Aovate: (begisi aovate) [be.ˈɰi.si a.o.ˈva.te] soulmate, destined partner (lit. betrothed by the hand of the world spirit)

Bancha: [ˈbaɲ.ca] empty, free of, lacking, fool, idiot, stupid

Barachi: [ba.ˈɾa.ci] warachi, baracheo, from kumquat (lit.: orange-berry)

Besēla: [be.ˈseː.la] Jerk, bastard

Bohhibe: with toothed beaks, flying bug, eats cloth

Buchiveru: stabilizer, plant

Daí: Sound often used by natives of Danū, used to represent a sound made in speech in a variety of situations, often used to ask for something to be repeated or explained or to elicit agreement.

Drakon: Ancient Greek dragon with a serpentine body. Can both swim and fly, and pop in and out of the Aō dimension.

Garisi: drinkable potion, as opposed to explosive potion

gembe: ['gem.be] catching, capturing, seizing

gembella: [gem.'bel.la] from gembe, prisoner, inmate

gembella chacheang: comfortable prisoner

Gichang: currency, money

gichang rīrō: money from Danu, pressed ruby

gichang riwao: money from Wands, pressed amethyst

gichachi: mark

Hn: A sound made by an Ipani when thinking out loud.

Helāni: Descendants of the Ancient Greeks who crossed the portal with the Moera

hū raku (raku): [huː 'ra.ku] poison gas: poisonous breath

iá: [i.'a] hailing; hello, ahoy, greetings

Iéle: [i.'e.le] moon

Imboe: [im.boe] Ancient Greek-Ipani creole spoken in Ipa.

Indakepoa: [ˌin.da.ke.'poa̹] translation potion, liquorice

Ipani: [i.ˈpa.ni] of the World; the language of the World. Ipani (singular and plural)

Ipononchi: [i.po.ˈnoɲ.ci] cookie, pastry (lit.: little baked)

Ko: Negative, soft no

Koj: [koej] No, none, no! don't!

Mei: Sound often used by natives of Oleanu, used to represent a sound made in speech in a variety of situations, often used to ask for something to be repeated or explained or to elicit agreement.

Moera: The Ancient Greek Fates

Muse: [ˈmu.se] spider

Neyuro: [ne.yuro] brave

Ouma: [ˈow.ma] magic; magical

Oumala: [ow.ˈma.la] mage, practitioner of magic, magic user

Rikorō: [ˈdik.oro] soul thief, plant

Rikwa: [ˈdik.wa] thief

Ruh: [ɾuo̥] wolf

solerie: [so.le.ˈɾie̥] soleri'g, solerigo (i) peppermint (lit.: ice-leaf), give you transparency, spectre, can be used for people and objects

Taevenye: [tae.ˌˈʋe.ɲe] cinnamon (lit.: cloud-wood), gives ability to fly, float, can be used in potions for people, and objects

Utwa: [ˈu.twa] scout, spy

PLACES

Ahan Alēla: ghost forest, haunted forest

"Ahan Rī. "Crystal forest"

Bilu Laoguro: "Broadneck lake"

Chong Alēla: Spirit Mist, in the ocean

Danū: "Six suns." Farthest Southeastern Island. Currently called Pentacles, Danū by the rebels.

Dempu Yuni: trading post island; Dempu: foot; (i) standing, located; (i) river mouth; Yuni: transparent, pure, clear

Eyuo Sāgirang: "Torn Earth Temples" The Karst Temples.

Ipa: ['ee.pa] the global ocean, the World

Oleanu: "Highwater" Island to the East. Currently called Wands, Oleanu by the rebels.

Piupeki: "Steelrock" Island farthest to the North. Currently called Swords, Piupeki by the rebels.

Ruta Helāni: Prefect's Tower

Rutavenye: "Cloudwall" The Floating island, location of The Tower

Sāgirang: "Tornland" Island to the West. Currently called Wands, Sāgirang by the rebels.

Sotiria: Salvation, ancient greek, island off the southern coast of Wands

Jōtenko: "Big Open" village name

PHRASES

Imboe translations:

E onī, Iéle. Pitano to kivenete a eki iesī.: Get back
  Iéle (Moon). The captain probably has questions.
N'twa'r a n'eakeang?: Where did [she] come from?

Ipani translations:

A twakom palo?: What do you make of her?
Ko nalo utwa, kum.: She doesn't seem to be a spy.
Dira'y e sao raí.: She might be telling the truth.
Nong gichachi?: And the mark?
Hāyan tileni muni?: Distant descendant?
Helāni poé a sesirang onje n'unne ipa, mollisi.: The
  Greeks came from another world, after all.
Kh. Hehive.: Myth
Ko kwela mū: It doesn't make a difference
Ja e'r a la cā n'jamae poé: I do this for my kind

www.ingramcontent.com/pod-product-compliance
Lightning Source LLC
Chambersburg PA
CBHW050944210726
48287CB00004B/1130